F. G. Trafford

Too much alone

F. G. Trafford

Too much alone

ISBN/EAN: 9783337047351

Printed in Europe, USA, Canada, Australia, Japan

Cover: Foto ©Andreas Hilbeck / pixelio.de

More available books at **www.hansebooks.com**

TOO MUCH ALONE.

A Novel.

BY

F. G. TRAFFORD,

Author of "George Geith of Fen Court," "City and Suburb,"
"The World in the Church," &c.

A NEW EDITION.

LONDON:

TINSLEY BROTHERS, 18, CATHERINE ST., STRAND.

1865.

[The right of Translation is reserved.]

CONTENTS.

iv CONTENTS.

TOO MUCH ALONE.

CHAPTER I.

TREATS OF AN UNFASHIONABLE LOCALITY.

In the City of London—to the east of Gracechurch Street, on the wrong side of the Monument, between the Mint and Fish Street Hill, and the River and the India House, lies a little tract of over-built and over-populated town, a *terra incognita* to all save those who reside or rent offices in the neighbourhood: may I be permitted to introduce my readers to it?

It is not now an aristocratic neighbourhood I must premise —its streets are narrow, its lanes dirty, its houses old, its inhabitants poor; its warehouses dingy: its air not pleasant. Its trade is not general, but class. As stockbrokers abound in Threadneedle and Throgmorton Streets, so colonial brokers, shippers, and people who are known on the Corn Exchange, have stores and offices here. Great fortunes are made apparently out of nothing but hard work, in dark little dens, up courts and down alleys, and at the back of church-yards—for this region is rich in churches; there is one in almost every lane—there are two or three in every street. Men do not pay such high rents for premises here as they do in some other parts of London; and there is not the same show and pretension required for carrying on business east of King William Street, as on the other side the Mansion House. People take mean offices in out-of-the-way corners—put up name-plates at the side of a common gateway, leading perhaps to a hundred other strange places—begin to write briskly—get business by some inexplicable system of push or connexion, and behold! in a few years they emerge from lodgings in Hackney, Dalston, or Newington; furnish bran new villas at Peckham, Brixton, or Stockwell, and stand out before the world of suburban

London as prosperous and prospering family men, whose wives dress well, who keep their carriages, and pay their tradespeople out of money made in some odd nook of that mysterious locality into which ladies never dream of penetrating, which is given over by common consent to importers and exporters; to the Mark Lane merchants, and the ship chandlers further east; to the fruit and fish dealers of Thames Street, to the sailors from the docks, and the soldiers from the Tower, and the poverty, and the misery, and the vice that comes from beyond the Minories and Ratcliffe Highway.

It is strange to reflect that this quarter of London, which is now so completely deserted by all who are not compelled either by business or necessity to pass through its streets, was once fashionable.

In the time of the Henrys, dukes and earls and young popinjay sprigs of nobility were plenty down East, as fishmongers and lads with trucks are now; there was great state held by men of high degree in these old world streets before, aye, and after the great fire which, according to tradition, began in Pudding Lane, and ended in Pye Corner.

It is indeed hard, spite of diary and history, and ancient records, to believe that the place ever was anything—as hard as to realize that the poor threadbare creature who asks alms from you to-day, once owned a property worth two thousand a-year, and lost it through no fault of his.

We are all apt to imagine that what is, always has, and always will be; and thus, but for the Tower and the Hill, but for the lives dragged away in those dreary dungeons, and the noble blood that was poured out like water here—just here. where we stand—we might forget that all around us is ground hallowed by suffering, sanctified by grief; where the best and the bravest of former times played out their tragic parts, and went forth at last, with proud step and unblanched cheek, to meet their fate.

Here, where we stand—where children are romping, and making a Babel of the blessed air; within sight of the then silvery Thames—out under God's pure heaven, men and women died—heads that once were held high in the land have rolled aside; and long fair tresses, for one of which, perhaps, some sighing lover would have perilled his life, have lain here at the feet of the executioner, soaked and steeped in blood.

Women's hearts have been broken, and men's tears have flowed just where we stand, out in the middle of this broad horseroad, with the yelling of ragged urchins sounding in our ears, and the evidences of trade, hard - working, bargaining practical trade presenting themselves on every side. For this place was famous once—yea, and spite of daily profanation, and the chances, and changes, and mutations of time and fortune, will be famous for all time to come.

So the neighbourhood, as I have before said, notwithstanding the depth of the valley in which it is now reposing, stood, in the days that are gone, on the very summit of the hill of fashion; and there still remain a few of the ancient houses, that speak, with their wide staircases and massive balustrades, and spacious chambers and strange carved chimney-pieces, voicelessly yet eloquently, of the wealth and magnificence that once abode in them.

There are not many of these places now left, but there were more a few years since; great mansions, looking mean and dingy outside, but wonderful places to wander through, nevertheless; and it was in one of them that Maurice Storn, head clerk, manager, general factotum, what you will in fact, to the Messrs. Colke and Ferres, lived, or rather vegetated, all alone.

I will not specify the precise spot of ground his abode then covered—indeed it would be useless for me to do so, as the old building being condemned was pulled down some time since, and replaced by a staring red brick warehouse, that looks sadly put out of countenance by the dirty locality in which it finds itself. It will be sufficient for my purpose, and for yours too, dear reader, to state that though the house was not in East-cheap, nor Tower Hill, nor Lower Thames Street, nor Fish Street Hill, yet that it lay close to all these thoroughfares, to several churches, and to a Company's Hall. It was a strange old mansion, placed back in a large courtyard, and protected from invasion by heavy iron gates, and huge pillars, and a high wall. In the days when it was inhabited by nobility this court-yard had been a clear space, where horses could prance, and great family coaches rumble up to the door; but time and commerce had changed all that, and built a counting-house as high as the first floor windows, which reached away from the building, out to the very sphinx himself, who, without a tail, kept watch and ward over an entrance that had in his recollection known better days.

The house was built of bricks, with stone facings, and having stood out in wind and smoke for some two centuries, looked weather-beaten in comparison to the counting house which Messrs. Colke and Ferres had finished off with white cement, and roofed with lead. This incongruity, however, was only noticeable from the courtyard, or between the iron fretwork of the gates; for pedestrians, passing along the opposite side of the street, could merely see the dirty red of the mansion itself, and from the narrow foot-path nearest the house nothing was clearly discernible excepting the high wall, the old gateway, and a bran new office door, bearing the inscription, " Colke and Ferres, Manufacturing Chemists."

There was a passage from the office right through the house into a yard at the back, which had once been a pleasure garden, but which the firm above mentioned used for storing their stock of manufactured chemicals. The only waggon entrance to this portion of the premises, was from a lane running parallel to that on which the house fronted ; and thus Maurice Storn, residing on the premises, was master, so to speak, at one and the same time, of two positions ; and holding the keys of office as he did, nothing could come in, and nothing could go out, without his being cognizant of the fact.

Beneath the principals of the firm in wealth and actual worldly position, he was in that house and yard really above them. They paid him his salary, and a high one too ; provided in a sort for his daily wants ; found the capital for conducting the business, and spent the money gained in the business ; yet still, where the money was made, where the business was conducted, Maurice Storn was master over them.

If they had interfered he would have resigned ; he took on men without consulting them on the subject, and dismissed servants at his own pleasure. When people came on business they asked not for Mr. Colke or Mr Ferres, but for Mr. Storn. Colke and Ferres left blank cheques signed for him to fill up ; he took orders and he supplied them ; he sent out travellers and collectors, he bought and he sold ; he had clerks under him, and he dictated letters ; he was in the yard by six o'clock every morning, and he left the counting-house last at night.

He toiled and slaved, and was master over a business out of which, after all, he had only an upper servant's pay. He had commenced as errand boy in the very establishment in which he now was ostensibly chief : for twenty years he had been climbing slowly but surely ; and thus it was, that having reached the highest rung of the ladder of servitude, he lived in the old rambling house, with coals and light, and housekeeper's wages all paid for him, fast saving money out of his six hundred per annum.

He had neither chick nor child—no wife, no mother, no sister to comfort or annoy him. He occupied two rooms on the first floor, and the housekeeper, a snuffy old woman, occupied two on the second At the very top of the house he had a place he called his laboratory, where he spent all his leisure time trying experiments, and making smells, which set his house-keeper wheezing, and obliged her profanely to declare, she thought he must " be trying to raise the devil."

His life was spent on the " premises." He got up early in the morning and went out to the yard—then he had his break-fast, and passed into the counting house. Through the day he perhaps took an enlivening turn about the old-fashioned rooms, which were chock full of chemicals, and in the afternoon he generally spent half-an-hour on 'Change. This was the routine of his existence. Always " somewhere about," as the city phrase runs, the clerks could readily lay their hands on him in an emergency. When Mr. Colke, who lived up at their great chemical factory in the north, and only appeared in London like a comet, once in a way or so—flashed, without warning, into the old city warehouse, Storn was always found at his post.

He was never at dinner, nor out of town, nor sick, nor away west, like other managers; he was in the counting house, or—" about;" and Frederick Ferres, who was sleeping partner in the concern, and a great man at Mansion House dinners and government deputations, said he had never called at the place by day or by night that Storn was not either sitting in the office, or behind in the yard, or down in the basement, or up in the laboratory. He never went to the play—the opera had no temptation strong enough to draw him beyond the iron gates. Travellers, town and country, traversed London and the three kingdoms for orders—collectors dunned people for their ac-counts, great or little—carmen delivered the goods to customers. Messrs. Colke and Ferres, from their northern manufactory, sent the goods to London for delivery and warehousing. Beyond the office and the yard Maurice Storn never travelled, except to church and 'Change. If people wanted to see him, they had to come east. He was able to do more good business in an hour at home than in a day outside; for it is a fact generally received in city circles, that the trade which requires a principal or a principal's manager to go wooing for it is seldom worth the having. No, Maurice Storn was ruler over the warehouse and its belongings, and, like a prudent king, he remained within the shadow of his own dominions.

For twenty years—first as errand boy, then as trusty mes-senger, then as under clerk, then as assistant manager, and finally as head and chief over all—he had hardly slept a night out of the old city house, and its dingy walls were dear to him, —dearer than anything else on the face of the earth, except chemistry.

For, as I have said, he was alone in the world, alone as men

and women only can be in London; he had no wife or child, or
father, or mother, or aunt, or uncle, or anything.   He had two
people whom he called friends, one of whom was wont, when he
could spare time, to come and smoke by his fireside, and eat
bread and cheese by the pound, and drink beer *ad infinitum;*
whilst the other, a man of a different walk in life, residing far
away from London, brought his erect, soldierly figure, and mili-
tary contempt for trade, and strict ideas on the subject of rank
and one absorbing mania, rarely across the threshold of the city
mansion.

The last was a relic of the world Maurice's father had known
most about; the first, an almost exaggerated type of the class
by which he found himself surrounded; but as the tendency of
mankind is to fall rather than to rise, Maurice felt more comfortable in the society of his own friend than in that of his
father's.   If Mr. Glenaen were vulgar, he had once, at all
events, been chief over Maurice; if he knew nothing of con-
ventional politeness, there was, at least, scarcely a compound, or
a solution, or a test of which he was ignorant

He knew who was good or bad in the trade; the exact price,
value, and cost of every chemical in the market, raw and manufactured; he helped Maurice in his experiments; he could tell
him chapter and page for the precipitation of barytes and solution of silver.

He was making his thousand one year out of a dirty little
factory down at Bow, and spending it the next in fresh plant,
furnaces, and experiments.   He smoked enough to have passed
for a German, talked science enough to have set up a professor,
and drank beer and ate supper enough to have satisfied a plough-
boy.   When he came over on Sundays, he and Maurice took a
walk round by Fenchurch Street and the Minories, and so down
to Tower Hill or the Custom House Quay, talking all the while
of Long's Colour Manufactory and his new crimson, or Hull's
bankruptcy and stock, or the fire at Harding's, or the dissolution
between Hulme and Standing; and as it got later on in the
afternoon, they went back to the house and had tea, and after
tea Glenaen lit a pipe, and Storn a cigar, and through a cloud
of smoke they spoke wisely concerning impending bankruptcies
and the profits of new discoveries.   When Glenaen was not
with him on Sunday evenings, Storn went to church, perhaps
because his mother had taught him it was right to do so; but
the manufacturer voted church a bore rather than otherwise,
and declared he liked to enjoy the only day of rest he had out
of seven.   And accordingly he did enjoy it, by never letting the
shop drop for a moment.

Sunday after Sunday he kept up a perpetual conversation about drugs and chemicals, and the two men seemed to live in a mental atmosphere of chloride of this and oxide of that; bichromate of potash, acetic acid, oxolate of one thing, regulus of another, and heaven knows what besides.

And yet the reader must not imagine that because the friends stuck thus closely to their business, and wandered away through the mazes of conversation, holding so pertinaciously by the thread of their trade, that there was nothing mental in their talk, nothing improving in it to an outsider.

To know what they did, to be able to speak fluently on the topics which formed their staple, had taken years of practical experience, nights of study, and days of toilsome experiment. In both their houses tomes of dreadfully heavy literature and manuscripts, piled high as those in a publisher's office, bore testimony to the fact that no unread man can ever become a good chemist; they had laboured hard, and perhaps it was for this very reason that they talked monotonously, because every person who devotes his life to one particular study becomes tainted by it for ever after. Beyond this, it must be remembered that chemistry is a business of progression; he who is far a-head in it to-day, will be left a long way behind next year if he do not keep well up with the discoveries of the age. It is a business of eternal mental exertion, scanty bodily rest, and absorbing excitement.

First, to strike out at a red heat some spark of a new idea, then slowly and tediously to work it out to perfection, then to give your discovery to the world, and, above all, to keep your *modus operandi* secret; there is excitement enough in all this; interest and variety sufficient to excuse a man concentrating his energies and his thoughts on some novel combination, some possible process of manufacture.

Success to the chemist who devotes his time and his money to the completion of a darling project is wealth and honour; wealth almost fabulous acquired by a few years' hard work! Honour and renown world-wide, and fame everlasting, by the happy development of it, may be some perfectly random thought! And then, to make the play all the more exciting, there is a reverse to the picture—beggary! for when the game is played out, the furnace-fire extinguished, and the experiment a failure, the experimenter finds there are two extremes to chemicals, and that the one which he has met is the work-house!

Thus chemistry is, after all, but a species of mental gambling; and, as billiards and the dice-box prove sufficient to draw men together night after night, to furnish them with themes of conversation and subjects of thought, so new experiments were strong enough to form a link between Maurice Storn and Gordon Glenaen. They had one grand post of observation in common; their trade was the trade of their affections; their warehouses and factories were sun, moon, stars, planets, earth, and all to them. Most essentially they were of their shop, shoppy; and to have heard them talk, no human being would have imagined they had another feeling beyond chemicals.

And yet each was ambitious after his kind. There was an active passion for power and position ever at work in Glenaen's breast, which tempted him on to sink money in new machines, fresh buildings, improved utensils; he was sowing—to reap—while Storn, possessed of greater talent and more invention, contented himself with looking out on a vast fallow field of discovery, which was some day to be turned up for his benefit, and produce fruit an hundred fold.

CHAPTER II.

MR. GLENAEN IS SURPRISED.

IT was these two men then—Maurice Storn, manager, and Gordon Glenaen, manufacturer—who sat together one Saturday night in the first floor front of the old city mansion.

A December's snow had covered the court-yard with a carpet of almost unsullied whiteness; and the air being cold, with that sort of two-edged sharpness and rawness for which London is famous—or rather infamous—the two friends drew their chairs close to such a fire as no man ever sees in his house after he has slipped his neck into the noose matrimonial, and taken unto himself a partner in domestic concerns, who conceives her department of the business is to spend the money, and to stint the coals.

Bachelors had need have some oasis in the desert of their existences, and I believe good rousing fires to be it. There it —the fire of Maurice Storn's bachelorhood—went roaring up the chimney, making the dim old walls look dimmer by reason of their contrast to its bright face. It crackled, and made as much noise as if it were pleased with its performances, and wished to draw public attention to them; and it threw a ruddy light over the faces of the two chemists, and brought out each feature in their countenance, each peculiarity in their expression.

You have imagined, I daresay, dear reader, that these men living amongst dry goods, poking through musty ledgers, bending over smoky furnaces, handling filthy drugs and abominably smelling chemicals could scarcely be good-looking, could hold no claim on the estate of beauty; but in this supposition you would be wrong, for both were handsome—as they were—ambitious—after their kind. Glenaen's features were strongly defined, and cut with that peculiar sharpness of chiselling which nature seems best able to perform on those of an unamiable disposition; whilst Storn's face was more filled out than his friend's, and pleasanter to look at straight. As the manufacturer sate with his cheek resting on his hand, and his profile presented to view, one might have styled his countenance almost aristocratic; but the front view somehow dispelled all idea of anything superior, and gave the beholder a vague distrust of the man.

I could not tell you why: but few people placed confidence in Mr. Glenaen. He was punctual in his payments, and those he employed frequently remained a long time in his service; but, after all, the bond which united his business connexions and his dependants to him was solely a pecuniary one. He was a person who, if opportunity had presented itself and circumstances developed that part of his character, would have been powerful in hate; as matters stood, he was only weak in love. He loved no one thing on earth, he had not it in him; you might read that in his cold eye, and delicately cut nostril, and thin lip and small cornerless mouth; you might know he was selfish by the way he flung himself into the most comfortable chair in the snuggest position; by the intuitive manner in which he helped himself to the daintiest bits of meat; by the way he brushed past women and children in the street, and his total disregard of others' feelings; in fact, by his utter want of perception of them.

You might know he was selfish by these things: domineering by his tone and manner, prompt and energetic by his quick, decided voice, and vulgar by a certain indescribable something in his whole appearance. He looked at all events, characters, and sources of action through a darkening glass of low suspicion; he was a man of many contrasts—full of contradictions, yet not worth unravelling; a hater of aristocracy, but a worshipper of wealth. Everlastingly asserting he was (as our friends over the channel say) " as good as any man, and a vast deal better too;" he would have pulled every person of family

in England down to his level, but still have kicked any unfortunate artizan out of doors who claimed to stand on an equality
with himself; he never entered a place of worship, but he
hated Catholics, Jews, Arians, and Deists with the hatred of a
devotee. He thought all things fair in trade, yet he would
hold forth for an hour about the misdeeds of any poor devil
who was passing through that terrestrial purgatory the Bankruptcy Court; he was rather addicted to brandy and water,
but thought it a fearful thing to see a dandy drink a bottle of
champagne; he was always railing against the nobility, yet he
was meek as a lamb in the presence of a man of rank. He
was brusque but still not frank, plain but rarely pleasant; a
faint friend, a bitter enemy; a person who liked better to take
than to give, to talk than to hear; perhaps it was as well he
had devoted himself to chemicals, because he could not hurt
them nor they him; and they employed his mind, his time, his
capital, and his tongue.

It was this very intensity of interest in his profession which
bound him and Storn together; beyond their absorption to
the same profession, they had scarcely an idea in common;
gentle as a woman, Maurice never called the sharpest portion
of his friend's character into action. Clever, he appreciated
talent in another, whilst he forgot to exact homage for himself.
He was apparently less communicative than his friend, and yet
somehow Mr. Glenaen managed to get everything (not appertaining to his employer's business) out of him.

The intimacy was entirely one of habit and similarity of
occupation; and though to many people Mr. Glenaen's society
might have seemed a doubtful advantage, and his constant visits
almost an incubus, Maurice Storn not merely tolerated but
liked them, and looked with his clear, honest eyes kindly on
the face of the only friend he had in the city; refusing to see
his faults, and resolutely persisting that he was a " very good
fellow." They were neither of them young, as age counts in
London, where boys of sixteen are men in miniature. Storn
was close on five-and-thirty, while Glenaen stated himself
older by four years; and they looked fully as old as they really
were; for hard work and late hours, and much study and little
sleep, had traced lines across both their foreheads, and already
a few grey hairs were appearing in Maurice's head—hairs
which he had neither vanity enough nor leisure sufficient to
notice and remove. They never thought about their personal
appearance nor their clothes. It was Glenaen's practice to stroll
out of the factory and sit down, in all the dirt he had carried
away from it, to dinner· whilst Storn, Sunday and Saturday

wore an old shepherd-plaid coat, stained with ink and dyed with chemicals, which he never replaced with a better one but to go on 'Change, or to church. If you had offered all the clothes they stood up in to an old-clo' Jew, he would almost have refused to carry them away for nothing. It seemed, indeed, as though the worse they were clad the happier they felt: holes were of no account in their wardrobes; dirt hid darns, and grease cemented the whole mass together. They wore thick boots and short trousers, and never " did themselves up," excepting to go out into the city. In point of shirts, Mr. Glenaen was more respectable than his friend, who seemed afflicted in his buttons, whose collars were always fridged, and whose fronts had generally a long slit or two down the plait. He was unhappy, too, in shabby cravats and invisible wrist-bands; and altogether, Mr. Glenaen, who had a mother, able to make and mend, exulted over the lonely bachelor in the matter of linen.

Domestically, too, Mr. Glenaen was more comfortably situated, seeing he had a servant competent to wait at table and cook like a Christian, whilst poor Maurice Storn, dependent on the tender mercies of his housekeeper for raw chops, and beefsteaks burnt to cinders, had sometimes to stand for half an hour at a stretch, vainly attempting to draw attention to his wants by executing a brilliant fantasia by means of a key on the bannisters. Consider-ing all things, it appeared strange that Maurice Storn did not " make tracks," as Mr. Glenaen expressed it, to Bow, instead of the manufacturer coming to him: but the fact is, men always feel themselves easier for an evening in a house without a mistress; there is a rougher and a warmer welcome, a more unrestrained hospitality, a louder conviviality, a greater freedom of action, and, above all, a clear field for talk. You cannot talk freely to your friend about your difficulties when madam is netting at your elbow; you cannot light a cigar and pass on the match, without leave asked and granted from head-quarters; it is utterly impossible to bellow out for hot water and brandy in the establishment presided over by a lady; and you know well enough all the time you are eyeing that remnant of cold sirloin, that she is thinking, if you have another slice, there will not be enough left for dinner on the morrow. Mrs. Mullan, the housekeeper, might be deaf, but Mr. Glenaen knew his mother was not; so he chose rather to trudge through the snow than invite his friend home, because he wanted to have a good talk with him about things in general, and the bad state of trade in particular.

Trade of all sorts, in all parts of the country, was dull then.

On the Corn Exchange there was literally nothing doing; while in other branches of business, candles were quiet, and pigs flat. and milch cows dull, and tea heavy, and hides slow, and indigo gloomy; the only thing light at the time was the snow, and that only tended to make business heavier; and thus as the chemical trade proved no exception to the general rule, it need be no matter of wonder to the reader that the faces of the managing clerk and his *ci-devant* chief took their hue from the general complexion of outside affairs. Drugs being gloomy, so were they, and their features seemed lengthened out after the manner of all men of business when the things in which they deal and are interested look blue. With jaws dropped, and cheeks hollowed, and hair hanging loosely over their foreheads, they sate one on each side the fire, gazing dolefully at the blazing coals, and occasionally cheering one another with some dismal sentence concerning the universal depression.

"Holt has called a meeting," observed Mr. Glenaen.

"Came off this morning," returned Mr. Storn; "and he only offers half-a-crown."

"He was worth a hundred thousand clear this time twelvemonth," groaned Mr. Glenaen. "Who would have thought of *his* going? only he married some poor lord's daughter, and got into good society, as the fools call it; gave great spreads, and neglected his business, and played the deuce with his money. He carries a dozen little people with him too: Scott, I'm afraid, will close next week, and he owes me two hundred odd."

Mr. Storn having heard about a dozen times before, hints concerning Scott's suspected shakiness, received this fresh intimation in sympathizing silence, while his visitor produced his pipe and tobacco-pouch, and commenced stuffing the former with what air of resignation was possible under the circumstances.

"It's a lucky thing for you, Maurice," he broke forth at last, "that you are not on your own hook: a mighty safe fellow you may think yourself these times, sitting here, rent free, with your snug six hundred a year, paid quarterly, and a couple of principals at your back, who are just as good as the Bank of England. I can tell you, with things in such a state as they are, a struggling trader like myself has a hard pull. Wages to pay, and a house to keep up, and rent to settle, and taxes to meet—everything going out, and nothing coming in. I went to-day round to seven of my best people, and could not collect enough to clear the week's expenses."

"Where will it all end?" inquired Mr. Storn.

"God only knows!" piously ejaculated Mr. Glenaen, who

having by this time got his pipe fairly into working order, commenced puffing forth volumes of smoke, under cover of which he carried on a dropping fire of desponding remarks relative to recent and expected failures, the state of the weather, the aspect of politics, and the general depression of trade. No doubt he found solace in the occupation; for when he had at last exhausted his budget of casualties, and grumbled concerning things in general, and his own affairs in particular, to his heart's content, he drew his chair forward to the table, and asked Mr. Storn, point blank, if they were going to have any supper?

"Because," he added, "care killed a cat, and I am as hungry as a hunter."

"I thought perhaps you were too dull to eat," said Mr. Storn with a grave smile, as he walked outside the door and commenced operations with the key; the reason for which performance (I explain for the benefit of the uninitiated) was that as all the bells of the house rang in the basement, the master consequently might have pulled them to the end of time before Mrs. Mullan would have attended to his wants.

Even as matters stood, she frequently pretended not to hear either Mr. Storn's vocal music or its iron accompaniment, and every now and then Mr. Glenaen had to come to the rescue and "waken her up."

It was so on the present occasion; for after bearing till he could bear no longer, he strode out of the room to the bottom of the second flight.

"Kate, Catherine, Mrs. Mullan, and be hanged to you, I say," he roared up the staircase; and responsive to the well-known shout came a shrill treble from the landing above.

"Yes, sir."

"Supper!" bellowed Mr. Glenaen.

"What?" she shrieked from the first step.

"Supper, you deaf old adder," was the polite response. "Bring down whatever you have left, and some hot water—boiling, mind—and a couple of tumblers—now look sharp;" and having delivered these orders, the manufacturer, who only considered Mr. Storn was master of the house when he chanced to be out of it, re-entered the sitting-room, perfectly unmindful of Mrs. Mullan's mutterings, which came wafted to his ear from the upper storey.

"Kate wants a few more lessons," he remarked complacently; "she is getting deaf again."

"Poor old soul, I cannot shout at her as you do," said Mr. Storn.

"Nonsense; I have heard you speak loud enough to men," retorted Mr. Glenaen.

"But men are not women, are they?" demanded the other; which question presenting a new view of the case to Mr. Glenaen's understanding, he made no answer, but commenced smoking over it, until Mrs. Mullan, entering with the supper tray, diverted his thoughts into a new channel.

It might have astonished a plough-boy to see how that man ate; now demolishing a plate of beef, and then making inroads into an old Stilton sufficiently advanced in age to have been warranted "able to walk from London to Woolwich alone,"— meat, bread, butter, cheese, and ale, alike disappeared before his persevering appetite. Anyone might have wondered where he could put it all, and imagined he was laying in provisions for a month, had he not remarked in a contented sort of tone, as he pushed away his plate, and drew the brandy and water towards him—

"I hope you have a good supply of provisions in the house, Maurice, because I get so moped down at Bow these times that I think I shall come over and dine here to-morrow, if you can give me anything to eat; but, remember, I don't care to make a meal off bare bones;" and he pointed significantly towards the remnant of a once goodly joint on the table.

"I am afraid you won't dine here to-morrow," replied his host; "at least if you do, it must be alone, for I am going out of town."

"The deuce you are!" exclaimed Mr. Glenaen, putting down the tumbler he had raised to his lips, and staring with all his eyes at Mr Storn, who assured him that indeed he was.

"To the manufactory?" enquired Mr. Glenaen, almost in a whisper.

"No."

"I suppose one must not pump about business matters!" suggested the chemist, whose rapid imagination had created a difficulty somewhere, and beheld possible bankruptcy looming in the distance over the heads of that firm he had so recently pronounced good as the Bank of England.

"I am not going on business—at least not on theirs," said Maurice, reading his thoughts.

"On your own?"

"No."

"On whose then, in Heaven's name?" exclaimed Mr. Glenaen, who had by this time worked himself up into a paroxysm of curiosity.

"Well, I am not exactly going on business at all," explained his friend; "but the fact is, Captain Maudsley has been very ill for some time past, and he wants particularly to see me; so, as Sunday is the only day I have to myself in the week, I mean to start early to-morrow morning, and get back in time for work on Monday."

"Well, and what does he want to see you for?" queried Mr. Glenaen.

"That I really cannot say,' returned Mr. Storn.

"I would not travel forty miles to see a man who could not tell me what he had to say when I got there," Mr. Glenaen observed sententiously. "It's some fresh phase of the old mania developing itself, I dare be sworn; for nobody can deny he is as mad as a March hare, and as foolish and unreasonable as a woman."

"He is a gentleman, at any rate," said Mr. Storn, with a little asperity.

"He is none the better for that," was the quick retort. "Come now, Storn, be frank; don't you think the Captain, with his one everlasting topic of conversation, an awful bore? When he came into town didn't you wish him and that blessed Earnshaw place at the antipodes?—I am sure I have often. And then if one introduced some interesting topic of conversation, and told him of any new discovery, good Lord, how disgusted he looked. Do you know I really do believe he had a sort of contempt for both of us because we were in trade. I never said as much to you before; but I am quite sure, though I am turning over more money in a week than the whole of his half-pay comes to in a year, that he thinks I am his inferior."

"I dare say he does," was Mr. Storn's quiet response.

"Well, but you know he chances to be most confoundedly mistaken," said Mr. Glenaen with the air of a man who considered his information had not been received with all the respect it deserved; "because I am as good a man as he any day; indeed, if it comes to that, *I* look down on *him*."

"But I don't see why either of you need look down on the other," replied his friend. "If Captain Maudsley does cherish one ridiculous mania, I suppose it gives him some amusement and occupation. You know I have not the slightest idea there is such a place as Earnshaw on the face of the earth; but still if it please him to think that there is——"

"He is welcome to his notion for me," finished Mr. Glenaen; "however, I should like to know what he wants with you."

"So should I," acquiesced Messrs. Colke and Ferres' head manager.

"He has a daughter, has not he?" pursued the chemist.

"I believe so," was the reply.

"Perhaps he wants you to marry her," conjectured Mr. Glenaen forthwith.

"I should think that about the last want in the world Captain Maudsley would be likely to feel," returned Maurice, gravely; "for, in the first place, I am servant to a trader; in the next, Miss Maudsley is young, and I am not; and in the third, she is to be heiress of Earnshaw."

"Nonsense, man," retorted the chemist; "Earnshaw is a negative, you a positive: six hundred a year, and a free house, and coal and candle, would be a good catch for any one, let alone for a half-pay captain's portionless daughter. Depend upon it, Maurice, the old fellow wants to hook you; and if you take my advice, you will just stay where you are, and write him word that press of business, et cetera, detains you in town."

"No, I must go," persisted Maurice; "he was a friend of my father's in his prosperous days, and kind to my mother when she needed help; and no matter what he asked me, I should try to do it; for whatever other sins I may have, ingratitude, I hope, is not among them. I would rather not go down into Bedfordshire, for two or three reasons; but when he is ill, I cannot refuse. After all, it is not any extraordinary exertion to get up at four o'clock in the morning; and as I have nothing to do here, I may as well spend to-morrow in the country as in London."

"I don't exactly see the force of that reasoning," observed Mr. Glenaen; "but if you have to be up so early, I suppose you won't thank me for keeping you any longer out of bed; so good night, and don't get trapped, or it will spoil you for a chemist."

Having delivered himself of which piece of advice, the manufacturer buttoned up his great coat, stuffed his hands deep in his pockets, nodded with peculiar knowingness to his friend, and departed, slamming the hall door behind him with a bang which shook the house to its very foundation.

So Maurice Storn was left at last alone, and the first use he made of his liberty after Mrs. Mullan had completed the task of what she called " clearing away," was to pull a little note out of his pocket and commence reading it carefully.

There was not a great deal in the missive, only a few lines traced in a female hand, to say the writer's father was very ill, and wished Mr. Storn would come to see him, as he had something very particular to communicate.

There was little either in the manner or the matter to rivet attention, but it had a charm in the eyes of Maurice which makes most things attractive to all of us—I mean that of novelty. It was strange to him to read a woman's note. For years and years he had lived among men, talked with men, written to men. Masculine voices continually sounded in his ears; all the letters he received began with a formal acknowledgment of his esteemed favour; every correspondent was his obedient servant, or his faithfully; every epistle commenced Sir, Dear Sir, or Gentlemen.

The only females who ever spoke to him were Mrs. Mullan and Mr. Glenaen's mother; and so it came to pass, that the little note penned so carefully on perfumed paper, woke to life a whole train of dormant feelings, and set Maurice Storn thinking for the first time for years about other things than chemistry and its belongings.

First he wandered back to his mother in her widowhood, struggling between her pride and her poverty, and letting him go forth at last only as a choice between that and absolute starvation, to struggle with the world an errand boy.

He saw her for years subsequently toiling over her little drawings and pretty fancy-work, wearing her delicate fingers to the bone for him; he remembered how she had told him she permitted her son to become a servant only as a means to an end; he was to work his way up, keeping himself to himself; letting men know by his conduct, his manners, his integrity, his truthfulness, and his exclusiveness, that he was a gentleman.

And somehow, as he thought over all this, Maurice Storn's cheek flushed, not because he had failed to push his way up as she had desired, but because he had felt so thoroughly contented with his company by the road. Then Captain Maudsley became mixed up in his musings; Captain Maudsley and his young wife, whose fortune he managed to lose by foolish speculation. He remembered the presents he used to send his mother, and the periodical visits he was wont to pay her; and the kindness with which he first permitted reference to be made to him by the firm concerning Maurice's character, and the willingness he evinced at a later period to become security for him.

Step by step from that time forth he followed the officer's path, from his bubble share purchases to his latest mania; from the first vague mention of Earnshaw as a place which was to fall in sometime, to his wild-goose chase after an estate that might be situated in Peru, for any authentic information he possessed to the contrary.

From Devon to Cheshire, from Scotland to Ireland, and thence to the Isle of Man, still pursuing the one shadowy phantom of his life, Maurice, sitting by the midnight fire, mentally followed him; then there was a journey down into Kent, and finally a house taken in Bedfordshire, close to a village called Ermchaw, which name had been sufficient to lead him away from the Land's End, and set him studying the church books and local traditions in order to discover what claim he possessed on the lands, and manor, and woods, and gardens of Ermchaw Hall. He had spent two years on the hopeless study; and so, with a jump, Maurice came back from the man's mania to the man himself, his sickness, and his daughter. She was an only child; and Mr. Storn, hearing from Captain Maudsley, during his rare visits to town, how Lina was copying such a passage for him, or poring over musty old volumes for his pleasure, had formed a vague, dreamy, romantic picture of the girl whose young life was passed amongst dreary records of the past, and glorious visions of the future.

He had occasionally felt a curiosity to see her, though perhaps his desire never extended to a wish for an interview; for somehow—yes, there was no use denying it, even to himself— spite of all his kindness, Captain Maudsley and he had never been congenial companions. He had an uncomfortable sense of being patronized--of his calling being tolerated, of the people who were great in his eyes being looked down upon, that gave him a vague feeling of uneasiness and irritation; and thus, even whilst he entertained a most genuine pity for Miss Maudsley, he had a most wholesome awe of her likewise—an awe of that intense and overbearing pride of station which proves just as intolerable to the man of business as the pride of money does to the man of birth.

But now he thought of her somewhat differently. That little pink note, so essentially lady-like and feminine, placed her before him in the light less of a romantic heroine and more of a genuine woman. And then, in a sort of half dreamy way, he began wondering about her every-day life, and whether the officer were confined to bed, and if he had no one to attend to his wants but her.

From this point it was an easy transition for Maurice, who, by the way, had never had an hour's serious illness in his life, to marvel who would nurse him if ever he fell sick.

Mrs. Mullan being the only possible solution to this enigma which presented herself, Messrs. Colke and Ferres' manager woke up from his reverie with a sigh, and having first made a tour of inspection round the house, to see that the premises were safe, he came to the conclusion it was time to go to bed, and betook himself thither accordingly.

And next morning, having in a very miserable, forlorn, bachelor sort of way contrived to boil a diminutive kettle over a gas lamp, he sate down to his solitary breakfast, and after its completion, turned out into the snow, and cold, and unutterable dreariness of a winter's morning.

CHAPTER III.

A CHANGE OF SCENE.

Down in Bedfordshire, where the farms are not divided by wall, or hedge, or ditch, or fence—where people plat straw, not by the hour or the day, but by life—where the roads are bordered by nothing, and run on through lands that look like cultivated deserts—where the Chiltern Hills break the monotony of the downs that stretch off for miles and miles—far away in Bedfordshire, Maurice Storn found himself some eight hours after taking his seat on the top of the Highflyer, which started in those days from the Swan with Two Necks in Lad Lane.

The weather was wretched as the state of trade, and the roads being in a more deplorable condition than either, six miles an hour was considered good travelling, wherefore it was close on one o'clock P.M. before our traveller, thoroughly soaked through, descended from his uncomfortable perch, and was left by the Highflyer to find his way as best he could to the residence of Captain Maudsley.

"Up among the trees on the hill side," the coachman had replied in answer to his query, pointing his whip at the same time to some dark object dimly discernible through the wetting mist which was fast thawing the snow off the ground, and converting the road into water-courses; and accordingly along one of the dreadful Bedfordshire bye-paths Maurice pursued his way—now over the ankles in mud, and again almost up to his knees in water; until at length, in no very placid frame of mind, he arrived at a small gate, which he rightly concluded formed the principal entrance to his friend's abode.

"Not much of a place certainly," was Mr. Storn's mental commentary as he threw a hurried glance over the front of the house, which, with its small windows and red tiled roof, and broken brick front, assuredly had nothing distinguished in its appearance ; but the sharp, depreciating criticism was forgotten almost as soon as uttered ; for before he had time to reach the hall door, it was opened for him, and Lina Maudsley greeted her father's friend on the threshold.

"Mr. Storn—oh ! I'm so thankful you have come—it is so kind of you ;" and Maurice Storn, dripping like a Newfoundland dog, found himself standing in the hall, with his hand held in both the girl's, listening to her grateful welcome, and not knowing what on earth to say to her in return.

"The coach was so late, and her father was so ill, and Mr. Storn was so wet, and she was so glad to see him ;" thus, in truly feminine style, she ran on, leading him at the same time into a sitting-room, where Maurice felt thankful to see break-fast laid. "I thought you would be here a little after ten," she said, and then proceeded to say he "had better change his clothes, and have something to eat, and see papa afterwards, because he is asleep now, and I am afraid to wake him—the doctor thinks him so ill, so very ill." And as she came back to that, the point whence all her conversation started, Lina paused, and the tears came into her eyes, whilst her visitor, looking for the first time fairly in her face, thought he had never seen so lovely a girl.

There was a something, too, in the way in which she had laid out a change of garments for him in the only dressing-room their house boasted, which struck Maurice almost as much as her beauty. She had concluded he would be drenched through, and here was everything ready for such a contingency —warm water and easy slippers, well-aired linen and some of her father's outer habiliments. Unconsciously the Londoner began to think this looked something like home, and that Lina being very different from what his imagination had painted her, was a decided improvement on Mrs. Mullan ; and thus, in a very pleasant state of feeling, he returned to the parlour, and, relieved of his dripping clothes and soaking boots, and comfortably located before a blazing fire, he felt himself a new man, competent to converse on any subject, and make friends with Captain Maudsley's daughter.

From her he heard full particulars of her father's illness, which, though serious, she evidently would not look upon as dangerous. "A bad cold, caught on the downs, was its commencement, and then he did not take care of himself, and so it had settled on his chest and turned to a cough. A very bad one," she added, "which weakens him, and gives him very little rest ; but still it is only a cough, and I think a few days' nursing will make him quite well again."

"But the doctor considers him very ill," Maurice ventured. To which she replied, hurriedly:

"Oh, yes! doctors always make the worst of everything."

There was a sharp nervousness in her manner, however, as she said so, that showed her visitor she was trying to crush a fear out of her heart which had lately found a dwelling there; and perhaps to change the subject, or, what is more likely, because he really felt curious on the point, he asked whether she had any idea why her father wished so particularly to see him?

"Not the least," was the answer; "but he has been most anxious ever since I wrote to you. He said he knew you would come; and when I saw what a dreadful morning it was, I got quite fearful lest you might not venture. It would have been such a disappointment to him, for, before he fell asleep, I think he asked me twenty times if there were no appearance of you."

"He wished to see me so much as that?" said Maurice, as if speaking to himself; and three ideas crossed his mind almost simultaneously—one concerning Captain Maudsley's mania; another, that perhaps the doctor might be right, and the patient in considerable danger; and, lastly, Glenaen's supposition of the previous evening.

As his friend's words came back to him, he looked up and met Lina Maudsley's eyes fixed full on his face. He could not tell what there was in that clear, honest glance, which sent the vain, ungenerous suspicion cowering down within him; and after all, the thought did not belong to him—Glenaen was the father of it; the notion belonged to his mind and character, and was certainly one that Maurice never could have hatched by himself. He was scarcely self-opionated and obtuse enough to have imagined the possibility of Captain Maudsley desiring a plain, plodding business man, a trader's clerk, for a son-in-law; and though Lina was by no means the proud, cold, dignified, old-young lady he had been wont to picture her, still there was something about the girl sufficient to put to flight every fear of his having been brought down forty odd miles from London in order to be taken in and done for, in a sense matrimonial, at the end of his journey.

It was fortunate, perhaps, for Mr. Storn's vanity that, despite of Mr. Glenaen's friendly suggestions, he came to the conclusion no sinister design was entertained upon his liberty by either Captain Maudsley or his daughter; for if he had deluded himself into an idea that he would be considered an eligible *parti* for the lady, he must have been disagreeably undeceived during the course of his interview with her father.

When the invalid awoke, Maurice was ushered to his chamber, where, propped with pillows, Captain Maudsley sat up in bed. Death was written in his colourless face, in his drooping mouth, in the pinched nostril, and the restless hands. Albeit not much accustomed to the sight of mortal sickness, Mr. Storn felt the man was dying, and a whole crowd of softening memories and strange sensations came over him as he looked on the last frail link which still united his present and his past, his parents and himself.

It was in vain for him to try to conceal his agitation, or endeavour to mask with set phrases and false words the feelings that looked out through his face; and so, as in all cases where the heart is deeply touched, the tongue remained silent.

" It is even so, Maurice," said Captain Maudsley, speaking with that marvellous calmness which frequently enables the dying to converse without a change of tone when those about them are convulsed with grief—" it is even so; this is the last sick-bed I shall ever lie on, and I want you to break the truth to my poor little girl. I am not afraid to die, but I am afraid to tell her: it is coming so near now that somebody ought. Will you ?"

There was a pause, during which Maurice tried to get rid of a certain choking in his throat, which prevented his answering; at last he said : " Could the doctors not ?—"

" Ah, my friend," replied Captain Maudsley, " doctors take these sort of things as too much matters of course to be fit persons for the task. They get used to death, it is a part of the routine of their daily life; and so it is routine work to all but the dying and the bereaved. My poor Lina has never seen death—never seen anything, God help her! We were the world to one another, and now——"

Once again Storn made no answer. He was indeed a very Job's comforter to go to such a place ; he had too much feeling, and too little experience, to be able to string unmeaning sentences together, and flatter with soothing tones the ear of the dying. For the desperate state of affairs he had not been prepared ; for illness grievous, perhaps dangerous, he had made up his mind; but here was death, not afar off, but close at hand. That day week !—the whole thing seemed to flash through his mind at once : the dead man—the lonely girl—the desolate home —the loss of a certain income—beggary. A whole train of apparently incongruous ideas passed before him in a minute ; finally, he looked at the altered face, and taking one wasted hand in his, held it for a few seconds, still making no audible reply in words.

"Will you tell her?" said Captain Maudsley, after vainly waiting for some remark. "I would not ask you if I could do it myself."

Then Maurice answered clearly and steadily enough: "I am a bad person to talk, but I will do what you wish. Whatever you ask me to do, if I can, I will. I will try to tell Miss Maudsley."

"Just what your father would have said," remarked the Captain, whose sentences were frequently interrupted by fits of coughing and difficulty of breathing. "He was one of the most honourable men I ever knew, and it is because I believe you are as honourable as he was, that I have sent for you to ask your consent to become guardian to my daughter. Some day— at no very future one either—she will be rich. I have found a direct clue to my claim on the lands of Earnshaw, or rather Ermchaw. The whole of the papers are there; the genealogy, and directions, and everything. I only want one link in the chain; to make the thing perfect I must see an ancient history of Bedfordshire. My father always said, 'Never mind, Earn- shaw will fall in;' but that must have been meant for Ermchaw, for I find that the Croton family got Ermchaw through a mar- riage with Grace, co-heiress of Hugh Madsley, Esq., at one time Member for Bedfordshire, both of whom are buried at Dunstable. Thus, you see, as my father died when I was quite a boy, I have mistaken the name of Earnshaw for Ermchaw, and there can be no doubt but that Madsley has, in course of years, become corrupted into Maudsley. I was just getting into smooth water when this cold seized me. Maurice, you must finish the search and—"

At this stage of the conversation the Captain, who had grown quite excited by the brilliant prospects opening out be- fore his eyes, was attacked with a fit of coughing so long and violent that it brought Lina to administer his medicine and ar- range his pillows.

There is no place on earth where a woman shows to such advantage as the sick room—where the gliding footstep, and the soft hands, and the gentle voice, and the tender heart are seen and valued to the same extent. The noiseless love of a woman's soul makes itself felt the moment she stands beside the bed.

There is something about the way a wife or a sister hangs over an invalid and smooths the pillows, and moistens the lips, and pushes back the hair, and wipes the brow, that seems to place her in a truer and lovelier position before our eyes; and as Lina lifted the poor tired head on her arm, and gave her father his medicine, and looked at him as he took it, and then laid him down again to rest, Maurice Storn watched her like one fascinated ; for most graceful and most beautiful are the ways of women when with those they love. Beautiful in health, but fifty times more beautiful in sickness ; natural in their joy, but five thousand times more natural in their sorrow ; when they put off from their manners every conventionalism of society, every scrap of affectation, and stand before you pure and unselfish as God made them, unconscious of their charms.

So Lina stood by her father, now resting his head upon her shoulder, now stooping and kissing him, now straightening the counterpane, now cooling his forehead with her hand, whilst the poor old man, whose idol and stay she was, clung to her as a child might to its mother, smiled at her even in the midst of his pain, kept the little hand clutched convulsively in his, and never glanced at Storn but once, when he turned upon him a look of such unutterable anguish, that the man of business was fain to rise and walk towards the window, feeling the scene was unmanning him.

At last Captain Maudsley grew better, and then his daughter left the room. When Maurice had closed the door after her, and resumed his seat, the invalid, speaking in a much weaker voice than formerly, said—

"I have left a will behind me, and appointed you her guardian. Don't think I have imposed a troublesome task upon you, for she is as gentle and docile as a child. The greatest trouble you will have will be searching that old history I spoke of, and seeing to the establishment of her rights. I have stated in my will that she is not to marry without your consent, and I trust to you to see that she never allies herself to a person of inferior birth ; to one not her equal in every respect. As a man of business, you will be able to estimate the advantages which may be offered by any suitor for her hand. I think she knows better what is due to herself than ever to love below her station, but still she is very young, and may be deceived."

Here was a dilemma : the night previously Mr. Glenaen had spoken of Captain Maudsley as a lunatic, and proposed Maurice himself as a candidate for the daughter's hand ; and now he was asked to follow out the officer's mania to an end, and see that the heiress of Ermchaw did not demean herself by entering into any alliance below her rank. His age, his methodical business habits, his sedateness, and his quiet life (not one of them any recommendation for a lover) had clearly been the reasons why he was singled out for the important post of guardian to a young lady in her teens; the prospective possessor of a property then in the hands of people who might not exactly see the propriety of relinquishing it. From no point of view could it be considered a gratifying proposition, and Maurice accordingly endeavoured to get rid of the trust by hinting a few of his disqualifications for the task.

He had no legal knowledge, he had little leisure time, he knew scarcely anything of what was called the "great world;" he was not a man of general reading, he had never associated with women, and was as little qualified to guide the choice of a young English lady, or to provide a husband for her himself, as if he had been born in the South Sea Islands. He mentioned these obstacles, and begged Captain Maudsley not to overlook them, though at the same time he repeated his willingness to do anything in his power to advance Miss Maudsley's interests, or ease her father's mind. And this was no phrase of course; for if the officer had asked the trader to undertake any enterprise from which a shadow of good was likely to arise, he would have put himself to much personal inconvenience for the sake of obliging one who had been kind to his mother. Even as matters stood, he was ready to accept the trust reposed in him, and discharge it to the best of his ability, though at the same time he had not the slightest idea of devoting his life to a chase after Ermchaw; and ventured to hint that determination to the invalid, who simply replied,—

"My daughter is entitled to the estate of Ermchaw: there is only one link wanting, which you are sure to detect in some one of the Histories mentioned in a list which you will find amongst these papers; when once you have discovered that link, you can place the affair in the hands of a first-rate lawyer; and only see that she is fairly dealt by throughout the conduct of the case. I have saved money enough to defray the expenses of a lawsuit, and maintain her during the short period that must necessarily elapse before she acquires possession of the property. If you will therefore promise me to exercise a sort of general superintendence over her affairs, I shall die quite easy in my mind. I cannot talk much more," he added after a brief pause, "but you will find every direction written down; you have full powers under my will. I don't ask you to use them well, I only ask you to take them."

What could a man in his senses, conceiving the person who addressed him to be utterly mad on one point, answer to a sentence such as the foregoing? Nothing, perhaps, except what Maurice did do—suggest the propriety of associating another person in the guardianship—"the clergyman of the parish, or the lawyer who had drawn up his will, or perhaps some relative."

No, Captain Maudsley did not like the clergyman of his parish, and he had drawn up his will himself, and he had no relatives.

"Well, your doctor, perhaps," ventured Maurice.

"Pooh!" said the officer angrily, "do you think I would leave my girl the ward of an ignorant country apothecary—a young fellow who has not the faintest idea of the distinctions of rank, and might even want to marry her himself? Preposterous!" and having exhausted his strength by uttering this sentence more rapidly and continuously than any preceding it, the poor invalid commenced coughing so violently that Maurice imagined he would be suffocated, and was found by Lina supporting her father up in bed, lest in one of the paroxysms he should choke.

After she had given him his medicine, the doctor arrived—a good-looking, flippant young man, who said his patient must be kept quiet; and recommending that he should try to go to sleep, followed Maurice out of the room, and informed him, in a confidential sort of whisper, that "the Captain was far through, very far gone indeed."

"Don't you think," said Mr. Storn somewhat hesitatingly, for though he did not like the practitioner, he did not wish to seem to impugn his skill: "don't you think that in an extreme case like this it would be more satisfactory for you to call in further advice; I think some one with a larger experience, if you have no objection?"

"Oh! no objection in the world—if you like to waste your money, why I can have no objection to meet the whole college of surgeons. I can have a consultation with anyone duly qualified; but I really think it is sheer waste of money. Better keep the cash to defray the expenses of his funeral."

"That is a point on which I certainly did not ask your advice," remarked Maurice gravely.

"No, decidedly; but I gave it—gratis, you understand; no charge for a general opinion; everything has been done for him that could, and it would be just sheer folly to call in any one else; still, as you seem to wish it—"

"You are so obliging as not to throw any obstacle in the way of my desires," said Mr. Storn with a slight sneer. "However, though I agree with you in thinking Captain Maudsley is beyond the power of human aid; still, as it is always a satisfaction to know every means has been tried, I believe I shall ask you to meet some other professional gentleman."

"Always at your service, sir," returned the man of draughts

and pills : " I suppose Captain Maudsley did not consider me worthy the honour of an introduction. May I beg to know your name ?"

" Storn," was the reply, which the doctor made a mental note of, as a sort of harbour of refuge to which he could send in a tolerably long bill for attendance and medicine *ad infin.*

So he took his leave, and Maurice re-entered the little sitting-room where Lina and dinner were waiting for him.

" What does he say ?" was almost her first query.

" He thinks your father very ill," answered Maurice.

" He is such a croak," she said impatiently. " I quite dislike to see him."

" I have just been suggesting the propriety of calling in further advice," ventured Mr. Storn, after a pause.

" The very thing Mr. Ayldue was proposing yesterday," said Lina eagerly ; " but papa would not hear of it. He advised me to send for Dr. Gregson, and if you think it would be better too, I will write to Mr. Ayldue to-night. He said he would send for him if I liked."

" And who is Mr. Ayldue ?" asked her visitor curiously.

" Oh, our rector ; such a dear old man."

" Then I should advise you to send for his friend Dr. Gregson at once," said Mr Storn. " If I knew where he lived, I would go. Perhaps you may be able to direct me."

" No, no," she answered. " Janet shall run down to the rectory, and he will send a messenger off immediately ;" and so saying, she left the room, returning in a minute or two with a lighter tread, as if the notion of a fresh doctor had filled her with new hope.

Still Maurice looked grave—he could not help doing so ; the time for his departure was drawing on, and he had promised Captain Maudsley to break the news to Lina before he left. He did not know where to begin, or what to say ; and he would probably have sat on for another hour cogitating over some form of words fitting for the occasion, when his companion herself opened a road for him by remarking,—

" That she thought on the whole papa looked rather better to-day."

Mr. Storn shook his head.

" Do you believe he is *very* ill—seriously ill, I mean ?" she asked, after a pause.

" Your doctor says he is," he answered evasively.

There was a moment's silence, and then Lina, who had been toying and faddling with her dinner, laid down her knife and fork upon the untouched viands, and said,—

"Mr. Storn, what do you say?"

There was no deceiving the gaze of those earnest, anxious eyes—no use torturing the love of that loving heart, and Maurice answered in two words—

"I fear."

"What?" she asked, and she rose from her seat as she spoke.

"Don't think me unkind in telling you. I am not cruel—only—your father asked me to tell you what he thinks—he is afraid he will never be better."

"Do you mean," gasped Lina, laying a hand on the table as if to support herself—"Do you mean——"

"That he is dying—Good God, she will faint!" and as Maurice said this he caught her in his arms and placed her in a chair.

"I won't faint," she murmured. "Let me go, please—I—I must go to papa."

"You had better not," he said; but Lina would: so she got up, and walked about half way to the door; then faltered, staggered, and fell.

It did not seem, however, altogether a swoon, but more a sort of giddiness; for when Mr. Storn helped her to the sofa, she soon recovered, and said again piteously, that she must go to her papa.

"Not as you are," he said, "you would only distress him—besides, he may be asleep. Have you no female friend or relative you could ask to come and stay with you—no lady who might be a comfort?"

"No," she answered in a stupid sort of way; "she had nobody but papa and Janet."

"And who is Janet?" he enquired.

"My nurse—she was with mamma before she died."

"But, would Mrs. Ayldue not come and stop with you?"

"Mr. Ayldue is not married; and—and if you please, I should like to go to papa."

So, as she would, he let her—and when, half an hour afterwards, Captain Maudsley sent for him, he found the girl lying on the bed beside her father, crying as if her heart would break.

The old man, too, was sobbing, and as he implored his daughter to be comforted, he himself wept like a child. It was not the least use his asking her to leave him—to go away: she clung about his neck, and smothered him with kisses, and then buried her face in the pillow, soaking it with her tears.

"I wanted to speak to you," said Captain Maudsley, at length addressing his visitor; "but you see it is no use; I am sorry to have distressed you so much—these are things, however," he added, with a mournful smile, "which we cannot avoid—you won't forget my last wishes : may I trust you ?"

"Implicitly," answered Maurice, who at that moment would have promised anything the Captain chose to ask him.

"God bless you !" returned the dying man—then tremblingly extending his hand, he said, in a low voice, "For the last time."

If Maurice had tried to utter a word then he would have broken down—so he did what seemed strange to himself afterwards, he bent his head, and kissed the hand thus offered : then feeling that Lina would not care to be addressed, he was quitting the room, when she raised her head, and said in a husky tone, in a voice drowned and smothered with tears :

"Good-bye, Mr. Storn."

Thus he parted with them, and five minutes afterwards was hurrying through the darkness, feeling more wretched than he had ever done for years past. Days passed away ; and still, in the streets, in the counting-house, on 'Change, by his lonely fireside, his thoughts were always reverting to that sick room in Bedfordshire.

No news came from Ermchaw, either good or evil : sometimes he thought the officer, under the care of a more skilful practitioner, might perhaps be recovering ; sometimes he concluded that a permanent cure was impossible ; and he had finally made up his mind to repeat his visit on the following Sunday, when another note arrived from Lina, not penned on pink paper this time : nor perfumed, nor carefully written, but edged with a deep black border, and blotted and disfigured with the tears that had rained over it. Her papa was dead : he died on that (Friday) morning, at eleven o'clock, after suffering great pain, and she did not know what to do. ·

Immediately on receipt of which intelligence Mr. Storn drove to Mr. Ferres' residence, and laying the state of the case before that gentleman, asked leave of absence for a few days, if his principal thought the business could do without him for so long a period.

"Why, if you were sick, it must, you know, Storn," replied Mr. Ferres : "and under the circumstances, if no one else can supply your place, I will take it myself:" and thus cleared of his shackles, Maurice went down into Bedfordshire to make arrangements for his friend's funeral.

So at last it was all over, the death and the burial : and after a time Maurice formally entered on his duties as guardian, and made weary searches in dingy old volumes—all of which went to establish the rights of the Crotons, and cut those of the Maudsleys out of the property.

Still, although there was no possibility of bringing Lina in as heiress of Ermchaw, there were many duties which his position of guardian entailed upon him; and one of the most remarkable of them was a succession of visits to his ward, which were undertaken first for purposes of benevolence, and then for purposes of business, and finally, for purposes of pleasure; and as the summer advanced, his journeys into Bedfordshire became more frequent, until at last he might have been found on the Ermchaw road every Sunday, almost as regularly as the sexton himself.

CHAPTER IV.

NEW LIGHT.

THERE was no longer any perfume in the bean fields, the summer roses were dead and gone, the grain was all cut and gathered in; October winds had strewed the pathway with leaves, and the perishable glory of autumn was departing from the landscape, yet still Maurice Storn came on. More frequent than formerly were his visits to the old house near the downs; for the man of business and of science, of great commercial ability and curious experiment, was beginning to feel the power of love, and to entertain a faint glimmering of what was the matter with him. A person of a different walk in life might have made that discovery months before—but business people rarely analyze their feelings, and still more rarely express them in words, and it is perhaps for this very reason that they are the only class in the community who really and truly care to read about themselves. They like to have their feelings, causes of action, and modes of thought put into words. A novel about business, about their hopes, anxieties, joys, and troubles, throws a new mental light across the page of their life's history; they find everything written there which they have experienced in their own persons, but never dreamt of making a romance about. A story is to one sort and set of men a translation of their own feelings to themselves. After a fashion, the author turns into poetry the monotonous prose of their existence, and he writes words to that low, sweet harmony which has at times thrilled every chord in their hearts with pleasure. The rich talk to the rich, and the poor talk to the poor—both pour out their feelings on the smallest provocation like a deluge—they analyze their minutest sensations; they know why they are sorry, and they know why they are glad; they can tell you wherefore they dislike this person and are fond of that; but it is in the nature and essence of business to be secret concerning itself. Unless the wife of his bosom be a very model of prudence, the merchant dare not confide the state of his affairs to her. He will talk business over with a friend, but not *his* business; for if he be doing well, it is imperative he should keep his trade, his profits, his connexions to himself; and if he be doing ill, he must hold the knowledge of his concerns all the tighter, in order to keep up an artificial credit, and be able to " pull through." If he have let his wife become cognizant of any important failure or great crisis in his fortunes, he lives in an agony lest she should inadvertently whisper the fact to her dearest neighbour—sister, perhaps, to his greatest rival or largest creditor; he never can speak before his children lest they should repeat chance phrases to the servants; and at length the habit of secresy, which may have been at first irksome, becomes easy. A man acts, but says nothing; feels, but hardly thinks about his feelings, until some writer, skilled in the mystic lore of human sensations, writing of some imaginary individual, unveils the secret of his own heart before him; when he imagines that the portrait must have been drawn from actual life, and declares that the fellow talks as if he had been " down him with a light."

I have often thought it a singular fact, that men so quick at seeing a bargain, so ready to take advantage of a wrong move, such rapid inferrers of great events from little circumstances, should be so remarkably blind to the feelings that are at work, and the changes which are taking place in their own breasts. When a farmer's son, or the heir to a landed property, or even John Thomas, falls in love, you never find him long in a state of mystification or doubt as to the nature of his own emotions : but a man of business rarely discovers the fact until some considerable time after his state has become apparent to the world in general. Something is the matter with him, but he does not know what it can be; first, because he has never accustomed himself to an anatomical examination of his own heart; secondly, because he does not want to know; and thirdly, because love-making being an occupation beneath the dignity of a member of the great commercial world—an employment fit only for women, fools, and officers—it never enters into his head to imagine love can possibly be the thing that he wants to be at.

And thus Maurice Storn, travelling down from London to Bedfordshire, and back again, all in one day, never strictly took himself to task as to what these journeys meant. He drifted on with the current, perfectly regardless of whither it might be carrying him. The present was pleasant, he felt that; for a new light was gleaming over the routine of his daily life, and gilding its monotony with sunshine. Beyond and outside of his experiments he had something to look forward to; these visits to Bedfordshire, undertaken ostensibly in his character of guardian, for the better management of Lina's affairs, and the benefit of his own health.

For all at once he had made the discovery, that it is a good thing for a man to have an occasional change, and that there was no air in England which seemed to suit him so well, and invigorate him so much, as that of Ermchaw.

Going on fine mornings, he was generally on the hill-side by ten o'clock, and then Lina, poor little soul, was delighted to go with her guardian to church; and for his part, Maurice Storn had a foretaste of heaven as he walked along by her side, listening to that low, sweet, musical voice, and looking at her pale, fair face, framed in her black crape bonnet, and separated, as it seemed to him, from all the rest of the world by her recent sorrow, and her peculiarly desolate position.

So they went to church in the morning and afternoon, taking a walk over the downs between services, and dining generally late in the day; and as they passed quietly and decorously on their way, they were all unconscious that gossipping tongues had found employment in chattering about their affairs, that curious eyes were criticising their actions, and evil hearts thinking ill of two who had not the faintest notion of an idea that they were doing wrong. It never seemed, to their blindness, that any exception could be taken to their method of proceeding; if they had thought about their conduct at all, it would doubtless have struck them as eminently proper and decorous; for they knew what they talked about, as they wandered away along the bye-paths; and there was nothing in their conversation unbefitting the day or their position. Purely secular matters were rarely touched upon during these rambles, for Maurice (though he was Lina's guardian) had few money concerns to trouble her with; and to do him justice, during those happy dreamy hours, he flung all thoughts of his own worldly concerns overboard, and always went back to town feeling that he had spent a very quiet, good, and almost holy day: whilst Lina, who, like all true women, had strong religious feelings underlying the proprieties of Christianity, if I may so express myself, (which had been taught her by the Captain, and the observance of which had constituted his sole idea of serving God), felt, when Mr. Maurice Storn left her, that he was quite as good as a clergyman, and competent in all respects to fulfil the arduous duties of guardian. She thought it was very kind of him to come and see her, and she looked forward to his visits as to charming breaks in the monotony of her daily life.

Truth to say, he was very seldom absent from her mind; and of a Sunday, when the mail passed without leaving him at Ermchaw, Lina's spirits sunk below zero, and she moped about the house, not knowing what was exactly the matter with her, and wondering continually whether Mr. Storn were ill. Still, neither of them called all this, in plain, honest language, love. Lina did not think at all about the affair—Mr. Storn would not; and I cannot tell how long they might have gone on deluding their understandings on this point, had their eyes not been opened—as lovers' eyes often are opened—by the assistance of an acquaintance.

Enlightenment came in this case to Mr. Storn from the clergyman of the parish, who first left an invitation with Lina, requesting the pleasure of her guardian's company to dinner, and subsequently sent a more pressing note to the Londoner, informing him he had an especial motive for desiring to see him.

Then it was all made clear to Maurice—clear as the sun at noon-day—that if Lina would not marry him, he must give up that which had become almost a necessity of his existence, and stay away.

It was after dinner that the clergyman broke cover. Pushing the decanter away from him, and hesitating slightly in his speech, he said:

"I have requested the pleasure of your company to-day, Mr. Storn, for two reasons; one, because I was desirous of becoming better acquainted with you; and another, because I thought it only right to remonstrate with you about the frequency of your visits to Ermchaw."

Having opened the pleadings in which manner, the clergyman fidgetted on his chair, whilst Maurice, turning first red and then pale, muttered something about "in what way?"

"Well, you know, in one way, it is not my business at all to meddle in your affairs; but the fact is, I have lived a good deal in society, and I am much out in my parish, and as a man of the world," he added more confidently (and it is curious to think like what thorough men of the world the professed servants of God can speak on occasion), "and knowing how such things are looked upon in the world, I have thought it my duty to warn you that you are doing Miss Maudsley no good, in the estimation of her neighbours, by the frequency of your visits. You see, my dear sir," continued the parson, noticing how Maurice was stunned by the manner and matter of his agreeable speech, "you don't come down quietly as you might, and stay in the house whilst you are here, and go peaceably back by the coach; you are seen so continually out together, that it gives the girl no chance. You attend two services, and——"

"Good God!" interposed Mr. Storn, "you don't mean to say you think it a sin for us to go to church?"

"I don't mean to say I think there is any sin in any part of the affair," returned Mr. Ayldue, pettishly; "if I had, rest assured I should not have asked *you* here; but Miss Maudsley is a sort of pet of mine, and I don't like the way people are beginning to speak of her; and for that very reason I would much rather not see you in church on a Sunday till you have been there once on a week-day. Do you not understand me? Immediately after her father's death it did not so much signify, but now——"

"You seem to forget, sir, the position in which that death placed me," ventured Maurice; "as Miss Maudsley's guardian."

"Guardian to what?" demanded the clergyman. "If to her, you can only make yourself a fitting one through my assistance, or that of some one like me; and if to Ermchaw—— I fear I am only wasting time in speaking to you, as no man in his senses could talk of being guardian to the heiress of that myth.

"But Captain Maudsley left money behind him," persisted Mr. Storn.

"Very little," returned his host, "he *can* have left very little. The fact is, Mr. Storn, in small villages like this; everybody knows everything, and we are all well aware of the fact, that whatever amount Captain Maudsley may have left behind him, it will not suffice to provide for his daughter's wants for any length of time. Now I believe the fund to be not yet exhausted, but popular report is rather less charitable, and declares—shall I tell you what it says?"

"If you please," said Maurice; but he pressed his lips together while he answered, as if he felt sure beforehand of what was coming.

"Well, it says, or at least it thinks, that you are finding the money for the establishment, and that your conduct——"

"For heaven's sake do not say any more," interrupted Mr. Storn; and for a minute or two there was total silence—then Mr. Ayldue, who had risen and walked to the window, turned round and said:

"I will not disguise from you the fact, that I think this rumour has been caused not so much by your visits as by the dislike generally felt for Captain Maudsley. People might have tolerated his mania, but they could not tolerate his pride. Then, many of the farmers' sons here admired Miss Maudsley, and thought, perhaps, their few thousands in hand were better than Ermehaw in perspective. I can understand well enough why Captain Maudsley held them all at arm's length; because, as I said before, I know a little of the world, and comprehend thoroughly how a man of birth and education would shrink from giving his daughter even to the best of my parishioners. Still, they having as good coats to their backs as the Captain, and seeing their sisters at boarding-schools, and being accustomed to think themselves the equals of anybody who did not keep a carriage and pair, were naturally indignant at being treated like dirt under the officer's feet; and so now they are ready enough to say ill-natured things of you and your ward."

Maurice made no remark on this speech, though Mr. Ayldue paused long enough for him to do so, if he felt inclined. After waiting a moment or two, as though anticipating some observation, the clergyman proceeded.

"Captain Maudsley never was cordial even to me. I and a friend dined with him once, and he used to come down here and search the church books; but still we never were what such near neighbours might have been. In fact, I do not yet comprehend how he came to favour you with his friendship, unless, indeed, you never contradicted him on the subject of his mania."

"I never did," said Maurice, who was sitting with his head resting on his hand, and spoke without changing his position. "I never did."

"That accounts for the guardianship," returned Mr. Ayldue, "on his part; but did the position never strike you as somewhat ludicrous?"

"No," was the reply: "at first I felt rather embarrassed at the charge; but that soon wore off."

"And you never thought people were likely to draw conclusions from the readiness with which you accepted the post of a guardian to a portionless young lady?"

"I should have imagined that Miss Maudsley's youth, and

my seniority, would have preserved her from calumny," said Mr. Storn.

"Did they preserve you from falling in love?" demanded the clergyman, coming sharp to the point he had desired to reach; but to this question his visitor vouchsafed no answer.

"I must speak frankly," continued Mr. Ayldue; "the world judges as I should judge, that you would never take the trouble of coming so many miles from London simply to hear me preach, or out of pity for Miss Maudsley's loneliness; and there are few persons who would believe what I do now, that until to-day you never were aware that affection for your ward was the magnet which drew you to Ermchaw."

"It is not likely to draw me here again, then," said Mr. Storn, bitterly. "I ought to thank you, and I do, for driving me out of my fool's paradise, and for showing me how thoughtlessly I have given rise to village scandal. I must now bid you good-bye," he added, rising. "Should you soon visit London, I shall be very happy to see you there, as it is a pleasure I am not likely to enjoy here." And, as Maurice uttered these words with an affectation of indifference, which by no means deceived the person to whom they were addressed, he held out his hand, which the clergyman took and retained in a friendly grasp, while he said—

" You will want my services some day, I hope,—and not in London."

" Even were I a marrying man," returned Mr. Storn coldly, "Miss Maudsley would judge—and judge rightly—that I should be no fit husband for her."

Mr. Ayldue entertained a different opinion on this point, but he refrained from saying so; and bidding him a cordial good-night, permitted his guest to depart, feeling satisfied that he carried away with him ample food for present reflection and future action.

So, with the blood tingling through his veins, and at times flushing his cheeks, Maurice Storn went on his way through the darkness, feeling one moment as if he would like to knock somebody down, and the next as though he had acted like an idiot and a scoundrel. Fifty things passed through his mind in rapid succession; but the uppermost idea was that he should never see Ermchaw again; and with that thought came another—if Lina did not marry him, how, in six months' time, was she to be supported? Vaguely then, and like a half-forgotten dream, his promise to her father returned to his memory.

Lina was left him under a trust—the prospective heiress of

a ridiculous place that never existed. She must not marry beneath her—must not wed anyone but a gentleman ; and then Maurice stopped short, and asked himself whether he should come under that category, and if the present advantages of his position might not be fairly considered to outweigh all considerations of Miss Maudsley's future fortune.

Finally, Mr. Storn made up his mind that no promise made to Captain Maudsley was exactly applicable to himself. It was as likely as not that the daughter might go to her grave as the father had done, without even a sight of the promised land ; and although Maurice knew well enough, that if he asked Lina to marry him, he should not be acting according to the spirit of the dead man's injunctions, still he considered he was fulfilling the letter ; and, in fact, he felt that as the officer's expectations had not become realities, any course of action founded upon the supposition that they would, ought to be abandoned, as simply absurd and injurious. Yes, decidedly, there was nothing to prevent his asking Lina to become his wife, but there might be a great deal to hinder her doing so ; for, spite of their long acquaintance and friendly relations, Mr. Storn considered a refusal both possible and probable.

He had mixed too little with women to have ever found himself, like many others, an object for competition amongst them ; and moreover he was neither vain nor self-opinionated. Lina's extreme youth, her somewhat remarkable beauty, and, above all, the peculiar school of prejudice in which she had been educated, militated against his chances of success ; and besides, there was little about him—his appearance, his situation, his conversation—likely to captivate a girl's fancy or win her heart. He might possess some solid qualities desirable in a husband, but these were not exactly the sort most acceptable in a lover ; and so—and so—Maurice Storn almost reasoned away all his hope before he reached the dear old house, which from that night forth was to prove unto him either the sweetest or the bitterest memory of his life.

It was little marvel, therefore, that whilst thus his whole fortune hung quivering on a chance—on a solitary syllable of acceptance or rejection—he should still delay the final decision, and walk back a few steps to ponder over what he should say, to try to conquer his agitation, and seem like the quiet, tranquil guardian of old. For many minutes he wavered between one form of words and another, sometimes advancing resolutely to the door, then hesitating before he knocked ; at last, however, Lina hearing his step as he paced slowly over the gravelled walk, opened the door, and so settled the matter for him at once.

"Mr. Ayldue had kept him a long time," she said; "but tea was quite ready, and he could still have it before the coach passed by;" and accordingly Maurice reluctantly followed her into the little room, where his heart failed him once again, and he felt as if it would be quite impossible for him ever to tell Lina that which he at once longed and dreaded to say.

Almost in total silence he hurried over the meal, and then declaring he should miss the mail, got up to go. He had said good-bye, and was half-way across the room, when he stopped, irresolute whether to speak or write—whether to try his fortune then, or defer the evil hour a little longer. Just as he was debating the point, Lina asked him "when he would be back again?"

"Not for some time—never, perhaps," he jerked out suddenly.

"Never!" repeated the girl. "What is the matter?—what has happened?—what have I done? Oh! are you going to leave me too?"

"Not unless you bid me, Lina," he said, calling her for the first time by her Christian name; "but I have been here too much for my own happiness, and I cannot come to you again unless you will promise to be my wife."

It was all out and over at last, and Maurice gathering courage as he went on, took his ward to his heart, and proceeded—

"It all rests with you—I love you as I never loved anything before on earth. I did not think it was in me to love a woman as I love you. You have woven yourself into my very being, but still it all rests with you. I will go or stay, just as you will—only, Lina, if you care for me at all, will you try and love me well enough to marry me?"

What a quick, sharp pang it caused, that new birth into womanhood; how she shrank away from his touch with a new light dazzling her eyes; how strange it was, that for the first time in her life she felt afraid to speak to him; how slow he was to read in all this the first quiver of a new sensation through her heart, and how readily he accepted her silence as a rejection.

"It was all over," he said, after a moment's pause; "all—he had been mad, presumptuous, blind—he had offended her, but should never be grieved by him more: he would go—go for ever;" and Maurice's breath came quick and short, as he made this promise, for it was the life of his life he was relinquishing.

Then Lina looked up at him for a moment with a new fear struggling in her breast, which this time he fortunately read aright.

"Must he go—or must he not?   It all rested with her!" he repeated.

"Oh! she did not know—she did not want him to go, and she did not want him to——"

"Stay," she was going to add, only she stopped at the word, and began, poor little soul, to cry.

On the strength of which, Maurice led her to a chair, and sitting down beside her, poured out his heart to her as he had never before poured it out to the ear of any living being.   He told her about his prospects; his home, his love, his family, and his income; repeated what had passed between her father and himself the first time he ever visited Ermchaw; stated his belief that Earnshaw, if it existed at all, was unattainable; and finally (Lina never having ceased sobbing throughout the whole narration), finished by saying that he must for the future either exercise his duties of guardian at a distance, or take her to his heart, and shield her from every trouble there.

Still Lina never answered, but wept on like a frightened child; she would not be comforted, she would not make a reply: she would not look at him, and she would keep possession of her hands, one of which he had vainly attempted to retain; so at last, not knowing what else to do, he got up to leave her; lingering on, however, loath to depart without some sentence of hope, some slight sign of encouragement more tangible than an averted face and showers of tears.

"Lina, I am going—will you not let me have a word, or look of comfort, to take to my lonely home?" and he drew the little hands from before her troubled face as he spoke, and held them, so that she might not hide her countenance from him again.

And then, of all places on earth, she laid her head on his shoulder, and fell to sobbing there.

"Must he go?"

"Oh! she did not know."

"Did she love him?"

To this there came no answer.

"Did she hate him?"

"Oh! no."

"Would she ever be able to love him well enough to marry him?   Would she think about him a little through the week, and write and let him know if they were ever to see one another again?"

And still, as she vouchsafed no reply, he asked most entreatingly—

"Will you, Lina?"

"Yes," she said at last, in a little sobbing whisper.

"And will you try to be composed, and not be angry with me for grieving you?—and will you be sure to write? and don't, Lina, don't keep me in suspense any longer than you can help."

Thus, at last, he tore himself away, having no cause for despair, yet scarcely daring to hope; whilst Lina, after she had cried and fretted to her heart's content, crept away to her old nurse, and sitting down at her feet and laying her head on her knee, said—

"Tell me about my mother, Janet." Whenever she was in trouble that was the tale she always pleaded for; and it seemed to soothe her, as that voice might have done whose music had been silent for so long. When the story was ended she went quietly away to bed, and moped and pined about the house for days afterwards, never fulfilling her promise, however, of writing to Mr. Storn, who, waiting morning after morning for some precious word of encouragement, and feeling that rejection itself would almost be preferable to suspense, made his appearance on the following Saturday by the afternoon coach, and put Lina, who had not expected to see him until the next day, into a pretty flutter by his visit.

"I could not bear it any longer, Lina," he said; "I was hoping you would write."

"I could not write," she said, blushing scarlet and looking more beautiful than ever.

"Then would she speak?" Maurice suggested, in a low, anxious tone.

Apparently she could not do that either, for she stood with her eyelids drooped, as silent and immoveable as a statue.

"Was he to go again and be miserable?"

"No."

"Did she think she could love him?"

"Yes."

At which last monosyllable Maurice nearly spoiled all, by taking her in his arms and expressing his joy by such a shower of kisses, that Lina, who had not been accustomed to demonstrations of the kind, shrunk timidly away, and sought comfort once again in her old pretty trick of face-hiding, which Mr. Storn considered the sweetest performance he had ever seen in his life. It was such pleasant employment, getting the little hands away and gaining a glimpse of her flushed cheeks and long silky eyelashes, and then she had such numberless pretty little timid ways; and the affair of love-making was altogether so novel a one to both of them, that Maurice in this new state of existence grew quite a different being, and committed numberless extravagancies, which, having a regard for his character as a staid member of the business community, I should be uncommonly loath to chronicle. And the days and the weeks flew by with the rapidity of a new time given to them : and the darkness and monotony of the man's old life was dispelled by the glory and halo of the new light shining over all.

CHAPTER V.

MRS. STORN COMES HOME.

THERE is a drawback to every enjoyment in existence, an alloy in every lump of gold we dig out of the mine of human happiness ; and the bitter dross which Mr. Storn found at the bottom of his cup of earthly felicity, was having to tell Mr. Glenaen about the love mess he had managed to get into. It was easy work enough looking foolish for a moment, and then blundering out the fact of a wife in prospective, to Mr. Frederick Ferres, who, not having been especially fortunate in his own selection, wished Maurice joy in a somewhat rueful tone. This was easy, or, in fact, it was pleasant, work enough, because he not merely received permission to remain on in the old house, but also was empowered to clear many of the rooms of chemicals, and make them fit for the habitation of a lady. Painters and paperers were set to work by direction of the firm, and Messrs. Colke and Ferres requested Maurice to place a hundred pounds to his credit, and expend it in any article of furniture he thought would best suit his wife's taste. Also, when the time for his wedding came, he was to have a fortnight's holiday for his marriage trip ; after which the firm expressed their belief that he would resume his duties and attend to their interests with the same indefatigable zeal as heretofore.

Nothing, in fact, could be more flattering to a man's feelings than the conduct of his employers on this important occasion ; but Mr. Glenaen was a different and a much less agreeable affair ; for the manufacturer was a friend, and marriage being one of those matters in the joy or the bitterness whereof no one living has a right to intermeddle, seems to be the special event of all others on which friends delight to volunteer unasked and, in almost all cases, unpleasant advice.

Still there was no help in the affair, sooner or later Mr. Glenaen must know, and it was due to his friendship to make him early acquainted with the sacrifice contemplated. Accordingly, one night, when the pair were deep in the mysteries of a novel experiment, Maurice suddenly broke the chain of his friend's discourse by saying :

"I have got a piece of news for you, Glenaen."

"What is it like ?" demanded that individual.

"Well, it is like that I am going to be married," Mr. Storn replied.

"So it has come to that," remarked Mr. Glenaen ; "and it is the Maudsley girl, I suppose. Well, Maurice, I must say I did not think you were such a fool."

"I don't see any folly in the matter," answered the bridegroom elect, in anything but a mild tone of voice. "Most men marry some time or other, if they can find anybody to have them."

"Oh ! any man with a good coat on his back and a fair income, can have the pick of the nicest girls in England," replied Mr. Glenaen ; "that is my belief."

"And a very bad one too," retorted Maurice. "You make marriage an affair of pounds, shillings, and pence—a cash transaction in every sense."

"Well, and pray what else is it, ever, on the woman's side ?" demanded the manufacturer.

"Why, we flatter ourselves that affection has sometimes a share in the matter," was the reply.

"Yes, so far as this : that women love best those who can give them the handsomest dresses and the nicest houses. So far as that goes, affection has something to do with it ; however, I always knew how it would end with you from the first hour I heard the old Captain wanted to see you, and I am very sorry to find my fears have proved true."

"Your congratulations are certainly of the coolest," said Mr. Storn.

"And why, in heaven's name, should I congratulate you ?" demanded Mr. Glenaen. "A man at your time of life marrying a chit of a girl : a trader mating with a gentleman's daughter. Gentleman ! forsooth. If you must marry, why could you not ask some sensible girl in our own rank to take charge of your household, instead of a superfine young lady, who will despise your business, and look down on your friends, and think the city ground scarcely good enough for her to walk on ?"

"You have taken up a false notion altogether of Miss Maudsley," said Maurice, warmly ; "she is no superfine young lady, she will welcome all my friends for my sake, and like them, I trust, for their own ; and as for my marrying above my station, I have a fair income, and you seem to forget that my father was a gentleman possessed at one time of a large landed property."

"Pooh, man!" retorted Mr. Glenaen; "never mind what was, but stick to what is: what was, is nothing; what is, is everything. My mother says my father had the blood of the best border families in his veins, and yet any Bond Street cub, in the impudence of his heart, would look down on me, yes—and on you, too, Mr. Maurice Storn, and so will your lady wife, or my name is not Gordon Glenaen. Look at Mrs. Lindor, there is a specimen of a fashionable West End madam transplanted to the East."

"I will not have Miss Maudsley and Mrs. Lindor named in the same breath," said Maurice, vehemently; "neither will I hear you speak of my future wife as you are doing—I don't want to quarrel with you, Glenaen—but I should counsel you not to try my temper too far, because—"

"You think your ladye love a nonsuch," finished the manuturer; "so be it then—don't imagine I am going to lose an old friend for the sake of a woman, though I sadly fear there will be but a cold welcome for me in the old rooms, when the new mistress comes home. We have had many a snug talk here, but they are all over now, I suppose."

"I suppose nothing of the sort," said Mr. Storn; "the fact of my being married will neither make me a cold friend nor a formal host. I have told Lina about you, and she is quite prepared to like you as much as I do."

"Oh! ladies always like everything *before* marriage," returned Mr. Glenaen, laying a marked emphasis on the one obnoxious word. "However, the girl may be a very different creature to what I expect, and I hope she may, I am sure, for I should not like to see you miserable, with an extravagant, useless, delicate, flimsy butterfly; I know there is no use trying to dissuade you from the step, so I hope you will be happy in your choice. Now let us shake hands and be friends again."

With which request Maurice complied, though not so cordially as he might once have done, and he did not mind asking Mr. Glenaen to be present on the occasion, as he had intended; but let the old sexton stand father to the bride instead. And he fee'd that functionary and the clergyman, and the servants, and the postilions, to their hearts' content; and though he thought the marriage service the most solemn, sweet, and powerful composition he had ever heard in his life, still he was very thankful when it was all over, and he could take his beautiful child-wife to himself alone, and claim her by right—to have and to hold, to love and to cherish for ever.

Although it was mid-winter, they travelled away north, to the Westmoreland lakes, and then Maurice seeing the sun shining on the snow-covered hills, and the dark tarns; looking at the beautiful waterfalls, and the houses on the islands, and the deep ravines, and the grand old mountains, thought he was in fairy land. Everything was new and fresh to him as his love, and travelling about with his young wife, he felt like a boy let loose for the holidays. His had been long school hours, and this was the happy vacation of his life. Short it is true, only fourteen unclouded days, and then home, to the old city mansion, which he had told Lina was dark and gloomy, but which, nevertheless, he knew he had lightened and beautified for her.

There was much the same pleasure in bringing her back to London, that there might have been travelling with a child. She was so delighted with everything, with the lights in the streets, and the brilliancy of the shop windows, and the constant stream of passengers, and the everlasting succession of vehicles. Their way home across the metropolis to the Bank was one continuous expression of gratification; but as they drove on through Eastcheap, she grew quieter as the way grew darker, thinking, perhaps, of the house she was going to be mistress over, of the new dignity and fresh trust of matronhood that had come upon her.

"Papa was here, was not he?" she said at last, softly.

"Frequently," Maurice replied.

"Oh! dear, if he were here now, I should be so happy;" and she drew closer to her husband, as they got into still deeper darkness. "Are we near home now?"

"We are at home, darling," he answered, for at that moment the cab stopped before the iron gates; and so he helped her out, and hurried across the court-yard to the open door, where Janet was waiting to receive them.

Mr. Glenaen would not have thought there was much fine-ladyism about his friend's wife, had he seen her kiss her nurse, though he might have called the scene trash; but Lina, pretty stranger, trembling on the threshold of an untried life, frightened, thankful, and excited, was not thinking just then about anybody's opinion, but only about her own feelings.

She seemed to be walking in a dream, and as in a dream, she saw the large hall and the wide staircase, and the luggage piled along the wall, and then her husband led her up the stairs, and so into a well-lighted drawing-room, where, clasping her to his heart, he asked if she thought she could make herself happy in this strange place.

It is not for me, dear reader, to tell you what answer she

made, nor how pleased she was with everything about her; the carpet was beautiful, and the furniture handsomer than any she had ever seen before, and the old carved cabinets looked so strange amongst the new things, and the pier-glass was such a size, and the chimney ornaments so lovely. Then she was pleased to catch a glimpse of herself in the plateglass doors of the cheffonier, and she clasped her hands together in astonishment when Maurice showed her all the pretty things he had purchased for her, by desire of Messrs. Colke and Ferres. Why should I enlarge upon these things, reader?—for it is the same with all brides, who, having married for love, come home with the husband of their choice, to find bright fires and snug chairs, and easy lounges; and they don't think then about the weary days to come, when the roses will fade out of the carpets, and the mirrors reflect pale cheeks;—when they will sit in those chairs weeping their eyes out, and find that the softest couch ever sent home from an upholsterer's hath no power to ease the heart-ache. They are all alike in their joy and their sorrow, and Lina, being no exception to the general rule, looked at everything with bright, happy eyes, and never foresaw that the dull cold grey of a winter's morning might look into that then cheerful room, and find her lonely there.

It did, certainly, next day, seem very strange to her to be without her husband, but still he came in and had a look at her every now and then, and asked her if she felt lonely; and at six he returned for dinner and for the evening, and she tried her new piano, and made his tea, and looked prettier than ever.

Was that, could that be the dark half-furnished room of Maurice Storn's bachelorhood? I don't think you would have recognized it, dear reader, with a French paper and white doors, just touched round the panels with gold, and a rich carpet and a handsome piano, and heavy green curtains, and furniture all covered with damask of the same colour. Then, instead of the dreadful old supper tray, laden with bread and cheese and ale, there was a bran new tea equipage, at which Lina presided—a decided improvement on Mr. Glenaen.

There she sat in the full flush of her girlish beauty, half a child and half a woman, with the old clinging winning ways, merging into the shy dignity of early matronhood; a wife, yet still clear of the trammels of married manners; a girl, yet still with the coming self-possession of a woman. She had not been a wife long enough to feel either perfectly at ease in her new character, or indifferent to her personal appearance in the eyes of her husband, and accordingly she filled the place formerly occupied by the manufacturer, dressed out in rose-coloured barêge, looped up with lute-string ribbons, and ornamented with black lace. She was of that happy species of women, who never look either too fat or too thin, too tall or too short ; she had beautiful hands and arms, and was perfectly aware of the fact, and perhaps she might be a little vain of her neck and throat, and like to show herself off to perfection, with the aid of an evening costume. Her hair was black, and perfectly straight, as jet black hair usually is in women, and she had a way of gathering it all behind, and then wreathing it round her head, that might have driven any professor of the *coiffure* art distracted with envy.

She possessed tolerably regular features, dark blue eyes that at times looked almost black, and a complexion usually pale, though on the slightest provocation the blood rushed up into her cheeks and flushed them with a brilliant though perishable colour. She seemed to have no taste for jewellery, and but a very moderate ambition for cultivating finery about her head ; for the only ornament that contrasted with the jet blackness of her hair was a sprig of white artificial heath placed coquettishly between the braids. Maurice, too, seemed to have turned over a new leaf in the matter of dress, for he absolutely changed his coat before dinner, and washed his hands and brushed his hair, and came to table in much such apparel as any other gentleman in England might have been expected to wear. Perhaps it was out of compliment to his wife ; perhaps the new furniture and French satin paper had rendered some renovation in his outward man necessary ; at all events, he looked much the better for the alteration, and, all things considered, did not seem any more uncomfortable than most men who have been accustomed to go about home in rags, appear when any circum- stance compels them to don new clothes.

He felt wonderfully happy in his changed life, and moved about his house for the first time as if it belonged to him. He had done for ever with the roughly served raw chops, burnt steaks, and remarkable joints of his bachelorhood. If Lina was not much of a manager, she at least possessed an efficient " sub," who marketed and cooked, and instructed their second servant in the way she should go, and saw that the dinner table was properly laid out, and had an eye to household matters in general.

Hot water was left in his room every morning, when he re- turned from his first rounds, and shaved, preparatory to de- scending to breakfast. Occasionally some room in the house went through the process of scouring, and he was able to lay his hands on any article in the sitting rooms without being smothered with dust. His clothes were looked up, and aired and mended; and Lina took to "tidying" his most sacred repositories in a manner which filled him with horrified alarm. For eight whole days he had never visited his laboratory, when one afternoon he found his young wife recklessly plunging among bottles and vessels, and tubes and acids, and poisons, and all sorts of pernicious chemicals.

"How did you get in here, Lina?" he asked.

"Oh! I managed to find the key; and I have been working so hard," she answered; "I thought you would like to have the place put a little straight, so I have been clearing out a quantity of old rubbish, and leaving you a larger space to move about in. I don't know what the half of the things are; but I am sure the most of them are of no use."

And quite exhausted with talking, and dusting, and smelling, she got down from her step-ladder, and came with sadly dirty hands to Maurice, who said very seriously—

"Lina, this is my Blue-beard's chamber, and you must not come into it without my permission. You might poison yourself, or set the house on fire, or do some other serious mischief: I cannot allow my little wife to tidy here."

"But I have not done the least morsel of harm," she answered; "I have only washed out those dirty glasses, and told Janet to get the dingy old vessels bright."

"What vessels?" gasped her husband.

"Why, all the things that were here," she said, pointing to a marble slab.

"My dear child, you have put me back months.—She surely has not touched those?"

And Maurice, in an agony of fear, descended to the basement, where he found the scouring proceeding in full vigour, and half his best experiments either blazing in the fire or floating down the sink.

It was a scene calculated to try the patience of any man; but still Maurice did not lose his temper; he only rescued as much as possible from the hands of the destroyer, re-arranged the old rubbish which Lina had doomed for destruction; and then locking the door and putting the key in his pocket, kissed his wife, and told her she must leave his territories unmolested for the future.

And although she had not the faintest idea of the extent of the damage committed, she was very sorry and very penitent, and ready to eat humble-pie in any quantity. But Maurice could not bear to see tears in the dark eyes, and so told her what was a great fib, that he could soon repair his loss; and he went out and bought her a quantity of new music, and paid a year's subscription to a West End library, telling her at the same time he thought these things would amuse her more than rummaging amongst his stupid chemicals. And when he got clear in the evenings, he took her out for a walk through the brightly lighted streets, and answered as best he could her eager enquiries about old places and ancient times. His historical and antiquarian knowledge was of the smallest, but still he could shew her where the fire began, and where the city gates had stood; and he knew that through Walbrook there once ran a rapid stream, and that out on Tower Hill people had been beheaded.

Then on Sunday she dragged him first to St. Paul's, and afterwards to Westminster, and came home quite oppressed with the grandeur of the Abbey aisles, and the beauty of the chanting, and the thought of all the people that were buried there, and, last but not least, with the beginning of a very bad cold, which she had managed to catch, either at morning or evening service.

Soon a stop was put to the evening strolls, for the cold got so much worse, that Mrs. Storn could not leave her room at all, and for the first time in her life lay in bed ill and alone. It was natural to her age perhaps, that when she had swallowed under protest her medicine and her gruel, and dismissed both her doctor and Janet, and read novels till her head ached, she should begin to cry very quietly for her papa. For had she not been the light of his life to him, and had he not always had leisure to devote to her, and were not their interests and their thoughts and their tastes one; and was not he always beside her pillow if ever she had a pain, no matter how slight and unimportant? And the darker the room grew the faster her tears flowed; and as the fire sank lower and lower her spirits fell likewise, only to leap up again higher than ever when her husband's foot sounded on the stairs, and he came in so loving and so cheerful to cool her burning forehead with his nice cold hands, and tell her she was nervous, and that she must make haste and get well, because his home did not seem like home when his dear little wife was not flitting about it. He had his dinner beside her, and, in defiance of the doctor's orders, let the patient eat anything she fancied, and thought it was no wonder she felt low on gruel and toast; and the next night he allowed her to come down stairs well wrapped up in shawls, and petted and indulged her to a tremendous extent. Still, after a little, though Maurice undoubtedly did feel miserable when his wife was ill, there could be no question but that he felt his existence somewhat monotonous when she was well. He had now been for above a month thrown on her for companionship alone, and whilst there was no doubt but that she completely filled his heart, it was equally undeniable that there existed a void in his mind. She knew nothing at all of business, and as little of science. He did not care for music—the books they had read were on topics far as the poles asunder; he might as well speak to her about the chiefs of the Pawnees as of the great city firms in whom he was interested—better, indeed,—because the Pawnees had some picturesqueness in their costumes, and romance in their lives; but there was no romance about grey-haired old aldermen, who spoke London English, and were clearing their ten thousands a-year. They had no old recollections, no acquaintances in common: the affairs of their household ran too smooth to furnish the smallest topic for conversation. He loved Lina with all his soul; but he wanted somebody to talk to nevertheless, and accordingly he felt by no means sorry when Mr. Gordon Glenaen was graciously pleased to come over and pay an evening visit to his wife.

It was evident the manufacturer expected to find Mrs. Storn a something above the common by the way he had adorned himself. His hair was newly cut and oiled—he wore his best 'Change coat—he felt happy in a blue braided waistcoat, and was unexceptionable in the matter of boots. He had taken some pains in tying his cravat, and tossed over all his shirts before he could fix on that likely to sit the best about the collar.

Maurice, who greeted him in the hall, felt perhaps a little astonished at the improvement in his appearance; but the surprise was mutual, for the manufacturer had not seen his friend before in his new apparel, and as for the old house, he declared he should not have known it.

He was just saying this, when he reached the drawing-room, where Lina was waiting to receive him. From her husband's description of Mr. Glenaen as "a regular business fellow," "a blunt John Bull," and so forth, she expected to meet a good-natured, fat, vulgar-looking man, and accordingly, when she saw a tall, handsome, and sufficiently presentable individual enter the room, she stood for a second uncertain as to whether this could be the person she was to welcome kindly for her husband's sake.

"Mr. Glenaen, Lina," said Maurice, noticing her sweeping curtsey in answer to the manufacturer's profound bow— "Glenaen, my wife," and on the strength of this fresh assurance, Mrs. Storn shook hands with the new arrival, and said very pleasantly all she ought to have said, and fluttered back to her seat in a pretty, graceful way, while Mr. Glenaen offered her his congratulations, scanning the young wife curiously from head to foot all the time.

It was evident she was very unlike what he had pictured her. Maurice could see that, by the furtive glances he turned upon her every now and then during the evening. It was clear also he admired her; for Mr. Glenaen was as good a judge in the matter of beauty as any man in London, but still at the bottom of his heart he disliked the stranger, and the reason he did so, was, perhaps, because he felt—without the slightest assumption of superiority on her part—that she belonged to a higher grade in society than himself, and compelled him to take heed what he said, and how he behaved, and how he moved, aye, and even looked.

For a woman's glance is quick, and Gordon Glenaen somehow did not care to meet Lina's full and fair. Even as she answered his first salutation he felt she was "taking him in," and he knew a good deal which passed through her mind on that first evening concerning him, which she never analyzed for months afterwards. He ate less and he drank less because of her; he "cut the shop," as he would have said, almost altogether, and talked on those subjects which seemed to interest her most. He said his mother was going to call, and Lina replied, that she would be very glad to see her; and he asked Mr. Storn about Westmoreland, and got Lina to speak of the journey, and then asked how she liked the city, and business; in fact, he did with her what he tried to do with everybody—get all out of her, and perhaps he was disappointed, he had so little trouble in the process, for he set her down mentally as a chit of a child, whom he could see through.

Still there was a feeling of antipathy between them—a sort of repulsion in their natures, and although they parted very pleasantly, and seemed to Maurice's eyes quite cordial—Lina standing on the hearthrug and looking fixedly into the fire, felt that she did not like Mr. Glenaen, and that she must not say so.

He did not go out through the hall door, and she wondered why he and her husband went into the counting-house together, and staid gossiping there for so long. It may seem unreasonable, but still she could not help marvelling what they had to say that might not just as well have been said before her. She walked over to the piano and commenced playing in order to delude her own judgment as it deluded the understandings of the two men who heard her from their sanctum. Maurice thought she was amusing herself, and Mr. Glenaen imagined she was wanting her husband back, and that Maurice was wanting to go. Something of this feeling he managed to put into his parting words.

"You have got a very handsome young wife, Storn, and you are a happy man—but—a spoiled chemist."

CHAPTER VI.

EXPERIMENTS.

THERE was quite sufficient variety in City life to make the first few months after marriage glide rapidly away. Everything seemed pleasant to Lina: their house was so large, their means so comfortable, and the constant succession of novelties so great, that the young wife, happy in her new position, and in the possession of her husband's affection, forgot to yearn for the green fields, and flowers, and hedge-rows of the country, and made herself quite content amongst bricks and chimneys, smoke, and dirt, and noise.

She was pleased, as a child might have been, with the panorama of active life perpetually changing before her eyes. Till you get tired of it, there is no place on the face of the earth like London; no place where so much is to be seen and heard at so small an expense; no place where a stranger can pitch his tent and feel himself at home so soon as in this mighty Babylon, which it is the pleasure of some individuals to describe as a howling wilderness.

So Lina thought, at any rate; she dropped into her appointed spot in the great city, and found at first that it fitted her exactly. The scenes which old residents passed by unnoticed were all fraught with interest to her; the sights and sounds of city life, instead of giving her head-ache, and making her heart grow sick for a quieter home, amused and excited her. It seemed to give a sort of stimulus to her existence, hearing the carts roll by, and the cabs rattle past, and the shout and hum of human voices break on her ear almost before she was awake in the mornings. Everybody was busy—no one in London ever appeared to rest, and thus the contagion of business spread to her likewise, and she used to hurry on with her dressing, and rush through the day as if she had something really to do in it. Wear takes the gloss off all things—even of the sensation of being perplexed and amused by the whirl of life in this great city, but for months Lina never crossed the threshold of

her home without seeing some trifle that she would talk for
half-an-hour about at night.

The rector's wife, seeing her pretty face and graceful figure
at church, departed from the usual rule of clergymen's spouses,
and calling upon the young stranger took kindly to her; and
accordingly through the bustling streets, Mrs. Storn rarely
wanted a companion, who was delighted to show her all the
sights, and indulge her fancy for variety to the utmost.

Mrs. Kingston was a woman so sure of her own position in
society, that she did not mind in the slightest degree what the
business world of London might choose to say concerning her,
and she made no objection about standing for ten minutes
amongst a crowd of the lowest rabble in London, if Lina
wanted to see Punch and Judy, or get a glimpse of the fire
engines getting under weigh. This last was a spectacle indeed,
that Mrs. Storn never wearied of beholding; there was something in the magical quickness with which the engine was
pulled out, and the horses were harnessed to, and the firemen
took their places, that suited the hurry and activity of her own
nature.

"There it is again! do let us stop!" she used to entreat
Mrs. Kingston; and then that lady would stop, and watch
Lina following every movement of the men with her great dark
eager eyes, holding her breath, and gradually working herself
up into such a state of excitement, that when the policeman
answered "Yes" to the question, "if the first street was
clear?" and the four horses went galloping away, with the
driver and firemen hallooing and shouting at the top of their
lungs, she gasped like one who had made some tremendous
exertion of her own. She thought the finest sight she ever
beheld in her life was a fire engine dashing down Waterloo
Place, and sweeping round into Pall Mall—the carriages, and
carts, and vans, clearing off to the sides of the horseway, and
leaving a passage down the centre for that which came and
went almost like a flash of lightning; and once, when a fire
occurred at one of the wharfs, and her husband was too busy
to attend to her, she pleaded so hard to Mr. Glenaen for a sight
of the spectacle, that he absolutely turned out in the bitter
cold of a March night, and escorted her to the scene of action.

It was a fire worth seeing. Mr. Glenaen himself, who had
never beheld any but remarkable fires, admitted that; and as
the burning oil escaping from the casks went floating in little
islands of flame down the river, the manufacturer told her she
might live a hundred years in London without ever beholding
such another sight.

Then Lina went home and chattered to her husband about the volumes of smoke and the sheets of fire that rose up to the sky, and the long lines and stars of light that seemed quite to cover the Thames, and made all the boats and vessels scuttle out of the way as fast as possible, until Maurice and Mr. Glenaen fairly laughed outright at her enthusiasm, and said she ought to try and get enrolled amongst the brigade.

Then they went on to speak of the loss of property and sacrifice of life which might be expected, and Mr. Glenaen told about the fires he had seen in his time—the Houses of Parliament, the Tower, and the Royal Exchange, and made Lina jealous of his larger experiences in the matter of conflagrations.

The old churches too, and the ancient monuments; the odd, out-of-the-way old-fashioned nooks and corners which abound in that part of London, had their charms for the chemist's wife; and thus, as she found ample amusement for herself during the day, and had her husband to talk to in the evening, Lina's life flowed smoothly on, almost without a ripple. The only pebble in her course was Mr. Glenaen, who every now and then would take Maurice away from his fireside into that odious counting-house, and rouse the old wonder in her mind concerning what it might be they had to talk about. True, on many of these occasions Mrs. Glenaen was left for her company; but Lina did not like Mrs. Glenaen, who bored her about housekeeping, and the price of provisions, and the duty of being economical.

"Handsome! yes, she may have been handsome some half a century back," Lina acquiesced. "I dare say she was a vulgar beauty once, but all that has nothing to do with the way she harasses me now. She wants to do my shopping, and to housekeep for me, and to matronize me in the streets. Go out with her indeed! I would just as soon go out with a Guy Fawkes."

So the young wife said to her husband when she had seen Mrs. Glenaen two or three times; but as Maurice did not seem altogether to approve the tone she adopted, did not "back her up;" in fact, she never stated her opinion so broadly again, but contented herself with occasional skirmishes in the enemy's country, holding her own ground so well all the time, that Mrs. Glenaen never got the smallest control in the city establishment, nor could induce Mrs. Storn to make use of her experience in the matter of housekeeping.

Mrs. Storn, like most other women, thought herself very competent to manage her own establishment: whether she was, it is not for me to decide; my own private opinion being, however,

that she knew nothing whatever about the matter, but was
fortunate in possessing a servant who did; and it was concerning Janet's position in the household, and her general
capabilities, that Mrs. Glenaen and she had the most uncom-
promising "tiffs."

Hard, cold, unsympathising, and stingy, Mrs. Glenaen "believed" in no domestic who was happy and well fed; and
Janet, being one of those contented, comfortable-looking sort
of bodies who manage to make a house seem a home at once,
fell of course under the ban of her disapproval.

"She would advise Mrs. Storn to be careful and not to trust
so much to servants;" but Mrs. Storn would not be careful,
and would not live in her kitchen, and would not go out marketing, and declined Mrs. Glenaen's offers to market for her.

"If I were old enough to be married," Lina said one evening, "I am old enough to manage my husband's house; and I
would rather be dead at once than begin to suspect Janet, and
live in constant hot water with the people I employ. I am
sure I am not extravagant; indeed, Mrs. Glenaen, you are
mistaken in thinking I waste Mr. Storn's money. I try to be
economical, and Janet helps me as much as she can."

"You are very fortunate," sneered the manufacturer's mother: "if I were to trust my money to a servant I should soon
come to an end of it;" and she repeated that phrase "my
money" so often, that Lina said to her husband, "Maurice,
where does Mrs. Glenaen get her money from? what was Mr.
Glenaen before he died, and why does she not dress in black as
she ought?"

To the latter part of this question Mr. Storn replied that
Mr. Glenaen had been dead a quarter of a century, or thereabouts; that many widows did not keep on mourning after
the first two years; but the former query he was unable to
answer, for he knew nothing about Mr. Glenaen senior, nor
what he had been, nor the source whence his widow's income
was derived; he only believed she had one, which Gordon
Glenaen found very useful on occasion. Like many men, he
had never thought about the matter until his wife put it into
his head to do so; but then he did begin to wonder at the command of money Mrs. Glenaen seemed to possess, and at the
complete hold she had in the matter of cash over her son.
There was a discrepancy between her apparent antecedents
and her actual means; between her clothes and herself, her
income, and her general modes of proceeding; but there are
many discrepancies of the same sort in London, and Maurice,
being fully occupied, soon forgot all about Lina's enquiries.

Business, experiments, and the every-day wear and tear of city life, gave him quite enough to do, without meddling in the affairs of his neighbours; indeed, after a time he found he had too many of his own on hand to be able to bestow proper attention to wife and chemistry, and it was then Lina began, as the phrase goes, to "find the difference."

Not in his love perhaps, nor in his thoughtful attention to her wants and comfort; but after they had been married some six or seven months, she was left more and more on her own resources for amusement and occupation; and this proved especially unfortunate, because, as time passed on, her stock of both became pretty nearly exhausted. There can be no doubt, whatever romantic young ladies may imagine to the contrary, but that after a time the gloss of matrimony wears off, that the novelty of being mistress of an establishment cannot last for ever, and that when the house has been thoroughly put to rights, and the whole of the neighbourhood explored, and the requisite number of visitors received, marriage becomes as dull an affair as single blessedness, if wives have nobody to talk to and nothing to do, and little to think of.

Perhaps on the whole it is a duller affair, because, before the clergyman has done what is needful under the circumstances, there is always the possible husband or wife looming in the distance, or making a little excitement in the present; whilst, after the noose has once been pulled so tight that that which God has joined man can not sever, no change in an ordinary way ever takes place till the undertaker comes to escort Madam to that country where the latest fashions are unknown; and Mister to a court where protested bills and clamorous creditors are denied admittance. Wherefore, seeing that the chances of matrimonial existence are of the fewest, it seems to behove people to make the most of the certainties, and strive to render the life-long journey as little irksome to each other as possible.

Now this was exactly what Maurice Storn failed to do. He was emphatically a good husband; grieved if even his wife's finger ached; ready to gratify her slightest wish, and proud of her as man could be; but still he never tried to make a companion of her, and fit her to be a suitable wife for a chemist. He thought, because he gave her a well-furnished house, ample means for housekeeping and dress, a handsome piano, a perfect parterre of flowers, and books *ad lib.*, that she ought to be, and was, perfectly happy. He imagined, because he saw her occasionally putting buttons on his shirts, darning his stockings, and dusting some of her nicknackeries, that household affairs were as much an employment to her as chemistry was to him; and indeed it would have been much better for Lina had she cared a little more for the practical details of domestic management, or been possessed of any taste for some pursuit which might have occupied her time and engaged her attention.

As matters stood, by one o'clock every day she had given directions for dinner, dressed herself for the afternoon, watered her flowers, tried over two or three new songs, and dipped deep into the magazines and latest novel; and thus for the whole of the afternoon she had no amusement left, unless Mrs. Lindor or Mrs. Kingston walked in, except worsted work and looking at her watch.

There can be no doubt but that it is a healthier employment for a wife to black grates than to spend half her life yawning and wearying for her husband's return. If a man and his wife cannot work and think together, it is better for her to be a frivolous fool, capable of finding occupation for life in dress and visiting, than to sit lonely and desolate at home gnawing her heart out.

For to this pass it came at last with Lina. She did not know what was the matter with her; but she felt she was utterly wretched. In the joys or the sorrows of those about her she took no sort of interest. Her pride and her refinement made her look coldly on those ladies who pressed forward most eagerly for her acquaintance. They might be rich—they might be as good as her husband's wife had a right to expect to visit with, but still they were not the "set" her father had taught her she ought to encourage.

They were common; there could be no doubt about that; and at last she grew so intolerant of their society, their interference, and their modes of thought, that she told Janet never to admit any of them, Mrs. Glenaen excepted, to whom she was afraid of showing any open slight.

Thus before very long her circle narrowed down to Mrs. Kingston, Mrs. Lindor, and the Glenaens. When it came to this pass, she calculated that for seventy hours in the week she had really nothing to do, and nobody to speak to. Competence to a person of Mrs. Storn's character was one of the greatest misfortunes conceivable. Could her husband have ill afforded to buy new clothes, and she had been compelled to darn, and turn, and patch, and think about, and contrive in her house-keeping, she might have found the days pass pleasantly enough, because duty will shorten the passage of the dreariest hours to every one of us, men and women alike; and labour, after all, is the medicine that gives us mental strength to bear the daily burden of existence.

Maurice, perhaps, did not act exactly right even in the earliest days of his marriage, for, instead of making his wife a companion, he made her his pet; and all unconscious that after the first novelty of her situation wore off, Lina had put childish things away from her, and was ripening faster and faster into mature womanhood, he continued to treat her like a doll—love her, kiss her, make presents to her, admire her, surround her with every luxury his means would afford, anticipate her slightest wish, and do everything, in fact, except what she wanted—trust and confide in her.

This part of a husband's duty was as a sealed book to Maurice Storn. Had his wife been the most perfect stranger he ever came in contact with, she could scarcely have known less of his daily life, his future hopes, or present associates, than was actually the case.

He was a chemist—that was all she knew about him or his profession; of what chemistry actually was she had the very vaguest idea possible, except that it usually smelt very badly; her nose satisfied her on that point, whenever she opened her bedroom window, or ventured near the laboratory, or visited Bow; and as for experiments, the only conclusion she could arrive at concerning them was, that they occupied her husband during the time she hoped to have had him with her; and that no earthly good she could divine ever had come, or ever was likely to come, out of them.

Her husband was following one unintelligible path alone; and she having no path of her own, and not being permitted to tread in his, followed his course with weary, anxious, dissatisfied eyes, wondering where all this was to end, and thinking what a different sort of affair matrimony was to what she had pictured it.

In the long summer evenings, when Gordon Glenaen and her husband were holding their endless private conversations in the counting-house, she left her piano, and making her way out on to the roof, would sit for an hour at a time gazing at the forests of masts, and the distant Surrey hills, and the sea of crooked chimneys, and the desert of red-tiled habitations all around her. And she sometimes longed to be sailing down that river to some dreamy island of her imagination, untainted by trade, inaccessible to Mr. Glenaen; and then she wondered whether her husband's expectations would all be disappointed as hers had been, and whether experiments in chemistry were likely to prove more successful than those she had tried in life.

And thus she would remain evening after evening, looking out with her large dark eyes into the future of her existence, whilst Maurice as eagerly, but how much more happily, kept gazing out on the vast fallow field I spoke of once before, which was to yield him fame, wealth, and position.

The glory of that distant prospect blinded him to the morass close by; the glitter of the gold mine made him forget the pearl of great price he held in his hand. In his ears sounded the bells of the fairy chariot that was to bear him triumphant above his fellows; and their deceitful music deafened him to the low, sweet harmony of domestic affection that can at once soothe our sorrows and increase our joy. His home was so happy to him that he never considered it might be less so to his wife. She never intruded herself on his private concerns, his time, his attention, or his secrets. She never said she was weary or lonely; never asked him to relinquish his friend, or his pursuits, for her; never met him either with a tear or a frown. Most faithfully she discharged her duty to him, in all save this—that thinking to spare him annoyance, she kept her own petty troubles to herself; and after the first few months of her marriage, never asked him either for sympathy, or companionship, or confidence.

So far she was in the sorrowful state of martyrdom, and had not arrived at the irritable. It does not take long to make people dull and melancholy; but it requires a little training to get up a grievance; and as yet Lina looked upon her husband's absorption to business rather as a misfortune than a fault.

Besides, poor little soul! as the days and the months wore on, she could not avoid picturing herself in a new character; would her unborn child fill up the great blank in her existence? —was she fit to be a mother?—what would it be like to have an infant all her own to nurse, to tend, to rear? As the days grew shorter, Lina, relinquishing her old station on the roof, would sit by the evening fire, thinking of these things, till it was time for her to go to bed, and try to sleep.

And when at last a son was given to her, and Maurice's love again became demonstrative, as it always did in time of sickness, she laid her weary head down on the pillow, and wept tears of thankfulness; and gathering the little bundle of mortality close to her heart, blessed God for that which He had given her.

So Lina found occupation, and though it was a grievous trial to her to have her boy called Gordon, after Mr. Glenaen, still she submitted to it with a tolerable grace, and consoled herself by making the new arrival known "to all whom it might concern," under the name of Geordie.

For months he left her very little leisure for reflection of any kind; and as time went on, she found plenty of amusement in teaching him to walk, and tossing him about on the sofa pillows; and singing him songs; and showing him pretty pictures, and letting him tear them to pieces. And he gave her nearly sufficient occupation braiding up her hair, for he delighted in pulling it down five hundred times a day; and so long as he was a mere baby, dependent on her for everything, going through all the various stages of choking and crying, and teething, and sleeping, and yelling, the old grievance of Lina's married life was lulled to rest, and she forgot to remember she felt solitary.

Still the fact was so, nevertheless; and as years passed by, the gulf between the husband and wife widened frightfully. There was, perhaps, as much real love as ever, but association had ceased almost altogether. At dinner she sometimes saw Maurice, but more frequently she sate at table alone:

"I am perfecting a splendid experiment, dear," he said: "and every spare moment must be devoted to it "—wherefore he worked at it unremittingly; stealing minutes from his employers' time; eating his meals standing; putting three years of life into one—denying himself rest, food, comfort, for the completion of his darling project.

It was Mr. Glenaen's idea originally—indeed, he usually saw the good, and set Maurice to work it out; and many and many a little experiment which he had urged his friend to try had resulted in profit to himself. He made the bullets in fact, and Mr. Storn fired them: and just so it chanced on the occasion in question that it was the practical man who suggested the propriety of the theoretical considering whether there were no possible means by which the expense of making sulphuric acid might be diminished:

"Why, that has been tried fifty times," said Maurice, "and always without success."

"It will be done some day, for all that," answered the manufacturer.

"Very likely," acquiesced Mr. Storn; "but when you know how many people have failed, you can scarcely expect me to succeed."

"There is a fortune to be made out of it, nevertheless," returned Mr. Glenaen:

"And to be spent," persisted Maurice.

"Not if you can make a small quantity of spongy platinum do a large quantity of work," suggested Mr. Glenaen.

"No one has ever done so yet," answered Maurice; "time and money are articles few can go on wasting for ever."

"True; but still it is to be done—and when once you have

found out the way, you may say you have discovered a gold-mine. I have set my heart on the experiment. Suppose we go into it together. If you can see your way at all, I am willing to risk a couple of thousands in testing the thing properly: what do you say?"

"That I know a man who spent twenty thousand pounds, and shortened his life by thirty years, and failed after all."

"Yes; and you said at the time that if you had had his money and opportunities, you could have done it."

"Well; and I say so still."

"Then why can't you go into the thing as I ask you?"

"*Because* I have not his money nor his opportunities."

"But you are a better chemist,"

"Perhaps."

"Oh! don't turn modest man all of a sudden," cried Mr. Glenaen impetuously. "You know you have more cleverness in your little finger than he had in his whole body. I tell you I know the thing is to be done, and that you are the man to do it. If you wait to make your fortune out of something in which nobody has ever failed before, you may wait till the day of judgment."

"But still, this is an experiment in which so much money has been risked and lost, that I confess I do not care to try it," said Storn quietly. "If once I began, I should not like to give it up, you know; and I might spend your thousands and my own savings, all for no good. It is such an expensive experiment, and I really have very little leisure time on my hands."

"Hang the expense," answered Mr. Glenaen determinedly. "Yes, and for that matter, let your objections go hang too. If the money is wanted, why I suppose it can be had some way; and as for your time, you can try the smaller experiments after business hours, and if we have to perfect them on a larger scale, you must give up the shop here, that's all. You don't mean to remain Colke and Ferres' manager the whole of your life, do you?—spending all your talent and energy in the service of other people. If I were in your place, I should like to strike out some plan for my own advancement. You would not object, I dare say, to have your snug country box like Mr. Ferres, and to see your wife driving about in her brougham and pair. Your son too, will have to be provided for, and I can tell you these things are not to be done on a salary even of six hundred a-year."

So spoke Mr. Glenaen; and, though Maurice Storn muttered some sentence in answer concerning there being worse lots on earth than that of a manager on a salary, it was evident the manufacturer had contrived to throw a sufficient quantity of ambitious yeast into his friend's mind to produce, ere long, the precise chemical leaven he desired.

In truth, he had flung out a tempting bait, presented to view a brilliant, though dangerous prospect; for no man in England knew better than Maurice Storn, that to succeed in this experiment, would be to secure at one grasp wealth, and ease for life.

And as he looked at the picture before him, its dazzling brightness became greater, whilst the difficulties in his way grew less. What if other men had failed; was that any reason he should fail likewise? He passed all the beaten candidates before him in mental review, and saw they had each lacked some important essential for the task. One had too little money, another too little experience; this man had been too rich, that too slow. Where there was experience there was no capital or convenient testing room. Where there were funds and opportunities, there lacked knowledge, and beyond all things patience.

Patience, perseverance, or money, had in fact, he discovered, been the stumbling block of most; and sure of his own chemical skill, of his fertility of invention, of his unwearied patience and determined energy, Maurice, at last, after much mature deliberation and coy reluctance, and anxious consideration, agreed to follow Mr. Glenaen's advice, for him to go into " sulphuric acid and win."

From that day forth Lina's fate was sealed—in the wide world she had no female rival in his heart; but chemistry proved a more formidable and constant one than any passing flame could possibly have done. Bending over the laboratory fire, heating his sulphur, passing it through platinum, trying different preparations of platinum, and buying experience with its weight in gold, he laboured on night after night, till his cheeks grew pale and thin, and a settled melancholy came over Lina, who was not permitted to enter the sacred precincts, and who rarely ever exchanged a dozen sentences with her husband during the course of the day.

If he thought about her then at all, he remembered she had her child for company; and as Geordie was in the habit of racing about the counting-house, and making himself friends amongst the clerks, Maurice, to whom these juvenile visits were a change and relief, considered what a blessing it was he had a son to keep his dear little wife company, and provide her with amusement now he was compelled to be so much away.

And so time passed by, and still Lina believed chemistry to be the last profession on earth in which a married man ought to be engaged.   She considered all experiments a mistake, and if she could have looked down into her husband's heart, she would have learnt that he was coming round to be of her opinion, for he had almost worked himself to death, and was even then sickening of that " hope deferred " which brings down the mental strength of manhood sooner than aught else : which is the least endurable malady that the human mind can be called on to suffer.

He believed he had exhausted his resources, and still the cost of making sulphuric acid was not diminished one farthing. Where others had failed, he was unsuccessful too; he might just as well—or indeed better—have let all his experiments alone, and in fact he declared to Mr. Glenaen:

"I may give it up, for I am only wasting your money and my own health ; and I feel I cannot go on much longer."

To which the manufacturer replied, though not so cheerfully as he might once have done, " Hold on, my boy, as long as you can.   The thing is to be done, and you will do it, as sure as that I shall be a cool fifteen hundred poorer if you don't.   You work too hard—give yourself a week's rest, and try to sleep out an idea.   People may laugh at the notion if they like ; but by Jupiter, I believe all the useful notions that ever come to a man, find their way to him in bed.   Take my advice, turn in at nine o'clock to-night, and see if you don't get up in the morning with some fresh plan."

There was a long pause, during which Maurice sat with his head resting on his hand, and thus he remained silent until Mr. Glenaen said—

" Will you, man ?"

"There is no need for me," Maurice answered, looking abruptly up, " for I have got it now."

On the faith of that assurance the two men grasped hands ; but if Maurice were right—if it really were so—would there not have been pleasure to Lina had she known of his hope ? Had she been able to follow him step by step along his toilsome journey ; had she shared alike the anxiety and the triumph, the doubt and the joy, this story need never have been written. As it was, Glenaen's hand alone grasped her husband's, and of all the mistakes Maurice Storn ever made in his life, of all the false and futile experiments he ever tried, that of not trusting and confiding in his wife, of not strengthening her attachment and awakening her sympathy, was the most futile and false of any.

He found that out afterwards ; but it was a discovery not likely to be made then,—when haggard and thin, but still exultant, he stood with a flush on his cheek, declaring "he had got it." And clutching at that treasure, he forgot he already possessed one which might, even as he spoke, be gliding away from him surely, though slowly.

If any one had suggested that idea to him, he would have said hurriedly that Lina was strong, that Lina was well; and so she might be. And for the rest, was she not his wife—his own? Oh! yes; but then matrimony and affection are two different things. True, but she loved him, and she was very happy, and above all, she was his wife—his for ever.

CHAPTER VII.

FOUR YEARS AFTER MARRIAGE.

LINA was sitting thinking about the fact that she had been married many months more than three years, and that on the especial Sunday morning in question she was just of age.

It was still early, for Mr. Storn, according to the fashion of most London folks, borrowed hours from both ends of the day, and his wife was sitting there till it should be time for her to get ready to go to church alone.

Her chair was placed by the open window, and though the city was London, and the locality either the Ward of Eastcheap, or that of Allhallows, Barking, (I am not quite sure which,) fragrant odours came wafted to her senses through the casement, for in this as in all other things save one, Maurice had considered her nurture and her tastes, and covered the roof of the counting-house with flowers of all sorts and varieties. So close, indeed, stood the pots, that from Lina's seat she could not see the opposite windows. But for the distant roll of carriages, she might just as well have been miles away from London; Geordie was out amongst the plants, plucking off their blossoms, as was his wont, in a most reckless style, and running in every now and then to lay some flowers on his mother's lap, which, half unconsciously, she arranged into a bouquet, and placed in her bosom. She was dressed in a pink morning dress, with her dark hair, plainly braided, upon her pale, fair cheek; she was very pretty;—beautiful, perhaps, would be the more correct word, and she had a staid, thoughtful look in her face, that somehow made her appear handsomer than in the days of old, before she was married.

It was of those days she was thinking; of her father, and

Maurice, before he became husband; and she wondered whether it was the change in herself that had caused the change in him, whether he had imagined she would remain a girl always, and never ripen into earnest, thoughtful womanhood; she had read books that had strengthened her mental powers, and grown a well-informed woman, quieter and graver than of old, with more matronly manners, and a less easily interested and amused heart. The city had lost its charm for her, she was sick of the endless whirl of business, of the sharp, eager, careworn faces she met in the streets, of the all-devouring vortex of trade, of the utter absence of domestic ties and pleasures.

She, who had always been the assistant, the confidant, the friend, the *first* at home, was now a cipher in the busy world in which matrimony had placed her. She was given her toys as though she had been a child, and expected to amuse herself for the whole of the livelong day, with her flowers and her piano, her new dresses and her boy. She was to play with these things and never quench the thirst of her active soul with work of any kind—never take part in the labours of those around her—never know what was being done by the nearest and dearest she had on earth—never feel the fluctuations of hope and fear—never be more than an outsider in the struggle of life—never with the power and the will in her to be of use to attain to a higher position in existence than that of "suckling fools and chronicling small beer."

Mr. Glenaen had been so obliging as to quote the foregoing for her edification, once when she entered a protest against the practice of keeping women in utter ignorance of all business transactions, and Mrs. Storn never forgave him the kindness. Indeed, her dislike to the manufacturer seemed to be the only stimulant which kept her feelings alive, and helped her to bear up against the monotony of her daily routine; a routine which a woman in the country might have varied by visiting the poor, and making herself a sort of lady patroness in her own district —which a fashionable woman might have broken with visiting, driving, and riding—which an artizan's wife would have been too busy to find irksome, but which poor Lina, just comfortably off, and no more, without relations or many friends, or any occupation, imperative or otherwise, occasionally felt to be almost insupportable.

She could love her child better than anything else on earth; she could listen to his prattle and sing him songs, and build castles for him, and kiss him, and pet him, and ruin him, but she could not talk sense to Geordie, nor get up an absorbing interest in his latest plaything. He satisfied her heart, perhaps, but not her mind ; not that part of a human being which requires to be kept speaking, thinking, acting. If anybody in the house had fallen sick, or she could even have handed her husband his chemicals, and been permitted to take an interest in the progress of his experiments, Lina would not have felt lonely. As it was, she sate that Sunday morning in a very dreary, listless, discontented frame of mind, waiting till the bells should commence ringing—her usual signal that it was time to put on her bonnet and go to church.

"Now, Geordie," she cried, at last, "mamma is going to dress—will you come up stairs with her ?" And, obedient to the summons, Master Geordie came running in through the open window, and seizing hold of her gown with both hands, begged her not to leave him, because Geordie was lonely when she went away.

Then Lina sate down again, and taking the boy on her lap, told him, as she had done many and many a time before, about her Father in heaven, whose holy day it was, whom she talked to when she went to church, just the same as Geordie did at bed-time every night. And so she went on for a few minutes, speaking as many a mother had done before and since, till the young gentleman pulled her suddenly up with—

"Has papa no Father in heaven then, mamma ?"

For a moment Lina's cheek and neck flushed crimson, but she immediately answered :

" Papa's Father is mine too, and as he cannot go to church, I pray there for God to bless him and you. Do you understand, Geordie, just as you pray for papa and me every night and morning, I pray for you and papa in church. It is God that sends us every good thing we have in life, who takes care of us when we are sleeping, and preserves us from all danger and trouble, and sorrow, and so we go every Sunday to church to learn how we can please Him best : to thank him for all His mercies, and ask Him to continue His loving kindness towards us."

" Geordie go too," said that important personage, whenever his mother ceased speaking.

" My darling, you would be tired," said Lina. " It is a long time for little boys to sit quite quiet. When you are a year older, you shall go with mamma every Sunday."

" But Geordie can sit quite quiet—Geordie is quiet at Mrs. Glenaen's—Geordie is a very good boy always."

" And Geordie is perfectly ruined," said his mother by way of a finale ; but the result of the discussion was that she took him with her when she went to dress, and gave him in charge of Janet to be put to rights immediately.

I don't believe there was a nicer-looking young creature in London that day than Madelina Storn, as she walked out of her room dressed in a dove-coloured silk gown, black velvet scarf, and white chip bonnet, with pale pink flowers inside. That it is not the dress which sets off the wearer, but the wearer which stamps the dress, I believe to be a generally received idea; but although it is the fashion to run down the milliner's skill, and ignore the power of the haberdasher, I must beg respectfully to intimate, that good tasteful clothes, well put on, and worn with a grace, have more to do with the appearance than most women, handsome or plain, are willing to admit. Dress is not all, but it is a great deal,—I would have you remember that, young wives who treat your husbands to curl papers and wrappers at breakfast : your Adonis would be a sorry-looking creature in shirt sleeves, and minus a razor for three days ; and for my own part, I don't think I could admire Venus herself in a dirty cap and a bedgown. Mrs. Storn had a knack of putting on her clothes quickly, neatly, and with a certain style that made her look better born than her neighbours. Her dresses were perhaps not quite so gorgeous as those of Mrs. Green, the butcher's wife ; but there was more unity in her costume, and she never carried a flower garden in her bonnet after the manner of that worthy woman. Then Miss Hughes—co-heiress, with Lousine her sister, of John Hughes, Esq., Alderman of the Ward of Beadledom, Chandler, deceased—had lace to her handkerchief quarter of a yard deep ; but she carried the same to church in her pocket wrapped up as it came from the laundress, and made such a fuss about using the thing, that it gave one the impression she had perhaps not been accustomed to so costly a convenience in the days of her youth. And somehow, altogether Lina, with her well-cut features and pale face, with her quiet lady-like movements, her thorough self-possession, and her graceful carriage, looked so different to everybody else in the region where she resided, that few could have avoided marvelling what on earth brought her there—by what strange chance her lot had been cast due east.

Not but what many a well-born person lives there—it is quite a mistake to imagine that no scions of good families are toiling their lives away beyond Gracechurch Street and the Tower. Many a man, and many a woman, who were ushered into life with fair prospects—who have driven in their carriages, and called Deputy Lieutenants father—are now pent up in some narrow street, dwelling perhaps at the top of a four storey house, letting out offices, or acting as housekeepers for those who do.

The best blood in the land might find kindred there; but it would rarely meet with a connection like Madelina Storn—so young, so pretty, and so well to do—living in a great city house situate on the wrong side of the Monument. Janet was very proud of her appearance. She always watched her progress down the court-yard, and on the day in question she stood at the hall door to see that " blessed child going to church along with the mother she had nursed;" a phrase which was quite clear to the mind of the old woman herself, though it might have puzzled a stranger to make plain English out of it.

But if Janet had known all, perhaps she would scarcely have felt so pleased to follow Lina with her eyes until she turned out of the gates and got fairly into the lane; and perhaps if Lina herself could have read the future, she would have stayed at home that day, and read the church service and the lessons quietly to herself. One might have imagined that the House of God would be the safest of all places for a lonely wife—that from behind those massive pillars no glance of evil could fall upon any one—that under the arched roof of the Temple of the Most High, human passions would be lulled to rest, and security be assured to the weakest and meanest of His creatures. We might in the abstract imagine a kind of change to take place in all persons when they enter a church ;—a sort of soothing of the feelings, a stilling and quieting both of the hopes and the fears of mortality when it comes so directly into contact with Infinity. But yet, while we constantly find men altered for the moment by the sight of Death, we never find them awed by the presence of God. They who never prayed before will pray in the midst of a tempest ; but we see people careless and inattentive whilst praise is being given to Him who rebuked the winds and the waves, and who holds the sea in the hollow of His hand.

Men forget themselves occasionally when they become interested in the story of some fellow-creature; but they never forget themselves when they are listening to the narrative of dark Gethsemane, and the Crucifixion of our Lord.

We all carry some human hope, or joy, or sorrow, into the sanctuary with us. The curate is thinking about a living he has just bought ; and even while he is praying for the sick, cannot help wondering how the old rector is, and when the tithes will fall in to him. The vicar is marvelling, perhaps, about a vacant bishopric, or travelling off in fancy to his only son in India. Whilst they are singing the Te Deum, Mr. Green is settling the knotty question of how many joints will be bad by to-morrow, and the lady whose friends are coming for dinner, has many misgivings between the responses, as to whether cook will filch some of the fruit for the pudding, and forget to break the eggs separately for fear of one amongst the "warranted" being rotten. It is quite true—we all take a hobby or a skeleton to church, and pull it out for mental inspection there when we ought to be thinking about better things: and just so pretty Mrs. Storn carried her little sorrow into her seat, and thought about it so much, that a pair of dark eyes in the Rector's pew—eyes that had noticed many odds and ends and good-looking women in the world—saw there was something the matter, and felt interested in the owner of the secret, which made her look at times so pensive and melancholy.

You will not, perhaps, think much of Herbert Clyne, my reader, when I tell you he had appeared the preceding evening at the Rectory House—ostensibly to see his cousin, Mrs. Kingston, but really to get out of the way of bailiffs. He had cudgelled his brain for some place to go to—some haven of refuge from the approach of a gathering storm, and in a sudden moment of inspiration, he remembered his clerical relatives, and determined to repair to them, because, as he logically remarked to himself, "Nobody would accuse me of having friends in the city, and a parson's is about the last place on earth anybody would dream of looking for Herbert Clyne."

Wherefore, Herbert Clyne beat a retreat from his West End apartments, and came down to renew acquaintance with connections whom he had too long neglected. Taking these items, and placing them to the debit of Mr. Clyne's moral account, you will not, I repeat, be favourably impressed with the individual in question; and yet, in spite of all his faults, and weaknesses, and misfortunes, Herbert Clyne was a fine fellow —spoiled.

They were his eyes, that falling, in the course of a careless glance round the congregation, on Lina's face, took surprized notice of its beauty—they were his eyes she met fastened full upon her when she looked towards the Rector's pew at the end of the first lesson—and once again they were his eyes that were instantly withdrawn as if in deference to the feelings of one who had not been accustomed to be stared at in any place, much less in church.

"That is my friend, Mrs. Storn," whispered Mrs. Kingston, when the service was all over, and Mr. Clyne stood watching Lina's progress down the aisle, "is not she handsome?"

"What name did you say?" he asked in the same under tone.

"Mrs. Storn," was the answer so clearly and distinctly spoken, that he could have no doubt with regard to the first word, which was all he had been uncertain about.

Under ordinary circumstances he would have said, " Cannot you introduce me?" but on the present occasion Herbert Clyne had something the matter with him and held his peace.

He had been studying that face, God forgive him, intently for two hours; when Mrs. Kingston imagined he was attending to the sermon, he was really "taking notes" of Lina, and somehow it was a shock to him to find that young girl was both a wife and a mother.

"Her boy?" he queried carelessly, pursuing his conversation with Mrs. Kingston in the church porch, and still following the retreating figure of the chemist's wife; "Her boy?"

"Yes, her only child."

"She does not look much more than a child herself," said the old man of the world, who had not yet counted thirty summers. "At what age, in Heaven's name, was she married?"

"Oh, young, very young, too young," said Mrs. Kingston hastily; "she was only seventeen, I think. She is a great pet of mine, and we will go and call upon her to-morrow, if you like."

Of course, Mr. Clyne was polite enough to like anything his cousin proposed to do; but it so chanced that they met before the morrow, on the church steps at evening service, and Mr. Clyne was there introduced to Lina.

"Mrs. Storn, my cousin," said Mrs. Kingston; and Mr. Clyne made a profound bow, and Lina blushed a little, very becomingly; and so the first step was taken in an intimacy that was destined in after-times to bring forth fruit of sorrow unto both.

CHAPTER VIII.

SHEWS HOW PLEASANT A WEST-END ACQUAINTANCE CAN MAKE THE CITY.

INTRODUCED by Mrs. Kingston, possessed of birth and connection, backed up by all those advantages which city people pretend to despise, but which they bow down before and worship nevertheless; helped on by his own agreeable manners, and easy assurance of welcome, Mr. Herbert Clyne soon found himself almost as domesticated in the chemist's family circle as Mr. Glenaen himself.

How this came to pass it might have puzzled an outsider to say; for it seemed an intimacy fostered by no one in particular, which grew out of itself, and was neither forced on nor watered, nor taken much notice of, but just let alone.

To do Mr. Clyne justice, it was not an acquaintance he would have cultivated had he seen to what a pass it might ultimately bring him; for though he was weak, he was not bad; though he had lived fast, he was not a *roué;* and though he had gambled, and drank, and betted, and travelled far along that road which leads to ruin, there was really no active evil in the man; he had never committed a bad action in his life of malice aforethought.

Wherever the tide bore him he floated; he had his own class ideas of honour, but no fixed principle of action. He would not have told a falsehood—he would not have taken any-one in—he would not have hurt the feelings of a single person, or done an injury to the most persevering dun that ever rapped at his door—he would have respected his parents had there been anything respectable about them, and even as it was, he treated both father and mother with a deference of word and manner unusual in men of his stamp and genus in the world.

He had been accustomed to society all his life, and was blessed with that smooth, pleasant self-possession which nothing but constant mixing with the world, and an almost utter in-difference to its opinion, can give to any one. He did not particularly care about a single person or thing in the universe; all persons and things were very well as they came, but they were equally well when they were gone. He would have obliged anybody who asked him to confer a favour; he had tolerably keen powers of observation, and a low opinion of people in general, men and women alike. He was well read—was possessed of good taste—liked music—paintings, anything,—and had never been in love. If he had been a worse man, it would not have damaged Lina to be thrown into his society; had he not been such a thoroughly good-hearted fellow, Mrs. Kingston would have felt more chary about asking Mrs. Storn to the house when he was in it; had his manners been demonstrative, the rector might have taken alarm about the acquaintance; but as it was, nobody ever seemed to imagine danger could possibly accrue from such an intimacy, and Lina herself became entangled in a very pretty morass of difficulties before she put a solitary question to her own heart.

The elegant truism which states, that where the heart finds the will the devil gives a way, held good in this instance, for very shortly after Mr. Herbert Clyne had settled with the bailiffs and left his cousin's roof, Mrs. Kingston fell sick, and what more natural in the world than that Mr. Clyne should often enquire concerning her, and call at Mr. Storn's on his way back to the west.

Then Mr. Kingston was about to exchange his living, and Herbert volunteered his assistance in the matter, and went frequently to the Rectory to report progress; and Lina being much there in the summer evenings, it followed as a matter of course that Mr. Clyne saw her home, and afterwards, when the Kingstons were leaving the neighbourhood, they came at shorter intervals than formerly to the chemist's house, and Herbert accompanying them, he fell almost without an effort of his own into the very heart of Mr. Storn's family, and found himself for the first time in his life—at home.

Absorbed in the success of their darling project, neither Mr. Storn nor Mr. Glenaen paid any extraordinary attention to the new acquaintance. They only knew, as time went on, that he was a good fellow; for once, when the experiment was nearly giving up the ghost for want of funds, and they were both at their wit's end to know how to raise money—(Mrs. G. having turned restive on the question of finance)—Maurice laid the state of the case before Mr. Clyne, who, spite his own pecuniary embarrassments, managed to raise the wind for them, and filled the sails of their heavily-freighted bark with golden zephyrs destined to bear it safely into port.

From that time forth Mr. Clyne was free of the chemist's house; for Maurice, as he truly stated in an early part of this story, was not ungrateful, and accordingly he showed the young aristocrat every attention in his power, always excepting that of devoting much of his time to him.

It seemed, however, quite sufficient for Mr. Clyne that he possessed the *entrée* of the mansion, and called Mr. Storn and his wife friends; that he was occasionally asked to stay for dinner, and left *tête-à-tête* with Lina after tea.

"He is a weak, trifling sort of creature," Mr. Glenaen declared, in a patronizing manner, "just like all of his class, fond of killing time in any trumpery. He will stand beside a piano for an hour at a stretch, and look over books of pictures, and spin teetotum for Gordon. It is all very well for a fashionable butterfly, but as for a man——"

And Mr. Glenaen pulled off his coat as he uttered this last sentence, turned up his shirt sleeves, and went to work amongst those everlasting chemicals, as he would have expressed it, "like a rational human being."

Meanwhile, there was a change in Lina which ought to have

alarmed her husband, but he had no leisure to notice it. A new leaf had been turned over in her existence, and the monotony of city life had ceased to be irksome to her. Her old interest in external objects was revived as if by magic; she took again to her piano, and the clear contralto voice made melody once more in the city mansion; she became fonder of walking, and had more to say in the way of general conversation. A spur and an impetus seemed given to her life, and she went fluttering on after the deluding light, that like a will-o'-the wisp was leading her astray.

Pleasant days those for Lina, when she read the history of the city through with a new hand to point out the most interesting passages to her; when she and Mr. Clyne, and Geordie, used to turn out of their way down Seething Lane, to see where the Earl of Essex lived; or wandered off to Queenhithe, and paused by the house near Dowgate Hill, that belonged to the Scroopes, and wondered how long it was since a river ran through Walbrook; and traced the site of Sir Hugh Nevill's old house in Leadenhall Market, and talked about how changed London was since Stow, then a boy, went and purchased milk from a farmer in Goodman's Fields, at the charge of a halfpenny for three ale pints.

Formerly Mrs. Storn's knowledge of city antiquities had been limited to the scantiest and driest facts. She knew where the fire had commenced and ended; how many houses and churches were burnt, and could repeat Pope's sweet couplet anent the monument.

She had a *mélange* of ideas about the Tower, gathered from tradition, history, and novels; but the great domestic tragedies enacted within that dreary pile were new to her.

The tale of Lady Arabella Stuart had its own peculiar charm for the fair listener; indeed, there was interest attached to every narration—from the story of the graceful bow the Duke of Monmouth made to the Lady Harriet Wentworth on his way to execution, to that most sorrowful account which has been handed down to us of the death of Margaret, Countess of Salisbury.

I do not mean to say, dear reader, that if you or I had recounted these incidents even in our best manner to Mrs. Storn she would have been dangerously impressed with the eloquence of the description; but she was very young, and very unsophisticated, and had not sense enough to perceive that no man would have taken so much trouble to please a woman had there not been some deeper feeling at work than the amiable desire of giving her pleasure; that is—he pleased her, because it pleased himself to do so; and as Mr. Herbert Clyne was no flirt, we might easily argue from these premises that he cared a good deal more for Mrs. Storn than was exactly prudent, considering another individual called her wife.

And that other individual was blind as a bat to the little drama which was enacting beneath his eyes; as blind as Lina; as blind as Herbert Clyne, though not so wilfully as the latter. The extraordinarily innocent nature of their conversations, and their amusements, might indeed have deluded anybody; for what harm could there possibly be, in talking about literature and antiquities; about old London Bridge and the three grave-yards Sir Christopher Wren found under St. Paul's, and the remarkable period when mules used to be led right through the Cathedral. I should like to see the lady who would take alarm because a musical friend asked her to sing songs, and romped with her child, and sometimes read to her when she was at work. What was to frighten Lina in the affair? Mr. Clyne never paid her a compliment; never said a sentence all the judges in England might not have heard and nodded at approvingly; was quite as cordial to her husband as he was to her; whilst Maurice, in his turn, liked occasionally to have five minutes' chat with a man in a better station than himself, who had no prejudices against trade, and no mania to rub his hair up with the wrong way, as had been the manner of Captain Maudsley in the days of old. Mr. Storn indeed looked forward to the time when, with more leisure on his hands, he might cultivate Mr. Clyne, and Mr. Clyne's connexions, into very pleasant acquaintances. For there can be no doubt but just as the yeoman possessed, it may be, of more money than the squire, likes to be invited to that gentleman's table, so the East Enders of our great Babylon pine under an uneasy sense of inferiority to the West, and long to unite in their own persons two very essential qualities—viz.: the bone of the city, and the blood of the court.

In other words, Mr. Storn wished not merely to make a fortune, but also to found a family and secure a position—the dormant ambition of his nature was developing itself in the genial atmosphere of partial success—and accordingly Mr. Clyne's hand was cordially seized as a connecting link betwixt trade and aristocracy; a valuable stepping-stone over the stream of prejudice which grows so narrow just at that point where the withered banks of pauper gentility and the luxuriant fields of mercantile wealth front and face each other.

The only person, indeed, who spoke at all slightingly of the acquaintance was Mrs. Glenaen.

"Who is that young jackanapes Maurice Storn's wife has always dangling after her?" she enquired one evening of her son, after she had met Lina in the street squired by the new acquaintance. "A miserable, melancholy, sneering looking creature."

"Mr. Herbert Clyne," answered the manufacturer somewhat pompously; "son of Mr. Montague Clyne, of Scalands, in Hampshire, and grandson of Sir Hugh Clyne, of the Falls, in Northumberland. He will be a baronet some day, if he live long enough. But what's the matter, mother? what ails you?"

And indeed the abrupt question was warranted by the unwonted agitation of Mrs. Glenaen's manner. She flushed up to her temples, whilst a hot angry light flashed out of her evil eyes; and even whilst her son was speaking she clasped her hands so tight together that the long nails dug into the flesh and drew blood out of it.

The next moment she grew white-looking, and Mr. Glenaen repeated his question, though in a slightly different form.

"In Heaven's name, mother, what ails you?"

"The notion of Maurice Storn's fine friend ever living to be a baronet," she answered, with a bitter laugh.

"And what the devil should hinder him?" asked the manufacturer. "And what concern is it of yours, in the name of fortune, whether he does or not?"

"Maybe much, maybe none," replied Mrs. Glenaen; "only I know something of these Clynes—not of this young man, but of his connexions."

"Ah, indeed! and what may that be?" asked her son, carelessly.

"Something not to their advantage," she answered.

"Is it worth any money?" demanded Mr. Glenaen.

"Perhaps."

"Because if you could turn it to any account, it would be a capital thing for me just now. Storn and I are going to take the factory over the way there, just on the other side of the common; and if I could raise a few thousands we should not know ourselves. What is the secret, mother? let us have it."

"That you may go and repeat it to Maurice Storn, and let his lady wife tell it to her friend. No, no, Gordon, I am not quite such a fool as you take me for."

"And I am not such a fool as you take me for," returned her son, emphatically. "If you imagine I tell my private affairs to Storn, you are much mistaken. I would not give any man the key to all my concerns. I tell him just as much as suits my purpose, and no more; and—"

" You give him the use of all your own money, and of all my money," finished Mrs. Glenaen, in an excited manner.

"And shall I tell you what he gives me?" said Gordon, slowly; "what neither you, nor my father thought it worth while to enrich me with; what I haven't, and you haven't, and what, for aught I know to the contrary, my father hadn't either. Shall I tell you?"

"Yes."

"Brains—imagination—invention—cleverness. There now, don't begin that," he said, thus dutifully interrupting a sentence his mother was commencing; "for I know perfectly well what I'm saying, and why I say it. I am clever in my own way. I can see where a good thing is to be worked out as well as anybody: but I want just that quality which Maurice Storn possesses— genius. He does not know as much perhaps in some ways as I do: he is far slower about pitching into a speculation than I am; but I tell you what it is, mother; I would give all I am likely to make the next three years,—all this last venture must bring me in, to have Maurice's brains. I would indeed."

"Then you would be a great fool for your pains," suggested the amiable matron; "but why would you do so? just tell me that."

"For much the same reason that some one said he would give ten thousand pounds for a good character, viz., because he could make twenty thousand pounds out of it. And there is another reason, too. I should then be like a man who has the full use of his limbs; as matters stand now, I am lame of one faculty, and must have a crutch to lean on. I should then, in fact, be able to strike out ideas for myself, instead of having everlastingly to cry out to some one else 'there is a fine country on the other side of that river—ferry me over.' Why, even that fellow, Matson, who has not half my knowledge and experience, can invent processes I should never have thought of. I declare, I could kick him sometimes half-way across the common. Mother, in the name of heaven, why did you not give me brains?"

"You have brains enough," she answered, coldly.

"Enough, but not of the right sort," persisted her son. "I want genius—that is the best name for the thing after all— genius."

"It seems to me, Mr. Storn's genius is a very expensive one," said Mrs. Glenaen; "what good has it done—what will ever come out of it?"

"Wealth and fame, gold and applause. I see in the distance, thousands and thousands for both of us; I see riches for him and for me, but honour only to him."

"Who is imaginative now?" she enquired, with a sneer, sharply.

"I am not," was the reply; "these things are as surely within our grasp as if we held them there; my faith in Storn's capabilities was unbounded, and he has not disappointed my expectations, but we want more money; and if you know any means by which a screw could be put on the old baronet Clyne, or anybody else, I wish you would give it to me—I won't tell Storn, nor whisper a word of it to the lady wife, as you call her. What is it, mother?"

"I shall not tell you," she answered.

"Not tell me!" repeated Gordon, who was just in a temper to be annoyed by any opposition. "So be it then, I must e'en go and see if Storn can get any more money from this same Mr. Clyne—he is a good fellow for a gentleman, and—"

"Stop," commanded Mrs. Glenaen, laying a detaining hand on her son's shoulder; "I desire you not to take money from that puppy. Do you know what these Clynes are?"

"I know nothing more than I have told you," returned Mr. Glenaen, sullenly; "and how the deuce you happen to know anything about them, puzzles me most confoundedly."

"I come of a border family—they are of a border people too," she answered; "and I know all about them weak, false, and fickle fools. They will be friends with you one day, and cut you the next; look down on those better born than themselves, and take airs over them—play fast and loose—pick you up from caprice, and then crush you under their feet. Every one who has ever heard of the Clynes, knows they are not to be trusted, that they have ruined scores of people, and yet in the long run been no person's enemy so much as their own."

"Do you know, mother, I think some of these Clynes must have jilted you," was Mr. Glenaen's observation, as she concluded.

He spoke the words lightly, but he really started at her laugh, and the look that accompanied it.

"No man ever did that to Jessie Glenaen Gordon. I never stood any nonsense when I was young, from any one—remember that; and you may as well remember this too, that now, when I am old, I will not bear any insolence from my own son."

Which threat producing a visible effect on Gordon, he muttered something about not meaning to be insolent, and thinking more of her than of anybody else in the world, and at last wound himself round again so far into her good graces, that she promised to think about whether she could get him two hundred pounds by the following Saturday—he wanted it so sadly, he really did.

And having assured her he would repay all he had received, principal and interest, twice over, within two years, he got up from the tea-table where this conversation had taken place, and strode out of the room mentally ejaculating :—

"I wonder what the devil she knows about the Clynes, and where she gets her money from."

Which last clause containing a knot Mr. Glenaen had been trying to untie for years, he gave another twist to it on his way to the house in the city, where he now went almost every evening, to have a consultation as to ways and means, with his friend and colleague.

It was on the same evening that Lina Storn first woke up to a sort of consciousness of danger. So far she had been floating away with the stream, but all at once, as it seemed to her— a quicker movement—a more rapid flow of the waters of her soul—warned her there were falls and cataracts beyond; and accordingly from that time forth she began catching at the reeds and bulrushes by the side, to stay her progress, to retard even for a moment her passage down.

Thus knowledge, not to be answered, came to her ; after parting with Mrs. Glenaen, whose anger she had unwittingly excited, by looking uncommonly pretty, she, and Mr. Clyne, and Geordie, all started off to the Tower wharf, which in those days—it was long before the Crimean war—the public were free of.

More than one person turned round to look after the pair ; he so distinguished-looking—she so handsome ; he with that interesting melancholy face of his—she with a bright, happy flush on hers, which told tales, alas! for Lina's happiness. And so they sauntered up and down, till it was time to go back again to the house, talking about all sorts of old rubbish, and making romances out of particular windows and archways, and loopholes, of the Tower ; and Mr. Clyne had a great deal to say about Edward Osborne, the city apprentice, and Mr. Temple, and that remarkable animal the Earl of Southampton's cat, which made her way to him in prison ; and Lina listened ; and thought, as these things seemed to flow quite naturally out of her companion's mouth, how much he must know, little imagining he had read up and collected such scraps of the olden time for her especial edification and amusement.

Then, having been abroad, he had something to tell her about the lands to which she could journey, down that watery highway she had so often contemplated from the tiled roof of her own dwelling ; and as he spoke the poor child's soul went out from amid bricks and mortar, and stood for a moment free, amongst the mountains of Switzerland—only to come back with a gasp to its prison-house again.

So, broken with interruptions from Geordie, they rambled on through all kinds of innocent conversational labyrinths, till the short winter afternoon darkened, and Mrs. Storn declared she was afraid of keeping her boy out any longer; upon the strength of which, they turned their faces homewards, and when they reached the threshold, Lina did what she had never done before, asked Mr. Clyne to stay dinner.

"Mr. Storn would be so vexed if he did not come in—he would, indeed;" that Mr. Clyne yielded on the spot, and was sent into the drawing-room, accompanied by Master Geordie, till such time as Mrs. Storn was ready to join them.

She went up into her own apartment with a strange leaping and throbbing at her heart—then began with a sort of flurry to take off her things and prepare for dinner.

It was in her nature to be orderly at all times, but now she tossed her shawl, bonnet, gloves, handkerchief and veil, pell mell, on a table, and passing over to her wardrobe pulled out the most becoming dress she possessed, and laid it on the bed ready to put on. After that, a change seemed to come over her; for she commenced folding up her shawl, and straightening the ribbons of her bonnet—a grey straw, trimmed with pink ribbons, and ornamented with a white feather; ah! me, I saw one just the same, worn in the days gone by, by a happy wife, who is now a stricken widow—straightened the ribbons, as I have said, and stuck her slender fingers through the bows, and flattened out her gloves, and put each article away in its own appointed place; after that, she began to dress very methodically, and had just completed the operation, when Geordie, who had grown tired of being alone with their visitor, came dancing into the room.

"Mamma, beautiful mamma!" he cried, stopping short, and looking at her as she stood before the glass.

"It is only an old dress that you have never seen me in before, my pet: does Geordie like it?" she said; and opening her arms at the moment, her child scrambled up into them, asking in his point-blank way: "Why does not mamma wear that dress always?"

If a pistol had been discharged at Lina, it could not have given her a more violent shock than that simple question. Why did she wear it then?—The great mystery which had been disturbing her ever since she came in—aye, and for days before that, was placed before her in a human form at last. Why did she wear it? Lina put down her child, and smothered him with kisses—stooping over him to hide the flush that seemed to be burning up her face. Why did she wear it?—Master Geordie was just getting up breath to return to the point again, when Mr. Storn himself entered, to give with his hearty—"How handsome my little wife looks to-night;"—another prick to that same little wife's conscience—"Why don't you wear that dress every night, Lina? it is an age since I saw you in it before." And he drew her to his heart and kissed her as he was in the habit of doing whenever his mind was easy on the matter of chemicals; whenever, in fact, he lay in the trough of the experimental sea—having buffeted and conquered one wretched difficulty, and not discovered there was another just as difficult for him to buffet and overcome.

Why did she wear it?—Lina, with her cheeks scarlet, and her hands on fire, said something about the dress being too cold for any season except the height of summer, and then Maurice struck her another blow all unintentionally, by saying it was a pity such pretty things always were made far too cold and thin for ordinary house wear.

For ordinary house wear?—for whom, then, was she dressing?

I think the harshest being who ever lived would have pitied Lina, had he seen her pulling off that pretty dress as if the plague were in it—had he beheld the quick sharp snatch she made at the first bulrush growing beside the stream—had he noted the horror with which Lina blinded her mental vision, and would not believe she had been arraying herself to excite admiration in the eyes of another than her husband. In ten minutes afterwards, to Geordie's great disappointment, she made her appearance disrobed of all the finery he had been boasting about to Mr. Clyne; and as children's tongues cannot be kept quiet, he expressed his disappointment in words:

"Mamma, mamma, why did you put on that ugly dress? the other was so beautiful, and Mr. Clyne wanted so much to see it."

"I was cold, my pet," answered Mrs. Stone quietly—but her eye met with Mr. Clyne's as she spoke—and the tell-tale colour came back into her cheek. He seemed to read down into her soul: did he know what she had been thinking about upstairs—and a restless, fidgetty feeling came over the young wife—she felt afraid to look at Mr. Clyne, and yet still she had a nervous dread that when she did not he had his glance fixed on her.

It was quite a relief when her husband came in: nay, even Gordon Glenaen, who called during the evening, seemed a sort of God-send, till he told Mr. Storn he had walked over to have a talk about business, and would be glad to have a few minutes' conversation with him, if Mr. Storn and Mr. Clyne would excuse, et cetera.

"I must leave my wife as deputy," said Mr. Storn with a smile: "business, Mr. Clyne, like death, claims admittance at all hours and in all places: I hope we shall be clear of it some day:" and he passed out of the room after his friend, followed by Lina with a look which Mr. Clyne understood just as well to mean:

"I wish I had some one to talk secrets to, and see how Maurice would like it," as if he had possessed the power to read every thought of her heart; and perhaps he did pretty nearly. More was the pity!

CHAPTER IX.

FURTHER ON.

WHENEVER her husband and Mr. Glenaen left the apartment, Lina rose, and moving to the piano, opened the instrument. Just as she had done once before, she swept her hand over the keys, and defiantly drew harmony out of them; but it was not done now to soothe her own inharmonious spirit into tune, not done to satisfy that half unconscious dislike of the manufacturer which she felt at their earliest interview. Ah, no! there was a far different feeling struggling for mastery within her heart, in those dangerous later days; and so poor Lina, miserable and restless, struck the chords with her eager fingers to deceive him whom no art or artifice of hers could have deluded.

He came and stood by her as she played, leaning against the piano in that melancholy, abstracted way of his, which so frequently moved the manufacturer to contemptuous pity of his mental capacities: leaning against the piano, and seeming to be listening to the music, but really following the white hands over the keys, and stealing a look at Lina every now and then, which look seemed to turn back again into his own soul and trouble it. Then he asked her to sing, now some plaintive melody, now some lively canzonette—ringing, as it were, the changes on her heart at pleasure, and varying the time and tune of its music at his will. It was a strange power he had over her; and as Mrs. Storn went on turning over the leaves of life's volume, and singing songs out of all, making melody out of love, and hate, and sorrow, and joy, she forgot about her husband and Mr. Glenaen, about all but the dangerous present moment, which now came to her fraught so constantly with a new and pleasurable emotion —forgot all, till Master Geordie, who had tolerated his mother's absorption thus long in consideration of the charms of a pet kitten, interrupted any further musical efforts with:

"Mamma, Geordie tired. Come away; please come away!" Obedient to which mandate, imperative as that of the Autocrat of all the Russias, Lina left the piano, and drawing an easy chair towards the fire, commenced petting her child, and talking to Mr. Clyne.

Imperceptibly the conversation moved to business and business matters. Mrs. Storn did not like trade; Mr. Clyne thought it a necessary evil, a very important but still most disagreeable item in the well-being of society. Mr. Clyne spoke compassionately of merchants' clerks and others, seemed to consider them like omnibus horses—the victims of civilization; generalized about Londoners and shopkeeers, parvenus and men of that class, with the careless superiority of an ignorant aristocrat, and finally induced the remark from Lina, whose feelings he had carefully avoided touching, that—

"Country gentlemen could be occasionally with their wives and families, but that gentlemen in London seemed to have no time for anything. If they live at their place of business," she said, "it is business all day long; and if they live in the country, they do not get home till people in the provinces would be just going to bed; in fact, in London, a man's home is his office, and his family are his clerks, his ledger, and his business connection."

"Quite true," acquiesced the man-about-town, whose life had been such a peculiarly domestic one, that he was justified in flinging a stone at the drones of the earth; "quite true. I know men who, I am sure, have no idea of the ages of their children; some, indeed, who would scarcely recognize them if they met them in a strange neighbourhood. Money is very well in its way, but surely it is not worth such sacrifices as people make for it. For my part, I would rather see my wife dressed in simple muslins, and have a little more of her society, than I would behold her decked out as some of the London women are, like queens of Sheba, whilst I was poring over those wretched day-books, journals, and all the rest of the trash."

And as he concluded this speech, Herbert Clyne looked at Lina with a feeling of longing for a home such as he had sometimes imagined swelling in his breast. He could not have said exactly what was at work within him at that moment, and perhaps if anybody had told him, he could scarcely have believed the tale; but it was really a sickening yearning for a home, with Lina Storn for its mistress—Lina Storn, or some one like her, probably he would have added—a home free from trouble, and self-reproach, and debt, and anxiety, where he could persevere in the better life he had somehow already begun to lead, but which, nevertheless, was never destined for him on this side of the solitary house where there is rest at last for all.

I will not say Mrs. Storn did not notice the look, or fail to draw a meaning out of it, for she had grown conscious of something, concerning which she dared not question her spirit; but still, I must beg the reader throughout all this story to remember, that the power of the human heart to deceive itself is even greater than its capability of deceiving others; and that those, perhaps, who have been the most guilty in act have been the least guilty in thought; because thought prepares a man for evil, and should enable him to resist it; whereas if he resolutely refuse to believe there is danger, he glides into it almost without his own knowledge, and only begins to struggle when the time for struggle is over.

So it was, I imagine, with Lina; she had a vague sense of wrong somewhere, which kept rising up at uncertain intervals, and asserting its existence in her conscience, but she shut her ears to the cry that all was not well, and contented herself with a little effort of right every now and then, that never made her feel any happier, but only seemed to increase her embarrassment, and render her position a more difficult and trying one than ever.

Thus she merely smiled an answer to Mr. Clyne's observation, and then looked at the fire, and sighed. Her thoughts wandered away down into that never-ending counting-house, where money was made to dress her like one of the princesses of Sheba, if there were such people, and then up to the laboratory, where money was to be made to array her like the lady who visited King Solomon, and she contrasted these richer times with days when she had been twice as happy on one half the means; finally, she came back to the reality of her life, and compared it with the fancy picture Mr. Clyne had managed to give her of his visionary home; at this point she sighed again, and Mr. Clyne caught her thought ere it was lost for ever, and improved it for his own especial gratification.

"I have often thought," he said, "what a miserable life a merchant—a regular merchant's wife, I mean—must lead; fancy her living away in the suburbs, not as you do here, close

at hand, if ever your husband have a minute to spare; but
four, or five, or six miles from the office, killing the day with
visitors, finding occupation in scolding her servants, and trying
to make companions of her children; never hearing one sentence
concerning the things which interest the person who comes
closer to her than any one else in the world; for Mr .—— does
not dine with his family, he has a chop in town, and gets home
for tea, and reads the newspaper afterwards; and then he has
supper, after which he lies down on the sofa, and sleeps till it
is bed time, while his wife sits sewing on the other side the fire.
And what sort of a life is that for a woman?" finished Mr.
Herbert Clyne, apparently unconscious or unmindful of the
effect he was producing on his auditor.

It was the old sore touched lightly, it is true, and on the
very edge, but still it was touched, and opened accordingly.

"You have made my mamma cry," vociferated Geordie, who,
virtuously indignant at the proceeding, immediately drew public attention to the fact.

"Good gracious, Mrs. Storn!—I—I beg your pardon! I
am sure I had not the faintest idea!" exclaimed Mr. Clyne,
rising and advancing towards her; but she waved him im-
periously back, and then losing all self-control, all care for the
presence of a stranger, the torrent of years burst forth, and she
wept and sobbed as though her heart would break.

"Mamma, mamma, don't cry, don't," expostulated Geordie;
and immediately he fell to crying too, in a frightened, troubled
sort of way, that brought his mother back to her senses at
once; so with a mighty effort she closed the flood-gates as suddenly as they had opened, and laying the boy's head against
her shoulder, and smoothing his hair, damp and wet with her
briny tears, she looked up at Mr. Clyne:

For the first time since their acquaintance commenced, with
something like dignity: something that made Herbert Clyne
forget, for a moment, her youth and girlishness, and see in the
slight, graceful woman before him, another man's wife. He
had known she was so always—but he felt it more forcibly
now; and that feeling sent a chill through his heart, and gave
her a momentary advantage over him.

"She had been foolish," she explained, "and rude; thinking
of other things whilst Mr. Clyne was speaking."

Having said this, she went on with more ease and self-possession than Herbert had ever seen before in her manner towards
him, to answer his observation, and defend the merchants of
England against his sweeping accusation of absorption to
business.

He had trodden too close on Lina's mental corn to remind her she was now taking up another side of the argument—and so he let her go on, and acquiesced in what she said, feeling all the time a gulf had opened between them, as broad and as long as life.

Perhaps it was quite as much a relief to him as it was to her, when a new actor appeared on the scene, in the person of Mr. John Matson, head factotum in ordinary to Gordon Glenaen, clerk, manager, scapegrace; everything by turn, as it suited the manufacturer's purpose to make him. He had come in quest of his principal, whose presence was, he said, particularly required at Bow, and Lina accordingly sent him down to the counting-house; first, however, extorting a promise from him, that he would come back to tea. "You will be sure to come," Mrs. Storn said, so heartily, that the young man, who was not accustomed to such marks of attention from any one, more particularly from ladies, coloured with pleasure, and promised to return in quite a gratified tone of voice.

You, reader, might not have felt particularly honoured or gratified by an invitation to take tea in the city; but everything in this life is comparative, even pleasure and grief, and Mr. Matson was in some sense servant to Mr. Glenaen, and detested the yoke; consequently, it was a gratification to him to be civilly treated by Mr. Glenaen's friend's wife; besides, Mr. Storn was a man to be envied, and looked up to. What he was, Mr. Matson hoped some day he might become; and thus Mrs. Storn filled somewhat the same place in his imagination as Baroness Rothschild, or Milady Topofall, to you.

He had come of well-to-do people, who in their way and station were rich and comfortable, but bad times came, and John Matson had to give up horse and gig, farm in perspective and ease in possession, and leaving Hampshire, turn his face Londonwards to seek his fortune. Which finally came to him in the shape of a small salary and a hard master; notwithstanding which slight drawbacks on the happiness of life, he still managed to be happy in it, looking with that honest, open, country face of his, on the brightest and best side of his prospects, and feeling, that with youth and health, and a good clear conscience, no man who can work, and finds it, has a right to complain.

"Mr. Matson is a great favourite of mine," said Lina, whenever the door closed behind him.

"Indeed?" Mr. Clyne said this interrogatively.

"You should have added, and wherefore," Mrs. Storn remarked, with a smile, "for I am sure you were wondering why I liked him. Well, I will tell you; first, because he is under Mr. Glenaen, and I pity him; second, because I feel sure he does not like Mr. Glenaen, and I sympathize with him; third, because I think he has brains and uses them; and fourth, because, though it is impossible he can be comfortably situated, he always looks happy and contented. I appreciate that virtue all the more in him," Lina added, after a moment's pause, "because I know it is not one I should ever possess myself."

"Do you like very happy people best, then?" Mr. Clyne enquired, earnestly, and in a tone which brought the blood rushing into Lina's cheeks, but she answered immediately:

"I like those best, Mr. Clyne, who turn the bravest face on misfortune, and strike out nobly for themselves in times of danger and trouble; I think it is a sickly sort of sentimentality which sympathizes with a fictitious melancholy, and likes a sad face better than a cheerful one. There are real sorrows enough in the world without our making mountains out of molehills for ourselves."

"And your sorrows have been so numerous," said Mr. Clyne, with the faintest approach possible to a sneer, "that you feel yourself competent to decide how calamity should affect the countenances of your acquaintances."

"My life has been a peculiarly fortunate one," answered Lina, quickly; "but still I have had my share, a small one, of trouble. There is no day without a cloud—no life without a grief."

Right well her auditor knew that; no one in the wide world, not even Lina herself, better; and as he looked at her stroking down her child's hair, all the momentary bitterness vanished from his mind, and the old feeling of pity, and sympathy, and love, came back. For there was no doubt he did love her, as a man only loves once in his life. Whether well or ill matters not, it only comes once in a life-time, that all-absorbing, over-mastering passion, which lights or darkens, blesses or curses, the whole of existence; which leaves a mark on a man's heart that is never effaced till the grave closes over him; which brands its fire into his spirit, and traces in burning letters of anguish or joy every incident of that intimacy on his memory, till memory for him has ceased for ever.

Oh! there was no doubt he loved her, whatever he might think about the matter himself; and to have seen Lina holding her boy to her breast, holding him, as it were, betwixt herself and harm; straining that child to her heart as though he could protect her from some impending evil—a stranger might almost have guessed there would be a great battle fought some day in that woman's soul when the time came for her to decide whether she loved Herbert Clyne or Maurice Storn most— which she would choose, peace or dishonour—whether she would forsake child and husband, give up reputation and virtue, and go forth an outcast, and a wanderer with him. The struggle had already commenced—the brief skirmishes Lina had held with herself that very evening, proved it—and the way she laid Geordie's head on her shoulder, and every now and then clasped the boy suddenly in her arms, confirmed the fact. Lina knew she cared for Mr. Clyne, as it was not right or meet she should, and she was making feeble little efforts to set right the only clock that can never be put back for any purpose whatsoever—the human heart.

God help us—there are such struggles as these going on at many an honest man's fireside in England; a byeplay of affections, sentiments, quivering pulses, sleepless nights, and wretched days, such as he, snoring in his comfortable easy chair, never dreams of noticing. There are two terminations to them—one which the world sees, and one which it suspects not ; for the divorcée chooses her path through the law courts of England, and for the rest, no one save, perhaps, herself, ever suspects through what an awful ordeal of weeping, and praying, and suffering, many a matron has passed, in order to reach a port of safety in innocence at last. Many and many a struggle like this, I apprehend, is going on this night throughout the length and breadth of England ; but still, let us, fond husband and faithful wife, devoutly thank heaven they are comparatively but few.

If it were otherwise, woe for the land—for it is not in many natures to pass through such a fire, and still turn aside from Moloch.

During the course of this digression, Mr. Matson had descended to the counting house, and informed his principal that one of his best customers was waiting to see him at Bow. Which intelligence Mr. Glennen received in his usual gracious manner, remarking, "it was safe to happen so ; if he had stayed at home for a week, nobody came near the place—if he left it for half an hour, he was sure to be wanted." Having stated which novelty, and snarled a little at his employé, he put on his top-coat and hat, and asked Mr. Storn whether he would walk part of the way back with him.

To which proposition the chemist assenting, the three men proceeded together to the outer door ; Mr. Matson, however, bare-headed.

"Well," said Mr. Glennen, noticing this fact, "why don't

you come along, what are you standing there for, as if you were going to establish head-quarters at once?"

"Mrs. Storn was kind enough to ask me to stay tea," answered Mr. Matson.

"The deuce she was!" exclaimed the manufacturer. "I thought ladies generally left those sort of invitations for their husbands;" and with this agreeable remark, the manufacturer slammed the door between himself and his clerk, and, seizing his friend by the arm, hurried him off before he had an opportunity of saying a sentence to Mr. Matson, who stood for a moment or two just where his principal had left him, hesitating whether to return to the drawing-room or not.

Inclination, however, at last conquered prudence; and making sure of a cordial welcome from his hostess, Mr. Matson, with all the happy buoyancy of his nature, brought his good-humoured face into the drawing-room just at the moment when Lina was stroking her child's hair, and Mr. Clyne was saying nothing, but thinking a great deal.

With almost a gasp of relief Mrs. Storn hailed his return. There was something about John Matson she had always liked, and now it seemed to her as if he had brought more air with him into the apartment.

There was all the difference between Mr. Matson's mental atmosphere and Mr. Clyne's, that there is between heather and eau de Cologne, and Lina was not long in returning to her natural manner, when she had another person to talk to—a well-informed, unassuming man of business, whose heart was in his trade, but whose tongue was not; who could speak on general topics as well as Mr. Clyne, and who managed to introduce personal reminiscences, anecdotes, and experiences so adroitly into his conversation, that the West-Ender was absolutely surprised into taking an interest in the concerns of the East, and asked Mr. Matson questions as rapidly and curiously as though he had been an emigrant in some foreign country, seeking information about the colony from an old settler.

So far Mr. Clyne and Mrs. Storn had lived in the past of City history; they had chalked out old sites, and looked at ancient houses, and penetrated into once-remarkable places, where the inhabitants turned out in a body to see Lina and her escort, and to wonder what brought them there. They had poked through musty histories, and made romances out of matter-of-fact streets, and turned antiquaries, and utterly ignored the idea of a present at all; and consequently, it was somewhat remarkable in their estimation to be thrown into conversation with an intelligent man, who was all present, who ignored the past and voted antiquities a humbug.

CHAPTER X.

MR. CLENAEN'S DEPENDANT.

"I suppose it is a sad want of taste," said Mr. Matson, after tea, in answer to some question of Mr. Clyne's; "but I never did care about old ruins, or old houses, or old anything but trees. It quite amazes me to hear the interest people take in that sort of thing. I remember when I first came to London I was in a wholesale druggist's near Cannon Street, and for twelve months passed St. Swithin's church twice at least every day, except Sundays, but still I never noticed that ridiculous old stone in the wall, till a clergyman down in Hampshire asked me about it, and told me a long story about Jack Cade, and a whole host of other people, that had been dead hundreds of years, and were never likely to do me nor anybody else any good."

I hope, when I say Lina laughed approvingly at Mr. Matson's straight-forward speech, my courteous readers will give her the benefit of her sex, and lay no charge of inconsistency upon her shoulders. Mr. Clyne, not being quite impartial in the matter, and remembering all the mass of heavy reading he had waded through for information, felt somewhat annoyed, and enquired, accordingly, whether Mr. Matson meant to say he despised all memorials of the past?

"Indeed, I do," was the reply; "that is all old rubbishing memorials. One stone is just the same as another to me, whether or not Jack Cade placed his hand on, or Jane Shore walked barefoot over it. I have not a particle of what I suppose people call the faculty of realization about me. When the past has anything to show for itself, such as Westminster Abbey for instance, I can admire as much as my neighbours; but as for attaching interest to a place because a man was born in it, or was killed, or buried, or murdered, or tried there, I really could not do it; I want the power."

"But still many persons find both occupation and amusement in tracing out ancient sites, and monuments, and inscriptions."

"Every man to his trade, then," responded Mr. Matson. "I could just as readily get up an heroic about Blackheath, where, I suppose, some ancient Briton encamped in the days when complete suits were unknown, as I could about the Black Bear in Eastcheap, where Prince Henry used to drink in reputable company, as history informs us."

"You seem to know some few particulars about London antiquity, at all events," said Mr. Clyne.

" I wonder who could be long amongst its inhabitants and not
do so," returned Mr. Matson. " Each cockney tells one some
little fact connected with his own street, or warehouse, or shop,
which makes up a very pretty sum total of information, if a
man can only remember all he hears. There is nothing, however, the Londoners are so strong in as hangings and murders.
These things stand as landmarks throughout Cockaigne, and
point the way to many an out-of-the-way court, and yard, and
lane that nobody would ever find without these memorial bea-
cons."

" I should not have thought the Londoners had time to indulge in such reminiscences," remarked Mr. Clyne, with a polite sneer.

" Each man attends to these things as he attends to his own
business," was the reply; " he knows the history of his own
warehouse and his own shop, also of his parish church ; and it
is a surprising thing to see the sums of money men, who live
away in the suburbs, and never cross the threshold of their
ward church, will yet pay for its beautification, preservation,
and all the rest of it. The City churches put to shame the
country churches—and the merchants of London, who have to
pay high prices for pew rents in the suburbs, put to shame
country gentlemen who have their seats in their old parish barn
free of expense. I scarcely know a village church which is in
good repair : I do not know a City one which is not."

" You speak well for the London tradesmen, Mr. Matson,"
said Mrs. Storn, who had flushed a little during these praises
of a " set " she and Mr. Clyne had amused themselves by looking
down upon.

" And have every [right to do so," he replied. " I am a
tradesman myself, though almost on the bottom rung of the
trade ladder ; and I know both the virtues and the sins of my
class. A clerk," he added, laughing, yet colouring too, " cannot be expected to look on the best side of the men who rule
him ; but still I have seen so much genuine kindness, and open-
handed generosity, and straight-forward honesty since I came
to London, that I cannot but believe the English merchants
are as fine a set of men as the world could produce."

" I should think, however," said Lina, " you were not at present favoured with a pleasant sample."

" Now, Mrs. Storn, that really is not fair," exclaimed her
visitor ; " and besides, the topic makes you get technical—get
into our shop, in fact—I suppose there are better masters in
the world than he, but I know there are also worse. Mr. Glenaen is so wrapt up in his profession, that he is sometimes apt

to ride roughshod over what he considers less important things; human feelings—you were about to suggest, Mrs. Storn, and you would be right," he added, with a smile.

Once again Lina laughed, though foiled; but she was woman enough not to be beaten by a first repulse; so she said, in a pretty, coaxing way—

"Now, Mr. Matson, I want you honestly to tell me something; we are all here *en petit committé*, and I wish to hear your opinion of chemistry and chemicals."

"Chemistry!" he repeated, "what portion of it—chemicals!—gases—alkalis—metals—acids—which?"

"Ah now, you are only laughing at me," said Lina, petulantly; "I don't want to hear any more chemical technicalities, but just to know whether you who are so much amongst the wretched things, do not consider the whole science a great mistake—a terrible bore, in fact."

"No indeed I do not," answered Mr. Matson, bluntly; "I think it the finest science a man can take up; the best employment it is possible for him to find. It occupies mind and body; is at once a business and a profession; and whilst it gives a man a hobby, affords him the certainty, with ordinary prudence, of a competence, and most probably of wealth. Why, Mrs. Storn, it will give you a carriage and four, some day; a fine estate, and a handsome income. Mr. Storn is the cleverest and most inventive chemist of the day. He will be a great man before long. Is the profession which with one successful experiment can bring about results such as these, a bore?"

"Not to the experimenters, perhaps," Mrs. Storn returned; "but to me, if I do not care about a carriage and four, or a fine estate—or—or anything," and the poor little wife's voice faltered when she came to the last clause in her sentence, and John Matson's tone softened and quieted as he replied:

"Not for anything, perhaps; but for many people, this young gentleman, for instance," and he placed his hand on Geordie's shoulder; Geordie, who had long been friends with him, and who now sat on his knee: "and consequently whatever brings wealth and ease to those you care for will eventually look pleasanter to you. Chemistry must be dull work to persons who do not understand it; and really I think it would not be so especially charming to any one, if it were not so secret. 'Stolen fruits are sweet,'" quoted Mr. Matson, looking at Mr. Clyne, who did not particularly like the remark, though the honest eyes had no shade of double meaning or malice lurking in them.

"Is chemistry so very secret an affair?" he inquired.

"Secret as—as—what shall I say? itself. Only imagine in

a factory, one man stirring a back or vat, he knows not what for; another melting in red hot pots, and knowing not why either; go thus over a whole factory of seventy to a hundred men, each man going through a sort of treadmill work—only intelligible to his employer, who makes combinations, superintends, experiments, and brings, in fact, order out of chaos."

There was something in this sentence which excited Lina's interest. "Pray go on," she said. "I want to know a little more about manufactories. I never hear anything but dry details that I cannot understand. I should like to see a chemical factory."

"But that would not be allowable," said Mr. Matson, laughing; "we go a step beyond St. Senanus, and permit neither man nor woman to enter our holy island. You might carry alarming secrets off with you to the enemy's camp, to say nothing of other dangers; being suffocated with chlorine, or poisoned with minerals. When I first went into a factory I got a whiff of chlorine that nearly sent me to the next churchyard. It is just like having a rope round your neck, and a hundred fogs down your throat, mixed up with sand, settling on the lungs; I coughed till the blood poured from my nose, and I could not speak for three hours; and as for poisons, Mr. Glenaen only keeps himself alive with snuff."

"And what good in the world does snuff do him? enquired Lina.

"Why, it prevents the poison, the mineral dust which is constantly floating about our atmosphere, entering his brain. Pray don't look so disgusted, Mrs. Storn, snuff is life to us; I should be ashamed to confess here the quantity I manage to get through per week."

"I am rather curious to know, Mr. Matson, what sort of men you employ in such a peculiarly healthy and interesting occupation?" said Mr. Clyne.

"Well, our men are principally Germans, but I think I had better cry halt about them, for they are not interesting savages, Mrs. Storn. They are Mr. Glenaen's abomination, because they each and all desire to be aristocrats, Mr. Clyne: yes, and become such eventually!"

"How, in heaven's name?" demanded the gentleman addressed.

"By practising the great virtue of economy," answered Mr. Matson: "they come over here for one sole object, that of making money and buying land and a title in their own country; so when we are swearing at a man—I beg your pardon, Mrs. Storn, but we really can't help it sometimes—swearing at him for a thick-headed fool, he is thinking what a grand figure he will cut some day in his fatherland. Counts and barons (future of course) we pay no more respect to than to the spoons they stir our liquids with; save, save, and work work, for years to achieve one object; and the way they live, and the things they eat! Good gracious! the first meal I ever saw one of our men swallow, destroyed my appetite for two days."

And Mr. Matson pulled a face of the most intense disgust as he thought of the dirt and offal these foreigners planted down due east eat, and eat with a relish.

" Our people are all well paid, healthy, and strong," he continued a moment after; " no fit objects for pity, Mr. Clyne; but if you ever want to see London misery, not sin ; hopeless, abject, honest poverty, I should advise you to walk through Spitalfields at about three o'clock some summer's morning. You will then have a view of poverty in its quiescent state, whilst Bethnal Green, at say nine in the evening, exhibits rags in motion. The people all live in the street there, any place to be out of the house : they sit 'on door steps, lounge at the corners; the whole establishment turns itself neck and heels out of the house, and you may walk through street after street without being stopped by a thief, or asked for charity. The people have no heart left to beg or steal ; they just skulk out of the house and get their noses flattened against a cook-shop window. Spitalfields, however, to me is the worst; it is, like a dead beggar, the saddest, most pitiable sight I know."

" And can nothing be done for these people ?" asked Lina after a pause ; " could not I, and others like me, who have no employment on earth, be of use to them in some way ? it seems so dreadful to be comfortable oneself, while the poor are so miserable. Can nothing be done for them ?"

" Much has been done," was the reply, " but it is only a drop in the ocean ; there are schools and charities, and churches and reformatories, and all sorts of good institutions, but still they only touch the outside of the evil. The rich in London cannot reach the poor ; men are too busy to know anything of the misery lying close at hand, and so content themselves with a subscription, which is the easiest and the laziest way of bestowing alms I know. Five pounds distributed personally, would do more good than ten sent to a charity ; but, as I said before, there's no help for it; the rich never touch the poor in London, except at arm's length, patronizingly ; and yet there is good stuff in these men, a rich ore of human labour, if we only could manage to work it."

" And why can't you work it ?" asked Lina impatiently.

"Because of our English bugbear respectability," answered her guest; "and to make these people respectable would require time, which the rich would not give to the poor. Anything but that, they cry; and they pour out their money like water, and pauperize the land, and make beggars of men who would work, and are satisfied."

"And pray what other course would you have the aristocracy to pursue, Mr. Matson?" inquired Mr. Clyne.

"Oh, really I don't presume to dictate to the aristocracy," replied the young man; "I only know what I should do had I money. I would make every man work—except in case of grievous sickness—profitably for me, were it possible; but work, even if he dug a pit to-day in order to fill it up to-morrow."

"That is all very well in theory," argued Mr. Clyne; "but suppose a man with no place to dig a pit—an individual like myself, for instance, with a suite of three rooms, and no landed estate, not even a flower-pot in present possession, what would you have me do?"

"Either find work for them yourself, or get some one else to give it to them," persisted Mr. Matson. "The great stumbling-block in the way of the poor here, is, that nobody respectable can speak as to who or what they are. Suppose a man comes to us when we are in want of hands, the first question asked is, where he has worked? can he give references? No, he cannot; perhaps his old master is dead, or they parted on bad terms, or he has only had dock work, or he came up from the country seeking employment, or fifty things, quite consistent with the man being honest, and yet able to get no character. Of course, we cannot have him. He is able-bodied, strong, and willing to work, but he is not known, and we turn him from the door. Bit by bit his clothes go, then he takes to sleeping out, then he crawls to the workhouse, or turns beggar, or becomes a thief, and if he go in the long run to the gallows, I should like to know who is to blame; it is a monstrous thing in a town like this, for there to be thousands of men who are not personally known either to tradesman, gentleman, or clergyman. I confess were I in business on my own account, I should simply ascertain whether a fresh applicant were known to the police, and if not, I would just as soon take him without a character as with; a recommendation is no safeguard, I know, against theft;—but I beg your pardon, Mrs. Storn, I ought to have had more consideration than to weary you as I have done."

"I am not wearied," she replied. "I want so much to have something to occupy my time, that talking about work or any kind interests me. Do you know, Mr. Matson, I am dreadfully at a loss for employment, and should like to petition you to find me some."

Lina said this half laughingly; but Mr. Clyne saw how earnest was the feeling at the bottom of it. Mr. Matson, however, did not know sufficient of the state of affairs to be able exactly to appreciate the difficulty of Mrs. Storn's position, so he answered as men do answer particular cases with generalities.

"No person upon earth, Mrs. Storn, can make an employment for another. Whatever our hand finds to do, rough or smooth, we ought to do it, and sure am I that close to the hand of every one amongst us, lies some work that we sin in neglecting. Depend upon it, Mrs. Storn, you ought not to be weary;—God's world is a working one—you should be busy."

"Don't you think, Mr. Matson, though, that the work falls somewhat unfairly?" inquired Mr. Clyne. "For instance, you, happy in the possession of constant employment, can afford to twit Mrs. Storn and myself with a disinclination to labour. It really is our misfortune, not our fault, that we have never found our work in the world yet."

"Ah! well, you both will some day," said Mr. Matson, in a manner which seemed to say that he wanted to end the discussion. "Mrs. Storn, should you think me unreasonable if I were to beg for some music? I am so fond of music, and never have an opportunity of hearing any, but the chants on Sunday."

Lina would rather not have played, but she did, nevertheless, until Mr. Storn made his appearance, when she left the instrument and took up her netting quietly, whilst the three men talked about politics, and city news, and other matters of the same kind, which were interesting to them, though they did not seem so to her.

The chemist had not long returned, however, before Mr. Matson rose to depart. Mr. Clyne did not go with him, but said, as they shook hands:

"Mr. Matson, I think I shall ask you to be my guide through some of the places you mentioned."

"With the greatest pleasure," was the reply; "any time you like."

"What places do you mean?" inquired Mr. Storn.

"Some of the choicest spots of our East End," answered the younger man; "Mr. Clyne wishes to be formally introduced to Spitalfields."

"I wish him joy of his acquaintance, then," remarked the chemist; to which observation Mr. Matson made no reply, excepting by a laugh, that carried him fairly to the door and out of it.

It is not often that distance prevents a departing guest hearing pleasant things said of himself, but on the present occasion Mr. Clyne made a number of very agreeable criticisms on his new acquaintance, Lina endorsing his opinions.

"Well, I must say," observed Mr. Storn when Mr. Clyne came to a stop, "that Mr. Matson never was an especial favourite of mine; there is something, to my mind, too easy, offhand, brusque—I really don't know what to call it—in his manner, but I do not like him."

"And yet he seems both a good and a clever young man, who, I dare say, will rise to be somebody in city circles hereafter," remarked the West-Ender.

"Do you consider a flow of words a proof of talent then?" asked the chemist.

"Perhaps not," answered Mr. Clyne, with a smile; "but still, silence is not always wisdom."

He looked at Lina as he spoke, who was very busy saying nothing. Silence was wisdom with her then, and perhaps Mr. Storn had an uncomfortable idea of the fact, for he pursued the Matson question no further, but spoke on other matters, until Mr. Clyne left, when he went up into his laboratory, while Lina stole away to her old nurse, and sitting down beside her, as she had been wont to do years and years before, said:

"Tell me about my mother, Janet."

There was something touching in hearing the young wife going back to the story of her childhood for comfort, more especially as her tears flowed now, as they had never done in the days that were gone.

"Oh! I wish my mother were living now, Janet—I want her more now than ever I did in my life before," she sobbed; and then she laid her aching head down on Janet's lap, and rested it there.

There was something wrong; the old woman had known that for a long time past; but what that something was, she could not divine, and Lina never enlightened her. By some peculiar process of reasoning, she made a *mélange* of Mr. Glenaen, and living in town, and traced a grievance out of them.

"If my mistress lived out of this smoky place, and had even a few chickens to amuse her," she thought—"she used to be fond of feeding them out of her hand with barley and rice, and it would pass her time."

And so she rambled on into interminable country visions, forgetting, as people will forget, that the things which had amused and interested Lina once, would never amuse her more —that the child she had nursed was now a woman, with a woman's feelings, and sorrows, and temptations; placed in so unfortunate a position that no person in the world understood her thoroughly but one, and he should not.

That was the point of peril in Lina's horizon; she was striving to escape from its delusive brilliancy; she was standing midway between wrong and right; afraid of the one, disgusted with the other; only half conscious of the danger lying beyond: while exaggerating the sorrows of her life she was wearied of. Making little efforts and then losing ground again: giving place to new and strange feelings in her heart, and weeping over the painful pricks of conscience afterwards; blinding her eyes to the reason why she cared less for her husband's engrossment to business, and felt the time fly by when Herbert Clyne breathed the same air with her. Creeping away to bed, crying herself to sleep, and then waking with a fear and a horror to vow that she would make an effort to bring her husband and herself closer together; that she would take Mr. Matson's advice, and work: that she would strive to cast this awful something away from her, and flee from the evil to come.

If she never put that evil to herself in plain English, who shall blame her? If she was struggling feebly and imperfectly —ah! remember, it is harder to fight oneself than any other foe; that danger never comes openly, but steals into the citadel, and that there are few who have the mental strength and christian determination to keep up the strife through every hour and minute of the weary day for weeks and months together.

Lina, too, was awkwardly placed; she could neither tell Mr. Clyne not to come so frequently, nor explain to him by her manner that his absence would be agreeable.

She had nobody to place the matter in so strong a light before her as to make the relinquishment of his society a matter of duty. No one, in fact, seemed to notice the intimacy at all —there was nothing in their manner to draw attention to their feelings. Mr. Clyne was always quiet, gentlemanlike, and melancholy. Lina seemed more silent than formerly; but still she could speak on occasion just as well as ever.

To do Mr. Glenaen justice, although he did not like Lina, the notion of her flirting had never entered his mind. He thought her a very good wife—much better than he had imagined she would turn out. She did not care for society, and seemed economical; *au reste*, the manufacturer had no very discriminating notions of woman's feelings. He never troubled himself about a gamut of crime; the staircase of vice was a branch of architecture he had never studied; a woman was either virtuous or she was not; for delicate distinctions and minute classifications, he had no time or taste; from the street to the drawing-room it was all the same to Gordon Glenaen; when once a woman fell, why she had fallen, and there was an end of the matter. The result was the same in all cases; as for the motives, they were no business of his. So Mr. Glenaen, who, with all his own laxity in commercial affairs, had a very strict and good notion of what a woman's morals ought to be—argued the matter; and I am not going to assert his view was altogether wrong, but it had this effect; it prevented his noticing the port to which Lina Storn was steering.

If he had observed it, he would have set her down as bad then, and it was unfortunate he did not, as the harsh judgment might have spared her many an hour and day of weary suffering and fruitless struggle. Thus Lina was unfortunately situated in being surrounded by those who never thought of watching or suspecting her; but still she had a vague sense that it was necessary for her to do something; and after the evening when Mr. Matson stayed for tea, she might have been seen early in the mornings pouring over heavy books that were at first Greek to her, and that made her head-ache, and addled her understanding. Later on in the afternoons, about the hour when Mr. Clyne had been wont to make his way up into the drawing-room, Lina was generally out taking long object-less walks with Geordie, so that sometimes, for days together, she never saw her visitor's face. But with the effort to do right, came back the longing of old for things to be right. "If Maurice and I could be but more like man and wife," the poor heart which had such a store of love to give to some one used to think; and if in the long run the chemist's wife halted in her purpose and fainted by the way, there was none the less praise due to her for the mighty efforts she made in that the hour of her strength. It is easy to note the failure; but who may follow the struggle? Who, seeing the broken resolution, may tell how long and through what weary struggles it has been kept intact? Heaven knows, at all events, those days of Lina's could not have been borne in silence by an irresolute, faltering spirit; and if she had but spoken frankly, Maurice would have helped her on. Maurice, who, noticing her pale cheeks, began to wonder in the thorough trustingness of his heart what ailed her.

"She was tired of being alone," she said, in answer to a question from him one day.

"Alone! had she not Geordie?" Mr. Storn inquired.

"Yes, but Geordie was a pet, not a companion. I want to

take my part in life, Maurice," she added earnestly: "I feel useless, a cumberer of the ground. I wish to be at work—I want employment."

It was a puzzling problem for a man not used to analyze women's feelings, to solve what she really did require; and accordingly very kindly, but still very stupidly, her husband answered—

"My love, I do not exactly understand—you always seem to me busy about something. I do not think I ever come into the room that you are not occupied in some way or other. Tell me what it is you wish—I do not comprehend."

"Well, Maurice, I wish you to understand that I am not a child or a girl any more; that the things I used to care for have no interest for me now. I want to take my part in the world. I want to be more like a wife—like a help. Can't you be more with me—tell me about your plans and hopes? I think if you would, I should be well and happy."

"Well, but, my darling, you do know them all," said Maurice: "I am perfecting, indeed have perfected, an experiment which will give me leisure, and both of us wealth, hereafter. I shall soon be able to be more with you; and whenever I have any good results, I am always looking forward to the future time when we shall enjoy their fruits together. I want to place you and our boy beyond want; and if I work hard now, it is that I may idle at some not remote period."

"But now, Maurice—why cannot I be more with you now? why may not I stay with you for hours, as Mr. Glenaen does? why cannot I, your wife, know as much of your affairs as he does? and another thing, Maurice," she continued colouring, and speaking in a more excited tone: "I want to know why, when you are out, and Mr. Glenaen has a message for you, he cannot leave it with me, instead of writing a note? It looks as if I were not to be trusted, and I do not like it—I never have done."

Messages left with Lina on business! Woman mixed up in commercial affairs—an important communication about nitrates or brimstones thrown on the mercy of feminine discretion, to the chance of a false repetition! If Lina had been head wife to a Sultan, and proposed going out without a veil in the open streets, I doubt whether she would have astonished that worthy more than she did her husband. Pouring the *minutiæ* of his concerns into her ears as he did into those of Gordon Glenaen, and making Lina the *confidante* of this beautiful result, and that pretty experiment; it was not to be done—not even to be thought of! it was just like fretting because a freemason would not divulge the weighty secrets of his lodge. Generalities he would always tell her, but particulars would weary both her and himself. As to Mr. Glenaen, he frequently wrote to Mr. Storn concerning business matters of his own, which he would not care to mention even to Lina—and—

"And—and the meaning of the whole thing is this, Maurice, that Mr. Glenaen has come between us ever since our marriage; he has been the blight and the bane of my married life. He is first, I am second. I am the pet, the doll, the child. He is the friend, the helper. I have no one but him to thank for every sorrow I have felt, no one in the world."

That was not true. Lina knew so herself, as she sat sobbing angrily and petulantly; but it passed as a frank exposition of her feelings with Maurice, who, like all men that take their own way, in the long run could afford to be very quiet and gentle with impatience in others. He believed his path to be right and best; but that was no reason why he should not be very sorry for his wife not to agree with him; why he should not take the two wet trembling hands in his, and draw the throbbing head on to his breast, and take Lina to his heart, just when the calm had succeeded to the storm, to pacify her. She had got out part of what was on her mind, and was in precisely a fit state to receive bon-bons instead of meat; loving words instead of altered ways. Besides, did he not promise that in the future he would be more with her; and did he not explain, after his own fashion, the reasons why he neither asked her to sympathise with, nor assist in an occupation which was out of her sphere, monotonous, and tiresome in the extreme? And did he not somehow, with that calm, quiet, evenly balanced mind of his, contrive to still and soothe hers? and was there not, after all, as much consciousness of his superiority, as trembling doubt of herself in Lina's finishing speech?

"Oh! Maurice, how thankful I shall be when you can be more with me; I think you would make me better; I am not well—indeed I am not."

It was mentally she meant, but he took the sentence to the letter, and answered—

"I know you are not, my love! You ought to have change of air."

And so with this trite remark he settled a matter destined to be a weighty one to him—and so many another man decides more important questions. Change of air! Whenever a woman has anything the matter with her beyond the reach of the physician, whenever there is a disease too subtle to be touched by human finger, it is concluded that change is the one thing needful; and it accordingly is persevered in till there comes one change both of air and scene too many for the comfort of the survivors; and the sufferer is at home with Him who alone took cognizance of the nature and degree of her malady. So Mr. Storn, falling back on a convenient cure for all intricate and mysterious disorders, decided that Lina ought to go out of town; and out of town accordingly, spite of her remonstrances, she went, just at a time when Mr. Herbert Clyne received a summons from his mother to repair to Sealands without delay.

CHAPTER XI.

CHANCES AND CHANGES.

If I have hitherto made little mention of the individuals composing Mr. Clyne's family, it is because till it was actually needful to do so, I felt naturally reluctant to group the figures for public inspection. A man, now sot, now maniac—now sitting sullenly over his wine, and again screaming in *delirium tremens;* a lady with the word honourable tacked to her name, and mean engraven on her nature; a husband weak and silent—both hen-and-chicken-pecked—who had married for money, and sought refuge from his cares in forgetfulness—who never exerted himself even to cross his wife, and who yet offered a sort of donkey-dogged resistance to the scourging of women's tongues—a father who did not care for his daughter, and yet had her always in his sight; whose soft spot was his son, and yet who seemed really to dislike to look at him; a mother, fond of power, display, money, and visiting, are not the sort of people one feels remarkably solicitous of introducing; but still these different characters exhibited in two individuals, together with a married sister, whose vocation in life was scolding and rearing children, were the specimens of human nature that had been presented for Mr. Clyne's study, whenever he visited home, for years past. It was not to be expected, he taking his blood and his nature from a man so weak, and a woman so haughty as his father and mother, could come forth a perfect character; it was only marvellous, all things taken into consideration, that so much sterling good lurked far down in the bottom of his nature. Weak, but not bad; proud, yet not unkind; irresolute and amiable, with the vague consciousness of powers never used, and talents buried in a napkin,—Herbert Clyne seemed to have inherited the foibles and failings of both parents without the positive vices of either.

More kind-hearted than his mother, more gentlemanlike than his father, he was the hope of both sides of the house ; for Mr. Clyne senior stood in wholesome awe of his daughter's powers of speech, whilst Mrs. Clyne and she never agreed except when they were finding fault with the conduct of the head of the family. Mrs. Clyne held in her inmost heart a conviction that it was a hard case for her to have married a man whose uncle would not die, and give him a baronetage, whilst Mr. Clyne was quite satisfied that in wedding Mrs. C. he had made that mistake which men occasionally fall into when they mate with a lady possessed of a rent-roll and a temper. Mrs. Clyne and her daughter Mrs. Selfe were bent on keeping up the family; they were particular as to their associates, and thought and talked a great deal about who was who ; they were people who patronised county balls, and gave dreary parties ; they maintained they were buried alive in the country, and fancied altogether that Windsor or St. James's would have proved a more fitting sphere for two such luminaries.

If Mr. Clyne had not been formed of cast iron, he must have flinched under the attacks made on his constancy in the matter of a residence ; if he had been half a man, he would not have borne the side speeches and covert sarcasms, and endless scoldings and perpetual inuendoes, to which madam and her daughter treated him. But the fact of the matter is that Mr. Clyne was not half a man He had sunk from stage to stage of intemperance till he was a silent, reserved, taciturn, moping fool, who walked about the grounds with a weight on his mind, and never took counsel, either with himself or anybody else, as to how the trouble he bore might be mitigated or removed altogether.

For years there had been something the matter with Mr. Clyne ; people who had known him before his marriage, declared he was not the same man. Time had been, when a gay, dashing fellow about town, he was more handsome than Herbert, and as lively as that young gentleman was the reverse ; but all at once a change came over him, a shadow fell across his spirit. Perhaps his uncle lived too long, perhaps his marriage was not a happy one ; people could not affirm anything positively, though they conjectured much ; but this at all events was certain—as his children grew up he sank deeper and deeper into despondency, till that which had once been only a sorrow, grew into a skeleton. He shut himself resolutely up from society, left wife and daughter to pursue their own course, and conducted himself altogether in so indecorous and eccentric a manner, that many persons scrupled not to assert that whenever he came to his title, Madam would try to make a lunatic of him—and probably succeed in her endeavour.

As matters stood, he held the strings of his own purse so tight that nobody except Herbert could ever get a guinea out of it. Mrs. Clyne had money in her own right, which was strictly settled on the children; but during her lifetime she managed her pecuniary affairs for herself, and kept the cash so closely, that her son, who was both extravagant and careless, lived in a sort of swamp of debt, where he floundered about, clinging fast to his expectations, but feeling at times very insecure in spite of them.

The Clynes' was not a happy home—far from it—perhaps this might be the reason why the first-born so seldom crossed its threshold; and as he was in the habit of periodically receiving urgent notes from his mother whenever she wished to show him off at a state ball, or have the benefit of his escort thither, it is possible he would have paid little attention to her request preferred at the end of the last chapter, had he not fancied he perceived through all her exaggerations of language and profuseness of words unmistakable tokens of something being wrong at Sealands.

Thither accordingly he proceeded forthwith, arriving at his father's house on the evening of a calm and glorious summer's day. He was a man who loved scenery as he loved music; and while he walked leisurely up the drive, he paused every now and then to look at the view.

Green fields and luxuriant trees; the blue sea without a ripple on its bosom; the Isle of Wight; the Needles; with many a quiet village and church spire dotting the mainland on which he stood! Herbert Clyne could not help admiring the picture nature thus unrolled before him, and as he admired he sighed. *She* would have admired it too. She who was, who could be no more to him than the greatest stranger that ever lived.

And as he thought about this, he turned his back hastily on the view, and strode on, trying to forget her; but whichever way he travelled, in whatever company he found himself, Lina Storn stood before him. Had it been right for him to love her, it is possible he might not have thought one half so much about her; as it was—have I not said he was weak, and beyond all, was he not human?

So he vainly tried to turn his back on a pale sweet face, with smooth black hair braided simply upon it, but walked on with that memory still hanging heavy about his heart until he reached his home, where servants rejoiced at his arrival, and his lady mother positively thawed into affection when she beheld the hope of their house, her first-born, the future baronet, Sir Herbert Clyne to be, her son now.

After the first welcome, however, was over, she commenced a conversation, or rather a declamation, which was by no means an agreeable one. The moment Herbert enquired for his father, the torrent burst forth.

"Why, my dear, he is in bed, just as usual; and as things cannot really continue in this way for ever, I have sent for you to advise and assist me. One might as well be tied to a corpse as to a man who has utterly lost all idea of what is due to his family and himself—all perception of right and wrong. It really is quite disgraceful. We can invite no one here—we are utterly shut out from society—and, besides, as time goes on, it gets worse. It was not about his drunken habits, however, I wished to speak to you, my dear," continued Mrs. Clyne, dropping her voice to a *sotto voce* whisper, "but concerning a strange visitor of your father—a woman."

"A woman?" repeated Herbert, mechanically.

"Yes; a most vulgar, insolent creature; she created almost a disturbance amongst the servants, behaved quite rudely to Blanche and myself—insisted upon seeing your father, even though he were at death's door; and declared her business would gain her admittance if he were in the last agonies."

"And what name did she give?" enquired her son.

"No name at all," returned the lady: "she simply desired the servant to say *she* was there; and the most remarkable part of the affair is, Herbert, that though your father was confined to his own apartment at the time, she did effect her object, and was closeted with him for twenty-five minutes by my own watch."

"Were you in the room?" asked her auditor.

"Your father would not permit me to remain, and he persistently refuses the slightest information on the subject. Blanche wished me to leave the house at once, and take up my abode with her; but you know, my dear, what would the world think of such a step; besides which, I never will live in any house except as its mistress. However, some definite understanding must be come to between your father and myself, because I would not be subjected to the impertinence of that woman again for anything."

"Was she young?" demanded Herbert when his mother paused.

"Young! good gracious, no! she looked as old as——I do," the lady was going to say, but she just prevented that truth slipping out in time, and substituted as, "your father."

"And she did not give you the slightest hint as to what she wanted?"

"Not the faintest—she said her business was with Mr. Clyne, and Mr. Clyne alone ; that she must see him, and that she knew he would see her ; and you perceive, Herbert, the worst feature in the case is, that he did see her—would send her no message by either Blanche or myself—but desired Jones to show the lady to his room : Lady, indeed!" repeated Mrs. Clyne, indignantly.

"How was she dressed?" asked her son, pursuing his own course of questioning, which his mother rendered a somewhat slow one.

"Dressed ?—oh, respectably enough ; not like a servant, not like a person of any station. I will tell you, Herbert, exactly how she was dressed—and it never struck me till now—like a tradesman's wife, a well-to-do person of that sort."

" You never saw her before ?"

" Never in my life."

" It is very singular," said Herbert, after a moment's pause.

" Singular ! it is unprecedented ! beyond all rule. But now, Herbert, what would you advise me to do ?"

" I do not see you can do anything," was the reply, which brought down on the young man's head such a shower of words, reasons, injuries, complaints, and suspicions, that he finally promised to talk to his father about his ways in general, and his visitors in particular, and see whether anything could be done to render his mother's position more " suitable," to quote her own words, " to what she had a right to expect."

He stipulated, however, for a respite in the matter until his father should be quite recovered from his late illness, and perfectly able to bear a conversation on disagreeable topics ; and some of the young man's reluctance to enter on the subject wore off when he saw how ghastly Mr. Clyne looked, and received an assurance from the doctor that one other such attack would effectually place the patient beyond the reach of human help or human remonstrance.

Dreary days were those to Herbert Clyne, until his father was able to come down stairs and walk about again as usual. When he had to listen to his mother's complaints and his sister's tirades; when the acts and intentions of the poor weak soul upstairs, lying sick with the weight of a great mystery on him, were canvassed and criticized, and misunderstood ; when the young man, unable to offer any solution of his parent's conduct, had to remain neutral amongst the contending parties, and only assert from time to time that he was sure his father never meant to annoy any one, only he had contracted bad habits.

" Then let him cure himself of them," sharply interposed

Mrs. Selfe. "Really, I have not common patience with papa. He is quite enough to provoke a saint."

"Ah, Blanche, we should have patience with everyone," returned her brother; "we do not know how soon we may require the virtue extended to ourselves."

"Preposterous!" was Mrs. Selfe's gracious response. "Pray, Herbert, with whom have you been associating? you speak exactly like a Methodist preacher. Where can you have been in London to acquire such wonderful ideas about patience, and forbearance, and charity, and goodness knows what besides?"

"I suppose, Blanche, if I were to answer you as Goldsmith once commenced an anecdote, I should shock you very much. Amongst the beggars of Axe Lane—"

"My dearest boy, you don't mean to say you have turned philanthropist," exclaimed Mrs. Clyne in a tone of intense alarm; "for if there be one sort of people I dislike more than another, it is the so-called 'good;' they neglect their families and impoverish their relatives, and sink out of good society, and make their associates—their friends—of filthy beggar children and thieves, and wretched women. My dear Herbert, if you have any consideration for me at all, promise me never to become a philanthropist."

"Mother, mine, I am not good enough," he replied; "philanthropists are made out of other stuff than Herbert Clyne; but still I have been amongst the poor of London, and seen things that would, I think, sicken and soften any man. If the members of the aristocracy were to follow my track occasionally, I imagine it would be better for them, and for the nation at large."

"I trust the aristocracy have more regard for themselves than to do anything of the kind," said Mrs. Self emphatically; "it ruins anyone to come in contact with vulgarity and vice. I remarked at once you were much altered, and not for the better, Herbert; and it all comes, I see, of the manner in which you have been associating. People can't be too exclusive, can they, mamma?"

Mamma of course endorsed Mrs. Selfe's statement, and supplied a commentary on the text, by narrating the lamentable descent of persons who "had not cared" with whom they sate down to dinner, through the devious windings of which conversational labyrinth her son did not consider it needful to follow her, but employed himself in contrasting the city people he had been among with those nearest to him in blood.

Which were the most vulgar? which the most narrow-minded? Take the merchant's absorption to business; was it worse than his mother's devotion to society? Was Mr. Storn's care for chemistry more to be condemned than Mrs. Selfe's incessant effort to push herself into all sorts of circles where she had no business to intrude? Was the East-Ender's love of money to be considered more ridiculous and snobbish than the country lady's slavish admiration of birth? Was it less wrong to look down on a man because he had no ancestors, than to cut him because he had no capital? Was there not just as much intelligence, or more, amongst the traders, as amongst the gentry? Setting aside a certain ease of manner and general knowledge of *les convenances*, was not one set just as good as another? Could any one with the mask off show more uglinesses of mind and feeling than his sister? could any creature be a less entertaining companion than his mother? Only compare Mrs. Storn and Mrs. Selfe. Pooh! there was no comparison; and to prove the fact, Mr. Clyne favoured neither mother nor sister with much of his society, but passed the greatest portion of his time out of doors, wondering, when he was not thinking about Lina, who the woman might be that had come visiting his father; marvelling whether she would return, and making, as he often stated to himself, a very fair mountain out of a very small molehill.

For, after all, setting aside the comments his mother and sister had been pleased to make on the subject, what did the affair amount to? A person came to see his father, and saw him; that was the sum total of the grievance: she was not young, or pretty; she had never appeared before, never was likely to come again. Probably her husband, some tradesman, had sent her to speak to his parent on business; but then, no message, no answer; an audience in a bed-chamber, with closed doors; her admittance at such a time to such a place; Herbert went out to sea again on these fresh ideas, until his first conclusions foundered on a rock, and sank into a fathomless ocean of conjecture and uncertainty.

Nevertheless, spite of his curiosity about the mysterious visitor, the young man was far more uneasy concerning his father than his mother. He could see no great grievance in the feminine affair to her; but he believed Mr. Clyne's life depended on some radical change being effected in his habits. "If he have *delirium tremens* again, I would not give twenty-four hours' purchase for his life," had been the emphatic declaration of the family physician, and Herbert accordingly nerved himself up to remonstrance. He loved his father, though latterly they had been but little together; they had a common nature and a common sin; they were both amiable, and both weak; the father's character had descended on the son, and as Herbert was in no haste to become a baronet, and as he possessed human affections and human feelings, he felt that however repugnant it was to him to enter on the subject at all, he, who had more influence over his father than any other living being, ought now to try to influence him for good.

Like likes like, 'tis said; and perhaps it was for this reason, that as Mr. Clyne grew better, he seemed restless and miserable, except when Herbert was at his side. It appeared a comfort and a support to him to clasp his son's hand in his, and yet at times he would suddenly fling it away, and ask to be left alone in peace. He had changes and caprices which baffled the experience of his medical adviser—fancies which were no part of his malady—fits of silence, and excitement, and crossness, and affection, that were equally trying and equally inexplicable.

But still, through all, Herbert was patient. He had learned something, though not amongst the beggars, or in a good moral school, which enabled him to con slowly and imperfectly, it is true, but still with a will, the greatest domestic task of life, to bear and forbear.

Many a time in the future, when the story of the past was read by the clearer light of dearly-bought knowledge, Herbert Clyne thanked God that he had borne patiently and judged leniently; that he had not roughly touched the breast which carried a sore upon it, but pitied and forgave, as some one in those weary aftertimes forgave and pitied him.

By slow degrees the patient returned to health, and when he was able to walk out again, leaning on his son's arm, Herbert seized an opportunity of speaking to him on the subject which still kept the young man lingering at Sealands.

"You had a visitor during your illness, my mother tells me," he ventured one day, during a stroll through the grounds.

"Yes," was Mr. Clyne's reply.

"My mother seems anxious to know the nature of the business which procured her an audience at such a time."

"She asked me for information," the elder man answered.

"But you did not afford her any," rejoined his son.

"No."

There was no getting beyond these answers in any indirect manner, so Herbert came to the point, with—

"I am afraid, sir, you will think me as curious as a woman, if I say I really should like to know who this singular personage might be?"

"Well, Herbert, I cannot satisfy your desire," said Mr.

Clyne with a sort of unsteady quiver in his voice. "You must not ask me about that woman. I won't tell any one anything concerning her; and I can't tell you."

"Well, my dear father, then you shall not," replied Herbert soothingly; "I will not teaze you with any more questions on this subject, but I want to speak to you about another."

"What is that?" enquired his parent.

"Why, the matter has two sides," answered Herbert; "and the one side shows that my mother is not quite satisfied with her present abode, and the other that—"

"You are not satisfied with my mode of life. Is that what you would say, Herbert?" asked Mr. Clyne, as his son paused and hesitated.

"I should not have spoken," he acquiesced, "but for this; that Doctor Harrison declares another attack must prove fatal."

"The sooner the better, the sooner the better," interrupted his father. "I should not care if I were lying in the old vault to-morrow. I am tired of life, Herbert; I would to God I were dead and done with."

And as he finished this speech, the poor weak creature, who faced one existence so badly, that he wanted to face another, flung himself down on the green turf, and watered it with a stream of childish tears. "Better to be dead," he muttered, "far better than anything else."

Now was the time for Herbert to strike, and strike with a purpose; the iron was hot in the young man's kindly hands, and pliable as wax. Earnestly, though gently, he pleaded for the necessity of an alteration, the desirability of a change for all; he urged the benefits likely to arise from a removal to London, and the letting of Sealands for a term of years; he pointed out the fact, that the property was deteriorating in value, from the want of a person at the head of affairs competent to detect and punish dishonesty; he declared the whole parish lived on the produce of their lands; he said, if his father would come to London, he could safely promise to reduce his own expenditure, and spend a large portion of his time at home; he affirmed that society being all his mother wanted, she would be more satisfied in the metropolis than at home, whilst her own private income would amply meet any increased expenses caused by visitors; and finally, he wound up with an emphatic assertion, that his father would not find stimulants necessary, if he lived in the midst of more bustling, active scenes.

"In town," he said, "I am confident you would never require Dr. Harrison to prescribe for you; you might laugh at

all the doctors and surgeons in England; it is only a bad habit
—come to London and break through it."

"You do not know what you are talking about, Herbert,"
remarked Mr. Clyne, when his son at last came to a full
stop.

"But indeed I do, sir," returned the young man; and forthwith he went all through his argument again, and continued
adding fresh stories to his card-castle, until his father cut
across his discourse thus—

"It is of no use going on, Herbert, I can't come in to your
plan; but I'll tell you, my boy, what I will do. Let this
place, send your mother to town, and go abroad with you
alone. I'll do this, if you like, to please you; but for nothing
else under heaven."

CHAPTER XII.

CHANGES IN TOWN.

MESSRS. COLKE AND FERRES had given Maurice Storn notice
to quit. Lina was led to suspect this fact from various events
that occurred immediately on her return to town, and at last
she ventured to put the question boldly to her husband. Was
he dismissed?

"Yes, Lina, but you might have worded your sentence differently." Mr. Storn said this as if he were somewhat nettled.

"Is it not all the same when you are going?" she asked.

"Not exactly—going, means leaving of my own free will;
dismissal implies per force. Now I am not exactly dismissed,
because I should have left whether or no; my employers have
taken the initiative, however, and say it is better we should
part."

"And why do they say that, Maurice?"

"Because they imagine, and they are right, that no man can
do justice to two businesses; I ought not to have kept on the
situation so long: but that does not make my present position
any the pleasanter."

"Would it not be better to give up one business?" enquired
Lina.

"I am going to do so," he replied.

"Yes, but I meant your own—not theirs."

"No, Lina, I could not do that; I would not now remain
with Messrs. Colke and Ferres, and I could not give up my

own projects. I never go back from any work I once put my hand to; when I begin, I must go on, so long as health and strength last me."

It rose to Lina's lips to say—"Then you ought to be very slow about commencing anything;" but she had sense enough to know the observation would not be palatable, and accordingly contented herself with asking—

"And where do you propose going when you leave here?"

"I have taken a house at Bow," he said.

"Oh! surely not at Bow!" Lina exclaimed, flushing up at the word; "Maurice, do not ask me to go there—anywhere in the world but Bow."

"Why, what possible dislike can you have for the place?" enquired Mr. Storn.

"The same as I should have for any other on earth where a person resided who stepped between me and my husband," answered Lina. "I thought I saw little of you here, but I shall see less there. Wives generally think it is a fine thing to have no female rival. I would rather have one, than a business friend. There might be an end to her, but there is none to him."

And the wife's fingers trembled with anger as she turned over page after page of a book she held in her hand, fretfully and petulantly, whilst Maurice only said, gently—"Lina, you are unreasonable."

"Heaven knows I am not, Maurice," she replied; "no one but myself and God may ever guess the misery Gordon Glenaen has caused me in my married life. Only try for once, making a friend and companion of me instead of him. Oh! Maurice, you don't know the pains I have taken to fit myself for a chemist's wife; I have been studying and poring over your books—I know about most of the things you work with, I will learn anything upon earth to please you; I will find a pleasure in the driest employment you could name, if you will only let me be with you, and not leave me alone."

It was the old cry, but still uttered with a difference, and Maurice Storn's was not a nature to hear such an appeal with indifference, therefore he answered it lovingly and gently; and there was the old scene enacted again between a strong, calm mind, and an impetuous, unbalanced one; between him, whose love was unchangeable and undemonstrative, and her, whose affection was passionate and exacting. She had need of love, constant, unremitting, reciprocal; whilst for him, it was enough that he loved her, and that she was his wife; a negative blessing enough in such a case, God knows, but still amply sufficient for the need of some natures that never seem to conceive what treasures have been given into their keeping till they are going to lose them for ever.

The old scene over again, soothing, calming, promising—giving her all but that which her character wanted—justice; for though she spoiled her cause first by long and patient silence, and then by spurts of angry, tearful remonstrance, justice was all Mrs. Storn really required at the hands of anybody.

Treated fairly and sensibly, she might have righted herself; but no kind words or specious arguments could effect any permanent beneficial effect. So Maurice Storn acknowledged in later times with bitterness and pain; but then his inclinations and prejudices blinded him, and thus it happened that the sole result of Lina's remonstrances was a spur for a few days, and a falling back afterwards; that she acquiesced in the Bow house, and commenced packing up to go thither; that for two or three evenings Maurice remained with her, laughing at her newly acquired stores of knowledge, but never helping her to increase them; and then, after a little, things dropped back again into their former track. He was busy at the factory; Messrs. Colke's new man had come into the business, though the Storns were not hurried to remove from the house; and therefore, as his presence was not required in the city, he passed as little of his time there as possible. He was pushing his experiments on a larger scale: if they proved as successful as he anticipated, a few years of labour, then a fortune, then rest —as if it were in his nature ever to rest from labour till the grave closed over him.

Thus Lina saw but little of her husband in those days of waiting till the Bow house was ready; and if she did not feel lonely during their passage, it was because she was so busily occupied that she really had very little time to think about her feelings at all. For she had her domestic arrangements to see to, and sundry disposals of her private effects into trunks and boxes to make; besides which, all the friends and acquaintances she had in the busy world of city London came to call upon her and satisfy their curiosity on the subject of the change.

Her visitors were not many, but they were indefatigable; proffers of service, proffers of beds, proffers of vans, proffers of everything under heaven which Mrs. Storn did not want, poured in on every side. Idle hands were ready to help her to pack, matronly hearts thought of many a little difficulty the young wife ought to feel at such a time, and were surprised never to find her in a fuss after all. People she scarcely knew came and asked her to stay with them during the bustle of removing, and many a half-hour business men wasted with Mrs. Storn, trying to fish out the exact state of the chemist's concerns, which they thought afterwards might have been spent with about as much profit on the top of the Monument.

For she really had nothing to tell or to withhold; the errand boys about the concern knew a degree more of Mr. Storn's affairs than his wife; and thus people who came wondering how much credit might safely be given to Mrs. Colke and Ferres' co-manager, and tried to pump authentic information out of his wife, went away impressed with the idea that Storn was a very clever fellow, who told his better half nothing; and sighing, they wished for a leaf out of his book, and marvelled how he managed to keep her in ignorance.

In those days Lina saw more too of the Lindors than had been the case formerly. Mrs. Lindor had indeed always striven to "cultivate" the chemist's wife, but Mrs. Storn's reciprocal advances had been of the slowest possible kind; now, however, it seemed a relief to her to speak to any one; and as Mrs. Lindor and her three daughters were the most ladylike in their manners of all her acquaintances, she grew quite gracious in her demeanour towards the quartet, lent Miss Tryphenia music, did not object to gossip with Mrs. Lindor, and saw so much more of the family generally, that she at last found something feminine in it to like—an importation of recent date— Mary Cranstoun—Mr. Lindor's orphan niece.

She had come far to scant love and kindness; all the way from Scotland to cold southern hearts, a strange home, a strange people, and an unfamiliar tongue. It was her accent—slight though it might be—which first caught Lina's attention, and afterwards there was something in the sunny hair, and large blue eyes, and pure complexion, that made Mrs. Storn look again, and admire and pity.

For she had sense enough to see Miss Cranstoun's position could be no sinecure; poor—an intruder—not destitute of beauty—"the girls" both trampled upon, and were jealous of the interloper. When they agreed, it was in finding fault with their father's niece; when they quarrelled, she was a convenient scape-grace for them to expend the dregs of their anger upon.

Miss Tryphenia was a beauty—a star—a coquette—a fine, handsome, showy girl, with a voice and a tongue, and a flow of words, and an easy, unabashed manner; she was a person between whom and Lina there could exist no possible sympathy, and yet now Lina was always asking her to come over; and Miss Tryphenia came. It seemed, indeed, as Mrs. Lindor—a large, well-developed woman, who showed off good clothes, and was wont to sit swelling in her chair—remarked, as if they were only finding out a pleasant acquaintance to lose her; and then she would add a few other agreeable remarks, at which Mrs. Storn made an effort to smile, and succeeded wonderfully.

There was a bye-play in all this, and she knew it, for Herbert Clyne was back in town, and she was holding these people between herself and him. His visits were not frequent, it is true, for he had to be much with his father, who was in London, and whom he was going to accompany to the Continent, but still he called at the city mansion quite often enough to make the presence of strangers a relief; and Miss Tryphenia, dear innocent, was delighted to visit Mrs. Storn on the chance of meeting Mr. Clyne : and the dark ringlets used to be shaken over the handsome face, and the fine figure was displayed to the greatest advantage, and the well-shaped hands were carelessly exhibited in the most natural manner by the sweet creature, who had learned the noble art and science of flirting due East in America Square.

The Lindors thought it very good-natured of Mrs. Storn thus to put Treffy in the road to fortune ; and perhaps it was quite as much by way of evincing their gratitude to her, as for the purpose of securing the attendance of a real live gentleman at the affair, that they resolved to give a grand farewell party to the chemist and his wife; a dinner party, with ball and supper afterwards.

Now a party of any sort was just one of those things that Maurice Storn would about as soon have thought of attending as a levée or a state marriage, or any other ceremonial in which he had no earthly share or business. This peculiarity was pretty generally known amongst his intimates, but still it did not prevent the Lindors from making all necessary arrangements ; from taking up carpets, and hiring waiters, and inviting the guests, and asking Mr. Clyne and Mr. Glenaen, and Mr. and Mrs. Storn.

The manufacturer's mother was, for motives of their own, not forgotten either; and thus the preparations were all complete, when Mr. and Mrs. Storn's formal regrets arrived, and threw a damp over the group, who somehow had not expected it.

"Too bad, really."

"He could very well be spared, but she—"

"Mamma, you must make Mrs. Storn come."

"Shall I go over on Monday and try to persuade her ?" suggested Miss Tryphenia, who had her private reasons for desiring Lina's presence ; and thus, after much excitement, it was agreed that Mrs. and Miss Lindor should see, first thing on Monday morning, whether Mrs. Storn were invulnerable to their eloquence. Now this was on Saturday night, and Lina had then told Mr. Clyne she should not accept the invitation.

Man proposes, we are told: but it certainly was through no proposing on the part of little Mr. Lindor that he met Maurice and his wife on the day following the domestic consultation above recorded. Trotting out to Bromley, according to his usual fine Sunday afternoon custom, putting one short, fat leg before the other for that constitutional walk of his, to his cousin's house, he met on the city side of Stepney with Mr. and Mrs. Storn, who were returning from a pilgrimage she had urged to their new house at Bow. Just as eagerly as she once wished to stay out of it, she now desired to get into that delectable neighbourhood; and accordingly when the silk merchant encountered the pair, she was questioning Maurice about when they could move, when they would be out of the confusion she was living in, when they would be settled again.

As her husband was about to reply, Mr. Lindor stopped them.

"Very glad to see you—the very man I was wanting; not you, Mrs. Storn, though I was wanting to see you too. Mrs. Lindor and Miss T. are going to wait on you to-morrow with a round robin, signed by the whole family. You cannot be so cruel as to refuse. You don't know what a disappointment it will be if you do not come. Mr. Storn, pray use your influence with your wife. Mrs. Storn, I really must beg your kind offices in my behalf."

"I do not see, Lina, that there is anything to prevent your going," said Mr. Storn: "You know Mrs. Glenaen said she would call for you."

"If you would like to go—" she began, and then stopped short.

"Oh! you will come," fidgetted Mr. Lindor: "both of you, and come early."

"Thank you," replied Maurice, "but it is quite impossible for me; you must accept my wife as deputy."

"Oh, do come, both of you," persisted the plump little petitioner: "your friend Mr. Clyne is coming, and I told him you would be there."

"I really cannot go," said Maurice: "after a little, I trust I shall have more leisure; but at present not one hour out of the twenty-four belongs to me."

"And I am afraid I must decline too," added Lina, "as Mr. Storn cannot accompany me."

"Now that is really too bad," broke forth the merchant in

quite an injured tone. " What can you have to do, Mrs. Storn ? what have ladies ever to do ? I am sure you stay too much at home. A little agreeable society is necessary for everyone."

"I wish you would accept Mrs. Lindor's kind invitation, Lina," said Mr. Storn. "I am afraid you do stay too much at home."

There was something in his tone which made her eyes droop and her cheek flush ; then she said imploringly—

"Will you come then ?"

"My love, it is impossible," he answered.

"Then I would rather not go," she said. "I am a very bad visitor, particularly by myself."

"But you will be only amongst friends—my wife, and the girls, and Mr. and Mrs. Glenaen, and Mr. Clyne, and—"

"I wish you would, Lina," interposed Mr. Storn in that clear, honest voice of his that made his wife shiver. "I wish you would."

Thus urged, she at last said "yes," reluctantly, and Mr. Lindor bowed himself off to Bromley in a state of exultation, while Maurice and Lina walked slowly away in the other direction.

"Maurice, I would rather not go to the Lindors, please," she began.

"My love, I think you would be better if you went out a little more," he answered. "You mope in the house and grow pale and thin. Everybody says you shut yourself up too much, even Glenaen. I am sure you looked all the brighter for your trip to Southend, short as it was ; and I want you to try the experiment of visiting, at any rate."

" Could you not be a little more with me ?" ventured Lina.

"Not just now ; you know I have not twenty hours' sleep in the week, and every moment of my life is devoted to my new discovery."

"Will it be always so ?" she asked.

"I should be sorry to think it would," he returned. "I shall be rich and idle some day, Lina ; but meantime I must work."

"And when the wealth comes ?" she speculated.

"We will enjoy it together," he added.

It was a pity she did not say that it was of the blank between she had been thinking. As before, she held her peace, and thought that much more of the same would break her heart— that no future good could be worth so great a present sacrifice.

But men always delude themselves by believing that what they wish to do is precisely what they ought ; and Maurice

Storn imagined that the course he was pursuing, because he
liked it himself, was the best possible for his wife and child.

For although he associated neither in his efforts, he did in
their results. He saw Geordie heir to some fine landed property—Lina mistress of a grand establishment. He thought
he denied himself rest, society, amusement, and domestic comfort for the sake of those dear to him, and not for the sake of
chemistry—his beloved.

Science assumes to most a form of beauty arrayed in purple
and fine linen, glittering with gems, laden with gold and fame
for her most favoured followers, and men fancy that it is the
toys and the gewgaws they covet for their families, and that they
pursue her for the sake of others, and not for love of herself.

In many cases it proves a dangerous delusion, and so Maurice Storn found out later on; but in the meantime of which
both had spoken, he persevered resolutely in his way, and Mrs.
Storn went on hers.

"They were so fond of one another, and so happy," said the
world in general, and nobody but Mr. Clyne, and perhaps one
other, suspected that the world said false. Lina knew—she
knew that to the incubus of loneliness she was adding something else, and she shrunk back in horror from the thoughts
that would sometimes enter her mind. It was the common
story repeated, of a neglectful husband and a loving friend, and
she had no one in the world to help her feeble resolution—to
preserve her from herself.

She tried to keep herself right by the power of her own weak
will; already she was struggling to get out of the net of wrong
feelings which had entangled her; already she had a vague
sense it was sinful to quiver at the sound of Mr. Clyne's voice;
to shrink and tremble at his touch; to be lonely when he left
her, nervous when he returned. With her own feeble hands
she was trying to crush the monster in its birth; she was frus-
trating opportunities of companionship; placing others betwixt herself and him; endeavouring to darken the great light
that had latterly illumined her life; but after all, what did
these efforts amount to? Nothing more than this, Lina: they
dragged for a moment the wheels of a chariot which the strength
of Hercules could not have stopped. And yet what more could
she, poor soul! have effected—what more?

CHAPTER XIII.

FASHION IN THE EAST.

THERE was great rejoicing in the silk merchant's house when he duly announced the important fact that Mrs. Storn was coming. The first thing which seemed to strike everyone was, that now they were secure of Mr. Clyne; and therefore, in honour of his diplomacy, Lindor *père* was treated with more deference for some hours than it was the wont of his interesting family to evince towards him. Mrs. Lindor, who always wore black velvet and buttons about her in some place, swelled out under the influence of pleasurable emotions, and appeared to shake out and expand her plumage as we see hens do when they are making much of themselves. Tryphenia, in blue silk flounced to the waist, rustled about the room, and arranged her ringlets before the chimney glass, and thought how nice it would be to shake her curls tremulously under Limerick lace, and wear a wreath of orange flowers, and turn out of church Lady Clyne. Mr. Lindor considered how deucedly glad many a man would be to entertain a baronet's grandson; no common-place knight, or newly-created chandler baronet, but one of old blood, and fine estate, and aristocratic connexions. Not that he, Mr. Lindor, cared for birth—of course not; what city man ever did care for it? 'Tis all nonsense to suppose East-enders would give twopence for a genealogy, or that Westerns would sell a few of their ancestors for a thousand or two. These ideas are snares and delusions, and Mr. Lindor was wont to declaim against them. Nevertheless, facts are stubborn things, and human nature is wondrously inconsistent. Miss Try-phenia's nature was not, however; for she had always looked down on citizens, and even gone the length of snubbing Mr. Glenaen, who, heaven knows, never entertained any idea of proposing for her.

The hope of the Lindors took after her father and mother; she liked quality and quantity, money and position; she had been curiously brought up, on the edge of a note, to quote a musical phrase, and thus she seemed neither decidedly citizenish, nor decidedly a West-ender; she was neither sharp nor flat; she was willing to take the good things of both extremes, and to look down most decidedly on those who were either poor in purse or watery in blood; for the latter reason, she refused to fling sweet glances on Gordon Glenaen, and Gordon Glenaen laughed at her for her pains.

If we take into consideration the circumstances of the young lady's parentage, and of her education, her conduct throughout this tale will seem perfectly natural. We don't expect the plumage of the canary in a mule, nor the notes of a wild bird in a cage; and thus, because Mrs. Lindor had lived once on the verge of good society, and Mr. L. had not; because she was poor and pretentious, he well-to-do and vulgar, the children turned out that strange thing described by means of negatives, as neither fish, flesh, nor fowl, nor yet good red herring.

Now Miss Tryphenia, to a certain extent, was conscious of her deficiency, and wanted to become at once something or somebody in the shape of Lady Clyne, wherefore she bowed down before Lina, who seemed both able and willing to advance her projects—pretty Lina Storn, who was at last descending from her pedestal, to associate with the people amongst whom fate had cast her lot.

For, as is usual with those who hold themselves aloof, Mrs. Storn's society had been much sought after. Report, which exaggerates everything, had exaggerated her father's rank, and been good enough to give Lina a comfortable fortune. Besides this, she was young, pretty, graceful; her husband's abilities in his profession were of no common order; and these things, together with a certain easy indifference, hard to be imitated by those who have not been born something, sufficed to place her on an eminence above persons who, though they might be bringing up their sons and daughters to be ladies and gentlemen, were certainly neither ladies nor gentlemen themselves. Society in some parts of the world is a strange thing—strange due west in this metropolis; but a trifle stranger, perhaps, due east. Society down there had warehouses, and shops, and great old houses as large as those of any moderate abode; it mixed with suburban society which resided in red brick buildings, with plate-glass windows, and green venetian blinds; it went out in the summer time to ruralize at bay windows in verandah cottages, where it contemplated two vases on the twenty-foot lawn, and a grotto by the gate. Society, as Lina saw it, did not make the best of its furniture; it had no occasion so to do; it never looped up light cheap draperies, and made a room look stylish out of little. No, it went in for all things massive, costly, expensive; its upholstery was like its good manners, oppressive.

Everything money could buy for the people who constituted society down east, they had; but the money not having been in existence during the early portion of their career, all internal cultivation had been neglected. Some of the ladies, it was reported, could not write, and they were all innocent of French or any foreign language—indeed, they had only the slightest possible acquaintance with their own. Furniture and clothes, servants and plate, these things, the accessories of rank, they possessed in abundance; but they sat about as comfortably on them, and clothed the nakedness of the mental figure about as perfectly as the soldier's old jacket which the otherwise nude savage donned so complacently when he too went out visiting.

Amongst the blind, a squint is king; and for this reason, though my heroine would have been only one amongst more in any other part of the world, she was sufficiently nobbish, as a citizen, to be sought for at the "blow-outs" (so Mr. Glenaen called them) which the residents in that remarkable locality were in the habit of giving periodically.

Those who had the best wine and the greatest number of daughters, were wont to give "hops and spreads" the oftenest; and Mrs. Lindor having three young ladies to place out, got up these sort of entertainments more frequently than her neighbours.

Besides, was she not the grandest personage in all that district? Had she not associated with the Countess of Wisbech? and did she not even yet correspond with Lady Juliana Straightback? Was there any necessity for Mrs. Lindor to state she had been governess in the family of the one, and companion to the other? Why should she encumber her reminiscences of Rome with the fact of having travelled thither as nursery governess to Mrs. Debeyere's four children? Was it a sin of great magnitude for a lady who paid at the rate of a guinea an hour for Miss Treffy's music lessons, to omit all mention of the weary forenoons she had spent in the Countess of Wisbech's family, guiding stiff, yet sprawling fingers over the keys? Was it not more graceful to speak of the duets she and dear Lady Juliana sang together when she was visiting at Formality House, than to tell about that haughty woman's insolence and impertinence in the days of her servitude? It was a false gloss, and who may criticize her harshly for the deception. Have you never put a false gloss on anything either—you, or you? Have you never placed a fictitious ticket on the goods of your life, and exhibited them in the window which was to meet the eyes of your fellows? Have you never professed an intimacy which was not even an acquaintance; never implied you knew a man who would not speak to you in the street? Have you never talked grandly about your father's property in the country—meaning a cottage and paddock? never brought in a

sentence about his horses—to wit, old Dapple in the stable?
have you never lied about the extent of this transaction—the
largeness of this profit? You call all this putting the best
face on things. Mrs. Lindor did no more—she only said a
great deal which some folks believed, and which others did not;
but in the end she cleared a path for herself, and her career in
society was a success. Could she not count amongst her guests
Finsbury doctors, whom aristocratic patients visited in shoals,
and Bedford Square lawyers, men great in the papers, who
argued with Baron Bullfinch, and made troublesome interludes
in the courts. Was not her tri-monthly dinner party a thing
to talk about, a performance for the easterns to be proud of?
Did not people come all the way from Clapham to it? Yes,
best Clapham people, and in that select neighbourhood, be it
known unto you, readers, it is etiquette for one horse broughams
only to visit one horse, till the fortunate owners can turn out
a pair. Might Mrs. Materfamilias not be as sure as she was
living that her daughters would dance with no one objectionable,
in a matrimonial sense, at Mrs. Lindor's evening parties; for
had not that lady seen the world, and she was not so old as to
have forgotten the little affair between Lucy Debeyeres and
her Italian singing master, with whom the silk merchant's wife
knew she had once been rather in love herself.

She had altogether a very select circle, and nobody was
admitted to her receptions save those possessed of money, or
position, or talent. I do not mean musical, or literary, or
artistic, for Mrs. Lindor had too much sense to go in for
lions; but talent, which, like Maurice Storn's, was likely in the
long run to bring forth productive fruit. Talent valuable in
the commercial market, is that which finds most favour in
business classes; and it was this quality Mrs. Lindor was in
the habit of bringing in as a sort of spice to the more sub-
stantial city dishes set down in her bill of fare. She had seen
enough of good society to know how to mix up her ingredients
properly; indeed, but for Mr. Lindor, and the association of
twenty years with those who believed that money was power,
and a certain natural commonness about her, I might have said,
without any fear of contradiction, that Mrs. Lindor was a lady.

But though she liked the *éclat* of high life, she likewise
enjoyed the ease and plenty of a lower class in society. Thus
while her accent was free from vulgarism, and her manners
those of a woman who knew what was what; still, she was not
above listening to, and repeating, a very vulgar piece of
scandal, or laughing at a story which had better have been left
untold. She liked a good gossip just as well as a commoner

person, and she would chat with her servants, and be alternately distant and familiar as the fit came on her. Her eating
was the same as her conversation; an ice was a very nice and
proper thing to ask for beyond Charing Cross, and a jelly a
form of refreshment sufficiently lady-like and immaterial to
satisfy her at a company supper; but Mrs. Lindor would not
have cared to go to bed on such meagre fare, and accordingly
anybody learned in these matters, like Mr. Glenaen, might see
behind the ice, and the jelly and the champagne, a hot supper
laid out in a distant back parlour, where the silk merchant's
wife sat cosily down after her guests had departed, to saddle of
mutton and loin of lamb, and turkey and bacon, and Welsh
rabbit, and brandy punch. And to the charms of these vulgar
condiments, Miss Tryphenia, spite of her curls, and German
melodies, and latest waltzes, and pretty affectations, was no
more insensible than her mother. Wherefore, it might have
surprised many a sighing lover, fuller of sentiment than food,
to see what an appetite Miss Treffy could bring to bear on the
good things of her father's supper table. Talk about the
feasts of the ancients, about the extravagance of Lord M.'s
dinner table, about the waste of a nobleman's establishment!
Pooh! if you want to know what good living is, to see eating
in perfection, to comprehend why sons are left beggars, and
daughters are forced to marry anybody for a home; you should
come to London and take a cruise round the business supper-
tables of our metropolis. You have a very good cook, perhaps,
but she would stare at the richness of the pudding your boot-
maker eats up heaped platefuls of at home.

You fancy you live very well; but your tailor's wife would
not thank you for the best dinner you ever saw served up.

Quality and quantity; if you would see these things appreciated—if you would know what is thought of a biscuit and a
glass of wine—if you wish to look upon your own luxuries as
on herbs and spring water, get some kind fairy to lend you an
invisible cloak, and make a pilgrimage through the back par-
lours of monied second-rate London about nine o'clock at
night; see how the masters live, and the mistresses cater;
watch the servants making up messes for themselves, and the
children stuffing to suffocation. Good lack! it is the love of
eating which makes England the " happy and the holy," and
the gloriously free, for the people live to eat, and work to live
and if ever they grow to be fonder of books than of joints of
meat—of mental food than of bodily,—the country will go down.

Thus it came to pass, that because Mr., Mrs., and the Misses
Lindor liked to live, and lodge, and dress well, they revelled

among fatted beasts, and were arrayed in purple and fine linen, and received company, and put nothing by. Mr. Lindor had insured his life, indeed, for two thousand pounds; but what were two thousand pounds, as Mrs. Lindor sagely enquired, generally tacking a decided command to her query by means of the words—" Girls, you must marry;" and dutifully obedient to the maternal mandate, for marriage the girls lived, and moved, and had their being.

They were not, however, to marry anyone; and Mrs. Lindor was at some pains to explain to them by examples in point the precise meaning of eligible matches. Mr. Glenaen came under this head; but Miss Tryphenia and her parent differed so widely in opinion on the subject, that there were frequent wars in the land until Mr. Clyne appeared on the scene; when the stout lady and the slim one, the old manœuvrer and the young tactician joined standards together, and agreed to noose that gentleman, or die in the attempt.

To this end, wreathed smiles and bashful glances, new songs and old melodies; the production of portfolios; the intimacy with Lina Storn; white bonnets and pink bonnets, and costly dresses, and transparent sleeves; to this end, looks conned before the mirror, and waking dreams visioned on sleepless pillows. If women only took the pains to keep a husband which they do to get one, what light work the Divorce Court would find the adjustment of conjugal differences! If Tryphenia Lindor had only made herself as agreeable to Mary Cranstoun as she was endeavouring to do to Herbert Clyne, how much more endurable her cousin's life would have been. As it was, so it was. Tryphenia could not see the wood for trees. She was so busily engaged trying to captivate Mr. Clyne, that she never suspected Mary was looking out too, as a girl does look, tremblingly, yet hopefully, when she knows she has given her heart rightly, though not what the world calls well.

How did she manage to get engaged? she, who was under fire of five pair of eyes; who dare scarcely call her soul her own; who was " kept back" on all possible occasions; and who might well have believed that in all the earth there existed nobody ever likely to come and woo her. How did she manage it? Pray how do women generally manage such things, my fair reader? how is it that, spite of tongue and temptation, they can keep their matrimonial prospects such dead secrets when necessity exists for them to do so? How, beyond all, is it that quiet girls have such self-reliant natures, such determined wills?

They never ask advice, nor have nervous tremors; nor take society mysteriously into their confidence concerning the most ordinary event of life; they don't keep lovers waiting in agonies of suspense, nor make any trouble about saying and doing what is proper under the circumstances. They do not—seeing a husband in the distance—shriek out for the benefit of the public, " We are on the wing after him;" they have no consultations, no hesitations; they are never seen having love made to them ; they are set down as unattractive to men, old maids, and so forth ; and then they marry all of a sudden, and turn out, to the horror and indignation of their acquaintances, to have been engaged for some incredible length of time.

And so it happened, that Mary Cranstoun, spite her placid manner, and cheerful face, and unsentimental mode of proceeding, was nearer to a husband than any of her cousins; not that they would have married him if they could; and thus far there was no triumph nor success in the matter; but although they would have rejected an offer from him with scorn, that was no reason why they should make Mary welcome to her lover. They were regular dogs in the manger—would neither marry poor men themselves, nor let others do so; wanted to engross all the smiles, and sighs, and bouquets, and admiration for themselves ; and had no intention of letting Mary have so commonplace and prosaic a gift of heaven as a good husband if they could help it. All of which Mary knew, and therefore she kept two secrets to herself—for the quiet little girl had two—in the shape of a brace of lovers; one of whom she liked, and one of whom she did not.

A great old-fashioned house, with suites of rooms, and wandering staircases, and out-of-the-way corners, where many a vow had been made and broken in the days that were gone. Gliding along its passages, many a word was whispered in Mary's ear which it was never intended the public should listen to; and when mistress and daughters were out visiting, and Mr. Lindor was doing the honours to rough north-country men of business, who liked to come when Mrs. Lindor was away, Mary had many opportunities of hearing sometimes more than she liked, and of having love made to her—not by glance, and touch, and innuendo—but in straight-forward English, by plain, earnest men.

And yet the fair hair was never a bit less smooth ; the large eyes never looked as though they wanted sleep; no daily duty was forgotten or neglected because Mary Cranstoun was going to change her state; because she had refused wealth, and was going to mate with poverty. She did not flutter about in an agony of expectation like Miss Tryphenia; no brilliant prospects were blinding her vision; there was never a chance of her becoming my lady, or driving in her carriage, or receiving company, or becoming conspicuous in any way. Besides, she was sure of her husband, whilst Tryphenia's partook wonderfully of the 'two birds in the bush' character. There was much to be done yet by Lindor diplomacy before Mr. Clyne could be hooked and safely landed.

All that skill and experience could suggest was brought, for his sake, to bear on the party in question; and the interior of the old house, always handsome and heavy, became still handsomer by reason of the fresh arrangements Mrs. Lindor's taste dictated.

Three windows looking out into the street, four windows commanding the square, a blaze of light that lit up the whole neighbourhood, and gathered select parties of young Arabs from the vicinity of the Minories and Haydon Square to gaze on the splendours of Cockaigne society. Were not the hired servants men treats in themselves? the carpet across the pavement, the shrubs in the hall, the equipages and horses, and arrivals, almost equal to company nights at the Mansion House. And would any lord in Europe have asserted himself so obtrusively and created such a sensation as the retired rag* merchant from Clapton or the blacking manufacturer's son from Hackney? Was not each man, descending from his brougham, or dismissing his cab, a study in himself? from Simon Prentice, Miss Tryphenia's godfather, who had made a hundred thousand pounds out of upper leather, to Horatio Smyjthson, whose father, Mr. Smithson, commenced life by sleeping in an egg chest, and went out of it in a silver-mounted coffin covered with Genoa velvet.

If you are poor, reader, it would have made your heart ache to read over the catalogue of the visitors' names, with amounts of income appended; scarcely one who was not making his cool fifteen hundred a-year, or whose parent had not made it for him—fat, comfortable-looking citizens, spruce young dandies, who vainly imitated, however, the West-end drawl; brisk, lively lawyers, pompous doctors, stiff old matrons—it was a sight to see them all descend, and step cautiously over the carpet and enter the hall. How they did lord it over the servants! —they who had many a time swept out an office and washed a door-step in the days that were gone! What a gulf there

---

* For the benefit of the uninitiated, I beg to state that the above expression does not refer to a marine-store dealer, but simply to a dealer in Manchester goods, who is frequently thus designated in the City.

seemed between the ragged urchins outside and the wealthy diners-out within! How impossible it was to imagine Mrs. Harte, great in ostrich plumes and plum-coloured satin, a maid-of-all-work, at a shilling a-week! How hard to recognize in Mr. Grayne the boy who blacked your office stove every morning for twelve months, and who left you and went to Marson's because you refused him an advance of half-a-crown in his wages!

All honour to them! for the path they had trodden was one neither pleasant nor easy. All honour to them to have climbed so high, and climbed so well! But still, all shame that they should so soon have forgotten the weariness of the ascent, and refused to stretch out a hand to the toilers below!

I should like to tell you, young clerk, looking wistfully back at the turn-out of some man who has snubbed you, never to mind; for the time will come, perhaps, when in this world you may stand far above these people, and if not in this, why in the next, for in God's sight we are all equal. Besides, even here there is a balance; there is not one amongst them any happier than you. Mr. Grayne would give you half his money if you could bestow on him your youth; whilst Mrs. Harte, who married her first husband's apprentice, would retire on two hundred a-year, and make you over the remainder, if you would only reform her husband or lay him beside his predecessor.

In all things there is a balance of evil which matches the good. In your case it is the want of wealth, but remember money is always to be made. On the earth there is always some field of labour, out of which we can dig enough for our daily wants; but from what mine of the past can we conjure back the days of our boyhood, the hopes of our youth, and the love that made the mid-day glory of our manhood brighter?

Lina and Mrs. Glenaen were not amongst the first of the arrivals, a fact to be accounted for by a certain grimness of character in the manufacturer's mother, which prevented her hurrying to any place, or expecting much pleasure from anything. As for Lina, she went to that party like a sheep to the slaughter, and was not in the slightest haste to array herself for it. Nevertheless, she looked so pretty in her evening dress of black lace, with a scarlet camellia in her hair, that Janet was in ecstacies, and only wished she was going out to a party every night.

"Without Mr. Storn, Janet?" inquired her young mistress,

"Oh! he won't be so busy always, ma'am," she replied.

"Perhaps not," Lina said; and she went out of the room with a shawl over her arm, sighing audibly, and drove off with

Mrs. Glenaen to the Lindors' house in America Square, where the pair arrived, not amongst the first, but yet not amongst the last.

For a few people dropped in after them; and when the hands of the drawing-room clock pointed to ten minutes past the hour, Mr. Clyne had not arrived, and the guests and host and hostess commenced waiting for him as elderly persons, fond of having dinner good, hot, and punctual, do wait for some important individual who chooses to keep them on the tenter-hooks.

Poor Mrs. Lindor, frying between thoughts of a cook grumbling, of fish spoiling, of Mr. Prentice cutting them out in his will, of Mr. Clyne disappointing them, after all, enjoyed her position about as much as a hen is reported to enjoy one on a hot gridiron. A bright crimson spot came unbidden on the top of each cheek; she could not help looking uneasily to the time-piece; she was in agonies when no one spoke, and yet she dreaded each moment to hear Mr. Prentice open fire. The conveyances passing along John Street never ceased rattling for a moment, and yet still the lady strained her ears listening through it all, for Mr. Clyne's knock. She got into such a fuss, as the minutes sped by, that her kid glove was soaked with ungenteel perspiration; she glanced at Tryphenia, who bit her lip and tossed her head; then at Mr. Lindor, who pursed up his mouth and blew his nose dolorously. It was of no use trying to seem unconcerned, and carry on a light conversation with Mrs. Harte; she saw City men fidgetting uneasily, like dogs waiting her signal to make an onslaught on the viands below; she beheld Mr. Prentice draw out his watch and compare tables with the timepiece, and look at her. Worst of all, there was the fish.

"What shall I do, Mrs. Storn?" she asked Lina, *sotto voce;* and Lina, blushing up to the eyes, answered—

"I should order dinner."

"Oh, dear me, how provoking! I would not for anything commence before he comes, and yet the salmon won't be fit to eat!"

"Something may have prevented his coming," Lina replied; "and at any rate, he won't mind."

"You do not think he will consider it rude?"

"I am sure not; he is not easily offended, and besides, he ought to have been punctual. I should order dinner."

Upon which advice the lady acted, much to Lina's relief, who had felt only a degree less uncomfortable throughout the ordeal than Mrs. Lindor herself. What had prevented Mr.

Clyne coming ?—had not she ? Was it not because he thought she was not going that he likewise stayed away ? True, he had not said to her whether her presence or absence would be agreeable ; and besides, he would have sent an apology had something unexpected not detained him. She tried to reason herself out of the idea that she had any share in his non-appearance, but all would not do ; she felt guilty, and yet gratified ; uncomfortable to have caused so much annoyance, and still it made her heart throb triumphantly to think that out of all those present she was the only one he cared to see. No one else : she, Lina Storn, another man's wife !—and then the tide of joy swept back and left her heart bare.

Dinner was served at last, and in solemn procession the company moved down to the dining-room in pairs, and took their places round the table, which was covered and crowded with silver, and glass, and ornaments. The salmon was not spoiled, neither, as a matter of course, was the soup ; and Mrs. Lindor was just growing cooler and calmer, when a loud double knock startled her from her serenity.

"Here he is at last !" she exclaimed. "Dear me, I'm so sorry we began ! If we had only waited five minutes longer—"

"You would have spoiled the finest fish I have tasted this ten year," finished Mr. Prentice. "No, no, ma'am, never keep dinner waiting for anybody ; if a man cares for it, he is sure to come in time ; but young folks never do appreciate a dinner," and he glanced as he spoke at his god-daughter, whose appetite, never large in public, seemed utterly to have failed her.

And Mrs. Storn ! how well she knew that knock !—how well even she knew his step ! He had walked ; she heard him before he laid his hand on the lion's head, and yet she took not the slightest apparent notice of his advent, but continued a dialogue with Mr. Grayne while Mr. Clyne entered ; and after courteously apologizing for an unavoidable detention, took his place near Mrs. Lindor.

Then Lina recognized him, and bowed, and smiled across the table, and the excitement caused by his arrival having subsided, course succeeded course until at last the weary meal drew to a conclusion, and the final cloth was drawn, and the dessert placed, and the oldest wine produced.

After a little, Mrs. Lindor made that remarkable movement to Mrs. Harte, which always puts me in mind of the "call" in honours at whist, and that lady having graciously responded thereto, the ranks of the dining party were speedily cleared of petticoats, and the men proceeded to make themselves comfortable.

Upstairs meanwhile poured the stream of young life which had been invited for the evening. Girls in every variety of dress, with every variety of feature; dark-haired and light, blonde and brunette, tall and short, they still came trooping on, accompanied by aunts, mothers, brothers—the latter being all rising men—surgeons, brokers, manufacturers and the like. Mrs. Lindor had also contrived a Major from the Tower, and it was to this assemblage that Lina beheld, with no small astonishment, Mr. Glenaen and Mr. John Matson present themselves.

" Why John Matson ?" she wondered, for she had not been sufficiently intimate with business-people to understand the exact system of wheels within wheels which is at work amongst them ; she did not know that when Mr. Lindor wanted to buy drugs from Gordon Glenaen he went privately to John Matson ; she did not know that so insignificant a person as the manufacturer's manager could throw many a bargain into the rich silk merchant's pocket if he felt so inclined ; she had, in fact, no idea that it was her host's interest to be civil to her protegé ; and, accordingly, the fact of his presence puzzled and perplexed her not a little.

However, there he was, much to Lina's gratification, for she got him to sit down beside and talk to her, and when all the other single ladies were dancing, 'ticed pretty Mary Cranstoun over to join in the conversation ; and when the country cousin was set to play an accompaniment to a duet sung by Miss Tryphenia and her sister, she went with her to the piano and stood by her side until Mr. Clyne came to listen too, when she made way for him by taking John Matson's arm, and gliding back to her old position, which commanded a view of the instrument and of the performers at it.

Something fell on Lina's heart as she watched them ; something which seemed to turn her very blood into bitterness, and left the once full ocean of her life drier and barer than ever. As she talked on to Mr. Matson, gall and wormwood were dropped down into every sore of her nature ; she had no right, no cause to feel as she did, but still she could not help it.

Jealous, as she had once been of her husband's absorption to business, so she was now of Mr. Clyne's devotion to Tryphenia Lindor. How he bent over her music-book!—how he listened to her songs!—how he looked at her beauty !—how often he danced with her ! Lina saw it all, and felt, even whilst she was talking easily to her companion, as though some strong hand had clutched her heart, and was holding it tight.

She did not confess to herself she was jealous ; she only

thought it was a pity he should throw himself away on such a girl. And had she not herself brought all this about? Who had introduced them?—who fostered the intimacy? and what right had she to say nay to any intimacy or relation it pleased him to form? She, Maurice Storn's wife! she, Herbert Clyne's friend!—what was she to anybody, to husband, acquaintance, any one? And the tight grasp on her heart relaxed; and it seemed as if a rush of blood poured back into it which must have suffocated her. She sate alone at the moment, for Mrs. Lindor had seized Mr. Matson as partner for a rich maiden lady, who was old and ugly enough to mate with anybody, even a young clerk on a salary; and Mary Cranstoun was busily occupied in a conversation with Mr. Glenaen, and therefore not expecting any one to speak to her, she was startled at a low remark uttered from behind.

"I think our friend the manufacturer is over head and ears."

It was Herbert Clyne who spoke, leaning over Mrs. Storn's chair; and Lina, turning round, followed his eyes in the direction of Mr. Glenaen.

"Indeed! with whom?" she demanded, for it never struck her he meant Mary.

"*La belle Ecossaise*," he answered, laughingly; "he has been following her like a shadow all the evening—it is decidedly a hopeless case."

"Why, I always thought he had an idea of Miss Lindor."

"Or a bedlamite!" retorted Mr. Clyne. "No, no: take my word for it, Miss Cranstoun brings him here; and a very pretty young creature she is, too."

"The sweetest face in the room," criticized Mrs. Storn.

"Almost," he sighed; but Lina was not vain enough to take the compliment to herself.

"Will you not dance?" he asked, after a pause.

"I cannot," was Mrs. Storn's frank confession.

"I wish I could say the same," he answered; but the next minute was whirling round the room with Tryphenia Lindor.

He had spoken lightly to Lina, and as if he were enjoying the scene. She had not been enough in society to know that the real man never shows in a ball-room; she did not understand the difference between Mr. Clyne at her fireside and Mr. Clyne under Mr. Lindor's lamps; she saw he had come not expecting to meet her; that he seemed to admire Miss Treffy, and liked to flirt with her. Women's minds rarely are on the balance; a touch sends them either up or down, and it was some feeling of resentment towards everybody concerned in her annoyance which induced Lina Storn to say to Mary Cranstoun, before the evening was over: "I want you to do something for me, Miss Cranstoun."

"Anything I can, Mrs. Storn, anything," said the girl, with more earnestness than the occasion required, and with more vehemence than any one would have suspected to lie in her nature.

"Come and stay with me for a week or two; I want to know a little more of you."

"If I might—if I could—" began Mary.

"Shall I settle it with your aunt?" inquired Lina; and, to that lady's infinite discomfiture, Mrs. Storn presented a petition, couched in graceful terms, praying for her niece's company for a few days.

"I have felt somewhat lonely lately; Mr. Storn is so much from home," the chemist's wife explained; "and if your niece has been used to quietness, our house would just suit her."

"But Tryphenia would be so delighted to be with you," suggested Mrs. Lindor.

"Is not she much more agreeably engaged?" inquired Mrs. Storn, bent on having her own way; and the speech so delighted the mother that she gave consent at once. Mr. Clyne and they could now go on without Mrs. Storn's assistance; there was no occasion to meet him at the chemist's; besides, the Storns were removing to Bow out of the way of everybody; so Mrs. Lindor explained the reasons for her weakness to her daughters after all the company had departed, and no doubt she believed what she said, just as Lina did when she whispered to herself:

"Mary Cranstoun would make a better wife for Herbert Clyne than Tryphenia Lindor."

But it was nothing so disinterested as the desire for her friend to make a happy marriage which prompted Mrs. Storn's course of action. She thought it was, as she drove home beside Mrs. Glenaen and *vis-à-vis* to the manufacturer; thought and felt satisfied; but when she entered her own room, weary and jaded, and sat down for Janet to undress her, light dawned on her soul again.

"Mr. Clyne called, ma'am, about ten minutes after you left to-night; but I told him Mr. Storn was at Bow, and you gone to Mr. Lindor's."

"Good gracious, Janet, how you are hurting me with that hair-pin!" exclaimed Lina, as a sudden movement caused a thrust of the point into her head. "There, never mind; go on! Did Mr. Clyne leave any message?"

"No, ma'am; only to say he had called."

"And Mr. Storn sent word he would not be home to-night?"

"Yes, ma'am."

"And Geordie went quietly to sleep?"

"Yes, he cried a little after you went, but soon fell over."

"Thank you, Janet, that will do; now get to bed like a good creature. I declare it is nearly two o'clock."

And when she had shut out her nurse, Lina fell on her knees by the bedside, and flung out her arms over the coverlet, resting her head upon them. She remained thus for ever so long, trying to pray for strength, trying to pray for power to resist temptation; but when all was over, when she had thought, and struggled, and wearied, the only words she had been able to utter out of the depths of her despair, were, "God be merciful to me a sinner."

CHAPTER XIV.

BOW.

THE house which Maurice Storn had chosen for his future residence was situated on the edge of Bow Common, close to his new factory, and in the very midst of the smells for which that region is famous.

Bow Common is now a town; but not so many years since, it was a desolate-looking piece of waste ground, with footpaths running across, and undesirable roads surrounding it, dotted at uncertain intervals by the various factories which had been banned by universal consent out of decent society, and sent far east to ruralize, and stink, and make money at their leisure. Space was not quite so valuable there then as it is now, and therefore the houses and their belongings were better than the situation. Most of them belonged to the manufacturers, and had large gardens, stabling, coachhouses, and other conveniences of the same kind. The only drawbacks to them were the peculiarly low character of the neighbourhood, and the frightful stenches which came, now from east, now from west, now in at your drawing-room windows, now in a blast across your sweetest flowers. The factories and dwelling houses were all built of red brick, and the best abode in the place was disfigured with long low sheds and ranges of shabby workshops that formed connecting avenues between the rooms where the owners nominally resided, and the Pandemoniums where they really had their being.

It was a house of this description which Maurice Storn had taken; a large, roomy mansion, showing its eight windows in the front, with wide gables, and old-fashioned chimneys, and skylights in the roof, and fruit trees in the garden. Have I not the place before my mind's eye now, standing vacant in the dim light of an autumn evening, and speaking in tones which one or two, perhaps, besides myself could understand, of labour and anxiety, of hope and joy, of success and ruin?

Standing there and looking at the unlighted windows that seemed like blind eyes in the dusk, did I not think about the shadowy memories which hung around the untenanted rooms. In that chamber Maurice Storn used to read, and test, and try experiments, and rack his brain for fresh expedients. There he sat, pouring not alone chemicals, but health, and strength, and life-blood into his crucibles, and I leaning over the gate and watching the phantom pantomime of real events, while I have set at work in the now deserted house, cannot but wonder what the man thought of during all the hours and nights he passed alone with his books and his experiments.

Was he thinking of science all the time? did he concentrate all the powers of his mind—all the imaginations of his brain— all the hopes, fears, affections, anxieties of human life in sulphuric acid and cyanogen?

Was chemistry really and truly meat and drink, sleep, wife, child, friend, immortality, and heaven to that man whose profile I catch bending beside the lamp?

Was his world in very earnest the factory and the laboratory? Had he no visions of a quiet home far away, surrounded by woods, on the banks of some calm river—no longings for rest of body and ease of mind? Did he ever desire to be more with his wife, to mix freely amongst his fellow men? had he any wish to travel? did he ever get tired, impatient, fretful? did he ever feel misgivings about feebleness, sickness, death? Had he a feeling to spare to aught or anything besides chemistry when he shut himself into that room, and strode up and down its length, and put fact to fact, discovery to discovery, and idea to idea, till the end was gained at last?

And in another room I see Lina Storn, sometimes talking in the evening twilight to Mary Cranstoun, but oftener sitting alone, conning over the facts and fancies of her life, whilst Geordie is racketing about with the men in the workshops, and her guest and John Matson are improving the few stolen minutes that come so sweetly in the course of the days when people are engaged; when they settle the plans of their life and trace the outline as they list; when the shading of the future is all *couleur de rose*; when the peach is held in the hand of each, but still with the down on; and when, not having tasted the fruit, they never doubt for a moment but that it will turn out sweet, and last so all their lives long.

Can I not see the place and the people, though they dwell at Bow no longer, and though the house may not be standing now? Always with the same dim twilight about it as when I saw it last; always with the curtainless windows looking black even in the gathering gloom; with its great courtyard solitary, its workshops silent, its furnaces idle, its factories still. It was not thus, however, when Lina Storn came to take possession of her new abode; for the sun shone brightly as she and Mary Cranstoun entered the hall, and the greatest portion of the furniture having been removed from the city some days previously, things had been, to use Janet's phrase, put to rights before Mrs. Storn's arrival.

Carpets were down, and curtains up, and tables in their places, and Lina was able to find a corner to lay her bonnet and shawl, and then went to consult with Janet about dinner just as quietly and methodically as if she had been in the new house a week; whilst Mary Cranstoun made wonderful discoveries in the garden with Geordie, who came in brimful of delight to tell his mother that there were green strawberries in the beds, and that after a while they could gather gooseberries off the trees.

"A half stage to the country, Mrs. Storn," Mary said, with the sunlight streaming full on her un-English face. "Should you not like to go the whole journey?"

"No," answered Lina, "I have no quarrel with London. Five years naturalize one to any place. Besides, till lately I have been a wanderer on the face of the earth, and have no home ties anywhere. Do you know I could not tell where I was born. With you it is different; I can understand your dislike to London, and desire to return to Scotland."

"But I do not dislike London, and I do not wish to return to Scotland," explained her visitor.

"No!" said Mrs. Storn in astonishment; and for a moment she roused herself out of her usual absorption, and looked at Mary, trying to solve the riddle she had propounded, until the blood came rushing up into the young girl's face, beautifying it with burning blushes.

Then all at once light broke on her comprehension. "There is some tie that binds you here, then," she said slowly, and as if she were trying to reason a disagreeable idea out of her mind. "Is it not so?" and when she read out of Mary's face a reluctant, yet smiling answer, she said—"Then before I know further, I want to say that whoever it may be, I wish you and him joy and happiness. It is surely not Mr. Glenaen?"

"Oh! no."

"And are you certain—quite positive, dear, that he loves you?"

"Oh, Mrs. Storn!" and Mary forgot, in her surprise at the question, to look proper and modest as she answered it.

"I did not mean to annoy you, or say anything you would not like; only, you know, women are sometimes mistaken."

If Miss Cranstoun had not been pre-occupied with her own feelings, she must have noticed how strangely Lina was moved; how she seemed to wring the words out of her breast, and torture herself in doing so; how pale, how very pale she had turned; how the little hand clenched the arm of the chair, and how anxiously she waited for Mary's reply, which came out gently, yet confidently—

"I am not."

"Quite sure?"

"Oh, quite! you might not think it, but he never cared for anybody besides me in the world."

"False and fickle! more false than man—more fickle than woman! more unstable than water, weaker than a child; as shifting as sand, as little to be depended on as the winds of heaven! false and fickle." What right have you, Lina Storn, to murmur that sentence to yourself, and then to raise your cold, beautiful face, and say—

"It has been so sudden, you can have seen so little of each other."

"Not much, but still enough," was the brief reply; and then Mary, crouching down close by her friend's side, said, with those pleading eyes of hers turned up to the frigid, impassive countenance—

"You are not angry with me; you do not think I have been forward or hasty? Perhaps I have not done right to engage myself suddenly, and without my uncle and aunt's knowledge; but I knew it would be of no use asking their consent; and besides, I did not like. Indeed, I should scarcely have told you, if you had not been so kind to him; and, besides, he said it would be better."

"He did?" it was all Lina could say.

"Yes, he thinks there is nobody like you in the world. Sometimes, do you know, I have told him I was jealous; but that is not the truth; and—and—Mrs. Storn, would you have any objection to his calling here occasionally? I am afraid you will think me very—very—what I ought not to be; but it is all his fault—he said if I did not ask you, he would. It seems so hard to be so near one another, and yet still to be separated. And he does not like to come to the house without your permission."

"My dear child, if you are not talking of Mr. Glenaen, of whom are you speaking?" enquired Mrs. Storn, with a colour in her cheek almost equal to that which came into Mary's, as she answered:

"Why, John Matson, to be sure; who else could it be?"

Who else? Oh, blind, and guilty, and miserable wife, who else could it, should it be but the frank, buoyant man you had been kind to and forgotten? Was there but one in the wide world to love, or be loved? but one to think about? but one to care for, or to marry? What a little sinful world your horizon bounded, and yet what a light broke out over its wretchedness, when you heard that girl say the plan you had formed for her advancement, and his happiness, and your own salvation, had failed; when you found that wife to him she might never be.

Who else? why, where had her eyes been not to have noticed the attachment previously? how had they been darkened? what could she have been thinking about—or who?

And as the last question brought a train of ideas with it, she loosed her arms from about Mary's neck, where she had thrown them to wish her joy; loosed them quickly and sharply: for what right had she to touch her? what right to sympathize in a pure and innocent attachment, while she carried the plague-spot about with her, while she nursed and petted the disease that was killing her; while she made no vigorous effort to root it out once and for ever?

From that time forth she would try; she had a husband who had been kinder and truer to her than she had proved to him; a child she idolized, and who would grow up a companion and a friend; a staunch ally and adviser in John Matson, who had first shown her that idleness was a sin, and the parent thereof; who had told her that God's world was a working world, and that she had her share of occupation allotted her somewhere in it. Had she not been told from the pulpit, in words that seemed addressed to her individually, that an idler was a blot in the universe; and that to such, in the present day, as loudly as to the labourers standing still in the market-place of old, the Lord of the Vineyard was crying from his throne above the Heaven, "Why stand ye here all the day idle?"

Was her life not now a perpetual struggle, and an eternal

dread ? were not the gleams of joy that flashed across her path as rare as the darkness and gloom were frequent ?　Was not there something more faulty in herself than in her position ? had she no strength of will, no power of mind to set herself right, no matter who else might be wrong ? was she not competent to control her feelings as well as her actions, to think as she ought, as well as to do as she ought ?　Because her husband neglected her, was she to lead this wretched existence always ? because she cared for Herbert Clyne, was that any reason why she should not blot his memory out from her mind and thoughts for ever ?

Was he not going abroad ?　Were circumstances not about to separate them ?　"Oh, I thank God for that !" Lina murmured, as she thought all this over in the solitude of her own apartment; and because she was able to thank God at the prospect of her future loneliness; because, in the first flush of a newly-conceived resolution, she could stand there with both hands covering her heart, and still its starts and throbs, she thought she had gained a battle over evil, and was already on the road to safety.

As though, poor soul, she knew anything of the meaning of the word "temptation;" she who had never yet been tempted by him—but only by herself.

Still, as the days went by, and she began to take an interest in the progress of affairs between the lovers; as John Matson's plain, straightforward sense came to help her determination; as Mr. Clyne's visits grew still less frequent; as Mr. Glenaen's became imperative; as Geordie required keeping out of the workshops; and pale-faced women began to call her "the missus," and look to her for help; Lina grew quite strong in her good ways, and never thought of putting the question to herself: "How long will this last ?　When I have done watching Mr. Matson and Mary Cranstoun, and enjoying Mr. Glenaen's discomfiture—when I have no more quiet half-hours to plan for this pair to be together—when my visitor becomes Mrs. Matson, and Mrs. Lindor tires of coming out here—when all the outside scaffolding is withdrawn, and the props of my life are removed, how shall I then be able to stand alone ; I, who, Heaven help me, have scarcely, with all those aids and stays, been able to remain upright ?"

Have I not said that the human heart is weak ; a weathercock, which imagines, because it is still in a calm, that the tempest will have no power to stir it ; and who shall blame Lina for fancying she was out of danger ; that the worst was over ; that she was conquering ; that she would win ?

'Twas easy for her to conquer and win in those pleasant spring days, when Mary Cranstoun and John Matson stood as shields between her and evil, and Mr. Clyne stayed so much with his father, and Mrs. Lindor was always sending Miss Tryphenia and her sisters out to Bow, on the chance of meeting him.

It was easy for Lina, then, when, if ever she and Mr. Clyne did chance to be alone, he only spoke on general topics, or concerning Mr. Glenaen or Mr. Matson. For some reason or other, he took an immense interest in the engaged pair, and watched the bye-play between Mr. Glenaen and the young lady with unwearied attention.

" I want to see how the manufacturer will conduct himself under trying circumstances," he said to Lina one day. " If you give him a chance of proposing, it will spring the mine at once."

" Do you think so ?" she asked.

" I am certain ; *voila*—our friend does not like his manager, evidently, by that note. Perhaps he suspects an attachment— perhaps he does not ; at all events, let him once be refused, and then—"

" Am I to read this epistle ?" demanded Lina, holding the paper Mr. Clyne had given her unopened.

" Assuredly ; it furnishes a practical comment on the liberty and equality theory. I was foolish to direct my note as I did, but it would have been a pity to have lost that missive. It is a curiosity."

And it was—running as follows :

" SIR—If you have occasion to address my clerk, be good enough to put ' Mr. Matson' on the envelope, and not ' Matson, Esq.'

" Obediently yours,
" GORDON GLENAEN."

" H. Clyne, Esq."

" I wonder on what principle it is he Esquires me ?" said Herbert, as he folded up the note.

" Because you are not his servant," answered Lina. " Now, only fancy if Messrs. Colke and Ferres had ever treated Maurice or Mr. Glenaen himself in that way!"

" There would have been thunder in the air," remarked Mr. Clyne ; " and, if I am not much mistaken, we shall have lightning before long."

He was quite correct in this idea ; for, in the course of the following week, Mr. Glenaen had ten minutes' private conversation with Miss Cranstoun, and the very next day that young lady was required to repair forthwith to America Square, whence she returned, some hours later, with very red eyes and pale cheeks, having received the royal command either to give up Mr. Matson or else her relatives.

"And I have no place to go, Mrs. Storn!" she sobbed.

"Can you not stay here?" inquired Lina.

"Oh, I cannot do that! Mrs. Lindor would never speak to you again."

"So be it, then," replied Mrs. Storn. "I could live happily if I never saw your aunt more. I suppose she is offended with me already?"

"No; she said she should come over and tell you about my obstinacy herself."

"I shall be very glad to see her," Lina observed; "and for the rest, you will remain with me till you decide on marrying Mr. Glenaen—giving up Mr. John Matson or becoming his wife."

"Oh, Mrs. Storn! who told you about Mr. Glenaen?" questioned Mary.

"My own eyes," answered her friend. But it was hardly a true reply, for she would probably have never noticed the fact, had she not seen through another's spectacles.

"I am afraid it will do John a great deal of harm," said Mary, sorrowfully.

"Well, you must do him good," was Mrs. Storn's reply; for the chemist's wife never once thought of dissuading Mary from the match: first or last, she had never put a single obstacle in Mr. Matson's way; she had encouraged him to come and to stay; she had urged on the match with all her power; she had watched them throwing the dice of their lives with a sort of amusement. They loved—they would marry. As to money matters, she never thought about them; she had never known shortness herself, and it did not occur to her that they might; she saw no one cared for Mary at her uncle's; she felt satisfied Mr. Matson would make her a good husband; *ergo*, it was best they should marry. Of course it was; Mr. Clyne thought so too—Mr. Clyne, who had once stated a desire to see the affair completed before his departure.

"I have never been at a wedding," he said to Mr. Matson; "I should like to be best man at yours."

"So that you may know how to conduct yourself when you likewise are sacrificed," laughed the young man. "Ah! I fear mine will be a very dull affair; and when Mary intends to make up her mind as to her part of the performance, I am sure I don't know. We ought to have been married a month ago."

Opinions might be divided upon this point, but there was no question as to the necessity of doing something decisive when once Mr. and Mrs. Lindor became acquainted with their niece's engagement. For her to return to America Square without making a formal relinquishment of John Matson, was impossible; for her to remain quartered on the Storns' hospitality, was equally so; more especially as Mr. Storn, who rarely troubled himself about any other person's concerns, had thought fit to remonstrate with his wife on the opportunities she afforded Mr. Matson and Miss Cranstoun for making up a match.

"But what can I do, Maurice?" pleaded Lina, one day. "I cannot send her home, for Mrs. Lindor declines to receive her; and the girl is really fond of Mr. Matson, and he is very fond of her. It is a case of genuine attachment on both sides."

"Yes; but that, my love, will not keep their bread buttered on one side; and Mr. Matson has no means of maintaining a wife."

"He has health and brains," Lina remarked.

"A man cannot very nicely set up house on those valuables, Lina," answered her husband.

"Why, what more had you when you married me?" she asked.

There was something in the way she put this question which grated on his feelings, but still he replied quietly and gently, as usual:

"I had a good situation and a free house, and liberal and wealthy employers, besides a considerable amount in ready cash: John Matson has nothing."

"Except a situation."

"Which he will not hold long. He has been very imprudent in his manner to Mr. Glenaen, taken a lead in affairs which he ought not to have done, suggested alterations that were not agreeable to his employer; and, in fact, behaved in such a manner, that Glenaen says it will be quite impossible for him to remain in his service."

"I do not believe Mr. Glenaen speaks the truth," was Lina's sharp commentary on this summary of offences. "He is what I always thought him—a mean, vindictive, vulgar-minded creature; and so far from trying to stop John Matson from marrying to please him, I shall urge the match forward by every means in my power."

"You will repent having done so some day, then, Lina."

"It will not be the first thing of the sort I have repented," she answered: "one more cannot make any difference." And she was turning in a pet to leave the room, when Maurice caught her.

"Tell me what you meant by that, dear? Do you repent having married me? Are you sorry for that which was the happiest day of my life? Do you regret having ever met me? Oh, Lina, don't say that!"

With any truth she could not have said that; but there was something else which, with her face buried in his breast, she was struggling to tell, when the door was flung open, and Gordon Glenaen strode in.

"Oh, I beg pardon, I'm sure! Anything the matter? I hope you are not ill. Storn, if you can, come away immediately, the acid is perfect: Mrs. Storn will be glad to hear, I am sure, that there is no doubt now—that your experiment has proved a perfect success."

He spoke hurriedly and eagerly. For a moment she stood still, not knowing what to say; for it was the first time since her marriage she had ever been made the confidante of a great triumph or a great failure.

The little she ever knew had come to her when the first blush of success was over, and, therefore, she now remained looking first at Mr. Glenaen's excited face, and then at her husband's pale one, till the latter said, in a low, agitated voice—

"Wish me joy, Lina!—wish me joy!"—the man was literally trembling with excitement—"say you are glad about it, dear! Wealth for you and Geordie, and rest for me!"

Glad!—the incubus of her life seemed lifted off at the moment. Glad!—she flung her arms round Maurice's neck, and kissed him in a manner which might have scandalized any one who looked on such demonstrations less as matters of course than Gordon Glenaen—ay, and she could, in the joy of her heart, have hugged even him, had he not very prudently left the scene of action, saying to Maurice, as he walked out:

"I suppose, Storn, you will be after me when Mrs. Storn has done."

"Well, little wife, are you sorry now?" asked Maurice, as he laughingly held Lina back from him, and looked in her beautiful, excited face—"are you sorry now?"

"Oh, Maurice, I am so glad! But it is not for the money —I should never be sorry if you would only stay with me, and be like what you are now."

" After a little, you will be telling me I am too much about the house, and turning me out. But I must be off now, to see this wonderful acid."

" Let me go too !" she exclaimed; and for once he suffered it. Side by side they walked down to the factory; he with his rough coat all daubed over with chemicals, she with her light breezy muslin dress and garden hat; and Maurice Storn felt prouder and happier that day than ever—for was he not on the road to fortune? and was not that slight, graceful woman his wife—his own? Once or twice, indeed, lately he had been uncomfortable about Lina; he did not understand her occasional irritability, her fits of depression, her little fretful complaints, and petulant expostulations. Sometimes he had thought —sometimes, though very rarely—that she did not care for him as she used, that she really did regret throwing herself away on him—so he worded the sentence; and not being conscious of any change having taken place in himself, he could not guess at the reason of the apparent change in her: as for doubting his wife's truth and purity, Maurice Storn would as soon have thought of disbelieving his own honesty. He trusted her implicitly—first, because he was good himself; and, secondly, because he was blind—blind as only a business man ever could be to the fact that Herbert Clyne came to his house, not for friendship, but for love; and that Lina, spite of reason, and principle, and duty, was attached to him in return.

Blind as an owl, and like an owl too, with the broad sunshine tracing out the course of events under his eyes; while she had been within an ace of telling him all—yes, and but for the sulphuric acid, would have done it too.

As it was, she felicitated herself on her silence; all would come right again now. Maurice would be rich—Maurice would be idle—Maurice really did care for her, and in time might grow confidential. For the future they would be like man and wife, and she need never fight any more battles out alone.

She was strong, in her own belief, to conquer her affection for Herbert Clyne; she had thought herself able to travel the road alone; but now she should not have to travel alone ever again.

And thus the wife's thoughts ran on, whilst Mr. Storn and Mr. Glenaen stood looking admiringly at results; and when at last she retraced her steps to the house, it was with a lighter heart than she had carried in her breast for years. In proportion to the sorrow, was the relief; and in precise proportion in aftertimes to the relief she felt then, was her disappointment.

Not many days elapsed before Mary and Mr. Matson arrived at a definite understanding on the subject of matrimony, and they agreed—whether wisely or not, is no business of mine—to become one—blow high, blow low, without any further delay; which determination they communicated to Lina, and Lina conveyed to her husband.

When she had quite finished her news and comments, he said, "I think I shall have a talk with Miss Cranstoun myself."

And accordingly, wonderful for him, he had fifteen minutes' chat with a woman that same evening; and spoke to her—as the young girl declared afterwards to Mrs. Storn—just like a father.

"I am sure my own father could not have been kinder," she finished, "so thoughtful, and gentle, and sensible, and good; but then you know, Mrs. Storn, he could not understand everything exactly; and though I should have been very glad to follow his advice, still it was quite impossible. I hope he will not be offended with me; he was so kind and good."

No, Maurice was not offended, or surprised; but he did not like the match, more especially as it was unsanctioned by any of her own relatives. He should not have cared about the matter had Miss Cranstoun not been staying at his house. He had all a practical man's horror for clandestine love affairs, and he felt a sort of responsibility in the business, which was both irksome and painful.

Most heartily Maurice Storn wished to do right, and it did not seem to him right that the girl should marry from his house, and plunge herself into poverty, if he could help it. Acting upon these ideas, therefore, he went that same night to America Square, and had a long confabulation with Mr. Lindor, who, being out of reach of his wife's hearing, told the chemist that he did not believe "Mary would have any life of it all now, between Madam and the girls. My own impression of the matter is," finished the little merchant, "that she must marry either Mr. Glenaen or Mr. Matson for a home; and as she won't marry Mr. Glenaen, why I suppose it must be the other. I cannot appear in the affair; but considering the girl has no fortune, I really think she might do worse. Have to be a governess for instance," finished Mr. Lindor.

"What do you mean by marrying Glenaen?" queried Mr. Storn, utterly regardless of the conclusion of the merchant's sentence.

"Mean! why, bless my soul! did you not know the man proposed for her? Mary is a very good little girl, and I never saw anyone more in earnest in my life than Glenaen about marrying her. Would have made settlements, anything she liked, quite a scene here about it; for between you and me, Madam always thought it was Tryphenia he wanted; and I suspect that is where the shoe pinches most. Women don't like to be mistaken, and so they tell Mary she is a fool. But I must say—in strict confidence, you understand—I go with my niece, for Gordon Glenaen and I never were good friends. Were I a girl, I should not care to marry him."

"I suppose you know that Mr. Matson is not likely to retain his situation?" observed Mr. Storn.

"Well, I should wonder if he were; but what does that signify? I cannot appear in the transaction, you know, at all, because Mrs. L. manages these things, and she has set her face against the match; but you may just tell John Matson from me that Bunt's agent has bolted, and he is in want of another. He can write to him and mention my name, and I have no doubt he will get the appointment. Better refer to me at the office, not here, you understand;" and twisting up one eye in a manner which was intended to represent or disfigure a very knowing and confidential wink, Mr. Lindor shook hands with his visitor, and sent him out into the darkness, wondering not a little.

"Gordon Glenaen in love!" was the burden of his soliloquy; and he repeated the phrase over and over to himself, as though trying to realise an impossibility. "Gordon Glenaen in love—willing to make settlements—marry:" this then was the secret of his dislike to John Matson, for the master could not bear the man who had beaten him in the matrimonial market.

Lina was right, it appeared. Mr. Glenaen had not spoken quite the truth; and as Mr. Storn remembered this, that disagreeable feeling came across him which is always engendered by the first doubt of a friend.

"And yet," argued the chemist the next minute, "I could not expect him to tell me he had been refused, and it was quite natural he should dislike John Matson, and I dare say the young man was uppish, and there is no doubt it would have been a much better match for Miss Cranstoun. Still, as she does not think so, what business is it of mine, more especially as her uncle approves her choice. I won't meddle in the matter further, but just let Lina do as she likes."

A thing, dear reader, which I may observe *en passant*, ladies are in the habit of doing, whether they are let or not: a truth Mr. Clyne was fond of impressing on Mary Cranstoun, whom he rallied in his quiet way concerning sentimental fancies and romantic ideas of love in a cottage.

" Mary's cottage will be a very unpoetical one," remarked Mr. Matson one day, " a three pair back in some place in the city, with an agreeable prospect of twisted chimneys, and a nearer view of a stunted geranium on the window sill. Mr. Glenaen has intimated to me that my valuable services are no longer required in his manufactory; and accordingly I am now a free man, with a quarter's salary in my pocket, and no character."

" No character?" repeated Mr. Clyne, inquiringly.

" He declines to be a reference for anybody," answered the young man; " and as for the reasons assigned for my dismissal, they are simply—' I choose it, and besides, no married man shall hold a confidential post about my factory. I won't have any talking to women concerning my affairs.' Of course there was no use in argument; and as he told me to take my wages and leave the place, it was time, I think, for me to do so."

" If there be one person upon earth whom I do cordially hate, it is Mr. Glenaen," said Lina, with an intensity of bitterness which startled one at least of her auditors.

" Nay, nay, Mrs. Storn," he answered, " you must not do that: Mr. Glenaen has a perfect right to dismiss me if he likes. He is as much at liberty to change his clerk as his tailor; and I for one would be sorry to cross his inclination on the matter, though it does put a stop to my plan of living among the perfumes of Bow. I shall know positively to-morrow about Bunt's agency; and if I get it, my future is planned out for me."

" And for you, too, Miss Cranstoun," added Mr. Clyne, rising to depart. " I shall depend, Mr. Matson, on your letting me know the result, as I dare say I shall not see you again for some days."

He only came down once more to Bow during the course of the next three weeks, and then it was to tell Mrs. Storn that he believed his father would be ready to start for the continent almost immediately.

" Why he has waited so long, I cannot imagine," he added, " except it be to settle some law affair; for his solicitor is closeted with him for hours together. However, he declares he is going now positively, and I can only say, I am glad, and I am sorry."

Lina never asked him wherefore, and he did not care to enlighten her further. A faint colour came up into her cheek; but she made no comment—put no question. The rapid fingers only flew faster over some work she was finishing for Mary Cranstoun; and it was in reference to her employment that Mr. Clyne said, after a pause—

" When is it to be ?"

" This week," Lina answered shortly.

" Before I go ?"

" That depends on when you leave."

Herbert did not reply. He was tossing amongst the white ribbons and the bridal finery with a nervous, restless hand; lace, and bow, and flower, he lifted and cast aside. Then he asked—

" Shall you be there ?"

" I think not," she replied.

" Ah! Mrs. Storn, you told me so once before," he said; and at the remark Lina crimsoned to the temples, and murmured something about circumstances over which she had no control.

" But I shall not go," she added, " to this wedding, unless Mary particularly wishes it. Mr. Storn has promised to give her away, and I think the fewer persons present the better."

Whether Mr. Clyne endorsed this idea or not, he made no audible remark upon it, but contented himself with another ramble through the ribbons, after which he said he should go and see John Matson in the city.

" For the last time during your term of liberty," he remarked to that gentleman, who expressed a hope that he would take him to church : " for, do you know," he said, naively, " I think I should feel it exceedingly strange to go alone. Do come! We cannot afford a stylish wedding, nor a breakfast, nor any other nonsense, but I should like to see you at church. Nine o'clock sharp, remember, at St. Olave, Old Jewry."

For it was in that parish Mr. John Matson had lived for fourteen days previously, in two top rooms, destitute of carpets, and innocent of easy-chairs, from whence he made daily forays in quest of furniture and crockery, and little things which he thought Mary would like.

Meanwhile matters were in a very pretty state of bridal confusion out at Bow. Lina did not wish to go, and argued that point with her husband and Mary, whilst Geordie was crying his eyes out in Janet's arms, because his mamma was a bad mamma, who would not take Geordie out in a beautiful carriage to see Manie married.

Mary herself was in an April state of smiles and tears ; and Maurice Storn rose at four o'clock, in order to set things right at the factory before his departure. The result of which arrangement proved that, at six, he was carried back again into the house, half drowned and almost whole suffocated, having fallen into an under-ground vat filled with mother liquor, the contents whereof might have been expected to poison any man but a chemist.

"Don't mention this accident to Miss Cranstoun, Lina," he said to his wife. "I shall not be able to go, but you must. Make some excuse for my absence; I dare say she would rather have you than me as escort. Don't look so frightened, my darling; I shall be quite well before night."

And thus, at the eleventh hour, Lina had to take her husband's place; whilst, for the same reason, Mr. Clyne, instead of attending as best man, had to stand father on the occasion. A mighty dull affair, Janet, who viewed the ceremony from the gallery, declared it turned out; though Miss Cranstoun looked very pale and very pretty, and Mr. John Matson appeared as happy as if he had gained a thousand a-year. Still it was dull; for Mrs. Storn could not help being anxious and uncomfortable, and Mr. Clyne's face wore an expression rather befitting a funeral than a wedding.

Nevertheless, if it were not a gay marriage, it was an earnest one; for the promises were made by two who understood what they meant, and intended, with God's blessing, to keep them. Lina, knowing how they were situated, could not help being impressed with the way they both vowed to have and to hold one another from that day forward "for better, for worse; for richer, for poorer; in sickness and in health, to love and to cherish till death do us part."

There is a something solemn in seeing a pair marrying to poverty, in knowing that the promises do not fall from their lips as matters of form or matters of possibility, but as things which will have to be kept from the day of their wedding probably to the day of their death; and Lina felt every word of that service sink down into her heart and sting her conscience. She never once looked at Mr. Clyne during the ceremony; she dare not have done it there; and, standing before the rails of God's altar, her thoughts and feelings were right for the first time for months—with her husband, wishing to be by his side.

At last it was all over: the witnesses had signed, and the clerk given the certificate, and the clergyman had been fee'd, and bowed himself out of the vestry, wishing the newly-married couple happiness.

Then Lina went across to Mary Matson, who stood beside her husband, and gave her one long kiss, saying, under her breath, "God bless you, dear, and make you happy!" whilst Herbert Clyne handed John a packet for his wife.

When the brief congratulations were over, Mr. Matson led his wife to the carriage which had conveyed her and Lina from

Bow, and then they said "Good-bye," and drove off, leaving Mrs. Storn and Mr. Clyne standing alone at the church door.

"Five minutes to tie a knot which it costs a life to undo," remarked the gentleman, as the vehicle swept round a corner and out of sight.

Lina started at the observation; it seemed as if Mr. Clyne had put her own thoughts into words.

"I do not think they will want it undone," she answered. "I imagine they have every chance of happiness."

"I trust so. She will make a good wife, he a good husband; they are very much attached, and spoke out the vows as if they meant to keep them. But, after all, there is a something depressing about a wedding; I suppose it is because the chains then forged are life-long."

He paused as if he were expecting Lina to make some reply, but she did not, only remarked, as they walked along the street together, on the beauty of the day.

"Are you going to return to Bow?" he inquired.

"Yes; Mr. Storn is ill." And then Lina explained the nature of the accident which had prevented his attending the ceremony, and compelled her to act as deputy.

"Otherwise you would not have been there?" queried Mr. Clyne.

"No; but I am now glad it so happened—glad, not that Mr. Storn should be disabled, but that I was compelled to be present. I should not have liked to be absent."

"I suppose you plead the inconsistency of your sex as a reason for the difference between what you say now and what you told me the other day," he remarked, with a smile.

Lina blushed—she could not help doing so; but she answered, quietly:

"We are not inconsistent—at least I think not—only we change our minds sometimes."

They had reached Lothbury by this time, and Lina, as she concluded her sentence, turned her eyes towards the cab-stand.

"Shall I call one?" asked Mr. Clyne, on whom her slightest gesture was never lost.

"If you please. I wish to return home as quickly as possible. Mr. Storn may want something."

"And I will not say 'good-bye' to you now, as I had intended," said her companion; "but come out to Bow some time to-morrow, to hear how Mr. Storn is before I go."

"Are you going, then?" Lina did not add the words "so soon."

"Yes; on Thursday morning. I hope Mr. Storn will be quite recovered before I leave."

If that were the great desire of Mr. Clyne's life, it was not destined to be gratified; for Maurice, though better, was not well, when he called the next day at Bow.

As a balance to this disappointment, however, he had the felicity of finding the three Misses Lindor located in Mrs. Storn's drawing-room, and, for some private reasons of his own, asked, when they rose to depart, to be permitted to escort them home. And thus, when they said "Good morning," he said "Good-bye." Lina was just conscious of her hand being pressed convulsively, and something like the words "God bless you!" were murmured, whilst the Misses Lindor trooped down the old-fashioned staircase. No other human being, however, could have guessed, from Mr. Clyne's manner and appearance, that he cared one straw whether he ever or never saw the citizen's wife again.

She knew, however; and as she watched the quartet walking slowly along the pathway, a sickness like death came over her. Tryphenia and Mr. Clyne leading the van, the younger sisters following—all three with their muslin dresses flowing like trains behind them, and raising the dust in clouds.

Then Lina saw him turn as if to speak to Miss Sophy, and felt that he was looking back at the house.

Next minute she was at her husband's side, asking him if he were better? if there were nothing he required? whether she should read to him? whether he wanted any letters written?

She was quite eager in her desire to do something, and it seemed a disappointment when Maurice said he only wished to have a sleep.

The shock had proved a more serious one than either at first imagined, and he was still weak and exhausted. This Lina saw, and so she sate down quietly beside his bed, and remained there till the light of the spring day faded, and the room grew dark, and objects near at hand became first indistinct, and afterwards invisible.

Then Lina began to fret; very softly she laid her face on the pillow, and commenced crying about every grief she had ever known in her life.

Most probably it did her good, for when her husband woke, and dressed, and came down to dinner, she was bright and cheerful, and more like the wife of their earlier days than Maurice had seen her for years.

Leaning back in his easy-chair, with Geordie and his cat squatted together on the hearth-rug, with Lina sitting opposite, and a chemical work, just published, lying uncut at his elbow, Maurice Storn felt very happy and content. His experiments were successful; he saw riches coming to him; there was no sickness in his family, no cloud on Lina's face, no apparent trouble of any kind in any corner of his house. Peace seemed to have taken up her head-quarters in the chemist's house, and for once he thought his own fireside was a more pleasant place to pass an evening than any laboratory in England.

But it was not to last: it could not, though Lina Storn and Herbert Clyne had parted that day.

Parted unfortunately, however, *Au revoir !*

CHAPTER XV.

SUMMER DAYS.

YES, Mr. Clyne was gone, and Mary Cranstoun married; and Mr. Storn well again; and there was nothing left for Lina Storn to look forward to or struggle against.

Nothing even for her to do in the present save to make the best, with God's help, of the state in which it had pleased Him to place her.

Make the best! During the whole of those glowing summer days she tried with a will to do it.

Sunshine over the scrubby, burnt-up grass of Bow Common —on the red-tiled factory roofs—on one side of the blackened chimneys—on the dusty roads—in Lina's rooms—sometimes almost in Lina's heart.

Glorious sunshine! in which Geordie revelled and grew a strong, sturdy child, spite of Bow smells and Bow chemicals; whilst his mother's cheek changed from white to brown with constant exposure to the air. During those days she and Geordie lived almost entirely out of doors:—up and down the garden walks, when those little feet were motionless she heard them still pattering; shutting her aching eyes she saw the boy wheeling about his child's barrow, and plunging in among the weeds with rake and hoe. Many and many a time in the sunless future she woke in the night with his screams of delight ringing in her ears—sounds which were never to greet them more. What a time that was to look back upon out of the blackness of subsequent despair—a time flooded with sunshine—fragrant with flowers—a lazy, dreamy, happy life, without a cloud in its heaven save one—summer days—when Lina and her boy, and Janet would take long rambling country excursions—when the citizen's wife, provided with a book, sat contentedly under the shade of the old trees in Epping Forest, whilst the child and his nurse wandered away through the glades and pathways of that relic of the olden time. Summer days—when the mother took close to her heart something which belonged lawfully and rightly to her, and felt in the inmost recesses of her soul the power and pleasure of intense love without its certain after-sting.

Summer days, when she and Geordie walked slowly along that dusty side road to the old church which stands out in the middle of the highway to Bow; when the pair passed together down the aisle, and the boy used to look first at the clergyman, and then at the clerk, with an earnestness of attention far too stolid to last, that gave way about the middle of the service, at which stage he invariably fell asleep with his head on his mother's lap. Summer days—when she went visiting about amongst the labourers' wives, and gave Geordie sweetmeats for their half-civilized children—when the mornings were cool and pleasant, and the evenings long and happy, spent, as they often were, with Mary and John Matson in their little sitting-room, elevated high above the London pavement, where the newly-married couple lived, quiet and contented as a pair of turtle doves in a nest.

"I don't think the Lady Mayoress can be half as happy as you, Mary," Mrs. Storn said one evening when the three sate together by the open window, looking over a box of mignionette at the skylight of an opposite house. "I daresay you would not change places with her this minute, if you could."

"Indeed I would not, Mrs. Storn," answered Mary; "I would not take my lady's wealth, and have to keep as many servants as she does, for the world; only fancy when I find one so much trouble, what should I do with the tribe at the Mansion House?" And the young wife laughed gaily; for she had not had a long enough experience of matrimony to be able to treat otherwise than as a jest the trials that further on she found harder to bear with equanimity. It was all very well in those early days to make a joke of the dinner being uneatable, and the tea cold; of the endless succession of chops and steaks; of the uselessness of attempting any joint more ambitious than boiled mutton; and it might be very amusing —though I doubt it—for Mrs. Matson to have to wash up the breakfast-things, and make her bed, and run down three pair of stairs to answer the door when Ganymede had her monthly holiday.

Mary would laugh till she cried over the narration of her mishaps—over the one first-class servant she ever hazarded, who came on Monday night and left on Tuesday morning, because she could not have spiced ale for her breakfast; and who declared she never took more clothes to any situation than those on her back, till she saw how she liked it; there was nothing Mrs. Matson did not laugh at; her own trouble, her own stupidity, her own inexperience: she was so happy in her husband's love, so content to be with him, so glad to be out of her uncle's house, that she could not grieve about anything; if they were able to make the two ends meet, why, they could not be poor. If John were satisfied, why should she be discontented? if their rooms were small, why they would have larger some day, and if they had not, what matter? if the stairs were steep and many, the air was better at the top of the house; and if she had to be busy as a bee, why it prevented her missing John so very much.

"If I had time to sit on the landing looking out for him, he would grow too conceited, Mrs. Storn," Mary said, "and think I could not do without him. Now, when he comes in and finds me at work, mending, making, scolding, or otherwise usefully employed, he considers I could very well have spared him for an hour longer. Is it not so?" she added, turning to her husband, and sliding her hand gently into his. "Would you not grow too proud to live with, if you thought I could do with you more at home?"

"Probably I might, my dear," he answered, while Lina turned away with a sigh, and bent over the mignionette, to hide a feeling, the existence of which Mr. Matson had begun to suspect. Men are quicker in such matters than women give them credit for; and thus, long before Mary imagined Mrs. Storn was grieving about anything, Mr. Glenaen's ci-devant clerk had a glimmering that all was not well with her; that somehow or another she was a disappointed wife.

That aught else could be wrong he did not yet suspect; but it needed no conjurer to tell him that, for some reason or other, Mrs. Storn detested chemicals; that her very efforts to master some of their details were no labours of love; that she had a more powerful motive than any mere *bas-blueish* desire to acquire a smattering of chemistry in her endless readings and ignorant questionings, and womanish impatience of the difficulties that arose in her path.

Sometimes he watched her, as she flitted from article to article in the room, admiring all the ornaments wherewith his chemical skill had enabled him to adorn his wife's otherwise plainly furnished apartment. It was a sight to see Lina looking at the lead tree on the mantel-piece, and the crystals in the cabinet; weighing his monster piece of barytes, and gingerly touching his colours; whilst all the time she was thinking—"How happened it Maurice never grew a lead tree for me, nor made crystals, nor did anything?" forgetting that whilst he had not placed his profession, or the things appertaining to it, in any way prominently before his wife, the money he earned so hardly by the ceaseless toil of mind and body, was lavished most readily and cheerfully on her.

Maurice Storn was a man who had no "personal extravagancies," unless snuff and wearing apparel are to be classed under that head. A new coat lasted him for a fabulous time, and the garments he wore in the factory would have been a disgrace to any one but a manufacturer. After paying his wages, and laying in fresh stock, and renewing his plant, Maurice always found plenty of money to spare for housekeeping; and had Lina not been an unreasonable woman, who cared more for her husband's companionship and affection than for purple and fine linen, she might have taken thought of the fact, that no house she entered was so well and tastefully furnished as hers; no business man's wife more uniformly, handsomely dressed than she; no chemist's child so rich in toys and pets as Geordie; no husband so liberal in money matters as Maurice Storn. He had asked her once, soon after she "came home," what amount she should require for domestic expenses each week; and from that time forth her purse was replenished on Monday morning regularly as the day came round. Then, as for dress and sundries, she had a milliner's bill which her husband paid without a question or remark; and her rooms were full of ornaments which Maurice had seen in the shop windows on occasion of his short visits to town, and thought Lina would like.

And Lina did like them; but still they spoke coldly to her of her husband's constant remembrance. He never gave them himself—never came to be thanked for them; but told the tradespeople to send them home to her, and expected she would be pleased with her new vase, or clock, or work-table, as a child would be pleased with a Noah's ark, or jumping doll; wherefore, because all these things never brought the pair any nearer to one another, Lina would willingly have swept vases, and time-pieces, and mimic flowers off the chimneypiece, in order to make way for that remarkable lead tree, which had now become the "bodily presence" of her domestic grievances.

Poor soul! she imagined John Matson would go on for ever making curiosities for his wife, and that Mary would always find time to dust and care for them; that in the future she would have leisure to think about such trumpery, and to plant flowers, and watch the seeds springing, and water her geraniums, and keep her little room as neat as it was then; she thought she too could be quite happy living high up within a stone's throw of heaven, if Maurice would have stayed there all the evening, and talked about his business and his prospects to her.

And then something else came across her heart, something she had vowed to crush out of it; and as this idea entered her mind, Lina lifted her head from among the mignionette, and meeting John Matson's eye fixed upon her, blushed.

If any one in after-days had asked him what first caused the idea to enter his head that Mrs. Storn held a secret within her breast which she was ashamed of, and wished to preserve intact, he would have answered, "The expression of her face once when she unexpectedly found me looking at her." Then it was but a mere tracing out of a set of feelings which he perfected into shape and form at a subsequent period; a little ray of light let in on an obscure subject, a mere glimmering of a truth which Mr. Matson was slow to accept and realise.

Still the notion did glide into the man's head that Lina Storn was fighting some kind of a mental battle; and before very long, he arrived at the conclusion, it was well for all parties concerned, Mr. Clyne had left England. Perhaps the fact of Herbert's writing to him confirmed this idea, and induced him to inform his correspondent, accidentally as it were, and in perfect good faith, "that they frequently saw Mrs. Storn, who was well and happy;" which piece of intelligence piqued Mr. Clyne, and gave him an excuse for acting foolishly once again in his life when he had the chance. She had been happy in his absence; of course then his presence could do her no harm. If he had cared for her, it was evident she had never cared for him; *ergo*, he could not be wrong in persisting in a course which injured no one but himself.

Early days those for John Matson to jump to conclusions about the east and west end intimacy; for him to draw painful deductions concerning Lina's melancholy, and Storn's absorption, and Mr. Clyne's attention. Early days for him to guess at so much from so little; but still, after all, it was merely a notion—a thought—a fear which never revealed itself in any way, unless a more earnest desire to help Lina by every means; to give her information about her husband's profession; to aid her studies, and create an interest in her mind for experiments, could be called the revelation of a pity too deep for words; of a knowledge at once of the strength and the weakness of a nature which was fully understood only by one who had no business to have comprehended anything at all about the matter.

Most kindly Mr. Matson laboured to place the difficulties and excitements of the chemist's life before her in an intelligible manner; most earnestly he tried to teach her how impossible it was for an experimenter to be a domestic man; he showed her how her husband had to toil harder than a galley slave; to wait, and watch, and work, and be disappointed day after day, without even a Sabbath of rest to recruit his frame and invigorate his body.

"In some branches of chemical manufacture," he said, "there is no rest for labourer or employer; you know as well as I do, that not a man about Mr. Storn's factory but has to turn in to his work as regularly on Sunday as on Monday morning. If the furnaces were to be let down even for twelve hours, it would take six weeks to bring them up again. Mr. Storn cannot help this if he would. I am not arguing for right or wrong; for Sunday labour or against it—I am only stating facts: at Stratford, East Greenwich, Lambeth, Woolwich Marshes, and Barking, it is just the same as at Bow. There is no Sunday out in those places, only a sort of half Sabbath, like Good Friday or Christmas Day, when some people keep holiday and others don't. In chemicals, it is work, hard and sore, from the first of January to the thirty-first of December."

"And do you mean to tell me," said Lina, "that all chemists have to devote as much time to their business as my husband?"

"It depends on the branch of manufacture they are engaged in," he answered. "Most have to work just as hard as Mr. Storn."

"Then chemists ought not to marry," said Mrs. Storn emphatically.

"Nay, nay, you would not doom them to such a fate; you would not shut them out from all domestic ties, all comfort and happiness. They work hard in the present for wealth, and leisure in the future."

"Which may never come," persisted Mrs. Storn.

"But which may," he retorted, "and which in any case should be provided for. I know I should feel much happier, if by any extra exertion—yes, even by leaving Mary a great deal more alone, I could make enough to lay by. It must be an unspeakable blessing to a man to feel he has something to fall back upon in case of sickness, or accident, or bad times;" and Mr. Matson sighed as he spoke the last words, for bad times were coming gradually down upon him, and darkening the glory of that golden summer time.

Bunt's agency had never been a peculiarly lucrative one; the demand for his manufactures, always of the most moderate description, was growing worse day by day. An opinion had somehow got afloat that the flight of his previous agent had crippled his resources, and that his goods were not of the same quality as heretofore. Do what he liked, and say what he would, Mr. Matson could not retain the old customers, whilst new ones were slow of coming in. On the one hand, there were constant complaints of the inferiority of the articles offered for sale; whilst on the other, letters came pouring in, wondering why sales were so slack. Whenever an order did come, the money had to be collected and remitted to the manufactory forthwith. Mr. Bunt was short; but customers did not understand being dunned twenty times in a month for goods which had not been bought at "prompt." "Call to-morrow" was the constant reply in town; "send to-day" was the everlasting mandate from the country.

Altogether, as autumn blew on into winter, things were in a sadly unsatisfactory state; trouble was very plenty, and cash very scarce. Under these circumstances, Mary had to make a little do much. She was forced to cut and carve her house-keeping more than ever; count the spoonsful of tea, think about the butter, and look after the ends of bread. She had to save off her own dress, in order that her husband might look respectable when he went out money-hunting, or remained at home trying to make sales; and it was the natural consequence of the want of money, that she was obliged to superintend everything in her establishment, from the scrubbing of the door-step to the cooking of the potatoes.

As time went on, it was a real blessing that she had so much to do, as to render it next to an impossibility for her to fret and worry about business affairs, which were in nearly as bad a condition as it was possible for affairs to be. Bunt, there could be no doubt, was on the eve of bankruptcy—the concern in the country would, of course, be sold: the place in town would, as an equal matter of certainty, be shut up. It had taken every sixpence of Mr. Matson's commission to meet daily expenses; they had nothing either in the bank or the cash-box; there was likely soon to be another mouth to feed, as is always the case whenever there is little to feed it with; every situation seemed filled up—trade of all sorts was dull; and in brief, as Christmas drew on, Mr. Matson was sometimes almost in a maze as to where they should go, and what they should do when they were compelled to leave their present abode and turn out into the world anew.

No house was wanting an agent: no chemical firm a manager —Mr. Storn was in course of winding up, and John was just thinking that his prospects were running down, or doing something equally desperate, when Mr. Lindor came to his rescue again, with—

" You know, my boy, I have no money to spare ever—but I have a little influence; why don't you set up as chemical agent? I can get you a four or five months' run—say one month's credit and a three months' bill—that would give you time to look round, furnish you with stock, and keep things moving for a while. Suppose you try—you have nothing to lose, any way, that is a comfort."

" Except my character," remarked Mr. Matson, with a rueful smile; " if this plan landed me in the bankrupt court, should I not lay myself open to a charge of reckless trading ?"

" Not unless you sold under cost," explained Mr. Lindor, who had, in common with most Londoners, made a trade out of nothing, and feathered his nest by means of credit; " if you offer your goods at a fair margin of profit, of course you are not answerable for results. Thus, you buy to-day, say two hundred pounds' worth of goods at four months, and sell them at ten per cent. advance to-morrow, prompt—you see you get the use of that money for three months, and with common prudence and industry, might make a good thing per annum. It is the usual system, and a capital system too."

" For young beginners—scarcely for the wholesale houses."

" Why not ? you meet your engagements punctually, and your bills are just as good as cash to people who can get them discounted. The banks or bill-brokers will do large paper for great folks, when they would not touch a twenty pound acceptance for you, if it were to save you from destruction. The whole case may be put into a nutshell. The manufacturers have the use of your paper, cash to them, and you have the use of their goods, cash to you—it is a mutual advantage altogether, and depend upon it, if men of business did not find their advantage in it, they would not be so ready to give credit."

" But then I could not afford to give credit," argued Mr. Matson.

" Of course not, you cannot live without cash. Don't I tell you banks were made for the accommodation of great men, and in the same way great men are made for the accommodation of little; and little, again, are made for the benefit of less. It is the way of the world."

"Suppose," enquired John, "at the end of the four months, I had not been able to dispose of the goods: what then?"

"Why, then, they must either take them back, or renew," said Mr. Lindor, with the greatest *sang froid*.

"And suppose I had sold them, and spent or lost the money."

"In that case, you would have to put up with the consequences; but there is no fear of that; your expenses would be light, that is, I should say rent and all might be covered at first by five pounds a week."

"And in the name of heaven, where am I to get five pounds a week?" enquired Mr. Matson.

"Out of your sales," was the answer. "Surely you can sell two hundred pounds' worth of goods a month; well, you ought to get ten per cent. out of that, any way, and that would clear your expenses without touching the capital at all. I will tell you how I managed when I began; but then, to be sure, I had no wife. I had a warehouse, office, and cockloft, at a hundred. Light, coal, and wages, were close on thirty shillings a week more; that made one hundred and seventy-five—a heavy pull: but I saved off myself, lived in the cockloft, made my own bed, and cooked my own food; yes, and at a pinch took down my own shutters. It cost me twelve shillings a week for food, and twenty pounds a year for dress; and though I commenced without a copper, I knew all through that if I failed any day, I should get complimented by the commissioner, and pass unopposed by my creditors. I kept a cash account of every halfpenny I spent, even to a packet of blacking. Of course your housekeeping will be heavier than mine; but I should advise you to put as much down to 'trade expenses' as you can. Creditors don't care so much for money being lost, as they do for thinking it has been squandered. Every young man ought to keep his books with an eye to the 'court.' It was what I did, and many a sound night's rest I had on the strength of it."

And the little silk merchant, possessed of so much business knowledge and business sense, leaned back in his chair, and with a look of ineffable prosperity and self-satisfaction beaming over his rosy, vulgar, chubby face, regarded Mr. Matson, who was trying to see his way through the mist, and to make out exactly what was right and what was wrong.

"If I sell at a profit?" he began, after a long pause.

"Which of course you will, or not at all," interrupted Mr. Lindor, "for I suppose you would not be such an idiot to sell at a loss; you will, in fact, either get your fair per centage, or else keep the goods; so that settles the matter; and now, if you like, I will write to two or three people for you."

"I think it would be better for me to think over the plan for twenty-four hours, and consult with Mary," said John, hesitatingly.

"Very well, just as you like. I never consulted Mrs. L. about a business matter in my life, but I should not wonder if it be a good plan; besides, Mary is a quiet creature, and not quite so fine a lady as Madam," replied Mr. Lindor, who dare not in America Square have said his soul was his own, and who consequently was only too glad to keep business and house separate. "Give my love to Mary," he added, as he shook hands with his nephew, "and tell her the first time Mrs. L. is out of town I will come over and have a cup of tea; I would call in the daytime, but really I have not a moment— up to the ears, my boy; always labouring, never have done."

"Profitable labour, at all events," said Mr. Matson, half enviously.

"Yes, making, but not saving," was the answer; "and still, what is the use of slaving and earning money, if we do not enjoy it?" With which philosophic reflection he dismissed Mr. Matson, who wended his way home and repeated the gist of the conversation to his wife.

She was delighted— such a wonderful idea—so strange they had not thought of it before; of course they would sell, and of course they could not only live, but save. Suppose only ten people were to take ten pounds of goods a week, why that would leave five pounds clear, after paying all expenses; "and five pounds a week would be two hundred and sixty pounds a year, John," she concluded; "so you see, even at the worst, we should have three hundred pounds to lay by at the end of the first twelve months."

Which vision of wealth so blinded Mrs. Matson's understanding, that John found it impossible to make her see how extremely unlikely it was he should be able at first to find so many customers.

"Still, I think," he said at last with the air of a man who did not want to give way too rapidly to extravagant ideas, "that we might be able to make both ends meet; what do you say, dear? what is the least we could live on?"

Which question at once started Mary into a fearful calculation concerning pounds of meat, and pints of milk, and loaves of bread, and she commenced counting up odd items on her fingers until she got into such an arithmetical labyrinth that her husband finally took out pocket book and pencil, and saying—

"Now let us go methodically to work:" put down first rent

and taxes, and then a boy's wages; and after that, all the various amounts which Mary declared would be needed for the house.

And during the whole of this performance she leaned over his shoulder, and when the final addition showed the sum total of theoretical expenses, she declared—

"It was not so much, after all."

Heavens! what children they were, sitting there and making pen and ink calculations of outgoings and returns—such children as hope and inexperience are capable of forming even out of grown up-stuff; but though it may appear very foolish to record how Mr. and Mrs. Matson, even with their apprenticeship to poverty and anxiety, made preparations on paper for starting on their own account, I would put it to you, most clever and courteous reader, if there be one amongst us who, at some period, and in some way or other, has not done just the same.

You, sir, have gathered in and stored your visionary hay and oats long before the first is ready for the scythe, or the latter for the sickle; you have calculated your tons and your bushels, and put this yield against that payment. You sell your calves mentally before they are reared, and get your own prices freely so long as you are selling them to yourself; whenever you have sowed your turnip seed, you estimate the value of that four acres, whilst Madam your respected wife counts her chickens before they are hatched; and when she sees a new cow come home, has pleasant dreams of numberless cheeses, and countless pounds of butter, which sell at preposterous and outlandish prices.

And don't you know, Miss Beauty, that the ante-matrimonial views of love in a cottage, and pretty straw hats, and flowers, and sunshine, and sweets, and kisses, which please you now, are all dissolving; and cannot I inform those whom it may concern, that the best fruit tree in the garden never bears the number of apples it was thought it would: that no publisher's subscription of a new work ever exhausted the number of copies he had set apart for it: that no house-wife could say with any truth she was able to keep strictly within her average: no person to save exactly what he had proposed to lay by.

So it is in all cases; no practice tallies accurately with its preliminary theory: the sum total of the work we have actually performed in age falls sadly short of the work contemplated in youth; the clergyman has proved no apostle, the barrister but a poor orator, the author but one amongst more; no linguist is a master of every known tongue; no musician can play on every instrument. Yet we go on, each and all, figuratively or

literally, making, like Mr. and Mrs. Matson, pen and ink calculations, wherein the credit is always too much, and the debit
always too little ; for cannot you remember, long ago, a certain
pig in the farmyard being called yours, which said pig you
counted would bring you in fabulous amounts to spend amongst
your school-fellows, until one unhappy morning, when, if it
had not to be killed to save its life, it was yet carried to market
in such a state that it had to sit down on its hind quarters and
be sold in that interesting position ?

And since those days, oh friend, have you not sent many a
once thriving porker out into the political, or mercantile, or
literary market, which, when it came to be weighed and tested,
and bought, had not even hind legs to stand upon, but was
returned to your hands dead and unprofitable ?

If you doubt me, look at that old pile of love letters, at
yonder pyramid of manuscripts, at the dishonoured bills in the
bottom of your cash box, at the estimates, and enquiries, and
plans, and offers, and prospectuses, that fill your desk.

Withered leaves of the goodly tree Hope, which still to the
last puts out fair green shoots for the wretchedest amongst us,
and makes children of those who stretch forth their hands to
gather its delusive fruit.

CHAPTER XVI.

LIFE AMONGST THE CHEMICALS.

MEANTIME Maurice Storn was "achieving fortune." A pleasant business to most people under most circumstances ; though
whether its consummation usually proves worth the pains
generally taken to achieve it, is a matter on which I entertain
some doubts.

Mr. Storn had none, however ; without a breeze in the air
—without a riple on the tide—without a look to right or left,
or lingering glance behind, he steered straight on for the port
of opulence ; and most assuredly, if skilful seamanship and
ceaseless exertion give a patent right to wealth, Maurice Storn,
the chemist, the experimenter, and the manufacturer, deserved
all he made, and hoped to make.

In the " concern," as Mr. Glenaen termed it, he was at once
master and man ; there was nothing too great for him to
attempt ; nothing too low for him to do ; the word " cannot "
was excluded from his vocabulary. He told the people he

employed at once what could, and what should be done; after that, it was optional whether or not they attempted it; if one person did not work, another would; in any case it was but a question of paying John, Harry, or Tom. In his own dominions Mr. Storn became a perfect autocrat; an individual against whose mandate there was no appeal; a man for whom no work was too hard or too heavy; a person who having set out to win the battle of chemistry, was not going to sink and faint under the heat and burden of the practical fight, after he had laboured so hard and so continuously for years in theory.

No—he had tested and proved; the thing was to be done, and he knew how; and it was not the amount of time and patience required to perfect his goods for market that was capable of frightening a man who had staked his money and energies, and talents on this single throw, and—won.

I wish, dear readers, I could by a stroke of my pen carry you mentally into that charmed spot, where most of you, I know, may never enter—a chemical manufactory. I wish I could show you the apparently inextricable confusion, but real order, which reigns throughout the rough buildings and miserable-looking sheds, and half-filled vats, and ovens, and furnaces, and chambers, and offices. I would I could present in bodily presence for your inspection the pale German workmen, with their light hair and bloated, flabby faces; and their Irish co-adjutors, who look like a cross between human beings and dried red herrings.

I should like to be able to place before you, as in a picture, these men, shirtless, stockingless, and bareheaded, standing naked—save for a pair of light slippers, and still lighter trousers, before fires that would, to use Mr. Glenaen's constant expression, have "melted the devil," shovelling, drinking, cursing, and sweating. Really, a chemical manufactory is like the valley of desolation by day, and like pandemonium by night; and the men who get their livings in such places resemble ordinary mortals less than spirits in Hades.

Out of such materials a man of weak nerve and slight determination would not have the faintest chance of achieving successful results; true—chemistry is a trade which shows to a nicety how much work every servant occupied in its details has achieved; but the results of a single case of negligence might be so fatal that no master dare wait for results to give him information of what had actually been performed. As the work progresses he must see for himself that each furnace man and labourer is at his post. He must guard against drowsiness, carelessness, spite; he must give rein in some cases a little, and yet feel that he has the bit tight in every mouth notwithstanding; and above all—and most important of all—there must not be a detail, however subordinate, that he does not understand, that he has not knowledge and strength and will sufficient to "set on and do" at any moment.

Flaring out across the darkness I can see the glare of the furnaces when a door is opened; and flitting across the brick floors, and looking like spectres between the two contending lights, the flickering of the oil lamps, and the blaze of the tremendous fires, we may catch a glimpse of those white bodies, and black faces, and sinewy limbs, that give a sort of unearthly animation to the scene.

There, in the midst of them, distinguished by his dark coat, stands Maurice Storn; and beside him Gordon Glenaen, whose own business not requiring such unremitting attention, often left his own more immediate concerns and came over to assist in those of the Co., for the pair were now in actual partnership together—Storn, Glenaen, and Co., being the title under which the new firm traded in the chemical market.

Mr. Glenaen was swearing—his usual occupation when he got amongst the brimstone; he had no other idea of managing anybody but by violence; no weapons ever came so natural to him as a volley of oaths; and when he was alone amidst the Germans and Irish of the Company's factory, without another English ear but Maurice's within hail, he was wont to launch forth into a sea of expletives which might even have astonished John Matson, who said he had heard his employer curse till he got hoarse.

On the present occasion he had almost met with his match; a gigantic Bohemian, a Black Forester, who feared neither saint nor sinner—who regarded oaths no more than hail—who was willing to stay or to go—to lose his situation or to keep it—to bear abuse, anger, anything, always excepting the heat of a new coke oven, which Maurice had declared he should draw, and which he, with equal determination, declared he would not.

"Leave the premises, you blackguard!" yelled Mr. Glenaen; "leave them at once, if you don't want to be kicked out. Do you think either I or Mr. Storn will stand any of your cursed nonsense, coming in here, and picking and choosing your work as if you were master of the premises?—Clear out, I say, and be—"

"I am ready to do anything, sir, you order me," answered the man in broken English, "except draw that furnace; it is a new one Mr. Storn has put up, it holds six tons. No man could do it, sir. I could not myself."

"You not do it," answered Mr. Glenaen furiously; "you, who I verily believe could go through hell and be cool?"

"Yes," persisted the man, perfectly insensible to this last compliment, which I only repeat for the sake of being accurate. "Yes, even I could not do it; there is not a man living could."

It was becoming a serious question—not that of drawing the furnace—but that of maintaining subordination; the other workmen were closing round the trio, listening with greedy ears to what they considered the triumph of their fellow. Maurice saw it was of no use Mr. Glenaen blustering and swearing; he had found his own commands perfectly futile; and as he looked round the circle of eager, excited faces, he formed his plan, one which probably not another master in England could have carried out.

"You say no man could draw the furnace," he said, in a quiet sort of tone, which contrasted forcibly with Mr. Glenaen's vituperations.

"I do," was the reply. "I could not do it myself."

"Very well; sit down there, and don't move till I give you leave," answered Maurice, pointing to a bench beside the oven; and the man having obeyed, he flung off coat, waistcoat, and braces, tied his neckhandkerchief round his trousers, and went to work like a Hercules.

"You are not going to attempt to draw that, Storn?" exclaimed Mr. Glenaen.

"Indeed I am."

"You will never be able to stand the heat."

"We shall see."

"You will kill yourself."

"I am content."

"Then, for Heaven's sake, when you are at it, just pitch the fellow in; I will give you a lift with him."

"Let him alone—don't speak to him; and now stand out of the way."

Which Mr. Glenaen did, as the peel came slowly round, emptying its burning load on the ground; and thus Maurice worked resolutely through the fiery ordeal, whilst the Bohemian, who had thrown himself on the floor, and lay lounging there, with a couple of dogs beside him, watched with intense delight the perspiration pouring from Maurice's temples, and thought, as he listened to every gasp of exhaustion, that his master would give in.

But Mr. Storn did not give in. He would have dropped down dead before failing or fainting in the work he had set himself to do; and thus, as the peel time after time went in empty and came out full, the Bohemian's triumph changed into annoyance; and when, after an hour of pulling, and scorching, and shoving, and perspiring, Maurice at last saw his task accomplished, the man got up and stood before him beaten.

"Well," said Mr. Storn, when at last he brought his face out of an ale jug, and found he had a voice left to speak with: "will you take charge of that furnace and stay, or make any difficulty and leave?"

"I will stay," was the reply, sullenly, but still determinedly uttered.

"And the next time you want an advance of wages, you may find it better to ask for it than to refuse to work."

"Do you think no man could draw that oven now, you confounded blackguard?" asked Mr. Glenaen.

"You could not, at any rate," muttered the fellow, as he slunk away with his dogs from the scene of action, quickening his movements, however, not in the least, for a threat from Mr. Glenaen to kick him into some remote period of time.

It was a triumph certainly, and for the future Maurice found his men more easily managed; less given to raise difficulties and refuse work; and yet, in a bodily sense, it was a triumph pleasanter just in the moment of fruition than afterwards.

For a month he was unable to close his hands; when he crawled home in the daybreak of an autumn morning, he found his palms were raw and bleeding: that he could not stand upright: that he was so completely exhausted he had to fly to stimulants, and alternately get Lina to pour him out wine, and bathe his forehead with vinegar, and bind up his hands in oil.

Yet it was almost worth the man's while to get ill, to see how eagerly his wife nursed him, how she pulled off her rings and rubbed his arms till her own ached again: how she put pillows under his back to ease it, and ran up and down stairs like a lapwing for cotton and oil for his blistered hands, and lemons for his head, and wine for him to swallow.

And when he got a little easier, and fell asleep on the sofa, how quiet she was herself, and how still she insisted on Geordie's remaining; what a pretty thing it was to watch her, as Maurice did once with his eyes half shut, stealing softly across the room, and getting a mat to lay her scissors on, for fear their rattle on the table should disturb her husband; and, above all, what a significant fact it was, that although the poor young creature did all certainly out of her heart, yet that, still no less certainly, she did it out of her sorrow.

Was it altogether her fault that she had fallen away little by little from the Lina of old? Were her futile struggles, and secret tears, and imperfect prayers, of no account? were her eager clutches at every blade of grass growing on the side of the moral precipice she had commenced descending, no sign that the woman wanted to keep herself right? feebly it might be, but still most earnestly.

Was it not pitiful to note the strained, anxious way in which she snapped at every duty, performing more in the process of its discharge than was by any means needful? Was it not, above all, most sorrowful to consider, that let what outward event be passing before her eyes: let what procession of incidents be fleeting by; she was always and ever looking at the little tragedy enacting within her own heart.

Working for herself in the dreary present, a past sufficient to cloud the glory of her brightest future. I declare that, as I write the story of the woman's efforts and shortcomings—as I recall the days and the weeks of that frightful self-examination, and trace how each circumstance in the course of her daily life was either a fresh temptation or a fresh reproach—I am sometimes almost induced to wonder whether Lina's conscience was not scourge sufficient for her spirit—whether the fiery trials of the future were needed for her then.

Viewing her as she sits beside her husband, exaggerating even the customary quietness of a nurse, looking at that pale, melancholy face, I wonder, even whilst I know; and, above all things, I commence to marvel whether stiff, and weary, and sore, though he be, Maurice Storn would have slept on so quietly, had any one whispered in his ear whither his wife's affections were wandering.

I marvel—and Lina sighs softly and under her breath—and after a while, her husband wakes, and yawns, and gets on his legs, and says he must go down to the factory just to show himself, and see what the men are doing. Having accomplished which duties, accompanied by Geordie, who had been on the tenter-hooks at having to keep quiet for so long a time, the chemist returns back again to cotton and oil, and easy sofas, and woman's nursing. In all his repertory of science, he could find no cure for an aching back. There was no drug in his laboratory capable of easing the racking pain across his forehead; after all, it was very nice to have Lina's soft white hand touching his raw, blistered palms; very pleasant to know he had a home, and a wife, and a nurse, to come back to when he liked. Sometime he would be able to remain more with her, he thought, on the rare occasions when he was driven back by sickness from science to nature, and for the moment he really considered he was a very much overworked individual, who was compelled by a stern necessity to do that which he might just as well have let alone had it pleased him to do so.

Some of the benefits attending matrimony appeared to strike Mr. Glenaen when he came to see his friend; for he found Mr. Storn being doctored in the most approved feminine fashion, and the room, and fire, and sofa, and pillows, looking so snug and sociable, that the manufacturer, contrasting perhaps his own "might have been," with "what was," grew a degree more snappish and unpleasant than ever, and put Lina, who had tried, contrary to her wont, to meet his views, out of temper.

Considering, probably, that Mrs. Storn had aided and abetted Mary Matson in her absurd rejection of his suit, and believing that the chemist's wife had pressed on a match which ended his first and last love fancy, he had been ever since that time on somewhat cooler terms than formerly with her; and now, although she urged him to smoke his calumet of peace in her most comfortable chair, though she lit her husband's cigar and sat between the clouds of smoke they puffed out at one another; though she kept Geordie quiet, and would not let him teaze; though she ordered up supper for the manufacturer without being asked to do so by her husband, and made herself as generally agreeable as it was possible for a woman who disliked her guest, and hated his trade, to do under the most favourable circumstances, Mr. Glenaen was not satisfied; but wished to heaven, mentally, Storn had not been such a fool as to marry anybody, least of all Captain Maudsley's daughter.

Whilst he was eating his supper he managed to keep an eye on Lina, who kept urging and coaxing her husband to swallow this, and taste that, and was everlastingly softening his wounds and bandaging them up again.

Watching her doing her woman's work, whilst he cut himself slices of Stilton cheese, and ate them buttered, as another person might have done bread, Mr. Glenaen felt himself moved at last to say, for some strange reason, in an insolent, sneering tone—

"I did not think you had been so good a nurse, Mrs. Storn."

There was something in the remark which struck down to the festering wound below.

"Did you think women could do anything, Mr. Glenaen?" she asked, sharply.

"Very little," was the retort, and down went another tremendous mouthful of cheese, whilst Lina dropped her bandages, and turned towards her husband with tears in her eyes. Tears! Heaven only knew why.

" Never mind, dear," said Maurice, kindly, " Mr. Glenaen is only laughing at you."

" I don't like to be laughed at, Maurice," she remarked with a sort of gulp as she took to her doctoring once more, and then, (forgive her! she was but woman), her thoughts went wandering out again.

And so did Maurice's—to the time when he should see Lina, as he wanted to see her, oh! so rich, and surrounded by so many luxuries. There was nothing money could buy he would have grudged to her or the boy. Nothing on earth would have been too good or too beautiful for Lina. When she became associated with his plans, it was always as a participater in the wealth they were to yield; for he could not see, poor blind fool that he was, that even in the midst of their present competence, his wife was hungering and thirsting, not for gold nor silver, not for grander furniture nor handsomer dress, not for more servants to command, nor more money to spend, but for love and companionship. Mentally the woman was starving, for the only food she had ever had presented to her, though tempting, was poison, and she felt afraid to touch it.

As well she might, for setting aside all other things—never to speak of the loss she was sure to gain eventually—she knew there was not in England so leal and loyal a heart as that which beat in the breast of the man she had vowed to love unto death.

Passing over his one error of judgment—an undue absorption to a pursuit which had for years stood him in the stead of dearer and better ties—there was not a man in the whole earth from whom it would have been a greater crime to swerve in thought or deed, in honour or in law, than Maurice Storn.

The man was blind, he wanted a sense, he had no eyesight, and no human being, nothing but the oculists time, experience, and misfortune could benefit his case. Stupidly, he believed Lina to be all he wished her, and so he blundered on through all sorts of smells and chemicals, and sulphuric acid, which, turning out a lucrative speculation, he " went in and won," to quote Mr. Glenaen once again; sharing all the profits with that individual, and working like a dozen men instead of one.

But he saw his way—he made money—hundred to hundred, thousand to thousand—the new Co. was " known" by respectable bankers—people began to wonder at their success—manufacturers became curious—the necessity for secrecy grew greater than ever.

" How did it happen Mr. Storn's chambers were so small?" enquired chemists learned in the lore of sulphuric premises.

"How came it to pass, Mrs. Storn had blossoms in her garden : by what means did he prevent the sulphur destroying vegetation ?"

So it went on for a little while, and then it was boldly asserted he had discovered a new method. By some means or other he had done what was needful with spongy platinum, and was clearing his fifty per cent. on every transaction.

Then came the eager questioning and eternal spying, the feeing of workmen, and dismissal of employés, the careful standing on defensive ground ; the everlasting caution necessary to the very being of a successful chemist. .

Nevertheless, through all, Maurice Storn held his secret safe, he kept the process intact ; there was no other house in the market able to sell with his margin of profit ; there was not another man in England possessed of his plan but Gordon Glenaen.

"A little more of this and I can retire," he said one day, in a state of high exultation. "Look at the balance sheet, Glenaen,"—and he pointed to a complication of figures, which proved at the bottom that the profits had been tremendous. "What do you think of that ?"

The manufacturer was graciously pleased to think well of the statement ; but he was like the daughters of the horseleech —and in his mouth and in his soul for ever and always rung out the cry, "more, more."

Wherefore, as one thing had done well, he thought that another might do better, and in an evil hour whispered into Mr. Storn's ear the solitary word, ",Cyanogen."

CHAPTER XVII.

MR. CLYNE'S RETURN.

TAKING it as a whole, the fact of a man being clever may be considered as a dubious sort of blessing, seeing that, like the weathercock, he stands on an eminence, rather for the convenience of other people than for any positive benefit to himself." There is always some respectable thief at hand to pick the brains of any one willing to work for pleasure—always some speculator ready to drag him off the road he is pursuing, and suggest that another might be made more profitable. Through all changes, chances, and vicissitudes, the bird that can sing and will sing is made to sing, and gets in return for its pains the minimum quantity of groundsel and sugar accorded to any of its fellows.

Overfeeding is doubtless bad for inventors, as it is for piping bullfinches; and perhaps it was for this reason that Gordon Glenaen got the lion's share out of the profits of the sulphuric acid—the largest amount of money for the smallest amount of work.

After his fashion he certainly worked for his living: he got up at six every morning, he lounged about his factory all day, and made his employés "look sharp." He stormed, and cursed, and swore, as if for the pleasure of the thing; he handled this, and tested that, and paid visits of inspection to Maurice Storn; he twisted his wits about, to see how he could make the concern more profitable; bought in the lowest market, and sold in the dearest; knew to a nicety what discoveries would "pay" in the chemical world, and whenever he got hold of what might be called a fine egg, carried it to Maurice Storn to hatch; certain, that if the thing could be made to chip at all, the chemist was the person to bring it to perfection.

And Mr. Glenaen, through his mother, always managed to get money for what he termed "warming an invention," which was a lucrative thing for the Glenaens; for first, after rent and taxes were cleared, interest was paid for capital, and then, but not till then, Maurice and the manufacturer shared the profits. Fair enough, I know most people will say, and the writer has no intention of controverting their opinion. A bargain is a bargain—though one man be fool enough to neglect his own interests, and another be wise enough to take advantage of the oversight. And for this reason Mr. Glenaen burnt the partnership candle at both ends, and left Mr. Storn only the piece remaining in the middle. What the whole must have been, might be inferred from the amount Maurice himself received out of the concern. He was quite right when he said a little more of it would enable him to retire; and even in their domestic concerns, Lina soon began to feel the change which had taken and was taking place in business affairs. She had now her pony-carriage, her own especial servant-man, and Mr. Storn kept his saddle-horse, on which, at rare intervals, he might have been observed riding slowly out along the Stratford road, chewing the handle of his cutting-whip, and thinking about cyanogen. He had his groom also for attending to his quadrupeds, and as these two men lived in the house, it was necessary to keep another female servant to wait on them. Altogether, what with present alterations and hints of future changes, Lina began to feel they were getting into a different position. They were leaving simple competence behind them and growing rich; and with a sort of surprise Lina woke to the idea of wealth, just as she might to that of poverty.

An abrupt rise in the world is a strange feeling to any one, even to a person who has never been absolutely short of money; it alters the routine of present existence; it changes the plans and prospects of the future; it turns an individual out of the humdrum track of every-day life; it seems to give wider views over the coming years; to enlarge a man or a woman's duties and responsibilities, and cares and pleasures.

Thus when at last Lina felt the tide of prosperity lifting her bark into higher waters, she roused herself, and looked forth with a sort of vague interest at the ports to which the change might steer them. The first thing, almost, that occurred to her, was the possibility of Geordie being " a gentleman," in her own peculiar sense of the word. Hitherto, she had never thought at all about the boy's future, but now it seemed to come upon her first with a sort of shock that her child must grow up; and then with a throb of delight, that he need not enter trade. It was, no doubt, very wrong of Mrs. Storn to look down on that which had put bread in her mouth—given her shelter, clothing, comforts, luxuries—but still there is no denying the fact Lina did cordially hate and detest commerce in all its moods and tenses; and, what was more, she could scarcely have been her father's daughter had she not done so.

Commerce to her was typified in Mr. Glenaen; he was the first specimen of a trader presented to her view, for she had made Maurice's acquaintance under circumstances which hid the bugbear business from sight; and accordingly it can scarcely be wondered at, that she disliked the idea of transforming Geordie into another of the same, and was thankful at the notion of preserving him from such contamination.

Perhaps it was from repugnance to the subject, that she had never given it any consideration until now, when a probability of deliverance from the evil might be considered also; at any rate, one thing is certain, that she swallowed the poison and the antidote together, and with the idea of prosperity took also the notion of being at once proud and anxious concerning the future of her boy.

At this, the one solitary air-chateau of her life, she began forthwith to build ceaselessly: if her husband had been able to spare time enough to listen to her, she would have enlisted his imagination likewise in the service; as it was, in answer to her questions, he furnished her with foundations for her edifice,

and sometimes threw out stray hints as to the style of architecture to be adopted; for if Lina was prejudiced and fanciful,
there can be no doubt but that Maurice had his views and
wishes too. A chemist himself, he entertained no desire to
see his son follow in his footsteps; a trader, he still had a
fondness for the aristocracy—a man toiling early and late for
money, he nevertheless felt a hankering after rank; he liked
chemistry for itself, more than for its belongings; he was a
thorough enthusiast in his profession; but in a remote future
he had always a vision of something beyond it. An estate
perhaps, and a name, and money, and leisure to try experiments
for experiment's sake.

He did not much care what he did himself, but he was perhaps a degree more particular about his son than Lina.

He never looked pleased to see Geordie in the workshops:
he very rarely let the child go with him to the factory: he
never paid the slightest attention to Mr. Glenaen's remark,
that he was making the boy a milk-sop, but once remonstrated
with that important personage when he chanced to be unbur-
dening his mind of oaths before his godson.

He would not permit him to run about with the labourers'
children, or amongst the men; he was always sending him in
to mamma, and never permitted Geordie, who wanted constantly
to be at his heels, to follow him, when he could prevent it.

He was proud of the child—proud, and fond, and vain; and
he liked to keep him away from contact with his own rough,
though mental trade; wanting to preserve him still the little
gentleman he was, against the future, when they should not be
living at Bow, nor, perhaps, in London, any place.

He was quite content to leave his child with his wife; to let
her teach, and train, and spoil, and dress the boy, who was to
grow into somebody yet; and when he had leisure to think,
visions came up before the mind's eye of the practical chemist,
that might have astonished Lina, could she have got a glimpse
of them likewise.

For the middle-aged and the old have as wild dreams as the
youngest amongst my readers. And Maurice Storn, quiet
though he seemed, and mentally balanced though he was, cut
vistas for himself at times through the forest of future events,
that surpassed all the avenues of pride Lina formed occasionally
to her castle of romance.

Spite of Miss Charlotte Elizabeth, I hold day-dreams to be
fine things for helping us across the morass of life. Will-o'-
the-wisps and cheats they may be, but still, somehow or another,
they compel us to forget the weariness of the present, for the

sake of the brightness of the future; and if that future be dark, if the dreams are never fulfilled, if our schemes fail, and our fortunes darken, and our castles crumble into dust, still it is a blessing to have hoped once, for the man who has ever done so, will, on the slightest provocation, hope again.

At any rate, it came like a light in darkness, like water in the wilderness, this consciousness to Lina Storn of having something to look forward to, and hope concerning. It gave her a mental occupation, a sort of interest in passing events, a kind of trembling, yet pleasant anxiety about the future.

It helped her to pass the days, and (as she thought) to fight out the fight of old with greater energy and determination than ever.

"Mr. Clyne is nothing to me now," she whispered to herself at last; "it was a folly, a weakness, a sin, but it is all past now. How could I ever have been so wicked?"

How could you, Lina—you think—as you sit looking with those dark eyes of yours that first touched Maurice Storn's heart, into the blaze which is leaping, sinking, dancing, and rushing up the wide, old-fashioned chimney—How could you have been so weak once? and how, above all, does it come to pass, that you, who were so weak so short a time since, can be so mad as to believe yourself strong now?

By what process of reasoning can you arrive at the conclusion that you, who have been battling with that evil affection, and trying to crush it out of your heart for months, are safe at last? Do you feel as though a heavenly hand had taken the helm of your soul, and was guiding it to a pleasant haven?

Don't you know that in the ocean of life, as in the ocean of nature, there are troughs as dangerous as the highest billows that come dashing on the coast? Have you never heard there are in existence moments of dead calm, that lull one into a delusive security, and leave all at the mercy of the coming storm? Can you not feel, as you sit there, arguing out that little question of departed love, with your own conscience, something at the very bottom of your heart reproaching and warning you? don't you know as well as I do, that it is not memory alone, but anticipation, which is sending the blood oftener into your face, and making your pulse throb faster, and causing you occasionally to tremble and turn cold.

Poor wife! you are determining that you will not care for this man more, and therefore you are trying to persuade yourself that it is all past and gone—that you do not care for him now. And so you go out to face the danger again, half-armed, with a cowardly consciousness, spite of all your assumed bravery, that it would have been better he had not come back: that if Maurice had known all—all that you should have told him, even had you cut your heart to pieces in letting out the secret—he would never have come in with that frank, honest face of his, and said,—

"Mr. Clyne has returned, dear: I met him in Threadneedle Street to-day, and asked him to come out here for dinner to-morrow. It will be rather a leisure afternoon with me, and I thought you would be pleased."

Pleased! oh yes, of course Lina was pleased, though the news came upon her with a clap, and so she sat down before the fire to persuade herself the past had been but a miserable delusion, while Mr. Storn walked out of the room, happy in his ignorance of all that was passing through her mind, and perfectly satisfied with what was passing through his own.

He was thinking of the probable future—so wrapt up in chemistry and speculation, that he had no eyes left to see what was passing under his nose, visible even to the unprejudiced vision of Lina's friend, John Matson, who wished in his heart Mr. Herbert Clyne had never come back to London.

The first visit that gentleman paid was to the chemical warehouse Mr. Matson had stocked, by means of credit, in Coleman Street; and though Mary was foolish enough to believe he came to see her husband, and for nothing else, that favoured individual was not so blind but that he could form an opinion as to what brought Mr. Clyne his way, and induced him to stay so long and talk so much, and speak of the Storns so little. It is those alone who have trodden the road that know the marks and milestones by the way; and thus it came to pass, that because John Matson had been in love himself, he, though slow to pass judgment on another, came to the conclusion that Mr. Clyne was in love with Mr. Storn's wife.

A startling conclusion for a person like him to arrive at, because he belonged to a class amongst whom such things are of unfrequent occurrence, and who are accustomed to look upon affairs of the kind more as mere men, than as men of the world.

Perhaps it was because of some inkling of this feeling that Mr. Clyne ceased cultivating the Matsons, and, in lieu of either visiting them, or going out to Bow, contented himself with making fictitious journeys into the city, on one of which occasions he was so fortunate as to renew his acquaintance with Mr. and Mrs. and the Misses Lindor, and the same day met Mr. Storn, who was obliging enough to invite him into the chemical dwelling for dinner.

Thus it all came about simply and naturally, without any apparent pushing on the one side, or possibility of coolness on the other, that Lina Storn and Herbert Clyne met once more.

Through the filthy bye road which he had left, thick with dust, he drove back again to her; and in the self-same room whence she had watched his departing figure, and fancied she saw him look behind, Lina greeted him on his return.

And Maurice Storn, good, faithful, honest heart, so steady, and sterling of purpose, so trusting in his wife, so sure of her and of himself, stood by, and looking at the pair greeting, never felt the tremor that shook Lina's voice, knew nothing of the thrill that passed through his guest's heart.

So unsuspicious, so noble in his intense unconsciousness of evil; if he had but been jealous, Lina could have told him all! if he had but doubted, she could have given him reason for his want of faith; but as it was, she could as soon have thought of stabbing a sleeping man as of plunging the dagger into his undefended breast. In the present, as in the past, she could but determine to conquer herself—but try to fight out the everlasting battle with her own soul, and fail.

I should only weary your patience, dear reader, were I to go over the old ground step by step with you again, for it would be but repeating a previously told tale, to show the almost imperceptible degrees by which Herbert Clyne regained his former position in the house—his wonted supremacy over Lina.

The world might not guess it—he might not know it; but to Lina it was clear as the sun at noontide that Mr. Clyne and she ought to separate—that he ought not to visit at the house —that it was her bounden duty to tell her husband how matters stood, and leave him to arrange their course for the future as seemed best in his sight.

But then, what was there to tell? the cunning and trembling heart asked back. Was there aught she could not live down herself—anything that time, and reserve, and coldness could not cure? the sophist, ever at work in the human soul, argued: and Mrs. Storn was only too willing to accept the answer for gospel, and ask no doubting question more.

Besides, Mr. Clyne, after all, was not so very much at the house; he went to Bow when Mr. Storn asked him to dinner, and he called occasionally in the mornings, quite as frequently, perhaps, in company with the Misses Lindor as alone; for it was a fact to be noted, that Mr. Clyne now never paid a visit to the silk merchant's house, but Tryphenia and some of her sisters were "just going to see dear Mrs. Storn."

"The girls are so fond of walking," the parent bird remarked, "and Bow is such a convenient distance off. It gives them an object to visit Mrs. Storn, and she is a delightful acquaintance for them : perfectly unexceptionable in every way: the only city person I like them to associate with : quite above her surroundings, Mr. Clyne. I do not think she is looking well, do you ?"

"In health ?" inquired the person addressed, with a quiet smile.

"Of course. Do you imagine I think you would be so ungallant as to say a lady looked ill in any other way ?" replied Mrs. Lindor.

"I believe I must plead guilty to not having noticed any particular alteration in Mrs. Storn's appearance," he answered, noticing his hostess expected an observation of some kind.

"I fancy Bow does not agree with her," persisted Mrs. Lindor, "it is such a wretched place,—so totally out of the world; and the smell from those dreadful chemical manufactories is really insufferable. The girls say every time they return from visiting her, that they wonder Mrs. Storn can exist in such a place."

It was on the tip of Mr. Clyne's tongue to inquire why they made martyrs of themselves by going there; but he wisely refrained, and remarked—

"Mr. Glenaen declared Bow was the healthiest place on earth."

"I wonder who would take Mr. Glenaen's word for anything," retorted the fair Tryphenia, with more warmth than politeness.

"Mr. Glenaen is so wrapped up in his profession," hastily interposed Mrs. Lindor, taking the rough edge off her daughter's speech, "that he sometimes forgets chemicals do not possess charms for every one ; but still I have no doubt but that if he consider Bow healthy, it really is so, for he rarely speaks without due authority on any subject. I have a very high opinion of Mr. Glenaen, and so ought you, Tryphenia," she added, with a rebuking glance towards that young lady, who only replied by a toss of her head and conscious look at Mr. Clyne.

It was quite a sight to behold the Misses Lindor taking leave of their mother when they started with their escort for Bow ; it would have made any ordinary man go deranged with envy to see the kissing and embracing that had always to be performed before the young ladies could tear themselves away from the maternal bosom. They were so fearful lest mamma should be lonely, and mamma was so anxious that they should take care of themselves and come back safe ; and sometimes,

after Tryphenia had managed, without disarranging her curls
or bonnet-strings, to give her mother an expert kiss, the lady
was in the habit of blessing her *sotto voce;* and when they
were clear of the house there were lookings up to the windows,
and nods, and smiles, and wavings of hands, which demonstrations Mr. Clyne regarded with polite sympathy, but yet was
wont occasionally to cut short by offering his arm to Tryphenia,
and carrying her off along the pleasant streets, bordered with
sugar-houses, filled with children, and roofed with cranes, that
lead from America Square to the Commercial Road.

Pleasant peregrinations these, along sidepaths so narrow
that Mr. Clyne was usually walking in the gutter—pleasant
walks through vile stenches and a viler neighbourhood—healthy
employment for mind and body to trudge that weary road to
Bow, and talk about nothing all the way—agreeable for Tryphenia to pass by loathsome butchers' shops, and get jostled by
the roughs of Whitechapel—a happy thing for Herbert to
have a girl he did not care one straw about, hanging on his arm
and getting affectedly frightened and amused, and faint, and
conversational by turns.

A very desirable journey it must have been to both parties;
but what will not men pass through when they are in love?
and what will not women endure when they are in search of a
husband?

As for the two sisters who played second and third fiddles
to Miss Tryphenia, nothing but their love of exercise could
have sustained them through the ordeal: and with reference to
Lina, it must have been a shrinking dread of the old skeleton
in her heart which induced her to be cordial to her lady visitors,
who now invaded her privacy, in season and out of season, and
under cover of her toleration commenced a cannonade of Mr.
Clyne's heart with greater obstinacy and vigour than ever.

That the citadel must yield eventually, neither Mrs. Lindor
nor her daughter entertained the slightest doubt; but still the
enemy was slower about capitulating than might have been
expected: in fact, though the siege was persevered in with
terrific energy, though works were thrown up and grenades
flung in, though all the arts and stratagems of feminine warfare were called into requisition, the original breach got no
bigger; and Mrs. Lindor grew maternally uneasy about a flir-
tation which was damaging her daughter's prospects in other
quarters, and yet promised no speedy and satisfactory termination in itself.

"I tell you what it is, mamma," said Tryphenia energetically,
one night after they had all been taking tea out at Bow; "I'm

quite sure Mr. Clyne is not in love with me, but with Mrs. Storn."

"Good gracious, Tryphenia, never let me hear you say such a thing again," exclaimed Mrs. Lindor. "A married woman and a mother! Preposterous!"

"It may be," responded the young lady; "but still I am sure of it. He is only trifling with me—he has not the slightest idea of ever proposing, and I have more than half a mind to give Mr. Storn a hint of the matter, and see what he thinks of it."

Mrs. Lindor got up, locked the door of her bedroom, in which apartment Tryphenia had opened her mind in the manner above recorded, looked in the cupboards and under the bed, and opened the wardrobe to see if any one were hidden there; having satisfied herself on which point, she returned to her seat, and said—

"Tryphenia, I am quite serious. You must never hazard such an opinion again, even in jest. You do not know what it is to make an assertion of this kind with regard to a married woman. You might cause a separation between Mr. and Mrs. Storn, and completely ruin your own chance of becoming Mrs. Clyne. I implore of you not to give expression to such ideas."

"Well, mamma, I can only say what I think, and what you must think, too, unless you are stone blind," was Miss Tryphenia's dutiful reply, uttered in a tone which implied she was just on the point of bursting into tears. "I don't like to be made a cat's-paw by anybody, and I will not go again to Mrs. Storn's; and as for Mr. Clyne, he may go to Jericho!"

Having delivered herself of which speech with a sort of gulp, the young lady looked defiantly at her mother, who, sinking back in her chair, covered her eyes with her hands—and—thought.

Miss Tryphenia was right. Mrs. Lindor had entertained a glimmering suspicion of the Storn and Clyne intimacy all along. She knew quite enough of men and of manners, to be fully aware that his conduct towards the chemist's wife could not be explained on the supposition of mere ordinary friendship. True, his manners were, and had always been, irreproachable—there was not a sentence, look, or gesture, to which exception could be taken; he was not more attentive and polite to Mrs. Storn than to Mrs. Lindor and her daughters: she had tried him in twenty different ways, and yet could never produce an impression when she mentioned Lina's name—she had not found Maurice's wife ready to accept invitations in which her friend was included, neither could she say that Mr. Clyne ever seemed to be unduly welcome at Bow.

They must be indifferent or cunning, Mrs. Lindor had often reflected; but yet she was not able to reconcile cunning with their manners, nor indifference with their conduct.

Once she decided Mr. Clyne did care for Mrs. Storn, and had made, as she thought, that attachment a cats-paw for her purpose; but now the tables were turned upon her, and she found, as her daughter said, Mr. Clyne was making a cat's-paw of them.

Tryphenia was decidedly right—there could be no question but that Mr. Clyne was in love, and not with her; nevertheless, his attentions to the young lady were indisputable—there was comfort in this—things were no worse than they had ever been; they were much better, in fact, than at one time she could have hoped. Mrs. Lindor came to that conclusion at last, and when she did so, she spoke:—

"Tryphenia, do you really wish to marry Mr. Clyne?"

"To be sure I do—or rather did," answered she, pettishly; "but what's the use of talking about that now?—much notion he has of marrying me—you must see that, mamma, as clearly as I do."

"And you must see, my dear, that it is utterly impossible he can marry Mrs. Storn," remarked the elder lady, oracularly.

"I do not suppose he can," retorted Miss Lindor; "but that will not do me any good."

"At all events, it is better that if Mr. Clyne have any passing fancy, it should not be for a single woman: I do not say he cares for her, and I believe she does not care for him; but, even supposing that he do admire her very much, and like visiting at the house, still that is no earthly reason why he should not eventually admire you more, and love and marry you in addition. Situated as you are—though you might get a rich husband—it would be almost impossible, under ordinary circumstances, for you to hope to combine wealth and rank: our intimacy with Mr. Clyne has been perfectly providential in this respect, and it would be unwise to forget we first knew him through Mrs. Storn; besides, though there has been no actual proposal, still, as a man of honour, he has gone too far with you to draw back. There is not the slightest necessity for haste; you are very young, and Mr. Clyne is a long way from his baronetcy; a little delay cannot matter much on either side; and if he have any foolish admiration for Mrs. Storn—if he really have, which I greatly question"—repeated the cautious mother; "it is well to give that full time to die out before your marriage; and mark me, Tryphenia, the only way we shall ever get rid of Mrs. Storn, will be by remaining friendly with her, and holding our tongues."

With which prophecies, and reflections, and pieces of advice, Mrs. Lindor at length managed to soothe her daughter's ruffled spirit; and although, at brief intervals, the doses had to be repeated, still the silk-merchant's wife contrived to keep fair with all parties concerned. To Mr. Clyne, her manners were as kind and cordial as ever—to Lina she paid what might almost have been termed court; whilst with Tryphenia she was at once sympathising and confidential—adhering through all vicissitudes to her cuckoo-note, that Mr. Clyne was very fond of her daughter, and that it was utterly impossible for him to back out of the matter now—after all the attentions he had paid, and the manner in which he had chosen to compromise himself with the Lindor family.

But during this time, was Herbert actually deceiving them or himself? Was he using them as tools of malice aforethought, or was he really persuading his own heart he liked Tryphenia Lindor, and would wish to make her his wife?

A knotty problem, dear reader, one somewhat difficult to answer; and yet, from my knowledge of the man's character, or rather want of character, I should feel inclined to judge he never took the Lindors into his calculation at all—nor thought of them, save as useful and obliging stepping-stones to an object, that object being frequent intercourse with Lina Storn.

It was just like him to make use of Miss Tryphenia, without intending to play the hypocrite; just as much a part and parcel of the weak nature to visit at America Square, without thinking of possible results, as it was for him to be in love with another man's wife, and yet even in that love to be more foolish than wicked.

There is but one sentence I know of capable of giving an idea of the man—"He would not look forward;" and because of this one tremendous failing, he sowed seeds of sorrow and remorse, and desolation for himself in difficult places; and spent the best and most profitable years of his after-life in reaping, with bowed and broken spirit, the harvest of grief he had planted for himself, in the perilously happy and marvellously swift-winged days of old.

CHAPTER XVIII.

THE OLD FASHION OUT WEST.

CONSIDERING that Mr. Storn was a clever man, he certainly did a great many foolish things; and at the head of his list of errors might be placed the fact of his giving Herbert Clyne as many opportunities of making love to his wife as though he had really wished him to do so.

Once again at Bow, as in the old city-house, came the hurried dinner, where three people sate down together with the soul of one absent. Cutting quickly, and eating hastily, Mr. Storn never craved the carver's orthodox half-hour; but, having finished his repast as soon as anybody else, swallowed his regular two glasses of sherry, and, after a rapid apology for unavoidable absence, and an equally hurried making over of the guest to Lina, he was gone, leaving the most precious gem of his life's casket in danger.

And yet, to do him justice, Mr. Clyne never took unfair advantage of these often-recurring absences. Setting aside the fact that he ought never to have entered the chemist's house at all, feeling as he did towards the chemist's wife; there was nothing particularly reprehensible in his conduct. Herbert Clyne never said a word to Lina Storn during these long conferences that all the world might not have listened to. It was a thing to be felt rather than seen, that the pair cared for one another; and perhaps it was this fact, more than anything else in her position, which rendered Lina's course so difficult. She held a stake in the game of life, and yet still never had a fair chance of taking the cards into her own hands, and playing them out as she would.

Without telling her husband all, without confessing that though Mr. Clyne had never offended the dignity of her matronhood by word, or look, or tone, still she cared for him as it did not befit Maurice Storn's wife to care for anyone, there was no help nor protection to be expected from that quarter; and unless she took the initiative with Mr. Clyne, and made a step along the road of love, which is forbidden to all women, married or single, she could scarcely have got rid of him.

There seemed, indeed, nothing to check but her own growing fondness for his society—nothing to curb but the rebellious feelings of her own heart—nothing to be angry with, nor indignant about—nothing which she could resent, or repent, or take notice of, or speak concerning.

All through the affair Lina knew that she was wrong, and that he was wrong; but once she began to reason upon it, the mountain sank down into a mole-hill, and Mrs. Storn felt satisfied. After all, she was hypocrite enough to whisper to herself, " He only cares really for Tryphenia Lindor, and so comes out to Bow that he may have the pleasure of walking back with her again, or his home is not comfortable, and he is glad of any quiet fireside by which he can sit and talk for an hour at a time, or a hundred other things," Lina generally concluded with; for the woman was energetic and determined about nothing regarding Clyne. In the present she contented herself with making everlasting resolutions, that in the future she would take firmly by the throat and strangle a feeling which lived on through all her vain, frail, fluttering, struggles for deliverance.

And besides, there is not the slightest use denying it, the stolen cup was sweet. So felt Herbert Clyne, so felt Lina Storn, as he sate talking, she listening by the winter fire, in that old house, which I last beheld through the glimmering twilight of an autumn evening out at Bow.

He was confidential—she sympathizing: except a few stories of wild folly in former times, and of a vain, unholy love in the present, Mr. Clyne had nothing to keep back from Mrs. Storn. Uncommunicative to the rest of the world, he opened his heart to her like a scroll, and read out every feeling and anxiety just as it came uppermost. Mother, father, sister, were daguerreotyped for his auditor's edification; his troubles, his wishes, his fears, were uttered out loud. He had a great deal to say about his father, and Lina could not help but like him for the thoughtful, compassionate tenderness that was revealed in every sentence. Bearing and forbearing, he her friend was most assuredly in his domestic relations; and although the same weakness which marked his conduct towards Lina, was evident in his behaviour at home, still she was not the one to note the defect; she only saw through his frequent confidences that he was kind to his father, respectful to his mother; that he stood between the pair when it was possible for any one to be of use; that he was most anxious concerning the influence which some unknown individual exercised over his parent, and yet that he never pryed into the secret so sedulously concealed from him.

He found many things to tell Lina concerning their late visit to the continent; and the little restless soul, who would have been a traveller if she could, thought, as she listened, about the days when she had stood on the old housetop in the city, and let her eyes wander away over the dull red tiles, and the forest of masts—down the rolling river to a distant dreamland of her own.   This was before she knew Mr. Clyne at all; and now she knew him intimately, and what a difference his acquaintance had wrought in Maurice's wife.   Lina did not like to compare now with then, so she was wont to try to forget those first summer evenings after her marriage, when every sorrow she had in life was caused by her husband, and not by herself; when she dared look into her heart without fearing to face what she might find there; when she had no secret to hide from any one;—when, in one word, she had not met Mr. Clyne.

As matters stood, unfortunately Mr. Clyne's affairs, travels, and experiences were far more interesting to Mrs. Storn than any other things on earth.   He had such a knack of enlisting her sympathies in his narrative, such a frank, unreserved way of telling his troubles, such an easy, pleasant flow of small talk about the places he had seen, and the people he had met, that Lina could not choose but listen.

Besides, nobody else in the world talked to her as Mr. Clyne did; there was always, even with Mary Matson, a something kept back; something which showed Lina there was an inner shrine still, beyond that of friendship, into which she had no right to expect to penetrate.   Nobody on earth thought out loud before her but Herbert Clyne.   Her husband was everlastingly going long mental journeys by himself.   Geordie was too young to have any serious journeys to take, and after these —her husband and her child—who was left?   Her father could never speak to her again on this side the grave; there was no one else.   But yet it was scarcely fitting for her to occupy the post of confidante to a young, unmarried, unengaged man, like Mr. Clyne.   It was something less than fitting, if you will, dear reader, and she was very wrong—but still she did listen, and answer and listen again.

And it could scarcely be wondered at that Mr. Clyne found comfort in detailing his anxieties and troubles to so fair and sympathizing a friend; for his place in the world's army did not seem exactly to fit him, and beside this woman he had no comrade to bid him hold his head above the fray, and be of good cheer.

If there were one thing for which the man of worldly experience longed and pined, it was for a quiet, happy home; like one he sometimes pictured to himself, where the domestic music was not broken by discord; where no loud voices, and pale cheeks, and tearful eyes, might disturb the contented routine of existence. He longed and sickened for a future never to be—for a hope never to be gratified; for a rest never to be given; he had his vision, of which the reality of his daily life proved the very antipodes; and sometimes he turned away from the house where his parents resided, miserable and faint-hearted—sorry for his father, angry at his mother, and thoroughly hopeless of ever setting matters straight between them.

True to the task he had out of his affection set himself, Herbert kept such guard as was possible over his father, and endeavoured to soften down the acerbity of his mother. With the latter he had some success, for Mrs. Clyne usually became mollified after a long grumbling *téte-à-téte*. With Mr. Clyne, however, the case was different; he shunned his son as much in England as he had clung to him in France; he was always making excuses to get him out of his library, to prevent their walking forth together; to shake off, as it seemed to Herbert, a burden of inspection which was becoming unendurable.

"Sometimes I almost imagine my father dislikes me," Mr. Clyne would say, in his calm, melancholy tone, to Lina; and then, of course, it became Lina's duty to combat this idea, and to give reasons for her disbelief of the proposition, which reasons generally resulted in a mutual wonderment concerning the name and occupation of the mysterious female whom Herbert had never seen, but who was, he felt, nevertheless, exercising a most marvellous and pernicious influence in their domestic concerns.

"What the tie can be I confess myself unable to conjecture," he remarked; "she sent my father to France, she brought him back from Italy; I cannot ask him about her, because it seems to annoy him; but I should like to see her, and have a notion of who she is, and where she lives. My father is harassing himself to death about something or other, and if I knew more of this woman, I am sure I could help him. I feel most anxious in the matter, for it is becoming a serious affair."

And if Mr. Herbert Clyne were anxious and curious concerning his parent's acquaintance, Mrs. Clyne was no less interested on the subject.

Bringing her woman's wit to bear upon it, she guessed shrewdly enough that there were frequent interviews between the pair; that though the stranger did not come, she wrote; that she received money from Mr. Clyne; that he was being daily impoverished by an artful, designing adventuress—neither young, pretty, nor attractive, nor possessed of one solitary personal advantage, which might account in the slightest degree for the extraordinary influence she exercised over a man who had never been peculiarly open to influence from his wife.

Obtuse, violent, and untrusting, it became the one aim and object of her life to find out who the low creature might be; to this end, cross-questioning, and anger, and nagging; for this purpose, remonstrances, and tears, and hysterics; burnt feathers, sal volatile, and the family physician, were the mildest results of an interview on the subject with her husband, who at last declared to God, that if it were not for Herbert he would take the first ship for New Zealand, and leave things to shape themselves by themselves.

After which speech he subsided into silence, and only broke it again after a lapse of ten minutes, when he interrupted his wife's eloquence by remarking, " that he was master of his own actions, and meant to remain so; and that if he heard anything more on the subject, he would go and take lodgings"——

" Where this creature may reside with you, I suppose," said Mrs. Clyne; but he did not take the slightest notice of this innuendo. He only turned to the table and opened a book whilst Mrs. Clyne flounced out of the room, declaring, that before another month, she would know who the person might be that so occupied her husband's thoughts, and drained her husband's purse."

Mrs. Clyne had a great deal to say on the latter subject; she made frequent reference to the fact of her children's fortunes being squandered on suspicious characters; and in proof of her assertions, raised up hundreds of ghosts about Mr Clyne's conscience, and rained down coals of fire on his devoted head.

No doubt he had been wild once. When he was young, like his son, there could not have been found a faster liver, nor a more reckless character about town than Montague Clyne. The misdeeds of the past were neither difficult to find, nor pleasant to remember; and yet he bore all his wife's rebukes, and reproaches, and reminiscences with patience.

He never turned but once, and that, to do him justice, was when he was half tipsy, and whole wretched, when the miserably mistaken woman would persist in probing the length and depth of the tremendous sore which was killing him, and insist, in the midst of his agony, that he should name his disease.

" I met that insolent creature in the hall, Mr. Clyne," broke forth the lady, sweeping into his sanctum in full evening costume, and never heeding the fact, that her husband's head was resting on his desk; and that when, in answer to her loud and angry commencement, he raised his face, it was pale as ashes.

"I spoke to her, and she only laughed at me," pursued Mrs. Clyne; "I asked her how she dared enter any house of which I was mistress; demanded who she was, and what she wanted; and in answer, she sent me to you. And now, before I stir out of this room, I will have an explanation of the affair."

If she had possessed any eyes, she might have seen the imploring and deprecating gesture, the broken-hearted and despairing look, with which he strove to put aside her question; but passion and obstinacy blinded her; she had so long regarded the man before her as an infatuated, irreclaimable sot; had dwelt for such a length of time on her own fancied slights and grievances; that she was not to be stopped by anything. The mystery had been a mystery, so far, but she declared it should remain one no longer. She would write to her brother; she would employ detectives; she would have a separation; she would not live with any one who was made a dupe and a tool of by vulgar, designing hags; she was not going to have existence rendered insupportable by her husband's extraordinary conduct; she had married him for love, and she believed in her heart he had married her for nothing but money; and in fine, to condense the lady's determination into a sentence, she would know, by fair means or foul, who the intruder was.

"If it were anything right she came about, you would not hesitate to tell me," she said, in conclusion.

"God knows it is not right—it is all wrong," he said in a feeble sort of way, pouring himself out a glass of brandy, and swallowing it raw. She had not perceived the brandy before, but now she seized it and continued her harangue.

"He should not drink himself into delirium tremens again, she would have no more horrors with that: if Herbert were at home, he would not permit him to touch brandy; but he drove his only son out of the house. That wretched woman had alienated him from the nearest and dearest he had on earth; but it should not go on, she would write to Lord Neverdon that night;" and Mrs. Clyne was turning out of the room as if to do so, when her husband stopped her with a hurriedly uttered "Don't."

"And pray why should I not?" retorted the indignant lady, facing round on the poor pale wretch who stood in the lamp-light, looking like a corpse.

"Because you would repent it once, and always," he said.

"Repent! nonsense! it is you who should repent."

"If repentance were of any use," he muttered.

"Why, of course it is," she interrupted: "give orders to the servants never to admit the creature, send back her letters, and refuse to give her any more money."

"Frances, I cannot," he said.

"Then let me do it," she replied; "I will engage soon to rid you of the woman; why do you not order some of the men to give her in charge of the police? do something decided, for if you do not, I will."

"You do not know what you are talking about," he remarked; and the remark was like a spark among wool.

"Did not she?" there were few things Mrs. Clyne did not know, in her own opinion; and accordingly, her husband could not have chosen a more unfortunate form of speech. "She would never speak to him again on the subject; she would send to her solicitor; she would write to her brother; she would after that night stoop to ask no more explanations; she would know who the creature was, and what her claim, and what the connexion, she would—she would."

"Then, if you *must* know," said Mr. Clyne, and there was a something awful about the way in which he faced round on the angry woman, answering her in a voice which seemed not to belong to him, but to some strange being that was speaking through him,—"if you *must* know, she is my wife!"

"Your wife!" she gasped; "I am—"

"Not," he supplied, and then stood for a moment looking at her as she looked at him. The next he was pulling the bell, and calling aloud for help; when once she got the full meaning of his words into her brain, she dropped to the floor in a fit. No more anger or recrimination in that house; no more secresy or explanation; the old, old fashion—Death had taken precedence of all other plans, and projects, and fashions of this world, and through the valley of the shadow her most miserable husband for days and days watched her passing.

All in vain it was that they lifted her from the ground, and carried her to bed, and sent for the family doctor. It was something worse than hysterics or temper that ailed Lord Neverdon's sister now. All the drugs in England, all the surgeons on earth could have done nothing for the altered and stricken being who lay there, incapable of speech, incapable of motion, incapable of thought, with her limbs paralyzed, and her face drawn up to one side.

The physicians looked wise, said it was only what might have been expected from various premonitory symptoms raked up from the past by her regular attendant; they had no doubt the stroke had been pending for a considerable period; they did not consider there was any hope of life, nor, under the circumstances, could recovery be deemed desirable. The Honourable Mrs. Clyne was of an excitable temperament, and had latterly lived in one continual whirl of company and gaiety. The late hours and the constant strain on the nerves, had proved too much for their patient; so the learned men, who really did not know what else to say, assured Lord Neverdon and society; and society and Lord Neverdon, as in duty bound, were satisfied.

Not but what rumours got afloat, through the servants and her daughter, that other causes besides company and amusement had brought Mrs. Clyne to her present state.

"A sudden shock rather than a continued strain," it was whispered; but as there was nothing to support this proposition, it was soon forgotten by all, save those immediately interested in the affair. Herbert Clyne asked no explanation of the blow, nor did he receive any. There was a something about the way his father sat stupidly by the side of the dead alive, that might have hindered even a less considerate man from putting painful questions: of course he knew there was more in the affair than met the vision of the doctors; but at the same time, into that more he felt he could not then with any propriety enquire. He was the same man in his mother's sick-room that Lina Storn had found him in her lonely matronhood; patient, gentle, and forbearing; very womanly in his care of the sick, and in his watch by the dying; in his tread, and touch, and thoughtfulness; and yet still very manly in his persistent respect for a secret which had brought his mother to this pass, and caused his father to sit days and nights beside her couch, a changed man.

But at last the days and the nights of that cruel vigil were over, and Mrs. Clyne lay dead in her coffin.

The evening before the funeral, Herbert turned the key of the dreary room, which seemed so much more empty then, than if it had been tenantless; turned the key, and entered the apartment, and pushed aside the lid, bright with silver ornaments, and looked upon the face of the corpse.

He had never been very fond of her, but still she was his mother; and as he bent over the coffin, it did strike him as strange and hard, that she should have gone down to her last rest without being able to tell him what had stricken her; she who in all her grievances and troubles, in her self-created difficulties and imaginary sorrows, had poured out every thought and wish into ears that Herbert now remembered with a pang of self-reproach, had been often weary of listening to her complaints.

For a long time he stood there, thinking over the past, and speculating about the present, till at length he brought his reverie to a conclusion by kissing the cold, distorted face, and murmuring, as he did so, the words, " Poor mother !" Then he drew the lid into its place again, very gently and tenderly, and turning to leave the room, found that his father was standing behind him.

"Herbert," he said, "I killed her ;" and he put his arms out over the coffin, and resting his head upon it, began to cry.

For a moment or two his son let him alone ; but at last, when he had thought about what he should say, he began : "Father, if you would only tell me what you mean—if you would only explain to me the mystery that seems to have cursed your life and ended hers—I think it would be better for us all."

" No, Herbert, no."

" If there be crime," pursued his son, "rest assured I should not be the one to accuse you; if there be anything you have done that you fear the world should know, I would do my best to help and shield you. Anything, surely, is better than this wearing secrecy. I have thought dreadful things sometimes."

"I am no criminal," answered Mr. Clyne, raising his head and speaking rapidly, though in a sort of choking voice. " I never voluntarily committed a crime; but I made a mistake once, and for years and years past I have been eating its fruits."

" And what was that mistake ?" Herbert inquired eagerly.

" I cannot tell you," was the reply.

" But why not, father ? Why not give me your confidence fully and unreservedly ? Why not let me help, or, at all events, share the trouble with you ? At least, let me know who this person is that exercises so extraordinary an influence over you ? It seems to me," he added, with more decision and emphasis than he had ever used before in speaking to his parent, " that standing here, beside my mother's coffin, and taking into consideration the circumstances of her death, I have a right to ask this question, and to receive an answer."

" Look here, Herbert," said Mr. Clyne, hastily raising the lid and pointing down at his wife's corpse ; " she said the same —she drove me to tell her—she would know, and that is the result !"

" She knew all, then ?"

" Yes."

There was a pause. Herbert walked to the end of the room and back again, losing in that moment of vacillation the chance for the future which the present had given him. If he had pressed his father for an explanation then, he might have known; and if he had known, he could have helped them both; but it was not to be! Weakly and regretfully, in after-days, he muttered that comfort of the irresolute to himself: "Not to be!" He came back to his father, having decided on following what was the easiest, and what seemed to him the kindest, course.

"Is there nothing I can do for you in this matter?" he said, standing once again by the side of that dreary house in the centre of the apartment.

"Nothing, my boy," was the sorrowful reply.

"Do you wish me never to mention the subject again?"

"Oh! Herbert," said the wretched man, "you have always been too good and too forbearing. But for you I could have borne it all; and if I ask you to forbear, now and for ever, it is only that I may never hear you curse me."

"No fear of that, sir," answered his son, "*whatever* this secret may be; and I was going to assure you that if you say it is better for you and for me and for my sister that I should not know anything of the affair, I will never put another question to you concerning it. I will respect your wishes implicitly, though at the same time I cannot help thinking it would be a comfort to you, and a relief to me, if there were no mystery between us. Will you not trust me?"

"With my life; but not with that, Herbert, not with that."

"Let it be so, then," said the young man, in his calm, gentle voice, and he took his father's hand as he spoke, and led him out of the room.

Less dutiful and more determined, Herbert Clyne would have left the apartment with the knowledge that he was illegitimate; that to the wealth of his mother, the estates of his father, the baronetcy in the family, he had no claim; he would not have gone out into the world again trading on a position, a name, and a rank to which he had no title. Seeing himself as he was, and not as he seemed to be, he might have carved out a different destiny than that he had to go out to face in the dreary hereafter. With that stain on his birth, with that great change in his fortunes, he might have gone abroad, left his aimless life, his blasted prospects, his useless lineage, his barren hopes behind—wrenched himself away in time from friends, and relatives, country, and Lina Storn.

But it was not to be! Once again I am forced to repeat the consolatory sentence wherewith he comforted himself in the days that were then to come, and true to his promise, he never harassed his father by another question on the subject of the strange woman who, after Mrs. Clyne's death, seemed to have given up tormenting her victim.

At least Mr. Clyne's improved habits and somewhat less careworn face induced him to form this opinion, which was, however, somewhat rudely overturned one morning by a strangely hesitating, and yet still most urgent, petition for money from his father.

Herbert was rich now. He had succeeded to the bulk of his mother's property, which was secured, by marriage settlement, on her children ; and, accordingly, the sum required was given on the instant, without question or comment.

But the daughter of the horseleech was insatiable. More, more seemed the ceaseless cry, till even Herbert's filial patience was exhausted, and he determined, in his undetermined sort of way, to stop the pecuniary supplies.

"My dear father," he said, when he adopted this resolution, " do you know you are draining my banker's account quite dry ?"

There was no answer, but Mr. Clyne looked imploringly in his son's face—so almost pitifully—that Herbert could not choose but open his desk and draw out his cheque-book.

"There must be some line drawn in this matter, or else I shall not have enough left to defray my own personal expenses," he continued, looking back over the sums already advanced, making a rough memorandum of the amounts, and then handing it to his father, who put it away with a deprecating gesture, saying, in that feeble, frightened voice of his—

"It's not for myself, Herbert; it's not for myself."

"If it were, I should not utter a word of remonstrance," answered his son ; " but it seems to me some person is bleeding you to death."

"She is—literally and figuratively," groaned out Mr. Clyne.

"And are there any limits to her requirements," asked Herbert ; "or are her wants only bounded by the extent of our means ? If you assure me it is necessary to your peace and tranquillity that this woman should share our income, I am quite willing to pay for immunity from her visits. Let her name her price, and she shall have it, if anything like reasonable ; only the thing must be placed on some different footing because the Bank of England would not stand such a perpetual drain upon it."

"If you give me the money now, I will put the matter on a different footing for the future," answered Mr. Clyne. "I will do my best, Herbert. I will try—I will indeed."

And he held out an eager hand for the cheque, which Herbert gave him, saying :

"Are you quite sure, father, you are not being victimized by an adventuress or an impostor, or frightened by shadows ?"

"Shadows may frighten, but they do not kill, Herbert," was the painfully uttered reply, and with one hand crumpling up the cheque, and the other pressed against his forehead, Mr. Clyne hurried from the room, leaving his son to solve the riddle of his fears and persecutions at his leisure.

In due time, however, the elder man intimated that he had concluded an advantageous arrangement with the lady, who was graciously pleased to signify her acceptance of a given sum yearly for life, in lieu of the uncertain amounts she had been previously wont to draw at terribly certain intervals.

"Well, now we know the worst of it, at all events, Heaven be praised!" murmured his son, by way of comment on the agreement; for he did not imagine then that he knew but part of the worst, the whole being the greater portion of his father's income; mortgages and legal expenses enough to have overwhelmed any man.

Nevertheless, Mr. Clyne, relieved from the incubus of the woman's dreaded letters, and still more dreaded visits, seemed from that day forth to grow happier, younger, and more settled.

Father and son joined in one establishment, a few miles out of town, whence Mr. Clyne was in the habit of driving into London more frequently than was well either for him or Mrs. Storn, whose husband had grown much too prosperous and ambitious a man to have leisure to perceive that unless he noticed more carefully what his wife was about, he might find a thorn in the flesh of his future fortune—worse than poverty —sharper than death.

CHAPTER XIX.

THE PLEASURES OF TRADING ON NOTHING.

TAKING it as a whole, Mr. Matson did not find the practical carrying out of Mr. Lindor's scheme an easy affair; true, as the silk merchant had predicted, there was not the slightest difficulty about getting credit—the real battle was to keep it. Somehow, rise as early as he would in the morning—work as late as he liked at night—save as much as he could—John Matson never felt he was nearing the lee side of fortune by even a solitary point in the wind. It was in vain that he was bookkeeper, salesman, collector, and clerk to himself, all in one ; it was in vain that he eschewed omnibuses and wore out his boots—it was all to no purpose that Mary pinched, and saved, and took the most out of herself, as her husband did out of himself; it was of no use that both tried to keep trade, and house, and personal expenses at the minumum—that Mr. Matson counted the shillings in his errand boy's wages, and Mrs. Matson gave herself headaches over her badly-kept and wrongly added-up chronicle of weekly disbursements. To all appearances, they might just as well have been extravagant as saving—idle as industrious; for roll away at it as they would, the stone of their luck fell back, and, spite of every effort to keep his accounts square and straight, and orthodox for the " Court," Mr. Matson found himself compelled to use one man's money to pay another man's debt: the rent had to be met to-day, the taxes to-morrow—baker, butcher, and grocer urged claims not to be passed by in silence, and, accordingly, the cash which was to have been put aside to meet one person's bill, had to be broken in on for twenty petty claims, and then both husband and wife lay awake at night, wondering how the dreaded acceptance was to be met; and after it had, by some special interposition of Providence, been rescued from the hands of the notary, they had hardly time to catch their breath again before some other debt giant came stalking towards them.

And yet still the pair never repented marrying—still they were both happy and cheerful—still Mary kept her looks, and John his cheerfulness. I suppose proper mammas, and staid old capitalists, who look as if all the cares of Europe were wrinkling their foreheads, will consider this assertion doubtful, and, at best, unconventional; nevertheless, spite of their disapprobation, it is true. John Matson and his wife were happy; they could laugh just as gaily as their neighbours, and build better air-castles than old Mr. Millionaire Hundredfold. They were able at times to shake off the cares of business, and forget, when talking together over the fire at night, that a morning of work and trouble was coming. And then there were the Sundays—those dear, delightful, quiet Sundays, when the city was still, and it almost seemed as if everybody, except the parson and the clerk, and the charity children, and the beer-boys were gone out of town. Oh! surely, nobody who has not been in business in the city—I mean business beginning at seven o'clock in the morning and ending at eight, or nine, or ten, or eleven o'clock at night—can fully appreciate the blessing of God's day of rest.

Six long working days of complaining buyers, and tardy payers, and clamorous creditors; six days of early rising, and rapid eating, and dreaded visitors, and disagreeable letters; six days of incessant toil, whether business be brisk or business be slack; six days of the world, the flesh, and the devil, and then a seventh of rest and peace like Heaven!

Poor Mary! though all the days of her life sped by with that marvellous rapidity with which time appears to travel only through the heart of business London, still, for her mental and bodily well-being, the six were far too long—the one far too short!

Every weary week she came, fagged and tired, to that halting place in the march of existence, and thanked God, regularly as the Saturday night came round, that the next morning would be Sunday.

Some of Mr. Matson's business acquaintances wondered " he and his good lady did not take a run out of town somewhere, on a Sunday, to get a breath of fresh air;" which observation Mary somewhat scornfully criticised, by marvelling what possessed people to be running about on a Sunday; and where the fresh air was to be found, Londoners were so everlastingly talking of.

For her part, she thought the air in the city good enough; and perhaps, indeed, she did find it sweet, as it came to her, sitting by her open window, over the box of mignionette, which was all the garden John could afford, or that she required.

Sitting there reading, with the sunshine falling upon her hair, she never regretted the time when the sunbeams had rested on her in a different place—when she had looked out from her father's house at the gray old Scotch hills, and the fir plantations, and the gliding river, and the darksome loch—she did not want more scenery than the houses over the way, or the perspective of Cheapside, or the glitter and glimmer of the lamps, as they faded and faded away.

She had through the week the amusement of an exhilarating walk to Leadenhall market, varied by occasional visits of investigation to divers trades-people, who resided in out-of-the-way streets, in remarkable neighbourhoods, and sold their goods at something under city prices. It was a part of Mrs. Matson's theory of duty, that, seeing she could not make money for her husband, she ought to try to save it; and accordingly she did save it, or, at least, she did not spend more than she could help.

The young wife seemed to have two aims in existence—one, to buy in the cheapest market, and another, always to have a nice dinner for her husband; which laudable objects were continually taking her off on various mysterious foraging expeditions, that served the purpose of giving her plenty of exercise, even if no other good end were compassed by her numerous little excursions.

Still Mary was not a "walking woman," perhaps because, in addition to her exploring tours, she had to make many a journey from the top of the house to the bottom. She would never have dreamed of crossing the door-step without an object on the other side of it; and as for John, Heaven knew he had enough of compulsory exercise through the week without going voluntarily on the treadmill on Sunday; and thus their ramble never extended further on Mary's "evenings out," which were her servant's "evenings in," than a stroll after church up Broad Street, and home by London Wall, or round Finsbury Circus and down Moorgate Street to the Bank. Sometimes they traversed the narrow lanes off Cheapside, getting into Falcon Square and Addle Street; and once they reached Bartholomew Close, where Mary ever after wanted to live, on their way to St. Sepulchre's, remarkable for its fine organ, and for owning the bell which has tolled the knell of many a sinner who died no natural death. But, as a rule, they never strayed far from home on Sundays; up Coleman Street and along London Wall, as far as Aldermanbury Postern or St. Alphage Church, was about the extent of their peregrinations after service; and if you, dear reader, be of the "fast" school, and style this method of living "slow," I have only to remind you, that no doubt if you are smitten with the tender passion, any place seems to you delightful when accompanied by the lady of your affections. For the rest—John Matson, though married—and Mary, though wooed, and won, and wed, were sufficiently unromantic and unfashionable to love one another just as well, and perhaps, God knew, a great deal better, than if they had been single.

Think of the routine of their lives, then, as fast or slow— just as pleaseth you best—it is none the less true that the time came when John Matson, looking back from the midst of ease and plenty, at the grinding poverty and never-ceasing toil of his city days, felt, strong man as he was, the tears dripping down in his heart, when he thought of the walks, and the talks, and the gestures, and the tones of old. Rich and prosperous as he was, he would willingly have given up all, and turned him to the weary drudgery again, if with the cares he could have taken back the pleasures that were gone. For the wound of the future may, for all a man knows to the contrary, be big for him with every earthly blessing but one—the love of the past—which on this side heaven comes back to us—no more.

In that future of prosperity which came to him all too quickly, he said that the time he lived in the city was the happiest of his life; and no doubt he spoke according to his thought, truly, for memory hath one glass for blessings, and another for sorrows; magnifying the one, while diminishing the other.

There is not one amongst us who appreciates passing happiness like past; and it was, perhaps, for this reason that John Matson, in more prosperous and more indolent days, looked back with sickening regret of soul, and nervous prostration of body, to the active, fully occupied anxious time, when he worked hard in the day, and laid his head on the pillow of care at night; and looked forward as a not unlikely finish to his labour and struggles—to being accommodated with high-priced, yet not over-comfortable, lodgings in the Cripplegate Hotel.*

Nevertheless, it were idle to deny, that whilst making the best of his position, as he tried to do of everything else in life, John Matson found occasionally his position a little too much for him. Some days buyers were few, and creditors plenty; and then he came in towards evening, depressed, and care-worn, and resting his aching head on his feverish hands, declared he must give up; that there was no use struggling further.

At such seasons, Mary had but to pass her dear soft fingers through his tangled hair, and scold him for being desponding, and coax him to drink his tea, and the man got right again.

"To-morrow might bring orders," the wife always, in her hopefulness, suggested, and the husband at her bidding was always ready to believe; and, indeed, dear reader, in strict confidence between you and me, I doubt whether, as a rule, business-people could keep up heart to weather the adverse winds of trade, but for this glorious uncertainty of what the morrow may bring forth.

The wear and tear of struggling forward would be too much for any mind, but for the thought that any minute may smooth the onward road. Even when a man is trotting at the rate of twelve miles an-hour down the hill, he never knows but that something may turn up to turn him. Now into this scale, now into that, bad and good fortune fling their mites; and if in the long run the trader become bankrupt, he has at all events had the change and variety of watching during his descent the manner in which accident tried to baulk fate. Now up, now down—now a rope, now a hand—now a smile—now a cheerful word from the shore—and when he sinks at last off his feeble

* Whitecross Street Prison.

craft into the dark waters of ruin—he can amuse himself, until it is "all over with him," in catching at the straws which well-meaning, though perfectly powerless Samaritans throw towards the hand which shall never seize a fortunate chance, or miraculous opportunity to any purpose more.

It must have been some alternation of feeling of this kind, which preserved John Matson from utter wretchedness, as he pursued the tenor of his almost uniformly disastrous way. This week, customers passed him by; the next, longer credit was refused for chemicals; the third, duns became pressing; the fourth, he could not get a shilling of what was owing to him.

"Making off life," with a wife and child, and without a capital, is a mighty harassing business; and so Mr. Matson found it. Somehow, when the extra mouth was sent, the extra food was, as is often the case, omitted; and accordingly, just at the very time when most money was wanted, least money came in.

Very dolefully John mentally confessed he could not take more out of the "stuff," meaning, time and himself, than he had done heretofore. Very happy he tried to look up stairs, when a fat old woman, smelling of gin, presented him with a little bundle of red flesh, and told him it was his daughter; but very wretched he really felt, when he retired again into his office, and tried to look the expenses of doctor, and fat old woman, and additional nourishment, and heaven knows what beside, full in the face.

More miserable still he grew, when he saw Mary struggling up, long before she ought, dismissing doctor and attendant, and toiling about the house with the little bundle always in her arms. But what could he do in the matter? though affectionate, he was honest; and when Mary said that this, and that, and the other thing, ran into money, which they had no right to spend, Mr. Matson never contradicted her. He only looked grave and thoughtful, and retired amongst his books, where he enlivened himself with a pleasant ramble through debit and credit, and a cheerful analysis of outstanding debts that were all too few; and three months' acceptances, that were all too many.

Nevertheless, somehow, spite of the fresh burden, and the slender means, John and his wife rubbed on for a time, without asking help from anybody; fondly fancying, that though the world might not, (heaven save the mark!) think them rich, it might, perhaps, be so far deluded as to consider them solvent.

"How was the general public to know," Mary hopefully argued, "the number of times John's bills had been noted, since not one had ever been returned to the drawer dishonoured?

If customers did drop off, new ones would soon come in. Doubtless, all houses found that buyers changed about from one to another—trade had been bad—her husband was not much known among chemical consumers—fifty things;" and the woman looked bright and cheerful, and undaunted; and her husband gazing on the true state of his affairs, with a much clearer eye, had still not the heart to damp her spirits; but listened and smiled, and, spite of sense and reason, was encouraged once again.

Still there could be no question they were trotting down the hill; and looking at the state of his affairs, after months of toil and harass, Mr. Matson could not but perceive, that taking all things into consideration, he was decidedly in a worse position at the end than he had been at the beginning.

For some of the bills coming due, he had goods, and no money; for others, neither money nor goods, but only very uncertain outstanding debts.

It was a perpetual struggle trying to get customers; kicking his heels in outer offices, with the pertinacity of a place-hunter, he found was useless; for some inexplicable reason, he could not keep his old connexion; and it was no easy matter to make a fresh one continuously week after week.

And if it were hard to get people to buy, it was trebly difficult to get them to pay; though those dismal acceptances were everlastingly falling due, and had to be provided for.

Each person had his own day, ay, even his own hour for paying money; and if the man without clerk, collector, or capital, failed to present himself before one o'clock on this Saturday, at this office; or hail, rain, or snow, on the first Monday in the month at that—he had to wait till the next payday came round, with a chance, perhaps, of being then told his invoices were lost, mislaid, or incorrect; that the quality of his goods was bad; that a discount must come off; that Mr. So-and-So, who signed the cheque, was out of town; or that the cashier had gone home that morning dangerously ill.

Football of fate, the man who had tried the dangerous experiment of trading upon nothing, was kicked about from post to pillar—getting many a sore mental bruise during the process; but night after night he returned to the little sitting-room, which was not so neat as formerly, feeling the world held a joy for him, that it was beyond the power of lord, or commoner, rich citizen, or new-fledged snob, to touch or intermeddle with.

For there his troubles grew lighter, his hopes greater—they talked over both, till the first seemed trifles not worth speaking of; and the second, certainties only to be waited and worked for.

Little blinks of sunshine came dancing across his business-prospects every now and then; and it would have astonished anybody to behold what long summers the pair managed to spin out of the rays.

A new customer was a fortune—a possible order a probable turning point in their lives.

Mr. Matson himself, a sensible man of business enough, if left alone, might, indeed, have occasionally taken something more than a desponding view of his circumstances, even when sitting before the domestic hearth; but it so chanced that he was blessed—or unblessed, just, dear reader, as you like to read it—with a wife whose bump of hope was as incapable of depression as an India rubber ball is of retaining a permanent dent.

So quiet in manner—and even in temper too—hope in such a quarter seemed to be less a delusion than a mere effort of reason. How was it possible, I put it to everybody, for a man to be gloomy, whose wife would not be cast down?—who had only to talk about a thing long enough, to have all the arts of feminine argument brought to prove that his misfortunes were sure to turn out blessings; that wealth, and riches, and honour, were mere questions of time—things to be waited for with patience, but certain in the long run to reward his efforts.

"It was a struggle in the present," the lady frankly admitted, and how hard a struggle none but those two ever exactly knew. Even they, perhaps, were unable to tell the precise depths of the current they breasted, until firmer ground was reached, whence they could cast down the plumb line of memory, and gauge the abysses of the ocean of trouble across which they had passed.

How Mr. Matson worked few people had a notion—not even Mr. Ferres, who being, however, at last struck by his perseverance, determined to give the young beginner a trial, and commenced with an order for five tons of oxalic acid, which was wealth to the man who counted his profits not by hundreds or thousands, but by shillings, and who was poorer than any one of his constantly changing customers could have conceived.

"Now, if I can only manage Hone's bill on Monday, Mary," he said to her, on his return home, "and get the goods for-warded any way quickly from him, my drudgery is over. Colke's people want this for shipping, I know, and they always pay prompt; no difficulty with them about cash. I shall get the money in fourteen days, which will enable me to clear off this one transaction; let me see,"—and out came pencil and pocket-book, and with the help of an old envelope, handed to him by his wife, John made out a very desirable margin, which was as certain, he said, as a balance in the bank, if Hone's bill were only met without fail.

And of course, Mary thought there could be no "if" in the matter. Every bill had been met hitherto, and there were one, two, three days clear for John to see about it, besides Monday; and even if it came to the worst, till post time on Tuesday. She was confident Mr. Lindor would not mind lending a hundred pounds, under the circumstances, for a few days, when the repayment was so sure.

"They were not now uncertain about their future prospects. Messrs. Colke and Ferres' order had placed them in quite a different position."

So Mary said, and so John was only too ready to believe, though when Thursday and Friday passed away without either buyer or payer entering his office, his hopes fell considerably.

As did also his wife's, when Saturday, the last good collecting day, came, bringing a deluge with it.

"I hate a wet Saturday," Mrs. Matson said, pettishly, to herself, while standing looking out at the leaden sky, and the wet roofs, and the soaking flags. Poor soul! she was thinking of the sloppy pavement, and the dripping alleys, and the cold and wet, and misery through which her husband that dreary winter's morning was walking, in order to call at fifty outlandish places, for the whole or balance of his account.

When dinner-time came, and he sat down to table, tired and shivering, he had no good progress to report. Only thirty pounds received, and the next day Sunday, and the next that bill. Two or three people had promised to send round, and Mr. Lindor might be able to help him, but still Mr. Matson shook his head dolefully as he suggested these possibilities, and cut determinedly into his joint, with the air of a man who doubted whether he should ever sit down to a comfortable dinner again.

Directly he had finished he rose, and saying he must be off, descended into the counting-house, where he remained till everybody else had shut, and the street was cleared of all commercial passengers.

Then, and not till then, he reluctantly told his boy to put up the shutters, and so closed business for the week.

Closed business, but not trouble, for he ascended the stairs like one carrying a visible burden, and entering Mary's room, and sitting down, sick and tired, on the unfashionable sofa, said :

"I firmly believe if I were to turn baker to-morrow, people would quit eating bread."

"Has no one been in this afternoon, then," asked Mrs. Matson.

"Yes, one man, to ask his way to blazes, or some place else," he answered impatiently; then added, "I'm sick to death of it, Mary. Be hanged if I had not rather work like a navvy at half-a-crown a-day."

"We must hope for the best," she said; sighing, however, even as she spoke, whilst her husband replied—

"I think all the hope is knocked out of me by this time, and all the spirit too—there is only one comfort in the thing—that some day or other I suppose we shall be tucked up with a spade in the daisy quilt, and have done with it."

"Yes, but what is to become of us in the meantime?" asked Mrs. Matson—to my mind very pertinently.

"Perhaps the parish will take care of us," he replied bitterly; "where would that be?"

"Now, John, stop," said his wife; and she got up as she spoke, and crossed from her post at the window to the sofa, where she covered his mouth with her hand, and looking imploringly into his face, went on: "I cannot bear to hear you talk in that way; it is not good, and it is not right. You know help may come when we least expect it; things have turned round wonderfully for us many and many a time before, and you may be quite sure they will do so again. Messrs. Colke's order never came so opportunely—only that you might be unable to execute it. You feel dull and hopeless now, because you have fagged yourself to death, and the day has been miserable; but to-morrow will be fine, and Monday finer; and you cannot tell what the first post may bring, or what money you will be able to raise. Have you sent to my uncle?"

"Yes, and he went out of town this morning, and won't be home till Wednesday.

"And how much money have you got towards the bill?"

"I have thirty, and am pretty sure of twenty more, before twelve on Monday."

"How much does that leave deficient?"

"One hundred and sixty—the bill is for two hundred and nine—some odd shillings."

For an instant Mary's face changed. A close observer might just have noticed something like a shadow passing over her eyes, and then they grew clear again.

"John, we must hope," she said, very resolutely; "we have been as bad as this before, and got safely through after all."

"Yes, but each time seems to make the struggle harder, Mary," he answered; "and on this occasion you see there are two things to be feared at once—the loss of credit at Hone's, and the loss of the order from Ferres. Now, Ferres's order, if executed without delay, would have made me. I should have their money in fourteen days, and be able to pay off some of these pestering duns. Hone's would give me three months', and if I could not manage to meet their draft at the end of that time, it would be strange indeed. It would set me on my legs again, and give me new life, if only—only this confounded bill were met."

" Well, dear, don't teaze and torment yourself about the thing to-night; leave Monday to take care of itself. It is time enough to fret when the bill is actually returned ; besides, I am quite confident it will not be returned ; and you know, John, I never was much astray in my certainties yet."

And with that last modest clause came the pretty, coaxing gesture, and arch, yet supplicating glance, which made Mary Matson's confidences so different from the imperative assertions of less loving and devoted women.

She wanted her husband not to despond, and so she teazed him into cheerfulness, or at least into an admission that by some impossible chance money might be found to meet Hone's claim ; after which she was very glad to see his eyes getting heavy and heavier, and his head falling lower and lower, till at length he stretched himself out full length on the sofa, and dropped fairly off asleep.

When matters came to this pass, Mary stole to the hearth and made up a good fire, drew down the blinds, and closed the curtains, and then with one look over her shoulder at her husband, which it was a sad pity John was not awake to see, quitted the room.

CHAPTER XX.

OLD FRIENDS AND NEW.

In the days when Jews' eyes were valuable, it might have been thought almost worth one of them to watch the manner in which pretty Mary Matson conducted herself when once she closed the door between herself and her husband.

The trembling sort of restless way in which she ran to the kitchen, and desired her little maid-of-all-work to keep back tea for an hour, and on no account to go into the parlour and disturb Mr. Matson, was suggestive enough ; but no one who had chanced to behold her flinging on bonnet and shawl, and sticking her fingers into gloves which did not match, could have doubted for a moment, that she was bound on some enterprise not over-pleasant in itself, nor yet very certain in its results.

Down the interminable stairs again, through the hall, out of the house—bound for time, and urged on by her own hopes, fears, and impatience, Mrs. Matson walked along the sloppy, slippery pavement as though a dozen bailiffs were on her track. Now pushing, now pushed, now crossing, now picking her way as well as haste would let her, the brave little woman found herself almost directly in Leadenhall Street, where she looked wistfully at an omnibus, and hesitated.

She had never fallen into the practice adopted by London women of her own grade in life of trudging through the streets by gas-light; and felt, poor simpleton, when people stared at and elbowed her, as if she did not like it, as though she were doing wrong. So she looked at the omnibus and hesitated, and thought, and shook her head, in answer to the conductor's insinuating wave.

The sixpence would be saved when the disagreeables were forgotten; so, true to her economical creed, she argued, and forthwith, without another look into the carriage-road, started determinedly on her four miles' walk to Bow.

I wonder whether any one who has not paced every step of that weary road, can imagine its insufferable tediousness, its intense monotony of badness.

The Aldgate Jews, and the Whitechapel butchers, and the Whitechapel thieves, and the Commercial-road sailors, and the Limehouse roughs, form even, in the best of times, a set of curiosities rarely to be met with, and studied seriatim; but that which seems in daylight simply questionable and disagreeable, becomes on any night pretty nearly intolerable, whilst on Saturday nights, when the inhabitants of the adjacent deeper depths turn out *en masse* to purchase provender, the road is a pandemonium, at least, so Mary Matson thought.

"And all for the value of sixpence," exclaims the criticizing reader. Well, I concede the woman was an idiot; but still that there were more such idiots in the world, you and I, and thousands more, might pray.

For wives and mothers know no medium, they are always either in their devoted economy, or their unthinking selfish extravagance, in excess; and, besides, there can be no question but that where people are occasionally short of shillings, pence become matters of serious calculations in the female domestic mind.

For this reason, past the butchers' shops, past Whitechapel church, past the flaring public houses, streaming out their bright light over the ghastly faces at the doors, Mary hurried on foot, without let or hindrance.

Some turned to see why she walked so fast; but the majority were so intent on their own affairs of business or pleasure, that they took no notice of the plainly dressed figure flitting by.—So along the Commercial Road, to Limehouse Church, and then across Bow Common, to the Storns. Janet opened the door, and said her mistress was at home, alone, disengaged, and in the drawing-room; would Mrs. Matson walk up stairs?

Lina was sitting all alone, when Mrs. Matson came in flushed, tired and excited. She had no hesitation in laying the state of the case before Mrs. Storn; and before five minutes, the chemist's wife was in possession of the facts, the narrative of which finished up with—"Do you think Mr. Storn—" and then poor Mary stopped.

Lina looked grave; Mr. Glenaen did not like Mr. Matson; Mr. Storn took his opinions from the manufacturer; she had never asked him during all her married life for money; never once; and this was a large sum to petition for, unless she assigned a reason for the request. All this flitted through her mind in a moment, and then after that pause, which seemed an age to the eager, anxious woman before her, she said, she could but try; Mr. Storn was in the house "for a wonder," Lina added.

Out of the room went the one wife, and in it stayed the other, with that peculiar sinking at the heart which waiting for anything engenders, making her feel sick and faint. Heaven help her; she had not a constitution like Lina, nor the money, nor leisure to mend a bad one; a frail body, with a strong spirit, which, some way, however, in those latter days, did not always keep strong enough to prevent the sense of pain and weariness. Mrs. Matson was ill, there could be no doubt about that; but she was not thinking about her health, whilst she sate waiting with what patience she might for her friend's return.

It was not long before Lina came back, looking stately, Mary thought; but through all her frigidity, a close observer might have noticed signs of a storm. "Mr. Storn could not raise so much in so short a time," she said; "but Mary, dear, would this trumpery be of any use to you?" and down on the table she threw all the jewellery she possessed in the world, her wedding presents, watch, chain, everything. "Take them, if you can make use of them : I don't want to see them ever again," she said. hurriedly, whilst a burning spot came on the top of each cheek. " There are ten pounds too, Mary, every little may be a help ; I am sorry I cannot give you the whole amount but—"

"And I am sorry I asked you, Mrs. Storn," said Mary ; " but I dare say I can get it elsewhere. I only came to you first, because—because I thought I would rather. I cannot take these things, but thank you just the same ; and don't," Mary added quickly, " don't be vexed with your husband for me."

"I am not vexed," answered Lina ; " but you must take these things ; I never wear them, never see them, and shall never want them ; take them ; they must be worth some money ; take them, Mary, do—to oblige me."

"I will not," Mrs. Matson declared, pushing Lina's extended hand from her ; " it is of no use following me," she continued, as Mrs. Storn pursued her to the door, while rings and brooches were scattered on the carpet. " It is not that I would not take any kindness from you ; but I have a particular reason for refusing this, and besides, what should I do with them ? If I were to try to turn them into money, the police would take me to the station-house, and you would have to come in the morning to bail me out. It is of no use, indeed, Mrs. Storn, forcing them on me ; for I would not take these things from you, if it were to save John from prison to-night."

"And why not pray ?" demanded Lina.

"Because I know very well you would be sorry in the morning ;" and Mary having unburdened her mind of this speech, ran away down the stairs, and out of the house, and took the most direct route to Mr. Glenaen's abode, across that dismallest of earth's dreary places, Bow Common.

"Is Mr. Glenaen in ?" she demanded of a servant. "I want to see him on particular business."

Even in her hurry and agitation, she had sense enough left to add that word—the open Sesame of Mr. Glenaen's doors, at all hours, to all people.

"What name ?" asked the woman.

"My name is of no consequence, it would be of no use," stammered Mrs. Matson ; and accordingly—announced simply as " a lady wishes to speak to you, Sir "—she walked past the maid, into Mr. Glenaen's office.

The manufacturer was seated on a high stool, writing at an old desk-table, covered with green baize and ink spots ; but when Mary entered, he ceased his scratching over hard paper, and turned round to see who his visitor might be.

For a moment he seemed uncertain, for Mrs. Matson wore a veil, and the gas-lamp being shaded, to throw a stronger light on his ledger, left part of the room in semi-darkness ; but the instant after, recognizing her face, he laid aside his pen, brought the palms of his hands down on his knees, and exclaimed, in a *sotto voce* of unutterable amazement,

" Well, I'm—"

I leave the reader to supply the word Mr. Glenaen brought slowly out from between his teeth. It was not an encouraging salutation ; but his visitor having prepared herself for something of the kind, merely remarked—

" I cannot expect you to say you are glad to see me, Mr. Glenaen ; and I do not wonder at your being surprised."

" I never thought I should have seen you in my house, Mrs. Matson," he answered, without rising, or offering her a chair.

" I imagined this was about the last place on earth you would ever have dreamed of coming to."

" So did I once," she said ; " and yet I do not know why I should not come to you, or why I should have hesitated at all about the propriety of the matter. Mr. Glenaen, I come to you, as a last resource for help."

" What is it that you want ?" he asked, and there was something in the tone of his voice which made Mary's heart leap for joy, as she fancied she saw deliverance at hand.

" I will tell you," she replied ; and forthwith she commenced placing their position fully, and, for a woman, clearly and quickly before the manufacturer.

He listened to the whole narrative without a remark, interruption, or change of countenance, still sitting with his hands on his knees, his feet stuck back through the rail of his stool, and his eyes fixed intently on her face ; he heard all she, standing beside his desk, had to say. When she had done—quite finished—he remarked :

" Your husband sent you to me ?"

" He did not," answered Mary. " He does not know I am out."

" I don't believe you," was the reply.

There was a struggle for an instant between prudence and temper, and then she said, quietly but firmly :

" Mr. Glenaen, I never told a falsehood in my life."

It was more than the person she addressed could have asserted, at all events ; and Mr. Glenaen, feeling, perhaps, an uncomfortable conviction of that fact, turned round on his stool and commenced pulling the feathers off his red ink quill.

The time he devoted to this amusement seemed an eternity

of suspense to Mrs. Matson; but she stood her ground manfully till he spoke, which he did at last, flinging the mutilated pen impatiently from him:

"Mrs. Matson, do you remember what passed between us, one evening, at Mr. Storn's house?"

"I do; but—"

"Don't go on," he interrupted. "I know all you had on your tongue to say. I only wanted you to answer me a question or two—I wish no remarks—you remember that. Do you recollect that I asked you to be my wife? that I offered to make a settlement on you? that I promised to keep you independent during my life, and leave you so after my death? Do you recollect all this?"

"I do," she replied.

"And do you remember what you said in answer?"

"Yes," acquiesced Mary, and a deep blush came over her pale cheeks as she did so.

"And what I said afterwards?" he pursued.

"Perfectly."

"Yet, in the face of all this, you come to me for help?"

I could not express, by any form of words, the concentrated bitterness Mr. Glenaeu managed to fling into the foregoing sentence: the malice and spite he contrived to put into these few words might have startled any one, and certainly effectually silenced Mary.

"I told you," he went on, "that you were an idiot to refuse such an offer; that if you married John Matson you would marry a beggar—a man who had no money, and never would be able to get any; that the time would come when you would want clothes for your children and bread for yourself; that when it was too late you would repent your folly and obstinacy in sackcloth and ashes; that love was all very well before marriage, but that money was better after. I told you I had never cared for, never thought of any woman but you, and still you refused me; and now, when it has all turned out as I prophesied, you come to me."

"I acted rightly by you then, Mr. Glenaen," she answered, "if I have done wrong to myself now. I did not exactly understand—I made a mistake—I did not comprehend—few people, I imagine, could have comprehended, that because I did not *love* you, you were for ever after to hate me. If I had known—"

"Why did I dismiss your husband from my service?" interrupted the manufacturer.

"Because I liked him better than you," she replied.

"And because I hated him," he said. "Had you forgotten my sending him adrift—"

"No; but that was when you were irritated—just after I had—"

"Dismissed me, you would say," he finished. "Well, Mrs. Matson, listen to me. I am a man who never changes—I am not angry to-day and forgiving to-morrow—I don't blow hot and cold; and when I dismissed your husband from my service, I only did what I would do again to-night, if I had a chance. So now my answer to your request is, that I would see John Matson at the devil before giving him a copper. That is all you have gained by laying the state of your affairs before me, Mrs. Matson; so now I hope you are satisfied with the result of your journey to Bow."

And Mr. Glenaen having concluded this pleasant speech, dropped down from his perch, plunged both hands into his trousers' pockets, and commenced striding up and down the room, whilst Mary walked to the door and turned the handle.

Holding it for a moment, however, she said, "Mr. Glenaen, perhaps you may not be able to understand what I am going to say now—but the day must come when you will—I feel thankful to have been here to-night, for you have reconciled me to poverty. I would not take your nature for the wealth of the world; and God knows, rich as you are and poor as we are, from the depths of my soul I pity you."

Before he could answer, she was gone out into the night, sobbing and crying. For all she had held out so bravely before him, he had mortified and hurt her through the most vulnerable point of a woman's nature, her husband; and she was disappointed and tired, and the excitement was over, and the reaction had commenced, and she began thinking what she should say to John when she got in, and how uneasy he would be at her absence; and so, as I have said, sobbing and crying so that her tears blinded her, she ran on past Mr. Storn's house, and along the lonely path leading to the highway, till she came with such force against a person she had not noticed walking before her, that she was almost thrown to the ground, and only saved by a strong hand which caught her as she staggered and kept her from falling back.

"You are not hurt, I hope," said the person to whom that hand belonged.

"Oh! no; not in the least. I beg your pardon, it is so dark, and I did not see. I was not looking. I—"

"Mrs. Matson, what are you doing here alone?" asked Mr. Clyne, for it was he. "Stand still for a moment, till you recover yourself. Where have you been? Surely not at Mr. Glenaen's?"

"Just there," she replied.

"But you did not get the money?" he said, eagerly.

"No; but how do you know? Who told you?"

"Mrs. Storn. She was in such grief about you when I went there. Never mind Mr. Glenaen's refusal. We will manage the matter without his assistance."

"We! You! Oh! Mr. Clyne," and the revulsion was so great that Mrs. Matson could not speak another word, but suffered Mr. Clyne to draw her arm through his, and walked on with him in silence.

Thus they re-traversed the whole of the interminable road from Bow, poor Mary's lightened heart rendering her unmindful of fatigue, headache—everything.

Her companion wanted to take a cab, but she would not let him. "If you are not tired," she said, "please walk. I feel so strangely confused, that I should like to get a little settled down before I see my husband. The cool air does me good. You are not tired, I hope?"

He was not; he assured her he liked the walk, and had only proposed driving lest she should be fatigued. Many a man would have urged her to get into a conveyance, and annoyed her by doing so; but Mr. Clyne had that quick perception of others' feelings and motives of action, which seems to belong to some people intuitively. This was one of his greatest charms, and nothing about him had ever touched Lina's heart like it.

He knew what she felt without giving her the pain or trouble of speaking. He caught even the shadow of her thoughts, and shaped his conversation accordingly; and thus it was that evil never came openly in Mrs. Storn's path. Delicately and sensitively every thorn was removed from the road of wrong she was pursuing—for Mr. Clyne rarely uttered a sentence calculated to annoy any one—and as for annoying Lina! Would you, sir, grieve your bride elect? would you, miss, commence now the system of nagging with which you mean to wear your husband's life out hereafter?

Alas! for that hereafter which brings to all of us the naked realities of our lives. When it came to Lina Storn and Mary Matson—the latter, remembering the events of that night, could not wonder at after-results. Looking back from the heights of experience, she only marvelled the *dénouement* had not come sooner. When the world was making itself busy about the Storns' affairs, and the bitter tongue of scandal was saying hard things of a woman whose course had not been easy, Mary thought of Herbert Clyne's almost womanly kindness, and his strong, masculine help, and, contrasting his conduct with that of others, she spoke of the man out of the fulness of her gratitude, in the warmth of her heart, as she had found him.

Little was said by either on the way back; but, as they neared the city, Mrs. Matson's steps lagged visibly, and when they arrived at last in Coleman Street, she leaned against the hall door till it was opened, declaring she was quite tired out.

"I shall get a scolding for allowing you to walk, and I richly deserve it," said Mr. Clyne, adding, as he entered the sitting-room—"Mr. Matson, I plead guilty to an unjustifiable act of weakness, in permitting your wife to have her own way; and, accordingly, I place myself at your mercy."

"My dear Mary, where have you been?" asked her husband.

"Oh! she had been all the way to Bow," and then the young wife was very rude, and whispered to John that she had brought help, by way of conclusion to which piece of intelligence she laid her head down on his shoulder and fell to sobbing there as naturally as a child.

Now, if Mr. Clyne had ever seen Mrs. Storn do such a thing —but, however, there is no use pursuing that question any further, for he never had; and so he watched, with that sort of interest which is excited by any new phase of human feeling, the husband untie Mary's bonnet and unfasten her shawl, and then lift her gently on to the sofa, and put the cushions under the poor tired head.

"My love, you should not do these things," he heard him say; and after that Mr. Clyne took the burden of the conversation on himself, and spoke so lightly of the sum that was salvation to Mr. Matson's credit, as to make that individual feel as if his head had suddenly been turned round on his shoulders, and various other liberties taken with his mind and body generally.

It was all true, however; the tremendous rock ahead could be safely passed on Monday, and John Matson breathed again. Another billow mounted—another respite given—and the man slept on an easy pillow that night; and Mary, every time she woke, first wondered if it were all really true, and then, with her eyelids dropping again with weariness, whispered a little prayer of thanksgiving to her Father in Heaven, who had been so good to her and her's from the days of her childhood upwards.

And Lina? long after Mr. Clyne had left, her husband came in, and kissing her, said—

"I am sorry, my love, I did not think before I refused that money to-night. When did you say John Matson wanted it?"

"Then," answered Mrs. Storn, shortly; "and I believe he has got, or will get it—in time."

It was not a particularly explicit or conciliatory answer, and it threw Mr. Storn back, more particularly as his wife left the room immediately after. Another opportunity lost for ever—swept from the shore of the present into the ocean of the past—that greedy, mournful tide which is always bringing back waifs and strays for us to look at and stretch forth our longing hands for, but which gives no lost chance into our keeping again—in the wiser and sadder future, never—more.

CHAPTER XXI.

MR. MATSON FALLS SICK.

HONE's bill was paid—the goods were duly forwarded to London, and shipped by Messrs. Colke and Ferres—the orthodox fourteen days had elapsed, and Mr. Matson, after waiting three days more as a matter of business courtesy, called at the new counting-house in the old lane for his money.

Which he did not get, however. Mr. Ferres was from home, the manager said, and had left a message, that before settling the account he wished to speak to Mr. Matson; on what subject Mr. Maurice Storn's successor either did not or would not know. The only definite information to be extracted from him being that he could not give a cheque, and that Mr. Ferres would be away from home for a week.

Now, there are times in a man's business existence when, to tell him to wait for his money for a week, is similar to saying to a starving horse at Christmas, "Live till the spring and you'll get grass;" for a hundred pounds in the distance will no more satisfy an awkward five-pound creditor close at hand than will the coming summer provide fodder for the present winter. In the land of Egypt the seven years' plenty preceded the seven years' famine; but in the city of London, amongst business beginners, the famine always precedes the plenty; and it would have needed a second Joseph to have been able to do otherwise than act as John Matson did, viz., return home sick and dispirited.

"He did not know," he confessed to his wife, "how he was

to get through the week; he had calculated on that money to
stop the mouths of a dozen clamorous creditors. He began to
think that really he had better face the worst, and call a meeting and try to get a situation. The harass was wearing him
out, and there seemed no end to it. He did not know what
to do."

Then Mary advised that he should do nothing until after he
had seen Mr. Ferres, who, perhaps, was waiting to give him
another order; but, though he followed her advice, he could
not swallow her comfort. In the matter of hopefulness, she
occasionally exhausted even his credulity, and accordingly he
worked and waited through the week, and when the day named
came round, walked down to the old lane off Eastcheap once
again.

Mr. Ferres was in the private counting-house and Mr.
Matson was introduced to the presence.

"Good morning, Mr. Matson," the town partner said, looking up from amongst a pile of papers and samples.

"Good morning, sir," answered the man without capital.

"Pray, sit down," continued Mr. Ferres, waving his visitor
to a chair. "I wanted to speak to you, Mr. Matson, about
that oxalic acid we purchased from you for shipment."

"Yes, sir," said John, as he paused.

"You remember the quality you sent?" questioned Mr.
Ferres.

"Perfectly."

"Do you happen to have a sample left?"

"I have about half a ton of the same now in stock."

"If you please, then," said Mr. Ferres, "I will walk round
to your place and take a look at it."

And, without waiting for Mr. Matson's reply, he lifted his
hat, opened the door, and with a courteous "After you," followed the younger man into the street.

If Mr. Matson's business had not been sick almost past recovery, that ten minutes' walk from Eastcheap to Coleman
Street, in company with the monied man of a great house,
might pretty nearly have set him on his legs again.

Six months previously, to have been seen in company with
Mr. Ferres would have given the young man a standing; but
now—John wincing, as even during that short distance he met
creditor after creditor—felt it was of no use; that ruin and
he were staring at one another, and the sooner it came the
better, perhaps, for him and all other parties concerned.

"Is this the same that you sent to us?" demanded Mr.
Ferres, after he had examined the acid in silence.

" Yes sir."

" Well, it seems a fair quality."

"I call it first-rate, sir; and I believe I am a pretty good judge," said John, decidedly.

"Then what is the meaning of what I hear on all hands about the inferiority of your goods?" demanded Mr. Ferres, facing point-blank on Mr. Matson, and looking as though he were trying to read him through and through.

" Inferiority of goods!—on all hands!" repeated his auditor.

"Yes; I hear your goods are never up to sample—in fact, that you never have a first-rate lot in your warehouse. Now look here, young man," added Mr. Ferres, "if this statement be true, the sooner you give up business the better; and if it be false, as from your face and this acid I feel inclined to believe it is, you had better try to sift the matter to the bottom, for your credit is bad in the market, and your character not worth a rush."

Having concluded which explicit and complimentary sentence, Mr. Ferres took John Matson by the shoulder and led him to a chair, where the man sat down, looking quite white and sick enough to justify Mr. Colke's partner in his earnest entreaty for him "not to faint."

"May I enquire," began Mr. Matson, the moment he could speak—"May I inquire from whom you heard these flattering particulars?"

"Our manager heard it, in the first instance, from Mr. Glenaen, of Bow."

"I did not think he had been such an infernal scoundrel," exclaimed John, which remark moved Mr. Ferres to ask in what way? and the question unloosed Mr. Matson's tongue.

Without a pause or hesitation, he told the whole story of his faithful servitude, his successful love, and his unsuccessful struggles through; he spoke of the points where he and Mr. Glenaen had come into rough contact together, and concluded his narrative by saying, in reference to his wife:

"I cannot expect you, Mr. Ferres, to believe the bare word of a man whose character you have heard blown upon—and if you care to satisfy yourself as to the truth of my story—you can ask Mr. Liudor, of America Square, Mr. and Mrs. Storn, and Mr. Herbert Clyne, to confirm it."

"Very well," said Mr. Ferres, dryly.

"And with respect to the oxalic acid, it left my hands as I received it from the manufacturer, and I am quite willing to let the matter rest till you hear from your correspondents abroad. If they are dissatisfied with the goods, pay me, then, what you think right, and I shall be content to bear the loss."

"Very well," said Mr. Ferres, again, and without another word, except "Good morning," departed.

Within the hour, however, a clerk came round to Coleman Street with a cheque for the full amount of Mr. Matson's account, which, for some unaccountable reason, that gentleman immediately converted, less commission, into a banker's order, and transmitted by the next post to Hone's great factory in the North.

He never made a better move than this in his life—though he did it out of his despair rather than out of his sense.

A week before, and he would have divided the money among twenty little people; but now he only, in a huff, looked out for the great man, and left the little people to shift as they could for themselves, whilst he crawled wearily up the stairs to his wife's sitting-room, where, complaining of illness, he lay down on the sofa, whence, in an hour's time, he crept with her help to bed.

It seems to be one of the established laws of nature that a man can play no desperate game with her without, in the long run, coming out the loser. Something like this idea passed through Mr. Matson's mind as he lay awake during the dreary night-watches, dizzy and faint, with that strange pain which comes so often to men of business, pressing on the top of his head, and, at times, stupifying him.

"Only a headache," he assured his wife the next morning, when he tried to rise, but was driven back to the pillows again ; and though Mary was not doctor enough to know that it was only that headache which sometimes precedes sudden death, and sometimes insanity, she yet grew mightily alarmed at his symptoms, and sent, like a wise woman as she was, for medical assistance at once.

Medical assistance came, in the shape of a ruddy-complexioned, round-bodied little practitioner, who creaked into the patient's bed room, laid his hand on what he called the seat of the pain, asked to be obliged with a sight of Mr. Matson's tongue, held John's thin wrist with his fat fingers, and then promising to send him round some medicine directly, got up to take his leave.

"One moment, doctor, if you please," said Mr. Matson, de-taining him. "What is it ?"

"Only a little congestion, my dear sir. We shall set you all right again in a day or two. You must keep quiet, though —perfectly quiet," said the little gentleman, lengthening the two last words as much as possible, in order, apparently, to shorten his journey towards the door and enable him to get out of it before his patient should have time to ask another question.

"Well, doctor?" said Mary, interrogatively, as he creaked into the sitting-room.

"My dear lady, you must exert your influence to keep Mr. Matson at home for a fortnight. Let him remain quiet, perfectly quiet," was the little man's energetic answer.

"And why?" she asked.

"Because excitement may be dangerous," he replied.

"Or—" Mrs. Matson paused.

"Fatal," he supplied; and they both stood silent for a minute.

After that pause, "Doctor," the young wife began, "my husband is no child, the best way to keep him at home is to tell him this—he would do anything in the world for me;" but at this point Mrs. Matson broke down in her sentence, and finished it with sobs.

"In that case," answered the general practitioner, "I cannot leave him in better hands; and I shall trust what I have said to your discretion. With rest and proper treatment, there is nothing to be apprehended."

Having given Mary which comforting assurance, he shook hands, and bustled off to another patient, leaving her the pleasant task of trying to keep a business-man "quiet."

"Short of a strait-waistcoat," she declared laughingly, "the thing was not to be thought of;" but, nevertheless, she managed to keep him in bed, and under the doctor, for a fabulous length of time, whilst she wrote entreating notes to tardy payers, and held frequent dialogues with duns.

Heaven, we hope, heard leniently the false glosses Mrs. Matson gave to John, concerning the true state of their affairs during that dismal period; according to her account, she had nothing to do but write to this person, and get back a cheque, or put off that, and have just as much time granted as she chose to ask for. She was a very boastful wife in those days, making much of her business abilities and powers of persuasion, proposing in quite a vaunting way to her husband, that she should take out samples, and try how many orders she could obtain, whilst he staid at home and nursed the baby, and looked up Ganymede.

Not till he was well again, had John Matson any idea of the wild way in which Mary managed business during the time of his great prostration.

Money had been got in, there could be no question about

that—indeed, he saw plainly that people had settled with his wife, to whom he might have written long enough, before he got an answer; but she had kept back all letters of all kinds from his knowledge, excepting those which contained some order or enquiry; and missives which should have been answered a fortnight previously, were only delivered up to him when convalescent, under a solemn promise that he would not worry about a word they contained.

"Have you kept a memorandum of the money you got in, dear?" he asked.

"Oh, no! but I gave a proper receipt for everything."

"How do you know then what you paid or received?"

"Why, I have got all I received, and I paid nothing."

"Nothing?"

"Not a solitary item, except the boy's wages and the stingiest housekeeping," answered Mary, gleefully. "I thought you would be having some great bill to meet, and I kept all against that. There were so many people wanting money, I thought it best to pay none. Here is what I got in;" and she unlocked a little box, and tumbled out gold, and notes, and silver, on his desk. "Count and see how much there is."

Dear little soul! she knew to a halfpenny how much she had stored away, but still she must needs have the pleasure of seeing her husband laying his notes on one side, and reckoning the gold, and piling the silver. She got up on the first rail of his office stool, and stood there with her arm about his neck, as proud as a peacock, of the amount of cash she had scraped together, in her unmethodical way.

"And now, John, there is another thing; you are sure you won't be angry," she said, when the counting was over, and she had received what she considered a sufficient meed of praise.

"Angry, my wife, with you?" he replied.

"Oh! yes, you might. I did not tell you at first, because I knew you would put yourself in a fever about it; and I did not tell you at last, because I wanted to keep it as a treat. Mr. Ferres sent another order."

"What for?" demanded Mr. Matson eagerly, as he seized the note his wife was tantalizing him with.

"Oh! Mary, this is dated days back. You should have told me at once. We may lose the order;" and he looked aghast.

"When Mr. Ferres has got the goods?" she asked in an ecstacy of delight. "I knew if I told you, you would be writing to Hone, and worrying about samples, and all sorts of nonsense; and you were very ill that day, so I just sent off a letter, saying you were ill; that the order had come in, and that Mr. Hone would please forward without delay."

"And the goods came?"

"Yes, and I asked Mr. Ferres to look at them, and he laughed, and said, they were just what he wanted: and he sent over his own carts, John, and I never had to employ a man.   He says, whenever you like to furnish invoice, you can have a cheque."

And as she concluded this triumphant finish of her exploits, Mrs. Matson dropped off her perch, and sitting down in the nearest chair, began to cry.

She said she did so because she felt so happy; but there could be no question but that it was really because she felt so weak.

During the whole of her husband's illness, she had slept little, and eaten less; she had over-exerted herself, mentally and bodily; and this was the result; languor and nervous prostration.

Nevertheless, she managed, in spite of occasional hysterical spurts of weeping, and a low pulse, and aching limbs, to get about the house for a few days more; at the end of which time, she had exhausted her remaining strength, and could not get up for breakfast, nor for dinner, nor for tea, but lay motionless in bed, wondering what on earth had happened to her.

And what might have happened to her, seeing that Mr. Matson had to be away all day, and was not, moreover, when he chanced to be at home, either a good nurse, or a professed cook, it is hard to say, if Lina Storn had not come in from Bow, and penetrated to the sick chamber, and taken a ramble through the kitchen, and conversed with Ganymede, after which she formed her plans.

"Mr. Matson," she said, making her way into that gentleman's warehouse, "I am going to take Mary to Bow to-day."

"But she cannot get up, Mrs. Storn," he answered.

"She will never get up unless she has different nursing," was Lina's comforting reply.   "If Mary have not change of air and better diet, she will be dead in a month.   Give her to me; I will nurse and cure her for you."

And Mrs. Storn, with tears in her dark eyes, looked imploringly in John Matson's troubled face.

"Can you not trust me?" she asked reproachfully.

"Yes, even with her," he replied, and took Lina's hand and kissed it gratefully.   "God bless you, Mrs. Storn," he said, "for all you have done in your life for me."

"I may take her then?" she persisted.

"Yes; but surely—surely you do not think her so very ill?"

"What Mary wants, in so many plain words, Mr. Matson,

is food. I don't mean full plates of meat, and loaves of bread, and loads of vegetables, which are strength to the healthy; but I do mean beef tea, mutton broth, light puddings, and all those sort of nourishing nothings, that are food, strength, life to the weak. I have always been a ridiculously strong woman myself," she added with a smile; "but still that does not hinder my seeing what your wife requires. In a fortnight you shall see her better; in six weeks on my regimen, well."

"Six weeks!" exclaimed Mr. Matson. "I do not know how I can do without her for so long."

"Try," answered Mrs. Storn, bitterly. "You should learn how happily men can live apart from their wives—not for weeks, but for years. Pardon me," she added, next instant, "I did not mean to vex you; but you know—oh, you know, right well—that something in my own life has gone all wrong."

"Not the love of your husband, Mrs. Storn, I am sure," said Mr. Matson, gravely.

"No—oh! no—I suppose not; something in myself; I am not what I used to be. Now let us go up to Mary."

How John Matson longed to stop her as she hurried before him up the stairs; how he longed to loose his tongue, and stretch out his arm between her and the path she was pursuing; how sentence after sentence chased each other through his brain, were things to think of afterwards and repent!

CHAPTER XXII.

CONVALESCENCE.

SLOWLY, very slowly, Mrs. Matson, in the midst of the Bow smells, regained her strength. Spite of Mrs. Storn's nursing and Janet's cookery, she did not recover so rapidly as Lina had promised, and Mr. Matson hoped.

All the day long she lay on the sofa wearily; all the endless night she slept uneasily, or not at all. She was miserable about her husband, miserable about his affairs. She was perpetually marvelling how John was getting on, and thinking concerning his unmended stockings and his buttonless shirts. Her daughter, Lina had brought off with them, and the young lady in long clothes was in the habit of rolling about the hearthrug in ecstacies, whilst her mother, with half shut-eyes, looked on.

Many a time Lina, who had a sort of taste for mental analysis, tried to get at the bottom of these long fits of sleepy musing ; all in vain. Mary, usually frank and communicative enough, would not tell what she was thinking about, and it was only in the sadder and wiser future that her friend, putting two and two together, was able to form a guess.

As she grew better, these reveries became shorter and of less frequent occurrence ; whenever she got strong enough to walk across the room, her spirits came back, and she would nurse her child and play with Geordie, and talk with Lina for the length of a day. That was a lazy time for the once active wife, when she had nothing to do, and did it thoroughly ; but after a time she pleaded so earnestly for needle and thimble, and cotton, begged so piteously for a sight of her husband's linen, and her child's frocks, that Lina relented ; and if she did not allow her to return to town, at least permitted her to have employment at Bow.

Once at least, during the course of every day, Mr. Matson stole an hour from his business to see his wife ; and by some singular chance, he rarely ever visited the Storns in the evening without meeting Mr. Gordon Glenaen, whose head, he informed Mary, confidentially, he should have " liked to punch."

Mr. Gordon Glenaen and Mr. Herbert Clyne, these two were almost regular guests at Mr. Storn's table ; the latter felt so anxious about Mrs. Matson's health, while the former was always dropping in to see his partner, as the cook dished the dinner.

Mrs. Storn might be uncharitable enough to think it was less her husband in his laboratory that the manufacturer wanted to see, than Mrs. Matson in her sickness and trouble ; but Mrs. Storn's thoughts did not signify in the slightest degree to Mr. Glenaen ; a fact which, for some reason or other, he was always trying to make apparent.

Still when John managed to shake off business, and get out at night to Bow, Mary enjoyed those evenings mightily, whether the manufacturer were present or absent. The music and the conversation, and the change of scene and variety of society amused and excited her.

Perhaps, knowing all she did, she had a secret pleasure in hearing her husband's enemy snubbed by Lina, and set down by Mr. Clyne. The tilts and passages at arms between the well-bred hostess and the unlicked guest—between the West-end gentleman and the East-end trader—made her occasionally forget her own anxieties and her husband's trials. She was not a very deep thinker on any subject, nor did she ever interest herself much in other people's affairs, or else she might have found excitement in the intimacy progressing before her eyes; but in Mr. Storn's absences, and Lina's loneliness, and Mr. Clyne's visit, the true-hearted woman saw nothing but that the chemist was devoted to his profession, and that it was a pity of his wife.

" I should not like it," she confessed to her husband, speaking of Maurice's constant absorption; and he, thinking of something else, answered—

" Neither should I."

Neither would he, to have had his wife worried by one man and wooed by another, whilst he sate in a distant room poring over his experiments.

" Were I in Mr. Storn's place," thought John, " I should kick Mr. Glenaen down stairs, and ask Mr. Clyne to follow him ; but being in my own, is there anything I ought to do in this matter : speak, or hold my tongue, or what ?"

Many a time, even whilst sitting by the chemist's fire-side, Mr. Matson propounded this query to himself—one, mark you, not to be easily answered by any one.

For he was not certain—he only feared—he had no facts; but merely ideas. He did know very much of Mrs. Storn's character, and he knew less of Mr. Storn's. He did not like to speak without being sure of his premises, and satisfied that good, and not evil results were to ensue from his interference ; and still he did not care to keep silent and see what he could not help seeing every time he went out to Bow.

But for the circumstance that he found his own affairs required all the time, and more, which he was able to devote to them, Mr. Matson might have taken up the Clyne intimacy, and argued the matter out himself with serious results ; but it so happened, that just about the time Mary was getting better, and talking of going home again, he had quite private business enough to transact, without meddling in Lina's ; in addition to which he had the pleasure of witnessing a scene which somewhat changed his opinion with regard to Mrs. Storn, and induced him to consider her more as an unhappy wife than as a falling one.

Perhaps, after all, he had been wrong, and that whatever Mr. Clyne felt for her, Mrs. Storn held no undue love in her heart for him—perhaps he had judged rashly in thinking Mr. Clyne's manner too polite. In comparison with Mr. Glenaen, any person must have seemed courteous; for the manufacturer was growing unbearable, and it was often a trial of Mr. Matson's temper to remain silent and listen to him.

On the evening in question he came in looking for Mr.

Storn. He was always looking for Mr. Storn, and yet never went away to find him. So Lina said, at all events; and it was with little hope of his availing himself of her suggestion, that she replied to his demand, of where her husband was.

"In the laboratory, I believe. Will you go there and see him ?"

"After a little," answered the manufacturer, taking a chair, and drawing it towards the fire. "Very cold to-night; though, judging from the fires I always see here, one would say it was cold in this house all the year round. Plain to be seen, Mr. Clyne, that Mrs. Storn has her fuel from the factory ; she gets all the lumps, and leaves her husband all the slack."

"Which is the only part of any use to him, Mr. Glenaen, you might have added," interposed his quondam-clerk.

"You know too much of these kind of things for me," retorted the manufacturer. "You remember, I always told you, Mr. Matson, you were too clever by half;" and without waiting for any reply, he turned and asked Mary, "when she intended returning to her town house ?"

"Do you mean our attic ?" enquired Mrs. Matson naïvely. "I really don't know ; to-morrow, if my husband allows it."

"What a remarkably obedient wife," sneered Mr. Glenaen, "quite a pattern among matrons. I hope he will exercise his authority when you return to Coleman Street, and not let you mope in-doors so everlastingly. It is destructive to women sitting over their work all day ; you should walk four or five miles every morning of your life."

"And in the name of all that's wonderful, Mr. Glenaen, where would you have me walk to ?" inquired the lady.

"To—anywhere," he returned. "I am sure there are plenty of lanes and alleys, streets and roads, in and about London ; you might walk four or five miles without going further west than St. Paul's, or further east than the Monument. A marvellous place is London ; no end to it."

"I believe there is not," answered Mrs. Matson; "but for mere walking's sake, I do not like to go out alone in the city."

"Not like to go out alone in the city ?" repeated Mr. Glenaen. "Are you afraid of anybody running away with you ?"

"Not in the least," she replied; "but I do not like walking about London alone, for all that."

"Pooh! Nonsense!" was the polite rejoinder; on which Lina, brim-full of indignation, burst in with—

"It's no nonsense at all, Mr. Glenaen ; I know by experience how extremely disagreeable the city is; and I think it says very little for the merchants of London, that their portion of it is the only part where ladies cannot walk unnoticed. They used to make observations on my appearance—whistle in my face—thrust their noses under my bonnet, and stare as if they had never in all their lives before seen a woman who was not an absolute fright. I am sure I do not wonder in the least at Mary's remark; for when we lived in the city, I should never have gone outside the door alone, if I could have helped it."

Having finished which neat speech, Mrs. Storn looked defiantly at Mr. Glenaen; whilst Mr. and Mrs. Matson laughed, and Mr. Clyne said in a voice which fell more like oil on flame, than like oil on the waters—

"I should think it must have been because the people you refer to, never saw a lady at home, that they stared at one when they met her in the street."

"Do you mean to imply by that," queried Mr. Glenaen, "that their wives and daughters are not ladies ?"

"I should imagine not," retorted Mr. Clyne, "or else their husbands would know how to conduct themselves like gentlemen."

There was no answering this observation, and, accordingly, Mr. Glenaen turned his attack on Mrs. Storn.

"Well, now, who were these people that tormented you, and what especial annoyance did they give, and where are they to be met with, if one were to take a leisure day and go out to look for them ? I never see anything of them, and I am sure I am out enough; and my mother, who has spent best part of her life in London, never makes a complaint of this sort. I never hear her say any one stares at, or is impertinent to her."

"Possibly, when I am as old as Mrs. Glenaen, there will be no necessity for me to complain either," said Lina, scornfully; for she detested her visitor's mother, and forgot—oh! many and many a score of times—the lesson taught in that Book, which she had long ceased to study, that "a soft answer turneth away wrath."

"I should be sorry to quarrel with you, Mrs. Storn," said her opponent; "but I will not submit to hear my mother spoken slightingly of by any one."

"I regret you imagine I have done so," answered Lina; "I only stated a simple fact, which is, that whilst I am still young, Mrs. Glenaen is not. I confess I do not see any harm in saying people are old, when they are so. If I live long enough myself, I suppose I shall prove no exception to the general rule."

"Did you mean that speech as an apology, or as a fresh cut ?" asked Mr. Glenaen, who, noticing a half-smile in Mr.

Matson's eye, and a sneer on Mr. Clyne's lip, was by this time quite ready to do or say anything.

"If you do not wish to consider it as an apology, you can take any meaning out of it which pleases you best," Lina replied.

"Then it pleases me to consider that you deliberately insult your husband's oldest friend; that whenever I come here, you set your visitors on me; that you would be civil to the greatest stranger sooner than to me; and that when you do ask me here it is only to provide amusement for your guests at my expense."

He had risen at the commencement of this speech, and at its conclusion, Lina rose likewise.

"Mr. Glenaen," she said haughtily, and with an air of pride, which Mary Matson could not have assumed to save her life—"Mr. Glenaen, as I never, to my knowledge, asked you to come here, I am quite innocent of the amiable intention you attribute to me. So far as you would let me, I have tried to be polite to my husband's friend, and make him welcome as I could; but as you will not permit me to be civil to you—as you seem to come here merely to try my temper, and to sow disunion between Mr. Storn and myself—as you seem never happy save when you are trying—God only knows why—to draw him from me—I think it would be better if, for the future, the mask were flung aside, and open war declared between us."

"You could have proposed nothing more gratifying to me," he replied. "You have voluntarily thrown me off as your friend, Madam," he added, bitterly,—"perhaps you may feel sorry yet for having done so."

"Whatever sorrow I may feel in the future, I trust I shall be enabled to bear the loss of your society with philosophy in the present," Lina answered bravely; but when he had taken her significant hint, and closed the door behind him, she flung herself into an arm chair, weeping passionately.

Mr. Clyne had never seen her so affected but once before; and this fresh revelation of a grief locked up in her breast, and only bursting its bounds at times like the present, moved him to such pity, that but for the presence of others, he might have committed some extravagance which would have warned Lina of the length and breadth, and horror, of her danger then.

As it was, however, he did what any other gentleman might have done under the circumstances—left Lina to her friends; and without more than a quiet shake hands with John Matson, quitted the room and the house.

When Lina recovered her composure, it was but natural that

the two should have a good talk over the fracas which had just taken place.

"What would Maurice say?" was almost Mrs. Storn's first observation; and her evident repentance for having done anything to which he could take exception, and her dread lest Mr. Glenaen should give a false colouring to the quarrel, filled Mr. Matson with the belief that she was right after all; that it was her husband, and not she, who was travelling so far wrong to get so little.

She made both her visitors repeat, twenty times over, the consolatory assurance that latterly the manufacturer's tone and manner had been insolent beyond endurance. She got them to say yes, over and over again, to her perpetually recurring question—"Now don't you think, did you not see I was provoked to it?" and when Mr. Matson at last suggested that it might be advisable for her to mention the matter to Mr. Storn, she rose immediately, and, in a sort of hurry, declared she would go to the laboratory that instant and tell him all, tell him everything.

So she went off—her silk dress rustling against the walls of the narrow corridor that led away to Maurice's sanctum, while John Matson, who had opened the drawing-room door for her, stood in the portal listening to her retreating footsteps, and wondering how the interview would end.

It was never destined to begin, unfortunately; for just as Mrs. Storn laid her hand on the lock, she heard voices within, and pausing for a moment, listened, till she felt satisfied Mr. Glenaen was closeted with her husband.

"Always before me," she murmured, angrily, as she retraced her way; "even before Maurice knew me he knew this man;" and somehow at the thought, all the confidence, and penitence, and sorrow, that had filled Lina's breast five short minutes before, departed, and the old unhealed sore burst out bleeding with all its wonted violence afresh.

"You did not go in then?" asked Mr. Matson.

"No, Mr. Glenaen has, as usual, forestalled me," she answered; "well, let it be so, his enmity can scarcely injure me more than his friendship has done. Now let us forget all about him."

"In a moment—just let me speak to you for an instant, please;" and Mr. Matson drew her a step or two away from the door. "It is not on this subject I had anything to say, Mrs. Storn, pray forgive me—but for mercy's sake keep Mary with you for a day or two longer —our landlord has just put in an execution, and I do not know whether I shall be able to arrange with him or not. I would not for the world—"

"You may rest content, Mr. Matson," Lina interrupted, answering his thoughts rather than his words ; and with this brief assurance that she had understood his meaning, and would comply with his wishes, she preceded him into the drawing-room, and saying, "Now let us have some music," opened the piano and began to play.

As she swept the keys, a memory came back in unison, as it seemed, with the sound of the music—of an evening long, oh, so long ago—when all alone she sat in another house, and played the same chords defiantly.

Had the very air she chanced on then been the first war-note of the battle of her married life? a battle in which she had sustained so many defeats, and made so many false moves, and permitted herself to be so fatally led astray, that Lina thinking of all these things at once, was compelled to turn over the leaves of her music-book, and try first one piece, and then another, to produce a mental diversion.

All in vain, till she began singing some verses of an old song that she had heard her father hum many a time, when she was but a child.

A mournful, plaintive, old-fashioned melody, that softened Lina's heart as she sang, and brought the tears into Mary's eyes as she listened.

"Don't go on, please," she asked at last, coming up beside her friend, and laying her hand on the white fingers that were straying so negligently over the notes—"I can't bear that song—it seems to choke me."

"You little silly simpleton!" said Mrs. Storn, getting up instantly, and tossing her music aside ; but as she turned from the instrument she muttered to herself—

"What an idiot I have been, too, to commence such a doleful ditty about death and partings, and all sorts of horrors, before a sick woman, fond of husband and child!"

Having finished which complimentary estimate of her own capacity, Lina proceeded to declare, in words audible and intelligible enough, that they were tired, that Mary ought to go to bed, that Mary must have a glass of wine and some chicken broth directly, and that she was going to be very rude, and turn Mr. Matson out.

"Do you see the time?" she asked, pointing to the mantel-piece. "It is no wonder Mary looks pale, and does no credit to her nurse, when I allow such hours as these. Now I shall just give you five minutes' grace, and then you must go."

"You are a perfect autocrat, Mrs. Storn," said John, laughing ; and whilst Lina went out of the room to speak with

Janet, he drew close to his wife, and took the dear hand in his, and twirled round and round the ring wherewith he had bound her to himself.

"I want to see that finger fatter, Mary," he said.

"Only that one?—You bad husband, you want me to have a whitlow," she answered; "but never mind about my being fat or thin now—tell me, is there anything new?"

"Let me see," returned Mr. Matson, great hypocrite as he was, bending his head as though culling among the unimportant events of the day for some piece of intelligence to tell his wife. "I have had no orders to-day; but one man was in for prices who I think will be a customer; and I got some money from Jones, and that old balance from Graham. I think that is all I have got fresh for you to-day, Mary—not much, but still better than nothing."

"And I may go home to-morrow, may I, John?" she asked. "I am quite well and strong again now, and I want sadly to be with you. There is no place in the world, after all, like one's own house, no matter how kind people are."

"There is not indeed," he answered, with a sigh; "but still, Mary, I should like you to stay here a day or two longer, if you are not inconveniencing Mrs. Storn. You look so much better for the change, that I think another week might complete the cure. I miss you grievously, my wife," he added, "but I would sacrifice anything on earth to make and keep you well."

And so the pair talked on; but as they chanced to be married and not single, I will spare the sentimental reader the remainder of their conversation.

The matrimonial *téte-à-téte* bears something of a domestic character all the world over. The Abyssinian speaks to his wife of the scarcity of raw beefsteaks, whilst doubtless the lady Hindoo has many remarks to make to her scantily-clad lord concerning the small quantity of food supplied by the rice-pot; and just so, in like manner, Mary had her inquiries to make, and remarks to utter, about the behaviour of Ganymede, and the state of their finances—about what John had for his dinner, and if his breakfasts were ready for him in good time every morning.

Very uninteresting and unromantic these things read in print, and to a bystander they are almost as bad in reality; but still, spite of theory, and romance, and fine writing, there can be no question that women do chatter such common-places, whilst men listen; and if you, dear reader, are inclined to doubt the fact, then you are either a bachelor, or else madam, your respected wife, sits in one room with her friends, whilst you sit in another with yours. She entertains her select circle with small talk, whilst you send round the bottle to laugh and talk as small, perhaps, though a shade more interesting, or else lounge to your club, or take a drag to Richmond, or do anything, in short, but stay at home and be bored to death with her.

Life is made up of a few great and a vast number of small occurrences. On the stage of no human life can scenes from a tragedy always be enacting. There are long stops and pauses when the actors stretch out their limbs and eat, and drink, and sleep, and talk about nothing, and are just like my characters, neither heroes nor heroines, but very common-place, every-day, ordinary sort of people.

So John Matson and his wife talked when they were together as any other respectable married couple might be supposed to converse, and Mary remained for very nearly another fortnight with Lina Storn, and was growing extremely difficult to manage and keep obedient; when one morning her husband entered, and exclaiming—

"I wonder what my wife will say to the news I have brought her?" sat down between her and Lina Storn.

"Good goods," it is said, "go in small bulk;" and we may presume the same adage applies to news. It did in Mr. Matson's case, at any rate, for a solitary sentence sufficed for his information.

"Messrs. Colke and Ferres have offered me their manager's place."

"Good gracious, John! and have you accepted it?" asked Mary.

"I did not waste much time over doing that, you may depend," he answered.

"And what about your business?"

"My business is *non est*," he replied. "I had to return my stock and put up the shutters. I have long seen ruin coming, but never expected such a deliverance from it as this."

"And why did you not tell me things were going wrong?" Mary asked, reproachfully.

"Because you were ill, dear."

"Only because I was ill?"

"For what other reason should I keep anything on earth from you?" he demanded. "But, Mary, you do not seem glad about the offer. What is the matter?"

"I am stunned," she answered, very simply. "I have not been used to good news; I want to hear all about it—how it came to pass—why you had to close—everything."

It did not take John Matson long to enlighten his wife on all these points. His landlord had brought affairs in Coleman Street to a crisis. To satisfy him, and protect the goods of various manufacturers lying in his warehouse, he had been forced to use money that had been laid aside to meet a promissory note. The holder immediately sued him upon it; and looking the state of his affairs straight in the face, Mr. Matson had thought it better and fairer to all his other creditors to clear his premises before judgment was issued.

The day he closed, Mr. Ferres passed the door, and stopped to ask the reason; and the young man told him in so many words that he was insolvent—his assets were not sufficient to cover his debts—a few of his creditors were imperative, and would give no time. He had come to the conclusion it was honester to close before he got deeper into the mud. He did not owe a great deal, but still more than he had any chance of paying. He feared there was nothing for him but the Court.

"What has been the reason of your failure?" asked Mr. Ferres.

"The want of capital, and Mr. Glenaen," answered John Matson promptly.

"Who are the people you have principally dealt with?" pursued his questioner.

The names were given without hesitation.

"And what do you mean to do when you leave here?" enquired Mr. Ferres.

"That depends on what I can get," was the reply; and thus they parted.

Four days afterwards, Mr. Ferres sent for him to come to the old house, where he found the two partners sitting in the apartment which had been Lina Storn's drawing-room.

"Mr. Matson," said the senior, "we had cause to be dissatisfied with our late manager, and so dismissed him. Mr. Ferres recommends that we should offer the situation to you. Do you consider you would be competent to fill it?"

"I am sure I could discharge the duties better than your last manager," he answered; "but I should not like to undertake to do all Mr. Storn did for you."

"Never mind Mr. Storn," said the other with an irritated manner; "we shall never expect any man to do the same work he did; neither shall we ever again place anyone on the footing he occupied. You will not have to fill his shoes; we shall not offer you his salary. Two hundred and fifty, with free house, coal, and gas, are our terms. You can think the matter over, and let us know to-morrow, if you like them;" which Mr.

Matson did first thing next morning, and then walked to Bow to tell his wife.

"We shall be nearer to you now a little," said Mary, turning to Mrs. Storn.

"I fear not," was the answer, gravely spoken. "We are going to move."

"Going to move?" repeated Mr. Matson. "When—where to? not far away, surely."

"No, not very—somewhere west. It seems the factory is not large enough for all purposes, and most of the rooms here can be made available."

"Oh!" said her visitor; then added, after a pause, "I wish I could get a leaf or two out of Mr. Storn's book."

"What would it do for you?" she asked.

"Make me rich," he answered.

"Would it make you happier?" Lina pursued.

"No, I think not," he replied, with that frank laugh of his; "now that I have got that situation, I am happy as a boy."

"What is the reason Messrs. Colke and Ferres offer you so much less than they gave Mr. Storn?" demanded Lina; something of a wife's pride and vanity in her husband prompting the question.

"Messrs. Colke and Ferres are wise men," answered Mr. Matson; "first, they know I am not to be named in the same day with your husband; and, secondly, they will never again give any man a salary out of which he can save a capital. I imagine they have had enough of that, and feel a little sore on the subject. Two hundred and fifty is wealth to me, however, Mrs. Storn," he added. "Do you think we can manage to make both ends meet now, Mary?"

Both ends meet! when they had almost screwed them together before, what might they not do now? It would have done Mr. Ferres' heart good to hear how the young wife laughed at the idea, and to know the amount of happiness he had been able to confer—ease of mind for John, rest of body for Mary. No more awful acceptances, no more impertinent duns; no more scanty meals and sleepless nights; nothing for the future, but regular work and certain pay.

"I have settled with a few troublesome people for you, Mr. Matson," said Mr. Ferres carelessly, the first morning John took possession of his new desk and stool. "The debts do not appear in the partnership books; so you can repay me out of your salary, as you find it convenient."

Thus the man without capital was pulled to shore at last, and entered on his new situation, whilst his wife made herself busy in the rooms Lina Storn had once glided through; and Lina herself, with the burden of old still resting upon her, and a presentiment of coming evil clouding her soul, very reluctantly, and not without much protest and resistance, took up her abode due west.

CHAPTER XXIV.

CYANOGEN.

MR. GORDON GLENAEN and Mr. Maurice Storn had come to the conclusion that the house at Bow was the best possible place they could choose for perfecting their experiments in cyanogen; and on the strength of this the royal fiat of the firm went forth. It was not meet that home, or comfort, or convenience should stand in the way of business, and therefore Mr. Storn told Lina he had chosen her a new abode, the antipodes of Bow, in the midst of wealth, and rank, and fashion, "away out," as the Easterns phrase it, " West."

I trust nobody will wish me to tell the precise reasons which induced the chemist to decide that a bran-new house in Belgravia, one brick thick in the walls, very thin indeed from back to front, and not much wider the other way, was the most suitable abode he could possibly, under the circumstances, have selected for his wife. He "thought it would be a change for Lina," he said; but the fact was, a change had taken place in himself. He had long worked for wealth, and now it was come, he desired to lay hand on some tangible proof that he had not slaved and toiled in vain, that his position was altered and altering; that some day, still further on in the visionary future, he should hold his head up amongst the famous of the land, and be known to thousands whom he did not know, as the discoverer of cyanogen.

The chemist was rising, and he felt it. A few years more and he could retire, buy property, devote himself to his family, relinquish chemistry as a profession, and study and experimentize simply as an amusement.

Looking back over his life he was a far different man to Messrs. Colke and Ferres' errand-boy, to Messrs. Colke and Ferres' clerk—aye, even to their manager—he was now a master over others, a servant in any sense no longer; old houses sent their travellers to him—new ones came, represented by one of the principals in person.

The best men in the trade cultivated his acquaintance, and were glad to talk five minutes with him on 'Change; and, accordingly, feeling that when the time came he had money and position to give in exchange for his first-class family ticket, Maurice determined, in his own mind, to hand his wife into the fashionable express, and let her keep his seat for him till he should be able to come and claim it for himself.

But Mr. Storn was not the kind of man to confess, or even to know, that dormant pride and ambition could have anything to do with him or his choice of a residence. It was for business purposes he moved his family from Bow, and it was for Lina's sake he selected a more cheerful and fashionable locality than any she had inhabited since she became his wife. It would be good for her to have more change, and greater variety. Mr. Storn had always entertained a slight misgiving that city people were not quite the sort of companions she wanted. Lina was to go West, and whilst he made money in their old home, she should be amusing herself by forming new connexions likely to benefit Geordie in the hereafter of boy and man that lay before him. For with the desire for his son to avoid low associates, had come also the wish for him to form high acquaintances.

Hitherto Mr. Storn had almost unconsciously aided his wife's endeavours to keep Geordie from contact with those amongst whom he was thrown.

Anything that held the child back from the very confines of boyhood seemed a pleasure to the chemist. His toys were all of the youngest description—his little books were not progressive. His laced and frilled trowsers, and braided frocks, and embroidered collars, which Mr. Glenaen said made him look like a little girl, were liked and countenanced by Mr. Storn. He did not want to make the boy a milksop, but he dreaded any change which might vulgarize him, and thus he imagined it was Geordie and Lina only he considered in his choice of a residence, forgetting that in Lina and Geordie was bound up himself.

So Mr. Storn chose the West End abode, and there in due time, with furniture and carpets, and hangings, with her carriage and men servants, and a number of other unnecessary appendages, Mrs. Storn, still a very young woman, was installed.

And society came to her. If that were what she had wanted to compass perfect felicity, Lina should in those days have been a happy woman.

Great chemists and wealthy manufacturers came to dine with Mr. Storn, and their wives and daughters drove in less ponderous carriages than those in vogue among the Easterners, to see the quondam manager's better half. The talk of these people was different to that of the people Lina had been ac-

customed to meet; they had much to say of the Row, and of
the Court; marvellous anecdotes concerning royalty were repeated amongst them—facts about which the queen herself was
ignorant, were patent to her majesty's most loyal subjects. In
those days Mudie's was not, but in lieu thereof the young
ladies had books from Bond and Holles Streets, and wept over
and criticized the works of men now famous, who were then
beginners. Mrs. Storn's visitors were learned in the fashions,
and knew every rag the most beautiful women in England had
worn at the last drawing-room—they went out to balls and
concerts, and flower shows: had boxes at the opera, and lovers
by scores; the young people had all been born to the station
such as it was they occupied, and were possessed, as a rule, of
easy, pleasant, lively, ladylike manners. To money and the
things it can purchase, they were well accustomed: and though
they stood quite as much, perhaps, on the edge of a note as
Miss Tryphenia Lindor, still it was a note of a higher key, and
they would have thought a contingent baronet a very poor
catch, indeed, for them to set their caps at. Their papas were
partners in houses that counted their capital by millions—they
had been educated at first-class schools, and learnt dancing with
future duchesses—they were to have fortunes and to marry
well; their brothers had entered the bar, the church, and the
army; all, except one out of each family, who was to step into
the father's shoes when he ceased wearing them, and accordingly, it was a natural consequence that Mrs. Storn's new
acquaintances should be more assured of their own rank, more
bound by *les convenances*, be more *au fait* in the ways of the
world, and altogether better informed—more fashionable and
less original, than the good people whom Lina had looked down
upon due east.

The Westerns entered into fewer domestic discussions; if
the mammas were their own housekeepers they kept the fact
quiet: if the young ladies had only one maid amongst them,
she was " still mine," to Laura, Caroline, and Jeanette.

Neither mother nor daughters knew anything of needlework
—a little knitting, netting, and cross stitch, sufficed to fill up
their few leisure minutes; flower painting, modelling, fantasias,
and *bravuras*, formed the employment of the unmarried portion
of Lina's intimates, whilst small chit-chat, maternal anxieties,
and not over-charitable gossip, passed the time for those who
having brought their accomplishments to a profitable market,
now considerately left the field open for another set of aspirants
for matrimonial promotion.

Altogether, without any special cause for complaint, Mrs.

Storn found general society out West, what, if she had seen a little more of the world, she might have known general society is in every place under heaven—a very vulgar, superficial, heartless, unnatural thing, well enough in its way, as a relaxation from mental toil or business anxieties or domestic duties, but nothing at all to fill up the void in a human life.

Something closer than society, nearer and dearer than well-dressed, well-bred women, we all need for the foundation of our happiness, and for this reason Mrs. Storn felt no less lonely in her new abode than she had done in her old one ; perhaps, indeed, she felt a degree more so, for Geordie playing with children of his own age, running about with other braided and frilled hopes of the nation, through the nation's parks, and going out to juvenile parties, was less her son than he had been in the garden at Bow, or under the shade of the ancient trees in Epping forest.   In the crowded West End churches he had now to sit up during the service, as other children did, and behave like a little gentleman, and it was but the natural consequence of "company," for him to be kept up-stairs in the nursery instead of sitting on the hearth-rug in the drawing-room playing with his cat.

It was pitiful to notice how Lina, through all, clung to her boy ; how she strove to get away from callers to walk out with her child—how she resisted all temptations to become a fashionable mother, and went up every night to Geordie's cot and made him whisper his prayers to her—how, through all changes and alterations in the household, she held to Janet as his nurse, and looked to his frocks and socks just the same as she had done in his babyhood, when she was but a manager's wife.

No change of abode, no variety of association could produce any alteration in Lina Storn's wants or wishes, virtues or defects.   The same, only undeveloped, she had been when Lina Maudsley as when she became Lina Storn, and she was precisely the same person as Maurice Storn's wife that she proved as Herbert Clyne's friend.   By no means a perfect woman, and yet still a very genuine one, possessed of a jealous, exacting nature, and a warm, devoted heart, with deep wells in her soul from which both good and evil were to be drawn, in the hereafter of her life, by some one.

In the voyage of existence she carried too much freight to be able to skim over the waters easily, and it was for this reason that a total change in every external respect produced no variation in her.   In the city, at Bow, out West, there was still the same sorrow and the same struggle—the old yearning for a love and a companionship that seemed never destined to be hers—the old warring against an affection and a congeniality which it was a sin and a shame even to think of.

Society threw up its barriers between the woman and her temptation, and she tried to thank it for its pains; but, at the same moment, society stole away a portion of that which had hitherto belonged exclusively to her—the sole blessing of her lonely matronhood, and the mother grieved, though she felt it was inevitable.

So Lina's life went on in her new house, whilst her husband worked harder and fiercer than ever, labouring over that new experiment as he had never, even in the most busy days of his active career, laboured before.

Hitherto he had never tried living away from his business—driving seven or eight miles for dinner—prefacing a long day's labour with a weary journey, and finishing it as host to a number of his new " connexions."

He had never before tried to unite the two labours of work and pleasure, never carried a feverish head into his laboratory, nor got himself mixed up in abstract questions that diverted his thoughts from chemistry. He tried to take too much out of himself and time—he endeavoured to be a manufacturer by day, a man of independent income in the evening, and an inventor by night—he strove to work the human machine too fast, and, at last, sank back in his laboratory chair, declaring there was something strange the matter with him : that he believed all knowledge and all sense was departing.

"Well, Storn, but this won't do at any price," said Mr. Glenaen, who sat opposite to him at the time. " We have too much risked in this confounded venture to play any tricks in the matter. I am afraid the sulphuric stuff has made you too confident of success. Remember, you did not discover that process in a day or in a night. You were not then beating out your gold over fifty different occupations. For Heaven's sake remember that, and don't play any tricks with this affair. We have made money, but we may lose it; and recollect that failure now would be ruin."

" I cannot help either," answered Mr. Storn, pettishly.

" Yes, you can," persisted the manufacturer. " The way you are getting on now is killing you, and doing us no good. You know as well as I do, that every day your bodily strength is decreasing, and your invention growing feebler : your expenses are heavy, and you are anxious, and nervous, and perfectly unfit for work. What the deuce you want with company, you who did without it, and did well, for so many years, I cannot imagine; but whether you want it or not, I must tell you plainly, Storn, that this West-end life won't do for an East-end chemist. If, as you say, your wife wants change, in God's name, let her have it; but take my advice, pitch the establishment, so far as you are concerned, over-board, for the present; never mind going home for dinner, have a shake-down here for the rare times when you want to go to bed; and give yourself up, body and soul, to this discovery. It's the devil for a man to live away from his business, and so I tell you."

"And yet it was you who first proposed breaking up my home here."

"Did I ever advise you to make a fool of yourself by going out West?" demanded Mr. Glenaen, defiantly. "I said, that with such an experiment as this going on, it would be well to have the premises clear of women, servants, and visitors. I said, we ought to have the two factories side by side, and that the garden might for a trifle be covered with sheds; but I never did advise you to cultivate a business connexion at your dinner table, nor to neglect your profession for your friends; did I?"

"I do not neglect my profession," answered Mr. Storn; "there is not a man in England works harder than I do."

"You work too hard," conceded the manufacturer, "and till you decide on taking that time for sleep, which you spend now in driving backwards and forwards to your home, and forming a connexion with people who will never do you any good, and who are not one bit cleverer than you—I see plainly the cyanogen will go to the wall; and if it is to go to the wall, the sooner you make up your mind the better, for the first loss will be the least."

"I am tired of my uniform want of success," said Mr. Storn, wearily.

"When did Maurice Storn ever before confess he was tired of anything?" inquired Mr. Glenaen, with some scorn. "When, till he was married, did he waver in any intention, fail in any endeavour? The first night I saw your wife, I said you were spoilt for a chemist. You may become a very fashionable man, Storn; but you will never be a remarkable one now."

"Yet it is since my marriage that I have perfected the acid," Mr. Storn replied.

"And confessed you were weary of cyanogen?" Mr. Glenaen added.

There was a pause—then the chemist said—

"You speak hard truths, Glenaen, in rough language; but still they are truths, and I will not quarrel with you about words. It seems hard that a man must go on as I have done

through years and years of work, and not be able at this time
to take even an hour's holiday. I have scarcely ever spent an
entire evening with my wife since I was married, and my boy
might almost as well be another man's child. I thought Lina's
spirits were suffering from the monotony of her daily life, and
fancied that if I removed the house entirely from the business,
I should be able to shake myself clear of trade, at all events in
the evening. I wanted to get some enjoyment out of my
labour, before the best of my life was passed; but I see you
are right, and that it won't do. I must slip on the harness
again. I suppose I shall die in it."

"Better wear out than rust out," retorted Mr. Glenaen;
"but for that matter, I don't see why you should die in harness at all. Perfect this experiment—work it out, and work it
up, as you alone can, and then retire. Devote twelve months
to your business, and after that as much pleasure as you will.
I confess it is beyond me to imagine what you want out West;
but that is your business, not mine. If you will only stick to
the cyanogen, I ask nothing more; but we have too much em-
barked in it, even to run the faintest shadow of a risk."

This was true; Maurice Storn had relied too much on his
previous success, and thought too little concerning the amount
of capital he was spending in his new undertaking. As fast as
the sulphuric acid brought in money, the cyanogen spent it;
and the cash which should have been returned to the other
concern in the shape of fresh plant, and improved utensils, was
now wasted in trying experiments that had not first been fully
tested.

He had swam out further than he was able to swim back,
and because of some unpleasant consciousness of the truth of
this fact, he did not refuse Mr. Glenaen's proffered help to the
shore. If twelve months of hard work and economy, and
shake-downs, and extempore meals were likely to make the
business answer, Maurice Storn was not the man to shrink
from the trial. But for the pride and ambition that wealth had
roused within him, he would have found even the best of his
new society very dull work indeed; yet it was in vain to deny
the fact, that the Bow manufacturer was a different person
from the city manager; that Maurice Storn, with a house in
Belgravia, was a far other man than Maurice Storn with a
house off Eastcheap.

Nevertheless, he determined, as he himself said, to slip his
head into the collar again, and to work less like a capitalist
than as a beginner. He went over and over his experiments
patiently, expended as little as possible in materials; gave him-

self up body and soul to the grand discovery which has baffled chemists of all nations, turned aside from his tests and his experiments, and his object, neither for business nor pleasure, but laboured on resolutely, till at last he felt himself in a position to say with certainty, " The theoretical part of the business is accomplished. I see my way, Glenaen—let us begin the practical."

And they did begin the practical. With the same energy as that with which he had fought his road through all sorts of chemical difficulties, and out-of-the-way experiments, Mr. Storn superintended the putting up of plant, and the laying out of money.

The garden was soon covered with sheds, the sheds were speedily filled with vats.

Workmen were hurried on—tradespeople looked up continuously; but there was one point still darkness to Maurice Storn—his furnaces.

" There is some better way of constructing them," he said to his partner, " and I won't build another till I have found the plan. We must have the newest and best of everything, in order to test my scheme properly. What are we to do, Glenaen ?—Where can any better furnaces be got at ?"

" Sharwood is in advance of us," replied Mr. Glenaen, after a moment's pause.

" How do you know ?" demanded the other.

" He was able to undersell me," said the manufacturer.

" Humph !" said Mr. Storn, to whom this evidence was conclusive, then added, " But how are we to obtain a sketch ?"

" Bribe his manager," suggested Mr. Glenaen.

The hint was conveyed in plain language, but apparently Mr. Storn did not like it, for his face flushed, and he answered—

" We should not care to have our people bribed, Glenaen."

" But they are, for all that you know," retorted the other coolly. " I could tell you half-a-dozen firms that have tried to get at our process through our men. If we had a manager to-morrow, our secret would be sold before seven days were out. That is one of the pleasures of chemistry. You must either work or trust, and if you trust you are safe to be beggared. It is the way of the trade, man—you can have your sketch at a price."

" I don't think it is honourable," hesitated Mr. Storn. " If other people do wrong, that is no reason why we should fail in the right. I wonder if Sharwood would give us a sketch in exchange for some good hints I could assist him with."

" Would he give you his head, do you think ?" demanded Mr.

Glenaen, with a sneer; "or would you tell him how you save
your spongy platinum? I think you are mad, Maurice. Is
not chemistry a game in which every device is allowable? Is
not every man's hand raised against you, and shall you not
raise your hand to protect yourself? A chemist is a very Ish-
maelite, and it won't do for you to commence standing on very
nice scruples at this time of day. It is not very often I open
a religious book, but the other Sunday, at Lindor's, I dropped
on a Magazine Madam had been making believe to read, and
the first paragraph I saw, contained an account of Foley the
fiddling fellow, you know, who went twice to Sweden, to see
the splitting mills. I am sure you remember all about the
thing. Well, the editor, after stating how he enriched himself and benefited his country, declares that it was 'the most
extraordinary instance of persevering self-devotement in modern
times.' Now I should like to be told, Storn, what difference
there is between bribing a manager, and blinding his master.
If that man were right, (and the editor of a good publication
certainly holds him up as an example to be followed,) you must
be right also. Suppose you succeed in taking the nitrogen
out of the atmosphere, you'll be a benefactor to the human
race—all personal feelings, or rather notions, should be thrown
overboard; the end justifies the means; besides, you don't
want to injure Mr. Sharwood's trade; you only want to benefit
yourself; you are certain this cyanogen won't interfere with
him, ergo, there can be no possible harm in tipping his manager
a twenty-pound note. It will be a help to the poor man, and
no loss to his employer."

"Do you know anything of Sharwood's manager?" asked
Mr. Storn.

"Not much."

"Well, I do; and I believe he is about as capable of being
bribed, as I should have been when at Colke's."

"Ah! then perhaps there is a foreman," remarked Mr.
Glenaen, with the greatest sang froid. "One man will do
quite as well as another, and the foreman will cost the least."

"You are a philosopher," said Mr. Storn.

"Or a tradesman," supplied the other: "fact is, if a thing
has to be done, I know it would never suit me to affect over-
niceness about the means. In business, I draw a distinction
between being honest and honourable. The first is the life of
commerce, the latter is death. Honesty answers to modesty
—honour to prudery—and—"

"Stop, for heaven's sake," exclaimed his partner. "Grant
me the thing is wrong, though necessary, and I'll do it; but

don't in defending the wrong, throw mud on the right. I suppose I am a fool, but I can't stand that."

"As you will," was the careless answer, "only tell me one thing. Is our cyanogen to fail because of these furnaces?"

"Not if I can help it."

"And what do you propose doing in the matter?"

"I will think, and let you know to-morrow."

"So be it!" Mr. Glenaen replied; and nodding a satisfied good-bye, he turned towards the door, and left Mr. Storn to his own reflections.

CHAPTER XXV.

A SLIGHT MISCHANCE.

THE morrow came, but brought with it no decision from Mr. Storn; indeed the reflections to which his partner left him at the conclusion of the last chapter, bore so little apparent fruit, that at the end of a week Mr. Glenaen's patience was exhausted, and he determined to get the needful sketches himself. It was but a natural consequence of this determination for him to present himself one morning before Maurice with a roll of papers, and the exultant words—

"Here they are, Storn."

"Here what are?" enquired the individual addressed.

"Why, the furnace plans, to be sure; while you have been asleep, I have been at work, and a deuced sight better my acting is, than your thinking—at least so it seems to me."

"How did you get them?" asked Mr. Storn, stretching out his hand for the drawings.

"Ah, you can take them now!" remarked Mr. Glenaen; "my fingers, I suppose, you thought were hot enough to pull them out of the fire; and now you seize them when they are cool. But hang it, what does it matter which of us ran the risk now that they are got? Make the most of them, my boy, for I was up best part of last night, and had to stand a ten-pound note besides. Holloa! you don't seem satisfied; what's the matter now?"

"These things are not of the slightest use to us," said Mr. Storn in a disappointed tone. "There is only one part of the plan we could adopt, and that is a very minor one. I am very sorry you should have had your trouble for nothing; but it would be folly to commence building furnaces like these—sheer waste of time and money."

"Then I wish I had my lost time and money back again," quoth Mr. Glenaen in an aggrieved tone. "I thought when I finished those confounded sketches, we were made up; and now we are on our backs again. Can't you contrive a furnace yourself? Come, set on, and draw one now."

"I have been thinking a great deal about these furnaces," said Mr. Storn, quietly laying aside the pencil and paper his partner thrust before him; "and after much hesitation and consideration, have made up my mind at last. I shall go north, to the only place, so far as I know, where this same experiment has ever been attempted before. They got a good many notions from Germany, I know; and at all events, I shall pick up some useful hints. Take the sulphuric acid off my hands, and let me go."

"Do you expect permission to go over any factory in England?" asked Mr. Glenaen slowly.

"Yes, I do."

"Then look you here, Storn; you had better stay at home and take a course of shower-baths, for I really think you are going mad. Have you forgotten what I told you about, the time I was manager here for Colke's house? Ferres sent me to their place to see after some wrong goods that had been sent forward for shipment; and of course I thought there would be no difficulty made about my having a look at the works. But, by Jove! I never was let put foot across the threshold. Sensible man, Colke, very."

"Nevertheless, I am determined to try my fortune."

"Do so, and fail then," retorted Mr. Glenaen.

"I am not much in the habit of failing in anything I attempt," answered Mr. Storn somewhat coldly; "but at any rate, succeed or fail, I am determined to try."

So spake the chemist: and as he had thought long ere he spoke at all, before night all his preparations for departure were complete, and late in the evening he sate alone in his laboratory waiting for Mr. Glenaen, and calculating in a sort of arithmetical way his chances of success and failure. He had bidden Lina good-bye—telling her he was going on a business journey to the provinces—kissed Master Geordie, who begged hard to accompany him—left behind him sufficient money to oil the domestic wheels in his absence—made every necessary arrangement for his wife's comfort, and the well-being of the sulphuric business—and had now ten minutes' leisure to sit still, and think about what he was purposing to do—and the possible and probable results of the step he was about to take.

At the bottom of his heart Maurice did not like the scheme,

though it was his own. It might be all very well to praise a man in a book for a discovery like that affected by Foley—but standing face to face with the enterprise was quite a different matter. It did not seem honest, it did not seem honourable, he thought, using in his own heart the word Mr. Glenaen had condemned as above the low level of his trade ideas—but still, spite of these misgivings, Maurice Storn never swerved from his purpose. The question of expediency seemed more important than a fastidious examination of right and wrong—too much was involved in the cyanogen for any nice scruples to be permitted to stand in the way of its success. If by this expedient he gained knowledge sufficient to enable him to perfect his plan—why, he should have done no harm to anybody—whilst he benefited himself and everyone connected with him. He would pilfer no secret, sketch no plan—but this—he would try to do a dishonourable thing honourably—and lend himself to evil, not for evil's sake, but that great good might come out of it. At all events he should not be tampering with inferiors —the matter would be settled betwixt himself and the principal—and if the principal were not sufficiently awake to see through the *ruse*, Maurice Storn could not be blamed for his stupidity. It was the all fair in war motto the chemist acted upon—and a very appropriate motto, too, for chemistry is a war to the death—and fierce to this hour is the battle among the contending parties.

With some such thoughts as the foregoing Mr. Storn amused and employed himself until the sound of his partner's heavy foot upon the stairs interrupted his meditations, and induced him to rise and open the laboratory door for his visitor.

It was getting dusk; and Mr. Glenaen, not prepared for the figure that met his view, suddenly pulled up with—" Mr. Storn engaged."

"No, sir," answered his partner, "walk in, if you please."

Mr. Glenaen did walk in, and slamming the door after him, stood looking at his friend with all his eyes.

"May I be hanged if I knew you, Maurice!" he exclaimed at last—"but what the deuce are you thinking of doing?"

"I am thinking of bettering my condition, and looking out for work in the North."

"Work!—what kind of work?" asked Mr. Glenaen.

"Any sort that is well paid—I am a strong, active, likely fellow—willing to turn my hand to anything. Do you think I shall find a man to hire me?"

"Storn, you are a trump!" was the manufacturer's complimentary observation, as he turned his partner round and round,

and surveyed him first near at hand, and afterwards at a distance. "Your own father would not know you."

"Nor my own mother," added Mr. Storn, sorrowfully. "I
don't mean in appearance—but in the part I am about to play.
I am quite sure Mabel Storn never thought she should bear a
child likely to turn spy."

"Turn gammon," was Mr. Glenaen's unsentimental conclusion. "Women know nothing of the necessities of business,
and therefore it is better to keep them ignorant of its details.
I dare say your mother would be shocked at many things you
have done—and there is no use turning soft about her now.
You have succeeded perfectly, Storn, even to the hands."

It was true:—a person more learned in such matters than
Mr. Glenaen might safely have pronounced Maurice's disguise
unexceptionable. In a workman's suit of fustian, the trowsers
short in the legs, and wide across the hips—the jacket mighty
short in the waist, destitute here and there of buttons—a coarse
shirt—strong, ill-made shoes, and a fur cap—Mr. Storn could
scarcely have been recognised even by a person let into the
secret of his metamorphosis.

And yet it was not even so much in his dress that the chemist had effected an alteration as in his appearance. He had
rubbed nitrate of silver into his face till it looked as though
begrimed with the dirt and dust of years. He had pared his
nails straight across, and stained his hands; he had cut his
hair short behind, and arranged it altogether differently upon
his forehead; he had shaved off his whiskers, and thrown back
his collar, leaving his throat partially exposed. There was a
stubble growth of beard upon his chin; he had left that pur-
posely.

"With a slight variation in my speech I shall do," he said,
when his friend had sufficiently examined and admired him.
"And now I must say good-bye for the present, for I mean to
catch the night mail for the North."

"Where shall I write to you?" demanded his partner.

"That can I not say," returned Mr. Storn. "I will write
to you; and just let me know how Lina and the boy are getting
on, will you, like a good fellow? thanks;" and the chemist
locked the laboratory door, and with a hasty good bye was off.
Before Mr. Glenaen, who followed in more orderly style, could
reach the front gate, however, he met Maurice running back.

"What have you forgotten?" demanded the manufacturer.

"Just come into the house again for a second," said Mr.
Storn in answer; and he darted up the stairs, taking two or
three at a time, entered his sanctum, struck a light, and com-

menced rummaging the pockets of the clothes he had thrown off a short time before.

"What a nuisance!" he exclaimed. "I must go home again; and yet still how on earth to do it with this stain on my face; it will take me half the night to get it off."

"Can't I go instead?" asked Mr. Glenaen. "Is it anything particular you have forgotten?"

"Yes, the key of a cabinet; in the hurry I am afraid I forgot to lock the place up, and it is full of all sorts of things—chemicals and poisons. But I won't go back, I will write to Lina, and get you to forward the note without delay."

"It shall be with her in an hour," said Mr. Glenaen; and thus assured, Maurice sat down and wrote:—

"DEAR LINA,

"I have either left in the door, or dropped on the carpet, or lost altogether, the key of that little cabinet on the right of the fire-place in my dressing-room. If you can find the key, lock the door and put it away carefully; but if it has been mislaid, send for a carpenter immediately and have a fresh lock put on; stay with him whilst he finishes the job, for there are some most dangerous poisons in the place. Don't delay, but see to this immediately. I shall be moving about for a week or two, so you must not be uneasy if you do not hear from me, as I expect to be very busy. Take care of yourself and Geordie.

"Yours affectionately,
"MAURICE."

"There," said the writer, as he concluded this epistle, "will you be sure to send this on to-night without fail?"

"I will," was Mr. Glenaen's reply; and with a grasp of the hand the men parted, and in another minute the chemist was hurrying through the darkness to his object.

"Grout," shouted Mr. Glenaen to one of his people, as he re-entered the factory, "take that note to Mrs. Storn; don't be three hours on the way, but deliver it into her own hands. Do you hear?"

"Yes, sir."

"And I shall send home your wages by your brother, to make sure you don't get drunk by the road."

"Very well, sir."

"And now be off, for I want her to have that as soon as possible."

Mr. Grout was off in an instant; but considering that his

employer's wishes could be just as well compassed by his eldest boy as by himself, he betook himself home, and dispatched that juvenile with the missive. And the juvenile, feeling somewhat exhausted by the time he reached Charing Cross, paused to recruit his strength by having a game at pitch and toss with a few kindred spirits recreating themselves in Trafalgar Square, during the progress of which innocent diversion one of his companions pulled the lad's cap off, and by so doing landed the note, which he had deposited there for safe keeping, on the pavement.

A very sorry missive it looked when lifted, muddy, and wet, and disreputable, so bad indeed that the boy, smearing it over first with his dirty sleeve, and then with the front of his ragged jacket, whimpered out that he did not know what to do at all; for if any complaints were made, he should get such a precious licking at home.

In a moment public sympathy was extended to his situation, and much sagacious counsel was proffered him by the friends of his adversity; the burden of the advice being, that he should not deliver the letter at all, but just drop it peaceably into the kennel, and let well alone.

Which advice the young Mercury followed but too closely, and then went in for all sorts of reckless amusement, returning in due course, and telling his father he had left the note all right. As he had in the mud of the horse-road, where it was trampled in the dirt and swept off into the scavenger's cart; while Mrs. Storn, sitting by her son's cot, did not dream a letter was lying out in the street which ought to have been delivered to her. She never received the note. Oh! woe for Lina!

CHAPTER XXVI.

MR. STORN ASSUMES A NEW CHARACTER.

MEANTIME Mr. Storn was posting off to the North, and twenty-four hours later found himself in the common room of a third-rate inn in Newcastle, waiting with what patience he might for the reply to a letter he had despatched about an hour previously.

"Suppose that after all they should not be in want of hands," he muttered to himself. "Suppose my journey should prove a failure, and that I have to return beaten. But no! that must not be, psha! what am I thinking of?"

He went out and stood on the steps of the hotel. It was a

wet, drizzling night; and as he looked up and down the dirty, sloppy street, a sort of desponding weariness came over him.

Even at the best of times, Newcastle-on-Tyne is not a remarkably inspiriting place; and seeing it as Maurice Storn chanced to see it, in bad weather, and not very good spirits, and moreover in a state of doubt and uncertainty, was enough to give any ordinary man the blues.

"Does he not think it worth while to answer me?" thought Maurice, forgetting for the moment the fact that he had dropped his actual station, and placed himself in a subordinate position; and so he went on chewing the cud of impatient, uncomfortable ideas, till he espied a groom bearing a letter, who first looked up enquiringly at the sign-board swinging over Mr. Storn's head, and then was about to enter the house, when Maurice stopped him.

"Are you from Mr. Madot?"

"Yes," was the curt reply.

"Have you a letter for me?" pursued the chemist.

"No; but a message for John Steinbach."

"I am your man then," said Maurice. "Now what is it?"

"Mr. Madot wants to see you."

"When?"

"To-night. Now. I am to take you to his house."

"All right," answered the supposititious Steinbach. "Lead the way. I will follow."

Off they started along the dirty streets, badly paved and dimly lighted, with the drizzling rain coming down faster and thicker every step they took.

"A nasty night to be out," remarked the man, as, suddenly turning a corner, they came close on the canal; whilst the lamps glimmered fainter, and the rain poured faster down upon them. "A nasty night!" but Maurice made no answer.

Through the darkness, he had discerned a block of buildings on the other side of the water.

"What place is that?" he asked after a moment. It was the first time he had opened his mouth since they left the hotel.

"Our factory," replied the man; and, at the words, Maurice Storn stopped and looked at the dark, shapeless mass curiously.

"It seems an enormous place," he said at last.

"Ah, you should see the factory Master is building at Earnshaw! It is twice the size of this!"

"And, in the name of Heaven, where is Earnshaw?" exclaimed Mr. Storn.

"It is about thirty miles from here," replied his informant. "It is not a town, but a property. The firm have a lease of it from Sir Hugh Clyne."

The words fell like a revelation on Maurice Storn's ears.

"Who shall say there was not some reason in that old man's madness?" he thought; and, as he travelled back in memory to the days of his managership, when he believed Captain Maudsley to be deranged, and had little sympathy with a mania different from his own, he fell into so profound a reverie concerning words and incidents long forgotten, that his companion could not get him to utter another sentence.

"Was it not strange," he asked himself, "that there should be a place called Earnshaw? Was it not singular it should be owned by Sir Hugh Clyne, and that they should know his grandson? Was it not beyond all things unaccountable that he should come down to Newcastle, and by so peculiar a chance hear spoken by a servant a name which he had forgotten for years, and scarcely believed in ever? Suppose there were a place called Earnshaw, of which he could no longer entertain a doubt, and that by some curious link Lina had a claim to it? How odd it would be for her to turn out an heiress after all! And how would it stand with him, and had he done quite right in marrying her? Was it a match her father would have liked? How would this discovery affect Lina, Geordie—himself? What ought he to do? How act in this matter? Clearly perfect his cyanogen first, and investigate her claims afterwards." And, as Mr. Storn arrived at this sensible conclusion, he lifted his head and found they had arrived at their journey's end.

"Wait here a moment," said his companion; and Maurice, true to his new character, waited in the hall, cap in hand, while the butler went to inform Mr. Madot of his arrival.

It was a new thing for Maurice Storn to have to stand on the mat in any man's hall, and a sort of proud, defiant feeling swelled up in his breast, as if he did not like it. He had scarcely time, however, to know that pride and prudence were having a hard struggle for ascendency, before the butler returned, and with a brief—

"Come this way," beckoned him forward.

Never, during the whole course of his life, had Mr. Storn entered an apartment that struck him so forcibly as the one into which he was, with scant ceremony, ushered. A long lofty room, with fireplaces at both ends; four draperied windows occupying the one side, and the other fitted with shelves, which were filled from floor to ceiling with books. A library table occupied the centre of the floor, and between the windows were statues that had been brought at great trouble and expense from abroad. The apartment was lighted with

shaded lamps, and, as Maurice walked down to the fireplace at
the further end, he could not help noticing that there was
scarcely a product of chemistry but was represented in some
way or other in the room.

On a couch, near the hearth, lay the man of whom he had
come in search. There were traces of sickness and care upon
his face, but Maurice was surprised to see how young he
looked.

"Not more than thirty," thought the chemist, as he looked
down on the slight, elegant figure that lay before him. He
was handsome too! with high forehead, and Grecian features,
and large, quick, grey eyes. Mr. Storn felt his pride die out
when their glances met, for the countenance he beheld was not
one that seemed capable of deceiving any person, and it was
hardly fair and honourable to try to deceive him.

"Sit down," said Mr. Madot, and he waved his white hand
towards a chair. "Your name is John Steinbach, I think,"
and he drew a small writing table nearer to his side, and took
Maurice's letter from it. "Where have you worked? What
can you do?"

His visitor had worked in many places, and could do several
things. Being out of a berth, however, he was willing to turn
his hand to whatever his employer might wish. If Mr. Madot
would try him, he was sure he could give satisfaction.

"It strikes me," Mr. Madot said at last, "that you write
better, and speak more fluently than I should have expected,
from your appearance. You seem to have received a tolerable
education."

"I was not brought up in so low a station as that I now fill,"
was the answer, spoken so slowly, that Mr. Madot, somehow,
felt he had hurt the man's feelings; "but my father died when
I was a mere child, and though my mother did what she could,
still she could not support us both. I had to turn out into the
world as errand-boy, and have since put my hand to anything
that offered. I want to do that now."

"What brought you down to Newcastle?" enquired Mr.
Madot.

"I wished to leave London, and a mate of mine told me this
was a place where I should likely get work, and good wages."

"With whom were you last?"

"With Glenaen and Storn, of Bow," was the ready answer.

"Oh!" exclaimed Mr. Madot, and he leaned back again on
the couch. "Those are the sulphuric acid people, are they
not?" he asked, after a pause.

"Yes, sir."

" In what capacity were you there?" was the next question.

" I emptied the furnaces, cleaned the vats; sometimes checked the men's time, in fact did anything Mr. Storn thought necessary."

" It is strange he liked to part with you."

" He does not care if he had to change his hands every week. I have often heard him say so."

" He must be a fortunately-minded individual," remarked Mr. Madot. " Why did you leave him ? I forget what you said was your reason."

" I was tired of sulphuric acid, and I wanted to better my condition. I wished to get a place where there would be a likelihood of advancement; but with Messrs. Glenaen and Storn, a man may stay at his five and twenty or thirty a week for ever. They do so much of the work themselves, sir, that they do not require to pay the wages, and employ the sort of people others do. The best man on the premises is no higher than a labourer."

" A useful hint to me," said Mr. Madot, with a smile; " but now for yourself. I have no vacancy at present likely to suit you. At the same time, I never like to let an intelligent fellow slip through my fingers, and if you like to work at odd jobs for a while, and prove to me that I shall find it my advantage to retain you in my employment, I will give you, should your late master's account prove satisfactory, five and twenty shillings a week, as a commencement."

" The wages are low, sir," said Maurice, in a tone of remonstrance.

" Work, and they will get higher," was the laconic answer.

" Well, sir, I suppose I must accept your terms ?"

" There is no compulsion in the matter," returned Mr. Madot. " If you don't like the offer, don't take it."

" How soon would there be a chance of an advance, sir ?" enquired Maurice.

" Whenever I see you deserve it," was the reply.

" Then, on that understanding, sir, I accept your terms," he said. " Shall I call again, or——".

" I will send for you," Mr. Madot finished abruptly, and with a short good night, in answer to the other's respectful bow, he dismissed his visitor.

" A most remarkably odd sort of fellow," he mused, when he began to think over the interview; " comes from a good school though, and may be made useful."

By the next mail, a letter was despatched to " Messrs. Glenaen, Storn, and Co., Chemical Manufacturers, Bow, London," making enquiries as to the abilities and character of the person John Steinbach, which enquiries being satisfactorily answered by Mr. Gordon Glennen, who signed for the firm ; the new hand was taken on in the Newcastle factory, and commenced his work and his investigations at the lowest rung of the labour ladder.

During the whole of his premature manhood and middle age, Maurice Storn had never been accustomed to spare himself; when there was an experiment to be tried, a discovery to be made, or a difficulty to be overcome, he had always thrust his shoulder to the wheel, and striven with a will to turn it. In Messrs. Colkes' yard, if a heavy cask of tartar, or an awkward carboy were wanted out of the way, the manager had never been above putting his hand to the lift; in his own factory he had never hesitated to fling off coat and waistcoat, turn up his shirt sleeves, and rush into any job, however difficult. He had always used his strength, and hardened his muscles, and accordingly thought there would be nothing difficult in the task he so fearlessly set himself to perform; but he found, before three days were over, that it is one thing to work under the spur of a moment, and another to labour from six in the morning till six at night. Hard and sore he wrought, conquering, with that giant will of his, the inclination to walk off and take to comparative ease again—to skulk away to sleep—to sit down and rub his aching legs and arms. "Every morning," he wrote to his partner, "I am wakened at half-past five by that confounded factory-bell, and from that time on for twelve weary hours, there is no rest for the sole of my foot." And it was true; Mr. Madot was trying him, wanting to see of what stuff the ready-spoken, superior-looking workman was made of; he put him to all sorts of jobs, and had always three or four awkward things laid out for Steinbach to do. It was an everlasting "Steinbach, clean out that vat;" "Steinbach, to-morrow I want that rubbish wheeled out of the yard;" "Steinbach, after dinner wash out those filters, and then carry the ashes away from the furnace." So sure as Mr. Madot caught sight of his new man, he set him to a fresh job, and through dirt and filth, and bodily and mental annoyance, Mr. Madot's new man steered straight on to his object.

Would Lina have recognized her husband as standing in the barge he emptied coals out on to the side of the canal. Black and heated, could she have believed it was really Maurice who stood there, taking pull about at the beer pot with his still blacker and more heated mate. "Twenty tons of coals to be shovelled over the side," Maurice had groaned to himself when he flung off his jacket in the morning, and twenty tons were really landed on the bank before he quit for the night.

How he could have sworn when Mr. Madot came to where they were working, and, in consideration of the quantity unloaded, doubled the ordinary perquisite given to the men over and above their day's wages.

"Steinbach, you can wheel a couple of hundred home with you," said the principal.

"May the devil burn them," thought Storn; but he said audibly, "Thank you, sir," and he loaded his barrow and wheeled his allowance to his lodgings, along the narrow streets, cursing every step of the road, and ready to lie down on the pavement with very weariness.

"Could I not have kicked the confounded barrow, with its load of rubbish, over into the street fifty times," he said to his partner next time he wrote; "I'd be almost ashamed to tell you how often it came into my head to give some fellow half-a-crown for liberty to turn the coals right down into his cellar. My landlady thought I was mad, I believe, for I left the lot in the middle of the pavement, and declared whoever liked to bring them into the house might have them. I went right up to bed, and without eating, or washing, or undressing, fell fast asleep. This is work, Glenaen."

As the days passed by, however, his position was bettered; first, he was employed by Mr. Madot to make purchases of tools, to wash out his own private chemical apparatus, and, at last, to lend a hand in his laboratory. As labourer, messenger, and assistant he laid himself out to be of use, and at length he so edged and elbowed his way up, that without being specially distinguished by any mark of favour, or having his wages increased or his hours shortened, he found himself standing at Mr. Madot's elbow as confidential man—the spectator of his experiments, successes, and failures.

One day Mr. Madot gave him a five pound note for a casual suggestion, the result either of remorse or carelessness, and Maurice Storn pocketed the money and comforted his conscience by thinking that his principal would make thousands by the hint.

All manufacturers know how to turn the brains of workmen to account, and, finding that Steinbach was a clever fellow, with plenty of head and lots of industry, the chemist determined at length on giving him some definite situation in the factory, with a proportionate increase of wages.

And the new situation landed Maurice Storn at the port he wanted.

Night after night, when he returned home to his lodgings, he sat down and wrote and drew for hours, sketching this section from memory, and explaining in notes at the bottom of his paper the meaning of the lines that stretched from A to B, or that rose from C to D.

When he had finished his supper of pig's cheeks and brown bread and weak ale ; when he had got rid of one or two mates who would come and smoke with him, and shut out his inquisitive and buxom landlady for the evening, he lit his candle and took his rolls of cartridge paper, and sat up till the small hours, trying to make his drawings as clear and intelligible as possible. It was in vain his fellow-workmen tried to entice him away to beer-shops, to lectures, to gaffs, or fairs, or shows, or anything. He got a name for steadiness and respectability which proved rather an annoyance to him than otherwise ; he was appointed member of one or two clubs, the chairman of divers societies ; he was offered four wives, and might have been as popular as a Chartist orator or the leader of a strike.

Had he stayed there, Maurice Storn might have achieved greatness—he might have been head amongst his fellow workmen— right-handed man to his principal—he might have worked his way up from servant to master, and climbed to the very highest rung of the ladder on which he had set his foot so low.

He might have reached out his hand to grasp most things he beheld within view, for Maurice Storn was no common man, and in that time of servitude and endurance he tested and proved his powers.

He might have made himself as necessary to his employer as fire, or air, or water ; he might have done anything—but it was not to be. One night he went home from his work and found a letter waiting for him. Within half-an-hour he was posting back to London.

The note, though directed by Mr. Glenaen, was from his wife, and contained but nine words :—

"For God's sake, Maurice, come home. Geordie is dying."

<hr>

CHAPTER XXVII.

GEORDIE.

MRS. STORN could not be said to have passed a particularly happy time during the first three weeks of her husband's absence. She thought — and who may blame her for the thought?—that Maurice should have left her his address, and told her where he was going. Perhaps the experience of years had taught her it was useless to expect information concerning the business which compelled him to leave London: but the old angry feeling arose within her when he said at parting, that Glenaen would forward all her letters if she sent them on to the factory; and she secretly determined, that if her husband never heard from her till the end of time, she would send no letter through Mr. Glenaen.

A very pretty piece of feminine petulance, that had, however, its root in the better and deeper soil of pained affection and misunderstood feeling. She made up her mind, in fact, to hurt herself and worry him, so that on his return she might have the pleasure of placing her grievance before him in an intelligible form : and the consequence of this resolution, and her adhesion to it, was, that she felt extremely miserable and dissatisfied with every person and everything, herself included; not forgetting Mr. Glenaen—never forgetting him. When he " dropped her a line," to say he was writing to Mr. Storn, and would forward any letters she might have, Lina returned for answer that " she had nothing particular to say which could not wait till Mr. Storn's return. Meantime, she and Geordie were well." This was her unvarying response to all the manufacturer's polite attentions, varied, however, at the close of a fortnight, by an intimation that she would feel obliged by Mr. Glenaen letting her know how her husband was, as she had not heard from him since his departure.

Poor wife, she was growing very anxious to receive some tidings of him, getting most anxious for his return; for in those days Mr. Clyne came too much to the house, and Lina knew it.

Frail though the breakwater of old had been to keep the waves of a sinful ocean from flooding her soil, and bearing her back with them to some distant shore, the name of which she was even afraid of whispering to herself—still it had been a sort of protection to her against him; but now she had no one to come in and interrupt those endless conversations—no one to divide the responsibility of that dangerous intimacy with her. She was alone then—more thoroughly and completely alone than she had ever been during the whole of her solitary wifehood with her temptation.

She felt it was such—she struggled against the power of the tempter : against the yearning of her poor heart for sympathy and companionship; against the seeming neglect and unkindness of her husband—struggled, because of duty and religion, for the sake of her husband, for love of her boy—struggled then, before she had forgotten God and man, before the night of sorrow darkened her understanding, before she was crazed with trouble—struggled then, armed with virtue and determination, and I am proud, for her sake, to write it, spite of the miserable defeat of the drearier future—won.

Feigning occupation, she denied herself to all visitors in the morning, and under pretence of an almost continuous headache, was rarely visible in the evening; she used to sit in her dressing-room after Geordie went to bed, in her voluntary solitude, crying as though some great trouble had fallen upon her. Perhaps the coming event was casting its shadow before; but Lina saw only the passing events of her life, and found enough in them to vex and harass her.

Why did not Maurice write? Not knowing how he was engaged, she might well wonder at his silence; not knowing that he would have been ashamed to send her his address, to tell her he was passing under a feigned name, she might well marvel at the channel through which he had asked her to forward his letters. Time passed quickly with him, but slowly to the unemployed woman waiting for his return; he could rest for a while satisfied with hearing that she and the boy were well; but every post that brought no letter direct from him, was a trial and a trouble to his wife.

At last she thought she would give in, and write; she would put her pride aside, and send a note to Mr. Glenaen, and beg him to enclose it to her husband; she would not write crossly, nor say a discontented word; she would only tell him she was uneasy at not hearing from him—that she feared he might not be well—or that something had happened; she would entreat him to let her know if he were ill, and to tell her how she might come and join him.

She would say she felt very lonely—she would put many things in the note; and as she sate thinking about them, Lina's eyes filled with tears, for now that she was in uncertainty about his health, now that absence had softened his faults, and thrown her altogether on her own resources, Mrs. Storn's love came back, and she would have given the world to be able to lay bare her heart before her husband, and ask him to spare her such another trial—to help her, and to teach her to be right.

She would send some kind of a letter to Maurice, so she determined, and had the pen between her fingers to accomplish her intention, when the post brought a note for her. From her husband! to be sure—how delightful; no matter now that it came in an envelope directed by Mr. Glenaen; she tore open the seal, and read—

"What is the reason, my dear, dear Lina, that you have never written me one line since I left home? But that I have heard from Glenaen that you and Geordie were well, I should have felt most seriously uneasy. Has my wife been busy, or lazy, or what? Do send me a note to say how you are. I have been so dreadfully busy, I could not write before, and I knew Glenaen would tell you I was well. I have stayed longer than I at first intended, but expect to make a good thing altogether out of my journey. If you are short of money, send to Bow for whatever you require. I hope soon to be home now, and most probably will not write again before leaving here. Be sure to let me hear from you immediately on receipt. If I had the heart to scold you, I think I should, for making me so anxious. Kiss Geordie for me. I shall bring him some pictures.

"Ever your own,
MAURICE.

"Did you remember about the cabinet?"

"About the cabinet?" Lina repeated to herself; and she puzzled her brain to recollect what cabinet she was to have remembered. She wondered if he had wanted any new article of furniture purchased—if he had ever named such a thing as a cabinet in her hearing—if he had left any directions to which she should have attended; but she could not think of anything; she would write and ask him what he meant; and accordingly, lifting the pen she had laid down when his letter arrived, began—

"My dearest Maurice," and was going on very rapidly with "I cannot imagine what you mean about—" when Geordie rushed into the room. "Mamma, mamma," he cried, "come and play at tip tap toe."

"After a little, my darling," she answered; "but I am busy just now, writing to papa: he has sent Geordie lots of kisses, and will bring him back such beautiful books; now run away and amuse yourself till I finish my letter."

It might have been as well for Lina had she never finished it; but she did not know that, as, scribbling on line after line, she told her husband why she had not written previously, and how sorry she felt for her silence, and how anxious she had been about him; and she filled three sheets of note paper before she thought of coming to an end, and she wrote on the inside of her envelope with two sharp notes of interrogation, "What about the cabinet?"

Then she sent her epistle on to Mr. Glenaen, and was just

going to call Geordie for his game, when a servant informed her Mr. Clyne was waiting in the drawing-room.

She could meet him now, no longer a neglected, solitary wife, but a very happy woman, with a letter from her husband safe in her pocket; perhaps she was glad to be able to say she had heard direct from Mr. Storn at last; at all events she ran down stairs, and entered the apartment where Herbert was waiting for her.

Not a bit changed in manner, or look, or nature from the Herbert who visited Lina in the city, who lent her husband money, who walked home from Bow with Mary Matson. Just the same weak, gentlemanly, womanly, loveable individual, who hung about another man's wife in the days gone by, and who hung about her still, no further advanced in evil, no better fortified in good. Just the same in all things save one—that he loved Lina more—that which had once been but a sentiment, a feeling, was now the one overmastering passion of his life.

He scarcely felt as if he existed when not in her presence; she was the one thought, the one blessing, the one curse of his existence. He dared not speak his intentions and wishes in plain language to himself. Subtly and skilfully he was taking advantage of every wrong move on the part of her husband, watching with the hunger of love upon him for every scrap of affection which the chemist blindly cast aside, secretly studying Lina, and winding himself by imperceptible degrees round that strange unequal screw, a woman's heart. He was sinning without thought, or, rather, because he would not think. A bad companion for Lina truly; one who lengthened the downward descent by such days and months of apparently innocent companionship that Lina scarcely felt she had left the heights of virtue till she saw before her the valley of vice; and, besides, and worse than all, he made the journey so pleasant that it would have been hard for any one to imagine it was leading to the devil.

This was Herbert, whom Lina had not seen for many days previously, and who was now anxious about her health, and to know if she had heard from Mr. Storn, and how that individual was, and a hundred other things which would only weary you to repeat, but which Lina listened to with interest, and answered with pleasure.

"And where is Geordie all this time?" inquired Mr. Clyne at last.

"Oh! dear me, I had forgotten him, poor child! he is in some place up stairs; he came teazing whilst I was writing to his papa, and I sent him away, and have not seen him since.

I dare say he is offended that I did not attend to him immediately, for he is sadly easily annoyed. I will go and fetch him though;" and so saying she left the room to find her child.

"Janet, where is Master Geordie?" she inquired, after searching her own room, and the nursery, and the dining-room, and breakfast-parlour. "Have you seen him? I hope he is not in the kitchens?"

"No, ma'am, he is not in the kitchens, for I have just come up from them; he may be in the spare room, for he sometimes goes in there and rolls among the pillows."

"He is not here," Lina said, after she had looked under the beds and in the closets, and behind the curtains, "Geordie, Geordie, my son, where are you?" and she walked out into the passage, calling out "Geordie, Geordie, my boy!"

Then like a very thin weak whistle through a reed, a little voice cried out plaintively—

"Ma!"

A sort of terror came on Lina as she heard the cry. "Can he be in here?" she said, turning the handle of Mr. Storn's dressing-room door. "Yes, it's not locked. Oh! Geordie, my darling, what have you been doing?"

She had hardly asked the question before she saw. At the other end of the room sat Geordie in an old-fashioned arm chair, and behind him wide open stood the doors of the cabinet to which her husband had referred. It was full of bottles. Lina perceived that instantly, and grasped the whole.

"My boy, you have not tasted any of these things?" she almost screamed, as she snatched him in her arms, and looked anxiously in his face.

"Geordie sick," was the only answer she received, uttered still in that thin, reedy treble. "Geordie sick," and he laid his head on his mother's shoulder, and let his limbs hang out limp, as if he was dead.

He was no light child, but she did not feel his weight then; down the stairs she ran, holding him fast to her heart all the time, and rushing into the drawing-room, implored Mr. Clyne to do something—to try something—to save her child.

She told him her fears in a moment, and as rapidly he ordered Janet to get him some mustard and warm water, and to send for a doctor: then proceeded without ceremony to Mr. Storn's dressing-room, and examined the contents of the cabinet. One bottle on the lower shelf attracted his attention. It was about half full, and the glass stopper had fallen to the ground; he picked it up, noticing as he did so, that where it had lain the colour of the carpet was changed, he turned the phial round and saw it labelled "Deadly poison;" he smelt it, and a sweet faint odour, as of flowers, assured him it must have been this which had attracted the child to taste.

It did not take him so long to master all these particulars as it has done me to write them, and recorking the bottle and placing it in his pocket, he returned to Lina, who had laid her son down on the sofa, and was watching him with a sort of stupid agony.

"He had better go to bed, Mrs. Storn," said her friend, looking at the child. "Let me carry him up, it is too much for you;" and lifting the boy, he bore him away, accompanied by the wretched mother, who secured one little hand, and kept kissing and fondling it all the way up those interminable stairs.

"Lay him down here," Mrs. Storn said when they reached the door of her own apartment, and Herbert carried him in and laid him down on the bed, and then stood looking at him.

"What do you think?" she asked almost in a whisper.

"We may do something," Herbert answered; but he felt his heart beating against the phial of poison, and knew it was almost a sin to delude her with a hope.

"The best thing we can get him to do whilst waiting for the doctor, is to swallow this," he added, pointing to the mustard which Janet just then brought in. "Now, Geordie, we are going to give you something very nasty, but it will do you good. Won't you take it like a man?"

"He can't speak," Lina exclaimed. "Geordie, my darling, take this to please mamma."

But he would not; every effort Mr. Clyne made to induce him to swallow the mixture was rendered abortive by a quick jerk of Geordie's head. He seemed very weak, but still he had strength enough to spill the mustard over the coverlid, and though ill, he kept turning an anxious sort of look on his mother, who did not know, poor soul, that the look was produced by no effort or feeling of his, but by the poison he had swallowed. She had not then learnt to know the various effects the different poisons produce on the human frame; she thought he was pleading to her to let him off from the dose, and she hardened herself, stricken mother, against the appeal.

"No, Geordie," she said, "you must take it, mamma will be very angry if you do not, do as you are told at once."

But Geordie was by this time as indifferent to her anger as he had been to her entreaties; he would not swallow, and Mr. Clyne turned at last to her with—

"Mrs. Storn, may I make him take it?"

"If you are not rough with him—if you don't hurt him—" she hesitated.

Rough with her child! Mr. Clyne could as soon have thought of hurting her! He contented himself, however, with assuring her he would be very gentle with the boy; but if they wanted to preserve his life, it was necessary to take some prompt measures.

On the strength of which assurance, Mrs. Storn gave him permission to do as he liked, and then buried her face in the pillow, whilst Mr. Clyne poured the contents of glass after glass down Geordie's throat.

For the first few seconds the boy struggled violently, but after that there was no trouble with him, and Herbert had just finished his self-imposed task, when the doctor walked in.

"Poison!" he said at the first glance. "What kind?"

Mr. Clyne handed him the bottle, which he looked at, uncorked, smelt, and shook his head over; he took out his silk handkerchief and let a drop of the liquid fall on the yellow border. It instantly turned the spot red.

"How came you to have such a poison in the house?" he asked sharply.

"My husband is a chemist," Lina explained.

"You, sir?" and he turned to Herbert.

"No! Mr. Storn is out of town. By some accident, the place where a number of these poisons were kept, was left unlocked, and the child got at them. Now, sir, what can be done?"

There was a something imperative about Herbert's manner, which compelled promptitude.

"What have you been doing?" asked the doctor.

"Giving him the only thing I could think of—mustard and warm water," answered Herbert.

"Very good; yes, very good! we must try something else though, and that immediately." Whereupon, the man of medicine set to work with a will to clear out the poison, which he told Herbert, in a confidential aside, would kill the child. "There is no hope; not the slightest," he said; "I saw that, the minute I looked at him. He may not die immediately— not for twelve hours, perhaps not for eight-and-forty. His father should be sent for immediately, and you had better break the news to his mother. It is of no use trying to save him, but we must try, for all that."

Tenderly and gently, Herbert Clyne broke the news to Lina, but he could not make her believe there was no chance of her boy's recovery.

"Send for Mr. Glenaen," she said, "he is so much among poisons, I daresay he will know better than the doctor what to do. Oh! please tell somebody to go for him fast. Let one of the men drive as quick as possible to Bow, and bring Mr. Glenaen back with him. I am sure he could save Geordie. I know Maurice could."

"Shall I go?" asked Mr. Clyne.

"No, no, pray don't go! Don't, for pity's sake, leave me alone now."

God help her, he did not. He staid with her in her trouble, never varying in his watch, never impatient with her sorrow, choosing, for her sake, the woman's part of sitting still, and watching, with idle hands, the course of events, rather than take his own man's path of rapid movement, and breathless occupation. It would have been easier far for him to go down to Bow, and bring back the manufacturer, than to sit still, watching Lina's despairing and passionate grief, and listening to her earnest entreaties for something to be done, and trying to make her forget how long the time was till Mr. Glenaen appeared.

When he came, Janet ushered him at once into the room where the boy lay; and the moment Mrs. Storn saw him, she rose and prayed him, in tones that went to Mr. Clyne's heart, for the love of God, to save her child.

"What's he had?" demanded the manufacturer. "I suppose you never attended to Maurice's note, but left that confounded chest of drugs open. Let me see what he took, though?"

"Maurice never told me that cabinet was unlocked," the unfortunate woman exclaimed, whilst the manufacturer was smelling and examining the bottle. "He said something in the letter I got to-day about a cabinet, but I could not understand what he meant;" and she stood sobbing and shivering before Mr. Glenaen, whilst he answered,

"Not know what he meant? I suppose he made his meaning pretty clear in the note I sent you the night he went away —at least I know he intended to do so."

"Mr. Glenaen." She caught his arm as she stopped, and literally gasped for breath. "I never got that note. What was in it? Oh! Geordie, my boy—my boy!"

"Mrs. Storn," said Herbert Clyne, gently, "pray compose yourself. Do sit down and try to be calm;" and he placed her in a chair, and took his stand beside the excited and almost maddened woman.

"You never got that note, you say, Mrs. Storn?" said Mr. Glenaen, still holding the bottle between his finger and thumb, and looking attentively at it and Lina.

"No, never," he answered.

"Then I'll kick Grout off the premises when I go home," was Mr. Glenaen's comment.

"But that will do nothing for the boy," remarked Mr. Clyne. "We thought, perhaps, your chemical experience might suggest some antidote—some remedy for this disaster not known to the doctors."

The manufacturer shook his head.

"What is the poison?" demanded Lina.

Very slowly Mr. Glenaen turned the label towards her, and pointed with his finger to the word "Deadly."

"It is not immediate. Mrs. Storn," he said, with a sort of slow, yet brusque reluctance; "and it is not painful, but it is *sure!*"

She had been pale enough before, but she turned, if possible, whiter and ghostlier, at the last word, uttered with so unmistakable an emphasis.

"Do you want me to believe," she exclaimed, "that my boy must die?—that with all your skill and knowledge, you know of nothing likely to save him?"

"I do not. There is nothing."

"Then of what use is chemistry?"

"In life of much; in death of none—and this is death!"

As he spoke, Gordon Glenaen walked towards the bed, and laid his hand on the child. There was silence for a moment in the chamber; all present felt there was something greater than themselves shadowing and sanctifying the place—the twin brothers, pain and death.

Then Lina rose, and stretching out her hand as if she were trying to put the phantoms aside, said :—

"Mr. Glenaen, I wish to send for my husband at once. I am sure if he were here he could cure Geordie. He knows so much. I feel if he could be told of this immediately, our child might live. Will you give me his address?"

"To what purpose, Mrs. Storn?" enquired the manufacturer. "Maurice could do nothing here. There is no antidote to this poison. Once swallowed, doctors and chemists are alike useless. If he travelled night and day, he could not reach here time enough to see Geordie alive. I am afraid you will think me very cruel for saying plainly, there is no chance for the boy, but it is the truth."

"I cannot believe it though," answered Lina, "and, in any case, I must send for my husband.'

"But why?" persisted Mr. Glenaen. "What possible purpose can it serve to bring him home to witness a scene like this? It is one he would spare you."

"But I should not want to be spared," Lina cried; "and neither would he. If he knew of the way Geordie is in, he could not rest till he was home again. I must send for him. Give me his address."

"If Mr. Glenaen will tell me where Mr. Storn is to be found, I will go in search of him immediately—not a moment shall be lost," interposed Herbert Clyne, whilst the manufacturer preserved a dogged silence.

He was thinking, Heaven pardon him, even in that death chamber, of his own selfish ends, and views in life. He was thinking, not of the great mystery of mortality, but of the great experiment of cyanogen. He was considering how to keep Lina quiet—to induce her to consent to her husband's absence—to gain his own purpose and foil hers.

"Will you tell me where I am most likely to find Mr. Storn?" repeated Herbert Clyne, finding no answer was vouchsafed to his former question.

"No, I cannot," Mr. Glenaen replied.

"Do you mean that you won't tell me where my husband is, when our son is dying?" broke in Lina.

"I do."

"Then, Mr. Glenaen," said Lina, very slowly, "listen to me. I know you are not acting now through any feeling of kindness towards either of us, but simply because Mr. Storn's return would interfere with some plan of your own."

"I assure you—" here interrupted the manufacturer; but she silenced him with a gesture, and continued: "And if you do not give me his address without any further delay, I will have my husband, on his return, choose betwixt me and you. Whether our child live or die, he must either break off all business connection with you, or I shall leave him. You have been the curse of my married life; and, but for my boy lying dying there, I feel as if I could curse you now."

Standing there, with her lips trembling and her hands clenched, and her whole frame quivering, she looked as if she could have done anything. It was of no use Mr. Clyne imploring and entreating her to be calm; she was far beyond the reach of reason or expostulation, and, finding her threat had produced a visible effect on Mr. Glenaen, she was about to speak again, when the manufacturer commenced:—

"I assure you, Mrs. Storn, you have fallen into a great mistake concerning my wishes and intentions. It does not make the slightest difference to me when your husband returns. I cannot give any person his address, because I promised him that, under no circumstance, would I do so; but I can send him any message, or forward any note you may desire."

"And you will do this at once?" she inquired.

"Certainly, if you wish it; but you must allow me to say, I think you are not acting wisely or kindly in writing for Mr. Storn to return under such circumstances."

"Mr. Storn will be the best judge of that himself," Lina said coldly, and, seizing a pen, she traced a few words on a sheet of paper, and handed it to Mr. Glenaen; remarking, "If anything should prevent this note reaching its destination, I shall ask my husband if Geordie's state would not have been sufficient to absolve you from any promise? Remember, Mr. Clyne has offered to fetch Mr. Storn."

"I will take that office on myself," said Mr. Glenaen, as he turned to leave the room, Herbert Clyne following him.

"You must be considerate towards Mrs. Storn," he urged, as they stood together in the hall. "She scarcely knows what she is doing, I think. She is almost deranged."

"She puts me much in mind of a tigress with her cub," was the manufacturer's feeling rejoinder, as, with a shrug and an angry sneer, he stepped out into the street, and wended his way to Bow.

There, the first thing he did was to walk straight into the factory, seize Mr. Grout by the shoulders, and deliberately kick him to the door. Once arrived there, he pinned him by the collar, whilst he said :—

"You told me you gave that letter into Mrs. Storn's own hands, and you know you told an infernal lie. By not delivering it you have caused the death of Mr. Storn's son, and whenever he comes home we'll see if there is no law in England can touch you. Now, never put your foot into these premises again, and take that, and that, and that," accompanying each word with a blow which might have felled an ox, and finishing the performance with a volley of oaths and a parting kick which sent the man reeling to the ground.

"Lie there, and be damned," said Mr. Glenaen, as though the one thing was the natural sequence of the other, and, much refreshed and invigorated by this act of justice, he re-entered the factory, and commenced preparing his letters for post.

Meantime Geordie got worse. Through the long night and the almost longer day, Lina watched his passage from life. The action of the poison was so slow, that it was difficult to tell when one stage had passed and another commenced. Only one thing appeared certain—that there was no hope.

Nevertheless, the poor mother could not choose but hope against reason—against assurance—against sight. She held on in a sort of blind, despairing way, to the weak spar which she had grasped in the first shipwreck of her life's treasure. If Mr. Storn would but come back, Geordie might be saved; she was sure he could give him something; he was so clever—he knew everything. And then, when the child lay quiet and slept, she stole out of the room and went down on her knees before the great God, and wearied him with frantic entreaties to spare her boy, changing her prayer whenever a look of suffering came over his face, to a supplication that the Almighty would spare him pain, and take him rather to Himself.

Still Geordie got worse, and when the second night wore towards morning, Herbert, who had never left the boy for a moment, saw that the end was near at hand. The eager, anxious look in the eyes, the white, parted lips, the drawing down of the features, and the limp listlessness of the hands, were all symptoms which the doctor had foretold as certain. There was only one thing else which might come before death —slight convulsions, and Herbert, fearing these, strove to induce Lina to leave the room.

But in vain. The nearer death came to her child, the closer she clung to him, the more feverishly she waited for Maurice's return; faithful to the end, she kept her dreary watch—hoping to the last, and fighting even against her own conviction to believe there was a chance that he might still be saved.

She was sure, she persisted, if her husband would but return, something might be done; but, as the hours passed by and still no tidings of him came, her heart grew cold, for the child was getting rapidly worse, and Mr. Clyne's face, as well as her own sense, told her that before another night she would be childless.

Why did not Maurice come? What could be keeping him? Had Mr. Glenaen forwarded the letter? She kept ringing out these sentences from time to time, and sent Janet fifty times to the door to see if there were not a knock, a ring—some sound of arrival in the hall.

"Ah! I feared so," exclaimed Mr. Clyne at last. The poor boy was in convulsions. "Mrs. Storn, do leave the room. Janet, take your mistress away."

Lina would not go; she was on her knees by the bedside, murmuring in a great agony:—"Oh! my darling—my poor, poor Geordie—would to God you could have died before. Oh! Mr. Clyne, can nothing be done to ease his sufferings?"

"He is not suffering now," said the doctor, who came in at the moment; "he has never suffered much; and this is merely muscular—it is the passing away."

There was a bustle on the stairs, and Mr. Clyne sprung out

into the corridor. There he met Maurice, travel-stained and haggard.

"Mr. Storn," he said, barring the parent's progress towards the room, "you had best not go in. He is just dying."

Pushing him aside without a word, Maurice Storn walked on, turned the handle of the door, and looked upon his son.

He did not say one syllable, he only looked on him for an instant, grasping the bed-post for support.

Geordie was lying quiet, his pupils dilated to twice their usual size, his arms and legs contracted, his face white, and his lips bloodless. All at once a slight quiver shook his body, the eyes turned, the mouth opened; in the dead stillness a little sigh or gasp could be heard, and in another second Geordie was dead.

Then Maurice cried out, "If I had been here I could have saved him," and, loosing at the same instant his hold of the bed-post, with a heavy crash fell fainting on the floor.

CHAPTER XXVIII.

AFTERWARDS.

It was all over, and Maurice and Madelina Storn were childless; the great suffering, the intense excitement, the tremendous shock were past; and when the boy was buried—when every act appertaining to that dreadful tragedy was played out —Lina tried to rouse herself, and look the reality of her bereavement and her desolation full in the face. Sitting by her lowly hearth, she wept for hours together; wept by day, and in the silent watches of the night, quietly, but ceaselessly, till her eyes grew dim, and the lids red and heavy, till it almost seemed as though she had wept the fountain of tears dry; for, at last, even when her heart was breaking, she had no more to shed; a lonely, silent, desolate grief; for she refused human sympathy, and sought for no comfort from God.

It had not pleased Him to grant the petition for life which she had poured out in very anguish before His throne. "If prayer were ever of any avail," thought the poor erring creature in her despair, "He would have heard me then;" and thus, because He had taken her idol to Himself, Lina, in her madness and despair, cast from her all thought or care for religion, and, wrapping herself up in a defiant sorrow, which was impenetrable to every consolation and proof against all remonstrance, set her sinful judgment at work to question the righteousness of God's decrees, and even in the very keenest agony of her bereavement refused to be comforted. No more anguished supplications now; no more prostrations of soul and body in faith that God would be gracious unto her; no more belief that He who raised the widow's son, and who had seen fit to take her boy, would comfort her, poor mother, if she asked Him to lighten her load; no more trust or hope in anything in earth or in heaven; no more struggles with despair; no more desire for aught but death. It was a mental trance, caused by the dreadful blow that had fallen on her unchastened spirit, for which surely, in the bitter repentance of after-days, she was forgiven, but which in the present time left her in such a state of helpless, hopeless misery, that it sometimes seemed almost as though God Himself had forsaken her, and forgotten that so utterly wretched an one of His creatures was suffering on the earth.

As for Maurice, the iron had entered into his very soul so deep, that he had neither words to speak of his bereavement, nor the power to console his wife. True to his profession— true to the instincts of his class, he was silent concerning his sorrow as about his trade; he locked up the great trial in his heart, and plunging into business and its cares again, endured in silence and made no sign. He could not bear to hear his son's name; after the funeral he never visited his grave; he put aside all the little evidences and tokens remaining to tell that a child had once lighted up his life, and went out into the busy world again, with no evidences of his trouble about him save a mourning garb and more grey hairs and deeper lines carved upon his face.

During the short time he remained in the house he avoided the room where the child had died—where the child had played —with a sort of horror; he never mentioned his name to Lina, nor she to him; the only perceptible difference the trial effected in his demeanour was to make him colder and sterner towards the outer world, and more gentle and tender than ever towards his wife. If there had not been something standing between them then, it is possible that the husband and wife might have drawn near to one another in their trouble; but as matters stood, Lina was in no mood either to give or demand sympathy; Maurice had not come when she wanted him most; when she was trying through sobs to tell him all about Geordie, he hushed her to silence, with the gesture as of one in torture: when she wondered where he had tarried, he said, "Don't ask me, love—I can never forgive myself for being away;" and when most, perhaps, in her life she needed the support of a stronger and calmer nature, and expostulated almost fiercely with Mr. Glenaen on the way in which he came and dragged her husband away to the factory, Gordon replied, and not without a touch of feeling in his voice either—

"That she ought not to wish Maurice to remain moping over the fire; that it was well to force him to take an interest in anything; and that it was selfish for her to try to keep him in misery at home."

"And I?" said Lina, turning her changed face towards the manufacturer inquiringly.

"Must bear, as he does," answered Mr. Glenaen, and he was right.

"Bear, Lina! bear!" It is the lesson of life that we must all suffer; it is the wisdom of life for us to learn to bear well. Bear! for it is of no use shrinking from the torture, and saying it is not to be endured; bear! for it only doubles the anguish to struggle and writhe upon the rack of mortal sorrow; bear! so that you may be able to perform the work God has set you to do; bear beyond all things, because it is His will. Bear! it is philosophy to lie quiet; it is Christianity to try to be content; there is no use in your raising your head and defying the tempest; it will beat you down at last; it is vain, and weak, and sinful to wish for death, and to ignore the duties of existence; it is well to sorrow deeply and through all time, but it is wrong to lie grovelling in the dust of despair for ever; wrong beyond all to give yourself up even at such a juncture to the mercies of the stream of circumstances which is hurrying you forward into an unknown ocean, faster and swifter than any earthly river travels to the sea.

She said in her soul, "I have lost the power either to bear or to resist; I have tried to face my misfortune, and find I am incapable of doing it; I should miss the only voice that has striven to comfort me; be ungrateful if I sent him away, to the only one who was not afraid to stand beside my boy; why should I struggle or fear any more? I know the worst life can bring me; I have buried my heart and my hopes with my boy—why should I strive or struggle any more?"

And Lina had got to such a pass, that she forgot to answer herself, "Because it is right."

Right and wrong, she had lost sight of them both. Floating away down that perilous stream, she neither turned her eyes to the right nor to the left, but listlessly she drifted on, perfectly regardless as to whither she was going, and only anxious to forget from what an ordeal she was coming.

Oh, weak and sinful! More weak and more sinful then than at any other period of her story. Lina, with no thought for anything, or any person, but herself, forgot all her good resolutions—all the perils, and prayers, and tears of old—and only recollected that Herbert Clyne had been kind to her boy—that he was kind and considerate towards her.

When others blamed her despairing grief, he tried to soothe it. When others tired of her sorrow, he was more indefatigable in his efforts at consolation than ever. When she liked to remain silent, he was so too. When she felt it a relief to talk, he was ready to listen. When Lina fled from other voices, his always fell soft and musical upon her ear. He seemed to know by instinct what she was thinking of at any moment, and was ready to follow her track whithersoever she led. Near, oh, very near! and dangerously dear she grew to him then, and many a time, the man who had never known what it was to love before, and who had been reclaimed from dissipation and indifference by the power of this one overmastering and sinful passion, used to think had he, instead of Maurice, been Lina's husband, would her grief have been so intense and distressing?

Could he not then have comforted her with the assurance that *all* had not passed away from her? Could he not have told her then—hand clasped in hand—how he loved—idolized her? Could he not, in that case, have said what Maurice Storn ought to have said now? And, as Herbert came to this last clause, he shrunk back appalled at the length and depth of the gulf of old that stretched between them, but which he was, almost unknown to himself, bridging over with broken resolutions, and daily companionship and mutual sympathy, and fresh stores and treasures of love. All these things, one after another, fell into the abyss of matrimony, forming future stepping-stones for Herbert Clyne to cross the boundary which now separated the two. She—Maurice Storn's wife. He—Maurice Storn's friend!

And yet he was not doing all this evil wilfully. He was only, like Lina, drifting on to an unknown sea, without making an effort to save either her or himself from sorrow and crime—a temporary gratification—an everlasting repentance.

Better sometimes in this world to be bad than weak, to do a wrong than to yield to a temptation. Better, so far at least as the opinion of society is concerned, to commit a sin than to forget *les convenances*. In the one case there is some chance of concealment—in the latter there is none; and because of this little peculiarity of propriety, who would rather, any day, be cheated than bearded, the bitter tongue, which had let many a

worse pair off free, came lashing down on Lina and her lover.
First, Mr. Clyne's frequent visits to the house began to be
remarked on by the servants, who, like crows on a corpse, are
always the first in at the death of the reputation of a master or
mistress.

There were smiles in the hall, and titters in the kitchen—
whisperings over area railings, and comfortable gossips at the
corners of the streets. "Mr. Clyne just worshipped the
ground she walked on," these domestic penny-a-liners generally finished off with; and if public opinion were divided on
the question, as to how far Lina cared for him in return, it was
solely because since Geordie's death her manner had left
people in uncertainty as to whether there was anything she
cared for, in heaven or in earth. "Not her husband, certainly,"
Mary, and Jane, and Betsy were so obliging as to believe.
"But then he was so horridly neglectful—never at home at all;
really, whatever happened, he had only himself to thank for it."

Having disposed of the affair in which summary and satisfactory manner, they proceeded to tell, with great *goût*, how
Mr. Clyne looked then—how he spoke afterwards—what a
handsome man he was—and how despairingly over head and
ears in love he was with Mrs. Storn. All of which servant-
maid gossip might not have done Mrs. Storn any harm in
London, where the strong curb of public opinion is rarely felt,
even by the most restive horse, till he has fairly kicked over
the traces, and thrown all regard for character aside for ever;
but it unfortunately happened that the scandal was true, and
thus, after a time, everyone who had the slightest acquaintance
with her, began to look upon the chemist's wife as a woman
compromised—a person who, though she *might* still be innocent,
had committed the unpardonable offence of seeming guilty.

"Could not take the girls there—utterly impossible; Mr.
Clyne, that fascinating man, is never out of the house. Quite
a Platonic affair, of course; but still, improper for so young a
woman. Mr. Storn is sadly to blame, too. Never at home.
Poor creature, it is a great pity! such a dreadful affair about
that child—she has never looked the same since. Mr. Clyne
was so kind to her at that time, no wonder she likes him;
but still——"

And with such like phrases Lina's character was whispered
and nodded away. Ladies looked wise and gentlemen foolish,
and people altogether made themselves remarkable busy about
the Storns' affairs, whilst the pair who were the most interested
in the matter, Maurice and his wife, had no idea that Lina's
character was being destroyed before its time; he was too busy

—she was too abstracted to hear or notice anything. If she ever remarked the absence of visitors, it was with gratification; if she ever marvelled why Mrs. So-and-So had dropped her—the true reason for a secession of acquaintanceship never occurred to her.

Mr. Clyne was the only one of the parties concerned who suspected what the world might be thinking; and, considering that he was a man of the world, who knew its curious modes of reasoning and various twists and turns of conjecture, he took, perhaps, the best means to avert the storm that could possibly have been discovered. He introduced his father to Mrs. Storn, and took to flirting with Miss Lindor. Seven days after he adopted this course, Mrs. Storn's West End intimates pronounced they had been mistaken; and just at the same time the East End came into possession of the story, which at last reached Bow.

"It's all gammon," Gordon Glenaen declared, when it came round to him, "some lie of that woman Lindor, I'll be bound. Mind you, Mrs. Storn never was any favourite of mine, but she is not that sort. The cap would fit old mother Lindor better herself, I've a notion. That's what people get by going and living away West—setting up to be fashionable. First, have a child poisoned, and then find a wife's character blown away. I don't believe a word of it."

"Well, I do," declared Mrs. Glenaen, to whom her son made this confession of faith. "The Clynes are a bad, weak set, and Mrs. Storn was always too fine a lady for the city, or for her husband. I wonder if Mr. Storn will get a divorce?"

"Get a confounded humbug," remarked her dutiful son. "I suppose you think Maurice Storn has nothing better to do than to drag his wife through the Law Courts. After all, what does this precious story amount to? Mr. Clyne is a great deal with Mrs. Storn. Well, he was always a great deal with her, and Maurice and I and everybody, down here, saw he was, and thought nothing about the matter. There is no more in the wind now than ever there was."

"Very likely," sneered the manufacturer's mother.

"May I be hanged, mother, if I don't think you believe Mrs. Storn to be bad—a regular out-and-outer; but now take a word or two of advice from me: you, and the Lindors, and all the rest of the busybodies here, had better hold your tongues about this blessed piece of gossip, for Maurice is a man much more likely to prosecute somebody for libel than to try for a separation from his wife. And, besides, the mere mention of such a thing would raise such a dust at the factory, that Storn

would be good for nothing ever after. If once he thought there
was any real danger with his wife, the experiments might go to
the devil; I know that well enough, and therefore, even for
my sake, mother, I think you ought to contradict this infernal
story."

"We are getting at the reason, now, why you refuse to believe it," sneered Mrs. Glenaen, who did not like the way her
opinions had been received.

"No," answered the manufacturer, "you are not. I believe
Mrs. Storn, though a crotchety woman, to have been, and to
be, a good wife. She never was a favourite of mine, and I
never was a favourite of hers; but still she has not had fair
play. If she had been my wife, I think I should have acted
differently to Maurice Storn."

"And, pray, who took Maurice Storn from her?" demanded
Mrs. Glenaen.

"Not I," was the quick answer. "The man would experi-
mentalize, and I thought he might as well do it for my benefit
as for that of anybody else. Maurice Storn is a fool, because
he likes his profession for itself better than for its results. He
is an enthusiast."

"And what are you?" demanded his mother.

"A man who knows how to use such," he said, with a grim
smile.

"And means to defend their wives till the latest experiment
be perfected. Eh! Gordon?"

"Maurice Storn can defend his wife for himself after that,"
was the reply, uttered coolly and bitterly. "Meantime I will
do so, and maintain Mrs. Storn to be an innocent woman."

"With Mr. Clyne always at her elbow?"

"Mr. Clyne is as much at the Lindors as at the Storns."

"I know which he likes the best, for all that," remarked
Mrs. Glenaen. "Still, I hope he may marry Tryphenia Lindor.
I hope from my heart and soul he may."

"Why, I thought you detested Mrs. Lindor, and such a
match would set all the flowers in her cap dancing with delight,"
he said with astonishment.

"For a time," she answered with a chuckle, "for a time."

"Mother, I wish you would tell me what you know about
those Clynes. It would really be a great satisfaction to me to
understand what you mean. What is the matter with them?"

"Nothing. Oh! nothing. They are highly respectable
people, of course: far above you and me, Gordon. There is a
baronetàge in the family, and they have landed properties and
good connexions, and are a most desirable family for East End

folks to marry into. The Clynes date back to the Conquest, or thereabouts; and if they are weak, why, weakness is no crime, is it? and if they are fools, why, they hurt nobody but themselves by being so. They are a most influential family, and it is a pity, Gordon, you did not pay court to Mr. Clyne when you had the opportunity. He will be a baronet some day; who knows? and then——"

"Mother, you are an oddity," was Mr. Glenaen's brief comment on his parent's mocking speech; and knowing, by experience, that unless she chose it, nothing was to be got from her by questioning, he marched out of the room and down to the factory, feeling from that day forth, whenever he and Maurice were having long talks about chemicals, that there was a little bit of gossip afloat, of which he ought to give him an inkling, were he really the friend he professed to be. But Gordon Glenaen was a friend to nobody but himself; and, besides, he thought Mrs. Storn could wait when the cyanogen could not, added to which, he had a very firm belief that the man who ventured to tell Maurice Storn the world's breath had blown upon his wife's reputation would have no pleasant task of it.

For all these reasons the manufacturer determined to let affairs "work themselves right," as he mentally expressed it, and so he permitted matters to go on their own course, whilst his mother thought she would go up West and call on Mrs. Storn, just to see and judge for herself at what precise stage in her downward progress that lady had arrived.

CHAPTER XXIX.

AN UNEXPECTED INTERVIEW.

IT is the fashion of the present day to disbelieve in the possibility of people being thoroughly and innately bad for badness' sake. No matter how ill-natured a man or woman may seem; no matter what crimes he may have committed, or with what *goût* she listens to, and circulates, the tale of scandal, we are requested by philanthropists to believe in a fabulous amount of virtues, which are sedulously concealed somewhere about the persons of those whom we are so unchristian as to dislike.

The greater the number of vices exhibited, the greater the number of virtues lying behind, seems to be the axiom on which it is customary, now-a-days, to build up all sorts of edifices.

"If you could only see your fellow-creatures as God sees them," exclaims this sect of tolerators—tolerant so long as the injury does not touch themselves—"you would discover good in actions that now seem wholly evil, and become more lenient to the stream of wrong when you discover that it probably had its source in some well of virtue."

Possibly we might ; at all events, it is devoutly to be prayed that we are not the same in the sight of Heaven as we are in the sight of one another ; but, having conceded so much, I cannot but think it a piece of sickly sentimentalism to excuse a score of bad actions on the plea of an equal number of suppositious good qualities.

In this year of grace, if a man embezzle, or thieve, or forge, or lie, he was such a good father, he did it all for the benefit of his family.

If he commit a murder—he is insane. If he place himself in an equivocal position—he has always borne an excellent character. If a woman "get on anyhow," to use a common phrase, a thousand impossible excuses are at once made for her conduct : In brief, it seems to be the universal opinion of the nineteenth century, that a man has only to be very bad to be very good ; and that, reversing an old adage, "the greater the sinner, the greater the saint."

Mediocre people are passed by in silence—folks with many virtues have their enemies sometimes ; but, excepting in the newspapers, even great criminals, in these latter days, seem to make no foes ; and if an individual be like Mrs. Glenaen, destitute of every Christian grace and kindly sentiment, she is at once stated by the world at large to be a very worthy woman.

It would require a philosopher to tell by what course of argument the world came to the conclusion just recorded. Mrs. Glenaen was a person who had a very accurate idea on which side her bread was buttered, and would have felt all the better pleased, in common, I apprehend, with most of us, to have found it buttered on both sides.

To the knowledge of mortal being, she had never performed a kind or generous act—never softened another's faults nor hesitated to reveal another's failing ; she had no gentleness— no love. If she cared for her son at all, it must have been simply because he was of her flesh and of her blood—a piece of herself, and a means to an end. Old as she was, she still retained traces of former beauty ; but it was of the "loud" and termagent pattern—that which makes a woman be called when young and in good action, "showy," and a "high stepper." There was a something hard in the very manner in which she folded her well-shaped hands together, and she had a way of walking as if she wanted to crush the earth beneath her feet.

A cold and cruel hand hers would have been to feel laid on you, either in vengeance or in anger—a hand not so heavy as relentless, which could not be satisfied with a smart and rapid blow, but must keep it resting on the raw for ever after.

Self-contained the woman was, too—she required no confidant, no assistant. If ill, she physicked and nursed herself—if well, she was just as content to be alone as with her fellows. She had plenty to say about other people, but never a word concerning herself, unless, indeed, certain revelations anent "my" housekeeping, "my" servants, "my" money, and "my" ideas of management, could be termed disclosures of feeling and sentiment.

Upon the subject of the late Mr. Glenaen, an inquisitor himself could not have gained any certain information; but somehow she managed to convey an impression that he had not been a "desirable" individual, and that matrimony with her had been synonymous with martyrdom.

Altogether her acquaintances concluded Mr. Glenaen's death must have been rather a gain than a loss, and that he had proved, while in the flesh, a very thorn in the side of a most worthy woman.

Heaven help a man afflicted with a worthy wife! It would be a comfort to throw a boot-jack at the head of a daughter of Eve so preternaturally perfect.

"A worthy woman" Mr. Lindor always called the manufacturer's mother, and poor Lina Storn had been wont to whisper to Herbert Clyne—

"Deliver me from her!" wherefore you, kind reader, can imagine the feelings with which Mrs. Storn beheld Mrs. Glenaen enter her drawing-room after the little *fracas* at Bow, which she fondly imagined had cut all intimate acquaintance between herself and the Glenaens for ever.

The old lady was very gracious—very preposterously civil, and touched so hypocritically on Geordie's death, that the poor mother burst into tears, and really felt for the first time in her life as if she liked the woman. Then she worked round by masterly moves to Mr. Clyne, but could not get Lina to look conscious; spoke of Miss Lindor's prospects, but failed to produce any effect. Great diplomatist as Mrs. Glenaen was in her own opinion, she had made a mistake by introducing the boy's death first; for what with swollen eyes, and tear-stained cheeks, and a pocket-handkerchief, Lina was able to hide her emotion, if she felt any—a fact which under the circumstances may be open to doubt.

For seated there with the black crape trimmings of her dress reaching to her waist—with her thin, white hands peeping out from under her black sleeves, with her pale face looking paler by contrast with her mourning bodice and collar, Lina did not seem like a person who was thinking of any human love, but only of that which she had laid down in the grave with Geordie. She was breaking her heart about the boy. Mrs. Glenaen saw that clearly enough, and was so far shaken in her opinion of Lina's guilt, that she had risen to take her leave without coming to any definite conclusion in the matter, when the servant opened the door and announced "Mr. Clyne."

"Now," thought the lady, "I shall see," and prepared herself to watch the meeting between the pair. Next instant, however, she was standing, looking, with her cheek, it might be, a shade paler, at Herbert's father, who stood, like one transfixed, gazing at her.

The whole affair, from the time of Mr. Clyne's entrance into the room to the sweeping and satirical curtsey with which Mrs. Glenaen made her exit from it, scarcely occupied two seconds; but short as was the interval, it sufficed to inform Mrs. Storn that the manufacturer's mother was Mr. Clyne's mystery—the haunting horror of his life.

Lina never had seen such a change produced on any one in so short a time as that which the appearance of Mrs. Glenaen effected in her visitor. When his eye fell upon her, he seemed to shrink down and diminish in stature, whilst his face grew neither a wholesome white nor red, but assumed a sort of leaden hue, that spread even to his parted lips. He watched her passage to the door like one fascinated, and then dropped into the nearest chair.

"Pardon me, Mrs. Storn," he said, "will you come near me, please?"

She went as he asked her, sitting down on an ottoman by his side, and bending that graceful, pliable figure of hers so as to catch his words.

"Is that person a friend of yours?" he asked, in a low, husky voice.

"An acquaintance—not a friend," Lina answered. "Neither she nor her son is a friend of mine."

Mr. Clyne might have noticed the emphasis she laid on the word "mine," but that almost before she had finished her sentence, he was on his feet, shrieking, yelling out, "Her son! Her son! Great God of Heaven! did you say 'Her son?'"

"Mr. Glenaen is Mr. Storn's partner," Lina answered.

"Glenaen! Glenaen! Ay, true," he muttered, in a more composed tone. "I had forgotten. Pray, Mrs. Storn, how old may this Mr. Glenaen, as you call him, be?"

"About forty-five, I should think," she replied.

"Forty-five," he repeated, and his voice grew louder and shriller again. "Forty-five. Has she other children?—more sons?—any daughters?"

"None."

"None!" He echoed her words as though trying to assure himself of the length and breadth of his great misery. "None! Now, Mrs. Storn, for Heaven's sake, tell me one thing more! You must have seen this man, Glenaen, often. Did you ever meet any one who resembled him—that he looked like—except his mother?"

"He is not like his mother in the least," she replied.

"Well, have you ever caught a resemblance to any one else—in feature—expression—anything?"

He asked the question eagerly and rapidly, pausing at last to look anxiously in her face; and as he did so, something in his countenance caught Lina's attention, and made her cry out almost in spite of herself—

"Oh! Mr. Clyne, I have never seen any one in the world whom Mr. Glenaen resembled, unless it might be you."

"Me!" He tottered somehow to the door; but Lina caught him there, and would not let him go; she clasped her hands upon his arm, and pulled him away from the staircase, and made him sit down again, intreating him to be calm, to be composed.

He did not answer her feeble efforts at consolation by a syllable; he did not seem, indeed, to hear her; at last, in the middle of the longest sentence she had ventured on, he stretched out his hand as if to grasp an imaginary glass, but then appearing to remember where he was, said with a painful twitching of the nerves—

"This scene has quite unmanned me, Mrs. Storn. May I be very rude and ask for a little brandy?"

"Brandy, I fear, we have not in the house," was Lina's instantly improvised fiction; "but wine will be better than nothing;" and she rose and rang the bell, and when the servant brought up the tray, she poured out some wine, and handed it to Mr. Clyne herself.

Thanking her, he drank it, then walking to the table, filled and emptied glass after glass till there was not another drop left in the decanter; Lina standing all the time looking on, not sufficiently sure either of his condition or of her influence to interpose.

When he had finished, he turned towards her calm and sober as possible. "I have given you a great deal of trouble to-day, Mrs. Storn, and I must give you still more. Will you promise me not to mention what you have witnessed to Herbert?"

"Certainly, if you wish it; but it seems to me—pardon me, Mr. Clyne, if I am intrusive—it seems to me your son should know of the matter, more especially if what I cannot help imagining should unfortunately happen to be correct." .

"It is not correct; oh! pray do not imagine anything. You are sure to be wrong; and as for Herbert, poor boy, I would rather he never knew anything about the matter. No; I shall write to Sir Hugh Clyne, and get the thing finally arranged. He, after all, is the only person who can be of any use. Yes, I will write to him, perhaps go to Northumberland myself. Good bye, Mrs. Storn. You will be sure to keep all knowledge of this from Herbert. Thank you—good bye—God bless you!"

With which benediction, which meant more from this man, who so rarely in his life had asked God to bless anyone, than it might from another sort of person, Mr. Clyne quitted the room, and Lina saw him no more.

Instead of writing to his uncle, consulting what was best to be done, or making any rational step of any kind in the matter, he took advantage of the fact of Herbert's being out of town, and fell back on his old friend and comforter—the brandy bottle.

It was to no purpose that the servants tried to baulk his mania—of no use for the family doctor, and the family solicitor, and, finally, young Mr. Clyne, to be summoned. They might just as well, save for the look of the thing, have stayed away. The man was determined to kill himself; and I should like to know of what use doctors, and solicitors, and sons are in such a case, unless they feel inclined to put a straight waistcoat on the patient, and tie him down in bed till he recovers his senses.

Through all the madness of *delirium tremens*, Herbert watched his parent, never leaving the room unless it might be to speak to the doctor outside the door, faithful to his father as Lina had been to her child—faithful unto death.

One day the doctor declared that Mr. Clyne was better. "If he can be but kept quiet and sober now," he suggested in an aside to Herbert, "he may get through safely, after all."

At the moment the patient was lying pale and quiet, with his arm flung out over the coverlid, and his eyes fixed half dreamily on the doctor's face; but all at once Herbert perceived a change in his expression. His eyes began to wander round the room, then he commenced dragging up the sheets, crouching and crying out to Herbert, "There she is again, lock the door, don't let her in ;" and he fairly hid himself under the bed-clothes, reappearing, however, in a few seconds, and commanding some imaginary individual to "come on."

"Come on, I'm not afraid of you now ; do your worst or your best, you cannot follow Montague Clyne any longer. There, doctor, don't you see her ? Come on, Madam, don't be afraid, speak out. Don't touch me, Herbert. Let me alone."

But Herbert would not let him alone. He saw something in his father's hand which he sprang to seize from him, whilst the dying man rose in his bed, and flinging his son back from him, drained the bottle to the dregs.

"Now, woman, what are you standing there looking at ?—do you want money ?—I have none—do you threaten me ? I am almost beyond the reach of your talons now. See here, I will tell you I know all—I was told of it by——"

What he meant to add, neither of those present ever knew, for he stopped abruptly with a kind of gurgling, suffocating sound in his throat. From the very shore of the sea of death, however, a long agonised wail, half of consciousness, half of penitence, came ringing back.

"Oh! Herbert, my son, my son!" echoed one instant through the apartment, and the next, Montague Clyne was lying dead, with his arms hanging over the footboard of the bed, and an empty spirit flask clenched in his hand.

"In the name of Heaven, where did he get this ?" asked Herbert, standing beside the corpse and trying to unloose the stiffening fingers.

"He must have had it under the pillow," answered the doctor reflectively. "It was useless to try to save him."

CHAPTER XXX.

GOOD RESOLUTIONS.

WHEN, after the interment, the state of Mr. Clyne's affairs came to be sifted, his son discovered that he had not left sufficient available property behind him to pay his debts and the expenses of his funeral.

Mortgage after mortgage rose up in fearful array at every

stage of the investigation, and interest and principal had both remained so long unpaid, that Herbert felt it was vain to resist the advice of the family solicitor, who declared it would be better to let the mortgagees foreclose than to try to keep the property together, burdened as it was with debt whichever way they turned.

"For what purpose do you suppose these liabilities were incurred?" Herbert enquired, after looking over a dreary list of creditors.

"For the purpose of keeping somebody or something quiet," replied the lawyer, without the slightest hesitation.

"Do you know who that somebody or something was?" demanded the young man.

"Well, the person was a woman; but as to the nature of the hold she had over your father, I am perfectly ignorant. All I do know is, she made his life a torment to him, and must have feathered her own nest very warmly out of his pluckings. Mr. Clyne was hopelessly insolvent for years past, and it all went to her, every penny."

"Did you ever happen to see this person?" asked the young man.

"Never."

"Did you ever hear my father mention her name?"

"No."

"It is a most singular fact," pursued Herbert, "that though I have carefully examined all his papers, I cannot find a single document, or letter, or memorandum, relating to this business. Is it not strange that he has left no clue behind him?"

"I should think it very strange if he had," answered the solicitor.

"Why should you think so?" enquired his client.

"Because it doubtless was a serious matter. It *must* have been a serious matter which could induce a man to pawn property after property, and, in plain English, kill himself to ensure secrecy. Mr. Clyne lived in an agony of apprehension lest a chance word should give anyone the slightest hint of the hold she had over him; and yet you marvel at his destroying all documents relating to the affair, burning, in fact, every possible witness of his crime."

"Crime, sir?" Herbert exclaimed, and his face flushed angrily.

"Crime!" repeated the lawyer deliberately; "a man does not generally pay for the concealment of a virtue."

There was truth in this, and the young man was forced to admit it.

"Notwithstanding," said he, "I never can think my father, even in his wildest days, did any person any harm."

"Very natural on your part," answered the lawyer; "but still there can be no question but that there was something in the history of his past life which Mr. Clyne wished to remain secret. I think, and always did think, it would have been better for him to have laid the whole matter before some disinterested and confidential person, and consulted as to what was best to be done in a bad business. I often urged him to do this with me; but he was inexorable, and you see the result."

"He had his own good reasons, doubtless," said Herbert.

"Possibly; he always said he had, and that his death would terminate the persecution. We shall see now whether he was correct in this supposition. If this person had any hold on your father, beyond himself individually, you will soon have her here, and I should suggest that if she do come, it would be better to refer her to me, or any other professional man you may choose. These kind of people often have a hold in feeling, when they have none in law, and I might be able to arrange the affair satisfactorily for you."

"I shall certainly not enter into any arrangement with the woman without consulting you on the subject," answered Herbert determinedly; but he was not destined to carry his resolution into effect, for after his father's death Mrs. Glenaen seemed to have cut the family. She contented herself with a visit to the Falls, frightening old Sir Hugh Clyne out of his wits, and extorting from the baronet a settlement of five hundred a-year, in consideration of her silence on a point which nearly concerned the honour and the legitimacy of the heir apparent to the property.

Meanwhile, Herbert Clyne lived on that portion of his mother's fortune which had descended to him. Freed from the constant drain of his father's necessities, he was comparatively wealthy, and with youth, birth, and the near prospect of an old baronetage at his back, he became, as was natural, an object of active competition amongst mammas, whose quivers were full to overflowing of unmarried daughters. But from the blandishments of manners, and the charms of daughters, Herbert turned coldly and unaccountably aside; and while some said he had no heart, and others that he was engaged to a city lady possessed of enormous wealth, everybody agreed that he was too much at Mr. Storn's house for the peace of that gentleman, or the good of his wife.

Poor Lina! from the hour matrons began to look Mr. Clyne up—her character was gone. It had been blown on before, but now it was worth no more, or indeed less, than if she had actually eloped with him. In the city, out West, it was all the same; and still, though the scandal went on from day to day, the rumour never reached Mr. Storn, who was too deeply engaged in studying the reverse of the chemical picture spoken of far, far back in this story, to notice how strangely some people looked upon, and what a marvellous amount of sympathy was evinced by others towards, him.

At last John Matson heard the story from his wife, who was grievously troubled whilst asking him if he thought there were a word of truth in the tale.

"Oh! John," she said, "I am sure if Mrs. Storn had been false to her husband, she would not stay with him an hour. I don't believe there is anything wrong about her. I think she has only been foolish and unguarded, and Mr. Storn left her so much alone. If I were to go and speak to her, and tell her very carefully what people say, don't you think she would listen to me? Would it be of any use? I know she has not been very friendly to us lately; but she used to be so kind, so good, that I am sure she would listen to me now. May I go?"

"It would scarcely do, I think," said Mr. Matson, "she has cut us so entirely since she went out West—not that I think she has grown fashionable; but I fancy, Mary, she knows I suspected this. Long, long ago I thought she cared too much for Mr. Clyne. I am afraid she is very fond of him."

"Oh! John."

"Don't look at me that way, Mary, don't think me uncharitable; put the case fairly before your own judgment for a moment, and see. What does a handsome, fashionable, marriageable young man want so continually in the house of a married woman without grown-up daughters or single sisters? and why is Mrs. Storn tolerant of his visits? can the thing be naturally accounted for on the supposition of friendship? Would Mrs. Storn like me to be in her house day after day? or do you imagine Mr. Clyne would sit hours at a time on that sofa, looking at you? We can only form a true judgment by bringing the thing home to ourselves. Can Mr. Clyne's conduct be explained in any other way than on the supposition that he is fond of Mrs. Storn? and if he is fond of her, she is fond of him."

"But you do not think that it has gone too far—that is, so far but that—"

"She may still be saved from herself and him," finished Mr. Matson, seeing that his wife paused and hesitated. "No, she may still be saved by some one. Now, look here, Mary," he added, after a moment's reflection, "I was once very nearly speaking to Mr. Storn about his intimacy, only, like an irresolute fool, I didn't. Before they moved out West, I thought I would just give him a hint of what I fancied I saw ; but Mr. Storn never much liked me, and I was afraid of venturing too far, and doing more harm than good. I am determined, however, to speak to somebody now, and I leave it for you to decide who that somebody ought to be, Mr. Storn or Mr. Clyne."

"Which do you say ?" she asked, without giving an opinion either way.

"I say Mr. Clyne," he answered ; "but perhaps I say that because I feel it would be the easiest. It is one thing to tell a stranger he is compromising a man's wife, but quite another to tell a husband that his wife is compromised. I don't exactly know how Mr. Storn might take it. The fact is, Mary, the same fear that made me hold my tongue before, makes me hesitate now. I might do more mischief in ten minutes than could be undone in a lifetime."

"Well, suppose you speak to Mr. Clyne first ; and if that does no good, it would be time enough to speak to Mr. Storn afterwards. I cannot believe there is anything wrong about Mrs. Storn. I could not, unless she told me so herself."

"Still, I am afraid, dear, she likes Mr. Clyne too much."

"And suppose she does, which is she or Mr. Storn most to blame in the matter ?" demanded Mrs. Matson.

"That is a question I really cannot answer," said John, with a grave smile. "I only know I should think it a very hard case that if my business compelled me to leave you to take care of yourself, you got into mischief on the instant. Mr. Storn could not remain constantly with his wife, and it seems to me she should have made it her business to preserve her honour and purity in his absence."

"Honour and purity, John !" repeated Mary, in a frightened sort of way.

"There is a mental honour and purity," he answered, "which, to my thinking, must be gone long before a woman gets talked of by the world. What sort of a heart do you think I should have if I found the love you swore to keep for me alone, when we were married, was being transferred, little by little, to a stranger ? Only consider for how long a wife must have cared in secret for some one besides her husband before she consents to leave home, children, reputation, and everything for his sake. To say that a woman is pure in soul till she falls in body, is all nonsense, and I, for one, don't believe a word of it."

"But, John, suppose a woman, suppose Mrs. Storn never thought about the matter at all? suppose she took the friendship and the companionship as both came—innocently, as from the bottom of my heart I believe she has done—how would it be with her then? Don't you think if she had any friend to point out what the world might say of their intimacy, that it would open her eyes and set her right at once?"

"Do you imagine it a thing possible, then, for a woman not to think?" he asked, doubtingly.

"I do; only consider—I was staying in the house for weeks and weeks together, and I saw Mr. Clyne there day after day, and heard him and Mrs. Storn talking, and never thought for a moment even, that the acquaintanceship was odd. Now that the idea has been put into my mind, I see that Mr. Clyne would not have gone there so much as a mere friend; but I never should have found this out of myself, and this may be Mrs. Storn's case at present."

"Possibly."—Mr. Matson uttered this very dubiously.

"But even if I knew she had cared for him," continued Mary energetically, "I believe still I should only pity her. Don't you remember his kindness to us? and then think of what she must have found it, when, but for him, she would have been quite alone at the time of Geordie's death. I almost loved him myself that night we walked home together from Bow. There was a something, so gentle, so considerate, so ————"

"I must take care who I allow to come and visit here, I see," John said, when his wife abruptly paused—some memory of that past time filling her eyes with tears. "It would scarcely do for me, Mary, to have you falling desperately in love with Mr. Clyne."

"Ah! Mr. Clyne would never fall in love with me," she answered, with a smile; "and not to be tempted is a great protection to some women."

Quite true, brave and faithful little wife, for there is no touchstone like that of temptation. Very good those may be, and little thanks to them for it, who have never come into contact with evil. Pure as snow—firm as an iceberg she may seem—who has never felt the sun of passion scorch her heart —who has never floated into the gulf stream of love, and been dashed to pieces in the vortex of its rushing waters. The blade looks well till it has been tested. The unsullied sword is brighter than the old tarnished weapon hanging in the hall— yet the one tells of hard-fought fields, where the enemy was met face to face—where, through waves of blood and groans of agony—with pain and toil and struggle—a battle was fought and won ; whilst its fellow !—it has a fresh and unsullied look —it is brighter than the other—it has no stains and spots marring its purity, and yet we know that had it been borne forth to bear the heat and burden of the battle, like its fellow, its temper might not have stood the first brunt of the fight, and instead of being brought home in triumph from the field with the rust and the notches of the fray upon it, the unproved steel might have snapped in twain, and been flung to the earth as useless and unprofitable in the day of trouble. So it is with women. In the hour of trial and temptation we find out what stuff they are made of. We learn the greatness of their strength—the extremes of their weakness. We know how to value the virtue that stands aloof; from afar, watching in safety and arrogance the war which is being waged below between frail human resolves on the one side, and the world, the flesh, and the devil, on the other. We know how to value the purity that has never been tested—the power of resistance which has never met a foe. While, on the other hand, we can tell how it is meet we should crown that woman who has struggled and won—who, putting her trust in the Lord, has fought and resisted temptation—who has borne the heat and burden of the day—who has felt the scorching fire of trouble, and the sorrow, and the weariness and the pain, and yet who leaves, at the close of her day, the battle-field of human life, only for the story of her trials, and her victory, to be stored up in our memories and our hearts, a hallowed memorial of a holy fight, like the tarnished weapon hanging in the hall.

And there are others still—the unrecorded ones who fall ! Those who either faint and falter in the first rush of the world over their souls, or who shrink bleeding and wounded from the fray.

For these——ah ! Pity them ye who are propped and stayed—surrounded by bands of relatives, and hosts of friends —whose life-stream goes flowing on to eternity, without a rock or pebble roughening its way—who stand erect, proud and firm, for most probably—God pardon me if I am wrong—if many an one amongst your glittering ranks had gone down into the battle-field, armed only with beauty and innocence, they would have fallen in the thick of the *melée* like the rest.

Some idea of the sort passed, at all events, through Mr. Matson's mind as he listened to his wife's half-serious remark, and he answered, after a moment's pause,

"Right enough, little woman. There's many a true word spoken in jest, and I believe it is more of a protection to many

a wife and maiden not to be tempted, than most of your sex
would be quite willing to admit. Nevertheless, Mary, I am
sure you do not need that protection—as sure as I am that
there is not a man in England who might not, if he knew you
as I do, be proud to call you wife."

"Now, John, don't begin to flatter, because it is not a thing
to be tolerated; besides, how do you know, supposing I had
been Mrs. Storn and you Mr. Storn, what might have happened? Oh! John, John!" cried out all the woman's heart
within her; "if I had been placed just as she was, I should be
very sorry to answer for myself."

"Well, I would answer for you among ten thousand," said
her husband lovingly; "and none the less willingly because of
your wide charity towards another. But now for Mrs. Storn.
To whom shall we speak?"

"To Mr. Clyne," she decided in a moment.

"And if Mr. Clyne will not be a wise man and listen to
reason, what are we to do then, my wife?"

"Tell Mrs. Storn."

"And if telling Mrs. Storn be of no use?" he asked.

"Nothing will be," Mrs. Matson said emphatically; adding,
next moment, "but I know, John, she will be true to herself
—true and faithful to her husband, as I would be to you."

Considering what he had seen, heard, and suspected, Mr.
Matson might be excused for not receiving the latter portion
of this sentence as absolute fact, and only half convinced by all
his wife's arguments as to the guilelessness and unconsciousness of Mrs. Storn's conduct, he told Mary he was just
going for a few minutes on 'Change, and should try to run up
afterwards to Mr. Clyne's house and have a chat with him.

With which intention he slipped on his out-door coat,
brushed his hat, produced a pair of gloves, pulled up his shirt
collar, and, having thus made himself look respectable, kissed
his wife and departed, thinking what he should say to Mr.
Clyne, and what Mr. Clyne might reply to him—picturing how
they would meet, sit, and part—considering what the result of
the interview was likely to [prove—in fact, acting out in his
own mind the little drama everybody amongst us composes
before she, he, or it comes into contact with other actors in the
piece, and finds the situations, and the looks, and the answers,
and the speeches, diametrically opposite to those of the brain-
play rehearsed so short a time previously.

Having settled what "I shall say," as he walked along
Fenchurch Street, Mr. Matson was just imagining Mr. Clyne's
reply, when someone struck him lightly on the shoulder, and,

turning, he beheld the very person on whom his thoughts had been running.

"You walk so fast, old fellow," said Herbert, "I thought I never should have overtaken you. Well, and how are you, and where are you posting to?"

"I am first going on 'Change, and then I was intending to visit you."

"Visit me! how fortunate that I chanced to see you, for I shall not be at home till all hours. I have an engagement for this evening; but if you will name your own day, I shall be most happy to see you any time. Bachelor dinner, et cetera; so now, Matson, you have your fare and its apology at once."

"Thank you; but I was coming to talk, not to eat. Fact is, I wanted to speak to you particularly; and if you can spare me five minutes after I have done on 'Change, I should really feel obliged. Are you pressed for time?"

"Not for three hours yet. I was just going to kill that interval at my club: but if you can perform the part of butcher for me, I shall take it as a particular favour."

"Will you, then," returned Mr. Matson, "walk up to the top of Cheapside and back again? I shall meet you before you reach Bow Church."

"Don't hurry yourself, my friend, nor lose a sale for my sake. This is a good hour for admiring the city belles looking in at the shop windows, and getting oneself hustled from curb to wall. I shall be lost, till I see you again, in astonishment at the beauty of the women and the politeness of the men. *Au revoir.*"

And, with a smile and wave of the hand, Mr. Clyne walked off, knowing, by a sort of intuitive quickness of perception, exactly what it was Mr. Matson had to talk about, and marvelling what on earth he should say to him in reply.

Strolling along Cheapside, where a line of splashed and draggled ladies blocked up that side of the footpath next the windows, and regiments of impatient men surged along the remainder, at times encroached on the softer sex, and treading on their dresses, and making unpleasant remarks about their length, by way of apology, Herbert Clyne steered his way among the belligerent parties, seeing but one face—Lina's; thinking but of one character—hers, and wondering how, in the world's eye, he who loved her better than life, or houses, or lands, should ever make that which he knew was stainless look pure again. God help him! he had been thinking about that for weeks past, struggling with his passion, struggling to save her. He knew matters between them were drawing to a crisis. He felt the pressure from without driving him at last to some decided line of conduct. He knew he must either leave her or speak of the love it was sin even to mention. He felt he must either urge her on to fly with him, and trust to the chance of a divorce from her husband, or fly from her for ever. He saw this Platonic intimacy, this dangerous friendship, could continue no longer; they must either cast their lots together in sin, or tear them asunder in sorrow. Lina was virtuous, and Mr. Clyne, who had seen more of her weakness than, perhaps, any other human being, knew it would be next to impossible to render her otherwise. All unknown to herself, that purity which the world refused to believe in had been a shield and a defence to her all through that long and insidious intimacy. It had been strong to preserve her from him, but it might not be strong enough to preserve her against herself when she heard that busy tongues had robbed her of her fair fame. Might she not, then? and somehow, as he contemplated the possibility, sparks of fire danced before Mr. Clyne's eyes, and he grew sick and dizzy. Might she not, then, fly with him—live for him—and, when divorced, marry him? Next minute, the dream vanished, and he was standing alone in his misery, seeing himself, and his wishes, and his intentions as they were.

He saw the lonely home, and the dishonoured wife, and the betrayed husband. His thoughts went back to the first time he had met Lina—he remembered all her guileless trust—recollected how cordially Mr. Storn's hand had always grasped his—pictured the shock, and the agony, and the awakening of that disgraceful flight, and felt he could not mention it. He would save her at any sacrifice to himself—at any fancied loss of companionship to her. The world had flung down its glove on the fact that he loved the chemist's wife, and, if need were, he would lift the gauntlet, and prove, by marrying another, that Lina had kept her vows before Heaven holy and pure.

Holy and pure! the man's brain reeled again as he contrasted the nature of this woman with that of the one he thought of wedding. But why should he have thought of her at all? the reader may inquire, and I answer, because Herbert Clyne was weak, and even in his strongest moments he could not help but let the current of his destiny drift him where it would.

There was but one in the world for him, and if he separated his lot from hers, what did it matter with whom else he joined it?

Eve, in Eden, might have been very well for Adam, but she could not have supplied the place of Lina Storn to Herbert

Clyne.   He was but a child in the world's nursery, and as he was forbidden one toy, he looked on all other toys as valueless. Perhaps he felt on the whole it was rather a fine and un-selfish thing to destroy his own future for the sake of Mrs. Storn's present; to live out a life of ill-assorted misery, so that he might silence scandal at once, rather than leave the woman he had compromised to wear down the idle gossip and battle with her sorrow all alone.

If the world talked much more he would marry, and having come to this determination and the end of Cheapside together, Mr. Herbert Clyne faced round and retraced his steps, feeling that now he could meet Mr. Matson on equal ground.

That individual did not keep his appointment either at Bow Church or further down Cheapside, but sauntering along the Poultry, Mr. Clyne espied his friend in the distance detained by stress of vehicles, making frantic plunges at the Mansion House crossing.   It was what the Londoners call a muggy day, —thick, depressing, miserable.   There had been rain, and the pavements were dirty.   There was going to be snow, and the sky looked black and threatening.   For all these reasons there were three times as many cabs, carts and omnibuses blocking up the streets as in ordinary weather, and ten times more women impeding the traffic than if it had been fine.

Thus it was some minutes before Mr. Matson could effect a crossing; and when at last he saw Herbert waiting, and reck-lessly joined him, the passage was only effected by keeping at the back of an omnibus, siding along with a brewer's cart, running the risk of being knocked down by a Stanhope, and ducking under the nose of a cabby's horse.

" A very creditable venture," said Mr. Clyne, laughing ; "I must congratulate you on your success.   How has business gone since we parted, and in what state are things on 'Change ?"

" Things are dull," answered Mr. Matson, " but still I have made a good sale.   It was that detained me.   I thought it would be a pity to miss a chance for the sake of a few minutes, and that you would not mind waiting."

" Mind ! I have been in ecstacies," Mr. Clyne replied; " I have been contemplating thick ancles and dirty petticoats.   I have seen gentlemen charging ladies at their proper peril, and ladies stopping up the side paths for no conceivable purpose, so far as I could discover.   I have been studying city nature and city manners in bad weather, and have come to the conclusion that there is something attractive to women in a rainy, sloppy day, and that if there be one time which they consider better than another for looking in at shop windows and for flocking out of doors, it is wet afternoons, when the poor devils who are forced to be out, but hurrying to be in, are wishing them anywhere. I don't think much of the city or the citizens on a wet day. What is your opinion, Mr. Matson?"

"I am used to it, you know," answered the person addressed; "but I do not imagine any place would be nice in the rain."

"Except one's own fireside," Mr. Clyne observed.

"A man can fill his seat there so seldom though, these times," remarked John, ruefully.

"What, are you beginning that cry?" exclaimed his companion; "surely you have not caught the chemical infection, and commenced experimenting?"

"Like Mr. Storn," finished Mr. Matson. "No, I stick to Colke's business like a limpet; but, talking of Mr. Storn, I was wanting—that is, I must speak to you about his wife."

"About Mrs. Storn?" The cool surprise expressed in Mr. Clyne's manner was perfect.

"Yes, you must try not to be offended with me. I do not wish to annoy you, but I feel I should be acting wrong to keep silence any longer. The world is making so busy with her name, that I feel, as a man who owes her much gratitude, I ought to try and save her."

He spoke hurriedly, yet emphatically, pausing at the end, and looking into Mr. Clyne's face for an answer. Herbert's eyes were fixed on the vehicles that kept rolling, rolling past, deafening him with their clamour.

"Is there a quiet spot anywhere in Babel?" he asked; "I cannot hear you speak in this roar."

They were just at the corner of Bread Street at the moment, and Mr. Matson turned down there and went straight on to Old Fish Street. Passing along it, he never spoke till he slackened speed in the walk that runs round three sides of the graveyard belonging to the churches of St. Andrew by the Wardrobe and St. Ann, Blackfriars.

"Will this do?" he asked, when they reached that cheerful promenade.

"Yes, it is quiet enough, in all conscience. Now what were you saying about Mrs. Storn?"

This was not an easy question to answer; it was harder to speak unpleasant truths there in the silence, where every syllable could be heard and understood, than amid the noise and bustle of the city thoroughfares, where the full violence of a harsh truth was broken and softened by the din of the traffic around.

Mr. Matson felt the change of situation was not a pleasant one for him, but still, after a slight pause, he managed to repeat his former sentence with a difference.

"I was saying," he began, "that people are making themselves busy about the Storns. At such a time it is the duty of a friend not to shrink from speaking the truth, however disagreeable the task of speaking it may prove. I would rather, however, not broach this matter to Mr. Storn, if the step can possibly be avoided, and therefore I determined in the first instance to talk to you."

"And wherefore to me?" queried Mr. Clyne.

"Because the world has been pleased to couple your name and Mrs. Storn's together, and it rests with you either to restore her reputation or blast it for ever. If it is a thing that still may be, Mr. Clyne, for God's sake leave Mrs. Storn to live in peace and honour with her husband. If common report lies, give it in the future no loophole for scandal. I would to Heaven I had spoken openly to you long ago, when first I suspected you were too much together. It might have saved her character—it might have preserved you both from sorrow and remorse."

He spoke strongly, for he felt deeply, saying, in the warmth of his friendship, more than he had at first intended; and when at last he stopped, he almost expected that Mr. Clyne's reply would not be a pleasant one.

It was not uttered for a few seconds; then Herbert said thoughtfully—

"I suppose, Mr. Matson, everything which passes between us this day will be held confidential?"

"You may rely on that," was the answer.

"Such being the case," pursued Mr. Clyne, "I will speak to you as I would to my own soul. I have heard the reports you speak of, and have decided that there is only one course open by which I can put a stop to this scandal. I must marry."

"Marry!" echoed Mr. Matson; "the very best thing possible."

"For Mrs. Storn, perhaps," said Herbert, bitterly, "but not for myself. A wife will silence the gossip, and alter my position at the Storns' house. As for the rest, before Heaven! Matson, whatever my own personal feelings may have been— I have never said a word to her all London might not have listened to. I have never by look, or tone, or touch, told her how she has blessed and cursed my life."

He was as pale as a corpse; and though he spoke quietly and gently, as usual, Mr. Matson heard a sort of quiver in his voice, that told of the struggle within.

"Are you really in earnest?" asked John, when he paused —"do you mean in very truth and honour, that in all the time you have known Mrs. Storn, in all the hours you have spent with her, in all the talks and walks you two have had together, you have never tried to alienate her from her husband, and draw her to yourself?"

"Never once," was Mr. Clyne's unhesitating answer. "The word love has never been mentioned between us. I tell you, if every sentence of our conversations, first and last, were written down, and published, the most jealous husband in England could take no exception to a single paragraph. I kept a guard on my lips, on my tongue, on my conduct; and if Mrs. Storn's character has suffered lately through me, the fault is not mine—for I have sinned no more now than in the old city days, when you all saw the intimacy, and held your peace."

"More shame for us, then," exclaimed Mr. Matson, "at least for me—if I had spoken to you long ago, as I am speaking to you now——"

"It might have changed my life," interrupted Mr. Clyne— "and saved some scandal concerning Mrs. Storn."

"The scandal is nothing," said Mr. Matson. "A wife can outlive, and a man disregard it. What I feared was that you had estranged Mrs. Storn from her husband, and that there was no hope of happiness for her domestically ever again."

"Shall I tell you the truth, Mr. Matson?" inquired Mr. Clyne. "Shall I say that, had Mrs. Storn been a worse woman, I should have been a worse man? Twenty times I might have said things to be repented of, but that there was always a restraining influence, hers, upon me. How often I have smothered whole sentences—trembling for the hour when I might lose all self-control, and be tempted to give utterance to them. I was afraid to show what I felt, for I dreaded lest the door of the only house that ever seemed like home should be shut and barred against me."

"That is, you thought, if Mrs. Storn knew your visits were rather those of love than of friendship, she might not have cared for their continuance," said his companion.

"Precisely; but so long as I did not enlighten her, so long as the intimacy was injuring nobody but myself, I argued there could be no harm in the affair. I did not remember there was a world possessed of a tongue till lately: in fact, Mr. Matson, I believe I floated on with the stream, and never thought about anything save this—that Mrs. Storn was friend and sister, confidante and adviser, all in one. Not a proper relation for a married lady and a single man I grant you," he added, with a bitter smile—" but still in our case most innocent."

They had wandered out of the graveyard by this time, and were pacing nearly in the dark, up and down some of the old passages that run through Doctors' Commons.   Almost unconsciously, Herbert's eyes took cognizance of the strange out-of-the-way places through which he walked, and he considered that they were just the sort Lina would have liked to explore.

Would she be willing to go through one of the Courts? Heaven help us !   Even in the midst of his good resolutions and his sincere penitence that evil thought crossed his mind—" and if she were landed on the other side, could not he meet her there, and——"|

His reverie was broken in upon by Mr. Matson.

" I am a business man," he said, " and we look at these sort of things simply as they are—matters of wrong instead of matters of romance.   I know that no circumstances could excuse your falling in love with another man's wife, and continuing the intimacy long after you were aware of the state of your own heart.   I know you have acted wrongly towards yourself, and most cruelly towards Mrs. Storn; and yet still, for the life of me, I can do nothing but pity you.   I am very sorry."

" And so am I," answered Herbert; " but there is no use in fretting about the past now—I will get married, and put things right for the future.   Mrs. Lindor gave me a gentle hint the other day, I was trifling with the young affections of Miss Tryphenia."

" But you will surely not marry Miss Lindor ?" exclaimed John, eagerly.

" And why should I not, my friend ?" inquired Mr. Clyne. " Whom else could I find in every respect so suitable ?   Miss Lindor wants a husband rich, and moving in a good station— she would like to be Lady Clyne, and she shall have her desire —one woman is just the same to me as another, save for this ; that whereas Miss Lindor wishes merely for an establishment, some one else might ask for the addition of a heart, and that I have not now to give to any wife."

" You will have it again, in the future, to give to a woman more worthy of your love than any of the Lindors," said Mr. Matson, warmly ; but Mr. Clyne shook his head.

" Of that you must let me judge," he answered.   " Rest assured, I shall always try to do my duty towards the person I may marry.   I will give her all she wants."

" But for you: I was thinking of yourself—"

"As I have sown, I must reap," was Herbert's reply. "So let it rest."

Meantime, Lina was lying on the sofa, in her drawing-room, weeping and sobbing, in the gathering twilight.

The rumour had come home to her at last; and with a sort of despairing agony she had suddenly been awakened to the truth that her character was gone—that she had compromised herself with Mr. Clyne—that Maurice would hear all—and that she and Herbert must part for ever.

It was Janet who had summoned up courage to tell her mistress that people said Mr. Clyne came far too much to the house—and that, if Mrs. Storn herself would not put a stop to the frequency of his visits, she must speak to her master. She would not be acting right by one she had served so long, she said, to keep silence another day. She was crying as she spoke, but Lina never answered a word, nor shed a tear. She heard all the woman had to say, and saw her leave the room, and then flung herself down in an agony of bodily and mental weakness, to weep and to think.

The battle of her life was drawing near; and yet still, knowing this, she lay on there for hours, disarming herself for the fight.

CHAPTER XXXI.

LINA'S LAST STRUGGLE.

WE are never closer to the wrong, than when we think we are nearest to the right. Just as the Mahommedan hovers over hell, when flitting across that bridge no thicker than a hair, and sharper than the edge of a sword, which leads to Heaven, so we are usually in more danger of falling when we imagine we stand perfectly sure, than at any other period of our existence.

For if "the heart of man be deceitful above all things, and desperately wicked," it is weak likewise, and there is no time when it finds it harder to leave the evil, and cling to the good, than when it has taken the first step in the right direction, and discovered the fearful barrenness of the road along which it will have to journey, in order to obtain an ultimate good. It is this that makes lovers' partings so frequently matrimonial meetings—that causes the infernal regions to be paved with good resolutions—that throws the thief back amongst his old associates—that tempts the speculator to try just one venture more, when he has had a fortunate hit, and all but forsworn chance transactions for ever; and it was the same sort of feeling which caused Mr. Clyne when, after leaving Mr. Matson, he went, for the last time, to Mr. Storn's house, in order to bid Lina farewell, to swerve from his purpose, and say within himself "that it was impossible they should part—that life without her would be unbearable."

He found her looking pale and troubled, with a greater restlessness and unhappiness visible in her manner than ordinary. No pleasant books—no sweet music now. Since Geordie's death, Lina had taken no interest in anything—reading, singing, walking, praying—she seemed to have done with them for ever. Some petty piece of needlework kept her hands employed—whilst she strove to avert her thoughts from the two subjects which were uppermost in her mind—her sorrow and her shame. Sorrow for the boy snatched so suddenly away; shame for having loved—yea, for loving another than her husband!—reserved, neglectful though he might be.

For some time there had been no pretence of congeniality in intellectual pursuits between the two.

There was no conversation about general subjects—about music, or art, or antiquities, or prose, or poetry, or any one of the other things that had been masks and snares to them in the earlier stages of their acquaintance. No! their scanty talk was now purely personal, concerning Mr. Clyne's affairs and projects, Lina's failing health, the chances of removal, and sometimes they wandered sufficiently out of themselves to speak of the Matsons, Mary and John, whom Lina never saw in these dreary days, and whose presence she avoided like a pestilence.

There was no attempt at disguise. Each knew what lay at the bottom of all this, though love had never been mentioned, nor hinted at by either. They did not try to gloss it over, nor to delude their own understandings, but sat silent, thinking about matters concerning which neither had the courage to speak. By small outward signs and tokens, an observer might have guessed there was something wrong, by the manner in which Lina avoided looking at Mr. Clyne—by an occasional pallor which came over her face when she felt his eye fixed on her—by a quick, nervous shiver that every now and then shook her frame—by the way in which she occasionally parted her lips to say something that was never uttered—by the fixed melancholy of Mr. Clyne's expression, and a sort of irresolution in his voice and manner. Looking at the two, as they sat, far apart, and rarely uttering a sentence, you might know a struggle of some sort was going on in both their breasts, likely to influence their future lives for ever.

And so the time crept by—each moment weakening his better purpose, and reducing her to a state of more abject fear. She trembled at every step—she shrunk at every word. And when at last she heard her husband's key turn in the lock, she started up, as if to go and meet him; then resumed her seat, and took that endless piece of work again into her shaking hands.

A moment or two elapsed before Mr. Storn entered the room, and when he did, it was with a slow step. He looked pale and haggard—so ill and anxious, that Mr. Clyne placed a chair for him, which he declined, with a gesture of the hand.

"What is the matter?" Lina demanded in a faltering voice.

"Nothing, dear, only a headache. I have had a racking headache all day. A night's sleep will set me all to rights though."

And he stood there leaning his arm against the piano, whilst his wife asked "if he would have nothing?—a cup of tea or coffee, or a glass of wine, or— ?"

"Only a good sleep," he answered—"if Mr. Clyne will excuse me"—and so he shook hands with Mr. Clyne, and turned to leave the room, followed by his wife.

"Don't come with me, dear," he said, when they stood outside the door. "I don't want anything, and I suppose you won't be long."

And then, in something of the old way, he kissed her cheek, and Lina's soul shrunk within her as he did so, and she thought of the morrow, with its horror, and its misery, and its shame.

She made no further effort to follow him, but crept back to the drawing-room, whilst Maurice went wearily up the staircase, thinking, almost for the first time in his life, that it was a nuisance to have a stranger constantly located at his fire-side, and that Mr. Clyne was, very decidedly, a bore.

It might have been just as well had Mr. Storn considered long before that time it was a possible contingency he would become something else; but he had not, and even at this advanced stage of the proceedings he only considered it a nuisance to have Mr. Clyne always in his house, even when, almost for the first time since his marriage, he wanted to talk to his wife. It is easy to understand how Lina feared to face such trusting unsuspiciousness—how she dreaded the shock of his being told that the woman he had never doubted was false to him in soul—that the rock he had confided in was shifting sand—that the first and best love of his heart was faithless and fickle—that the innocence he had trusted was turned into the consciousness of sin.

It is easy to understand why Lina dared not meet his anger! Why it would have been less difficult for her to encounter a jealous husband than a confiding one. Why, as time went on, she forgot the neglect he had shown, and remembered only the faith she had broken. Why she went back into the drawing-room with despair on her face, and agony in her heart!

Herbert Clyne, with his good resolutions scattered to the winds, rose as she entered, and taking her clammy hand in his, led her to the fire. There, standing beside her, he began :—

"I came here to-night, Mrs. Storn, to bid you farewell for ever. To say I was determined to break the spell which has kept me here so long. To tell you I would spare you, from this night forth, the pain of my society. To promise I would sacrifice myself to preserve you, but it may not be—may not be —I cannot leave you ; for though I have never said so before, you know I have loved you better than anything else on the face of the earth, and I——"

A gesture silenced him.

"Pray stop," said Lina, "I am ill ;" and she fell back into a chair, as if she would have fainted. After a moment, she rose again, as though to leave the room, but he would not let her. All the passion of his love was roused in him, and with that dangerous eloquence of which he was master, he pleaded his evil cause before her. Did she not love him ? He took that for granted, and she could not contradict him. Once granted, all the rest was easy. His own forbearing devotion—the wild-ness of hopeless years that lay before him—the notoriety of their attachment—the indifference of her husband—the life of happiness she might enjoy as his wife—they would fly that night—she had no need to face an injured husband—they would fly together, and he could return to chemistry—he would not miss her companionship, and how could Herbert Clyne exist without it—there were countries to which they might journey, where no taint or stain would rest on her fame. And Lina, with the thought of that dreadful exposure, listened, and her strength was shaken. She had only a dim sense of duty to guide her answers, and as, one by one, Mr. Clyne put down her arguments, and repelled her objections, she grew dizzy and faint—and wept !

When a woman takes to crying in the presence of her lover, it is all over with her part of the battle. So Lina felt ; he bore her down on all sides, and accordingly she made one last effort to break from the meshes of temptation he was weaving around her.

"She was a wife—she would stay with Maurice. Mr. Clyne must go, and she must stay——"

"To a life of greater loneliness than ever," interrupted Herbert; "to face your husband and the world—to be pointed at by people who, always ready to believe the worst of everyone, will believe, and do believe the worst of you—to be forced to confess to the man who trusted, even whilst he neglected you, that a stranger has taken the place in your heart he occupied—that you no longer love him, but me! Oh! Lina," he continued passionately, "I have kept silence for years, but you must hear me now. Come with me—I will love and cherish you, comfort you. Affection such as you have never known nor dreamt of shall be lavished upon your path—you shall never know a want nor a sorrow I can shield you from; do not send me out into the world a lonely, reckless man. Have pity upon me, and bless my life for ever."

He pressed his lips to her forehead as he ended, and Lina sprang from her seat with a thousand voices shrieking in her ears—'Lost! lost!"

"Let me go: let me go," she cried; then, the next moment, dropped back into her seat, muttering the one word, "Where!"

"Where!" He had words to tell her—he could speak of distant lands, of a foreign home—of a different nation, and a strange country. He could paint in glowing colours the raptures of that life and the agonized misery of this. He could show her years of love on one hand—years of scorn on the other. He could present two pictures for her contemplation, and compel her to love the one and loathe the other. He could plead as a man only pleads once in his life to a woman, with the irresistible impetuosity of a first passion, and, at last, he conquered. She would go.

And, as she gasped out her assent, Lina's good angel hid its face in the folds of its spotless garments, and shut her out from sight.

She would go! When, it mattered not—any time; she would meet him three hours afterwards—when all the servants should be retired to rest, she would meet him—he might be quite sure—he might go.

And he went; and Janet, hearing the hall door close so much earlier than usual, thought her remonstrance had produced an effect, and that her mistress would come right after all. Comforted with this idea, she went unsuspiciously off to bed, little dreaming that, while she slept, the child she had nursed was hovering on the brink of a more frightful precipice than any she had yet come to in her passage through life.

Over the rich carpet the little feet trod noiselessly, but ceaselessly, for hours. Up and down the darkening room Lina paced like an animal in some bodily anguish. She had no tears to shed—she had no prayers to utter—she had no friend to turn to in the wide world—she had no reason left to sway her—she was mad—mad as we have all been at some time of our lives or other—mad, at least, as all who have ever known an over-whelming joy, or an all-conquering sorrow—who have ever had the master passions of their hearts stirred by love, or hate, or fear.

At last, when the fire had gone quite out, she was startled in her monotonous walk by the sound of a neighbouring clock striking two. It was the time she had appointed. Lina woke up to that fact, and to a shivering consciousness of cold and misery at the same instant. Pushing aside the curtains, she looked forth into the dimly-lighted street, covered with wet, dirty snow. It was desolate without, but more desolate within; and, after a brief pause, she turned from the window, and, wrapping a shawl around her shoulders, went trembling to the door.

Another pause ere she turned the handle—a pause, but no return—reluctance, but seemingly no hesitation, for the next moment she passed out into the lobby, and then stole down the staircase silently—stole down to leave home and husband, peace and reputation, for ever behind her. Step by step she crept nearer to her ruin; but when she reached the bottom of the flight, a rush of old recollections came sweeping across her soul, and her good angel troubling the fountain of her soul, showed that the virtue had not all departed out of it.

It was but momentary, however, for with the memory of happier times the sense of shame in the present was too intimately connected to permit her to return. Though she loved Mr. Clyne—loved him, Heaven help her, with a sickening intensity of affection which she had never dared to realize to herself; still it was not for love of him she stood there trembling on the brink of destruction. It was not for the sake of that to which she was going, but rather because of the horror of that from which she was fleeing, that Lina had consented to leave home, husband, virtue, everything which women hold most dear and sacred in life, behind.

Oh! she did not know the nature of the man she was deserting; he had never permitted her to fathom the depths of love that lay in his heart for her, and she could not conceive—poor, weak, unbelieving soul—that, as the patriarch of old welcomed back his prodigal, so he would have taken the wretched truant to his breast, and kept her safe from temptation there for ever.

Tainted and soiled with the breath of unholy passion that had blown over her—with the love she had fought against, but which, nevertheless, she held in her heart for another than her husband—humbled and guilty in her own sight, though still what the world, in its wisdom, calls innocent of sin—Lina, leaning against the bannisters, remained for an instant feeble and irresolute, as the memory of another home she had once entered with him flitted before her eyes.

She saw the bride and bridegroom, the bright light and the wide staircase, and the blazing fire, and the cheerful faces; she felt her husband's kiss on her lips; she heard his welcome sounding in her ear; and then, with the agony of that other affection suffocating her, with other vows ringing through her brain, with another's burning kiss branded on her forehead, she rushed forward to change a present evil for a worse. Rapidly and silently she shot back the key and undid the chain, and undrew the bolts, and finally lifted the latch and opened the door. As she did so, something which had been sitting on the cold steps, leaning its head back against the pillar of the portico, rose and flitted away like a phantom.

What was it?

That which Lina might come to, but which she was not yet.

Out along the snowy street Lina's eyes followed her, and, as she saw the poor, shivering wretch skulk round a turning, light broke in on her darkened understanding, and the whole current of her thoughts was changed.

There was a worse than her present state, and that was it; through all the stages of infamy she followed herself to that; for if a divorced wife she married Clyne, what better would she be in the eyes of Heaven, in her own sight, than that lost sinner —what better? How much worse? Oh, God! oh, God! and Lina drew back into the shelter of her home, and falling on her knees, the poor, weak creature turned again to her Father in Heaven, whom she had forgotten, and was saved.

There, with her head resting on the stairs, she remained wrestling with her anguish and her despair until the light grew stronger in her soul, and she made up her mind to go, though not with him. Then and there for ever; without a companion, alone, always alone, the doom and the curse of old still clinging about her. Where or how she never thought, she never cared, only it came into her heart to look once more upon her husband's face before she departed. She was not so guilty now as an hour ago. She might do that.

I wonder—oh, happy wife and mother, pure maiden and unsusceptible man, if you, reading this record of a woman's struggles at your peaceful firesides, surveying her trials from the eminence of your own virtue, and knowing nothing of the love, and the shame, and the uprightness that had struggled together for mastery, can imagine what a victory it was Madelina had achieved; what a fierce, weakening battle had been fought within her by the powers of evil and the powers of good.

Ye who are good because ye have never been tempted, who are virtuous because ye had no need in your hearts for love, who stand erect in the sight of men and of Heaven, because God has been good to you, and never permitted your step to falter nor your eye to fail,—how can you, I say, tell through what an ordeal Lina had come forth; not scathless, but still safe.

For I am not one of those who hold that a woman can tamper with her own better nature, can trifle with the innocence of her own heart; can be wrong in feeling, though right in deed, without sullying that purity which Eve brought out of Eden with her, and which such multitudes of her daughters have been permitted to carry through the midst of a sinful world.

And thus it came to pass that Lina turned to her duty again with the marks and wounds of her struggle upon her, like some poor pilgrim, who, having blindly pursued the wrong road till it is too late for him to retrace the way, is compelled at last to force himself through briars and thorns, in order that, bleeding and weary, he may discover himself on the right path in the end. Along the track of error there is no return, no solitary step of that easy journey may ever be retraced; and it is only by means of the road of penitence, watered by tears and strewed with living regrets, that either man or woman can ever again get within sight of the point whence they started. So, weeping like one in some mortal agony, weary and worn with the length and strength of the unequal struggle she had waged, trembling at the darkness of the gulf she had so nearly walked into, sick with the memory of all she had done, with the thought of all she must do; seeing for the first time clearly the whole extent of her sin and her misery, Lina crept up the staircase, pausing and sobbing at every step, and feeling now, when she was sure she ought to leave her home for ever, like some poor fallen angel, who, having by its own act cast itself from its high estate, looks through the closed gates of heaven back at the land of peace and love for the last time.

So she went up, trying all the way to stop her tears; and when she had got, as she thought, quite calm and quiet again, she ventured into her husband's room, and, gliding to the bedside, stood for a moment watching him as he slept.

The light from a small night-lamp enabled her to see his features with tolerable distinctness, and, even as she looked, they seemed to change, to grow more thin and pinched than she had ever seen them before. It was not the face of the husband of old, but that of a changed and disappointed man, she was gazing at; and as this conviction forced itself on Lina, as she noticed the sunken cheeks and the dark hair streaked with gray, and the haggard expression revealing itself even in sleep, she bent forward, nearer and nearer, just to touch his forehead for the last time. While she was stooping, he moved restlessly, and commenced muttering some unintelligible sentences. At last the words, "My wife," struck distinctly on Lina's ear, and, cowering down at the sound, like one touched by some sudden pain, she covered her face with her hands and burst into a passionate fit of grief.

At that moment Maurice awoke with a start.

"Lina, what is wrong? What has happened? What are you doing? Are you ill?"

No, she was not ill, and there was nothing the matter, only she felt restless and nervous, and thought he looked ill in his sleep; and was he ill? he had been starting and talking. And Mrs. Storn stood beside his pillow, talking in a hurried, excited sort of way, which her husband might have observed, had he not been in the first stage of a fever, and almost incompetent to notice anything beside the most prominent facts.

"Would Lina not try to settle now, and have some sleep?" he asked; but no, Lina would not. She sat down on a chair by the bedside, and he put his hand into hers, and seemed to feel contented to touch her; but the heat of his burning fingers almost scorched her. In contrast to her clammy palm his skin felt like fire, and, involuntarily, she pressed both her hands over his, exclaiming:—

"How warm you feel! You surely must be ill."

"No, I am cold," he answered, "cold as ice."

"And you are shivering," Lina said, hurriedly. "Maurice, what is the matter?"

"That I am a beggar," replied the chemist; and as though he had in that one sentence exhausted all his powers, he sank back once again, shivering like one in an ague fit.

Instantly forgetting all about herself, all about her resolution, Lina darted off to Janet.

"Janet, Janet," she cried, shaking the old woman, "Janet, get up—Mr. Storn is very ill. I don't know what it is, but I am sure he is delirious. Get up at once;" and before Janet could collect her scattered senses, she was back with her husband again, piling blankets over him, and trying to get him to speak to her and say what she should fetch—what would be of the most use. All the great love of her heart was roused into action; for a few minutes she forgot herself, Mr. Clyne, and the dreary future and the wretched past; and when the memory of all came rushing back, it was too late to think of going, for Maurice was raving—maundering on through labyrinths of chemistry—shrieking about failure and ruin—addressing instructions to imaginary workmen, and calling loudly on phantom Glenaens.

At first Lina paid no attention to these muttered sentences concerning loss, beggary, extinguished fires, selling off stock, and such like phrases. During the early morning her ear was straining for the doctor's tardy step; and, as the day wore on, she started at every knock, lest it should be Mr. Clyne himself. She left out a note to be given to him, if he called; a little note, containing just one line:—

"We must never meet again.—L. S."

And when, towards one o'clock, he came, the missive was placed in his hands. He tore open the seal and read the enclosure, then turned from the door, and before two hours were over, had shaken the dice of his life's game for the last time, thrown them, and won a loss.

I wonder how many a husband and wife in England has been thus caught at the rebound—how many would now be single if they had only waited four-and-twenty hours, and cooled upon a fancied slight, or supposed hardness and coldness of heart. Herbert Clyne, at all events, would have gone to his grave a bachelor, had Lina only added a few words more, or the servant who gave him the note stated that Mr. Storn was dangerously ill up stairs. The great wheels of life spin round the merest atom of an axle; the mainsprings of our actions are set in motion by the faintest touch of accident, and the whole of a man's future may be made or marred by the chance of a word too little, or a word too much.

So Herbert Clyne, because Lina would be true to herself, went and proposed to a woman for whom he did not care one straw; and when he calmed down, and cooled, and repented, it was too late for regret or reflection.

And whilst he was hurrying to his ruin, Lina sate still by her husband's side, watching and waiting for the crisis. The doctor came and shook his head. As Maurice grew quieter, he grew graver. As day after day passed by, and the patient ceased to rave, the man of medicine seemed almost to cease to hope. The morning changed to night, and the night changed to morning throughout the whole of one weary week, and at the expiration of that period Lina found out the cause of his illness and the reason of his broken sentences. He had not been delirious when he said, "I am a beggar," for they were beggared. The sheriff's officers told Mrs. Storn so when they came to put men in possession of the house.

CHAPTER XXXII.

RUIN.

It was a new thing for Mrs. Storn to have to be up and doing —to feel that she had been born into the world for some purpose—to experience the full weight of the burdens that press so heavily on the anxious and the poor. It was new for her to be at once miserable and busy; yet the change proved beneficial—for what between doctors and medicine, nurse-tending, and management as to ways and means, she had scarcely a moment for thought or recollection.

When the men came, and, coolly taking possession of the best rooms in the house, said her husband was on the eve of bankruptcy, she stood for a few minutes trying to understand what they meant; but when once it became clear to her comprehension that some dreadful reverse had taken place, she spared no pains to ascertain the exact state of their affairs, to find out what she ought to do, and learn how, if her husband were well, he would wish matters to be conducted.

Though he lay there above stairs, sick unto death, though he could not speak, nor move, nor eat, though he was hanging to existence by the merest strand of the feeble rope of life, Lina knew her duties at that time, though they might begin, did not end with nursing him. Night and day she kept her loving and remorseful watch ; cooling his forehead, bathing his hands, smoothing his pillows, moistening his lips. But, through the intervals of that watch, she found time to master every particular of their position, and to meet their change of circumstances face to face

She sent for Mr. Glenaen, who came : and while she walked about the apartment, flung himself into the most luxuriant chair in her drawing-room, stuffed his hands in his pockets, and stared at her.

"This appears to be a bad business, Mr. Glenaen," she said at last, when she had conquered a sort of hysterical feeling in her throat.

"Deuced bad," acquiesced the manufacturer, with the most careless nonchalance.

"What has been the cause of it?" she demanded.

"Your husband's folly," was the polite reply.

"Mr. Glenaen, you would not dare to say that if my husband were well, and I will not listen to you say it when he is ill," she said, pausing in her walk.

"Well. Your husband's sense then, if that word please you better," answered the manufacturer, with a provoking smile.

Lina took no apparent notice either of the amendment or its accompanying sneer, but resumed her list of questions when he had finished speaking.

"What will be the result of the affair?" she demanded.

"Bankruptcy!" Mr. Glenaen answered.

"And what is bankruptcy?" she enquired.

"What is bankruptcy?" repeated her visitor. "Lord bless my soul! have you been married to a tradesman all these years, and don't know the meaning of bankruptcy?"

"I do not," Lina replied. "Thanks to your influence, my husband never enlightened me on business subjects. I believe it means failure. But it is quite necessary for me now, with Mr. Storn insensible in one room, and the bailiffs in another, to know exactly what failure involves?"

"Well, it involves everything almost," answered Mr. Glenaen, complacently—who, however it might turn out with his partner, was certainly failing with a "full hand"—"the sale of this furniture, for example. You will have to give up your watch, rings, and jewels, your plate, house, carriages—and, if the creditors are very strict, your wearing apparel, and the bed Mr. Storn is lying on too. In fact, it would be much easier to tell you what bankruptcy does not involve, than what it does. I can, however, put the matter, perhaps, into one word for you. —Bankruptcy is ruin!"

Ruin! It takes whole sentences to tell of a man's accession to property, of his newly acquired wealth, of his rise from poverty to affluence; and yet the whole story of his fall and his beggary, of the shattering of a thousand hopes, of the birth of a thousand humiliations, can be expressed in this little word of four letters—Ruin!

Ruin! Lina came to a halt when the manufacturer uttered the monosyllable. The state of affairs had been put before her, not in a business, but in a human form, at last; and when, next minute, she resumed her restless walk over the flowers on her carpet, it was with a more thorough comprehension of their position, than a hundred volumes could have given her.

"Then, if we are ruined, we have nothing," she said at last, reflectively.

"Except the property settled on you at your marriage," remarked Mr. Glenaen.

"What property?" asked Lina.

"That your father left you," he answered.

"My father left me no property, and that you know perfectly," was Lina's answer.

There was something about the straightforward manner in which she received and returned all the thrusts he had intended should go most home, which rather disconcerted the manufacturer. He had come to the house out of temper himself, and determined to annoy her; but he found she was not to be annoyed, and adopted a different tone accordingly.

"If you have nothing, Mrs. Storn," he said, in reply to her last observation, "and your husband have nothing, you should bestir yourself to get something. Days are coming, when shillings will be scarce, and pounds scarcer. You ought to be looking out for the future, for money to pay for lodgings, for bread and butter and tea. You should get a few sovereigns together, and keep them by themselves."

"But how should I get them?" asked Lina, earnestly; for she really had not a notion of what Mr. Glenaen meant.

"Good heavens! Women have about as much idea of business as cows!" exclaimed the manufacturer, pettishly. "Don't you see what I mean? A few days more, and we shall be in the hands of the Court. The official assignee will sweep off everything for the benefit of the creditors. Before that comes, however, you should secure as many valuables as possible. You must have jewels not in use. You might even put your watch aside, also any trinkets Mr. Storn may chance to have, and get some friend to dispose of them, and keep the money till you want it. The sooner you do this the better. You might pick out a few articles from amongst the plate— things not likely to be missed. I suppose only a portion of the furniture is down in the inventory; and if you were to give the men a trifle, they would let you remove what would make one room in lodgings comfortable, at all events. Do you not understand?"

"Yes; but, Mr. Glenaen, would this be honest?" and the clear eyes went looking with a puzzled expression into his face for an answer.

"Honest! to be sure it is honest. The things belong to you, don't they?"

"No, I think not; that is, if my husband owe as much

money as they are likely to bring in," she said reflectively. "I am afraid, Mr. Glenaen, it would not be right. I do not exactly see how I could do it."

"May I inquire, Mrs. Storn, if you exactly see how you are to live through your husband's illness, bankruptcy, and all the rest of it?"

"I do not. I can see nothing clearly. I only know I ought to do something, but cannot make out what that is. Cannot you advise me, Mr. Glenaen?"

She said this appealingly, and her tone might have disarmed any person under heaven, except Gordon Glenaen; but he remembered at the moment he had an old score to settle with her, and he paid it as he had never paid any money debt— willingly, in full.

"Can you not advise me, Mr. Glenaen?" was what she said, and he answered *con amore*—

"As you decline to follow my first suggestion, Mrs. Storn, the only other hint I can throw out is, that you should immediately apply for assistance to Mr. Clyne, who, if the world says true, would be only too happy to oblige his friend's wife in anything. The fact of his approaching marriage need not, in my opinion, disturb former arrangements in the least."

He had struck home this time, with a vengeance. When he mentioned applying to Herbert Clyne for assistance, Lina stopped and looked at him, the blood mounting to her temples; but, as he proceeded, the colour faded away from her face, and almost before he had spoken the last words, she was lying on the floor in a swoon.

When she recovered, Janet was with her, and Mr. Glenaen gone; but, in answer to the woman's inquiries as to what had happened, as to what was wrong—she refused all explanation.

Her first action was to look round the room, and ascertain that her tormentor had departed; her next, to totter to her feet, and somehow reach her husband's bedside, and crouch down beside it like one broken-hearted.

For hours she remained thus, never stirring except to attend to some little want of his; sitting on the floor, with her face buried in her hands, weeping, not with her eyes, but in her heart, measuring her shame and her duty, counting how long it might be before she should leave her husband—pondering and thinking, as in a dream, over all she ought to do for him in the meantime.

She tried to face their position boldly. She tried to look at herself without friends, money, or home; nursing her husband to health, and then leaving him for ever. She thought over

Mr. Glenaen's advice, considered that those trifles which the creditors would never miss, might help his recovery ; counted up the sum her knick-knacks might realize ; wondered whether it would be dishonest to sell things which were her own; then remembered they had been bought out of Maurice's money ; then considered again, that it would be wrong to risk her husband's life for a mere matter of honour ; then concluded that no question of expediency could make wrong right, or right wrong ; and finally wound up by a determination to do the best she could for each day as it came, and to let the morrow, so far as possible, take care of itself.

She would not think of the possibility of her husband dying —she would not think of the certainty of their separation— she would not suffer the bugbear of poverty to terrify, nor the spectre of death to affright her—she would try, without looking uselessly back, or painfully forward, to do right in the present—and, without changing her position, Lina prayed as she had never prayed but once before, since Geordie's death, that she might be enabled to see and discharge her duty.

She was not praying then for herself—for any deliverance from her own trouble, forgotten and laid aside, for a brief time, in the anxiety and hurry of sickness, and an overwhelming reverse—it had returned to her memory as a thing which ought to abide there for ever. Meekly and penitently she accepted her share of the sorrow, as a portion of the punishment she was to bear for the one fatal error of her life.—She had sinned ! It was meet that she should suffer—she confessed all this to her God, rather with her mind than with her lips. She could thank the Almighty that, though the world's breath had blown upon her fair fame, she had been preserved from the temptation to which she had so nearly yielded. Her soul spoke out in silence to its Maker, and Lina, who had for so long forgotten that there was a heaven above her, now sat alone in the stillness of that sick chamber, talking in very humiliation and agony of spirit to her Father, whom she had formerly denied in deed though not in word.

Grovelling there, in her grief and her poverty, amid the wrecks of her former pride—looking, with dry, tired eyes, back over the road of error she had travelled, Lina had no thought now of cavilling at the decrees of Providence—of questioning the justice of God.

"Oh, Lord, thou art holy, and I am a sinner !" cried out that spirit which speaks without voice or sound to the Most High, and it seemed to her as though she could hear her Saviour whispering to her soul—"Come unto me all ye that labour and are heavy laden, and I will give you rest."

Lina never exactly knew how it was, but she rose after this with a strange conviction that her husband would not die. Looking into his death-like face, she felt there was life behind —life to be preserved by her. She was to work for him till he got well again! She was to leave her tokens of how she had erred, and how she had repented on this page of her existence, and then go forth, hoping, perhaps, poor soul, even against hope, that when he knew—as he should know some day—all her faults and all her penitence, he would forgive the wife he was never to see more!

Lonely, miserable vigils were those which that wife kept by the sick bed—vigils broken only by the dropping warnings which were given of the rapid approach of visible ruin. In one day Lina dismissed all the servants except Janet, got rid of the sheriff's officers, and made the acquaintance of the bankruptcy messenger, who came to take possession of the things the previous occupants had thought fit to leave behind.

Plate, wine, pictures, carriages, horses, musical instruments, jewellery—as in some horrible nightmare, Lina followed him from room to room, seeing in the loss of each article of which he took possession, a sort of tangible poverty. Basement and cellar, kitchens, sitting-rooms, bed-rooms, attics, he went over them all *seriatim*—and, at last paused before the door of Mr. Storn's sick chamber.

"You must leave me this," Lina said, and, turning the lock, permitted him to enter.

He would have retired from the apartment when he saw the sick man lying there, but Mrs. Storn motioned him to remain.

"My husband does not understand anything that is going on," she said, "and I want to give you some things of mine. I have been sorely tempted to keep them, because they are mine, and because I did not know what we should do without furniture, or money, or home, or anything; but I see they belong, after all, to the creditors, so it is better for you to take them at once—only, don't you think if the people Mr. Storn owes money to, knew how ill he is, they would leave him just a few things till he got better—we will give them all up then, the minute he is well?"

During the delivery of this speech, which was uttered hurriedly, the messenger stood before a table, on which Lina had piled all her worldly possessions, looking alternately at the trinkets, and at her.

When she had finished, he said: "You do not seem to be aware, Ma'am, that there is always twenty pounds reserved for a bed, wearing apparel, and so forth; and, besides this, whilst the bankrupt is passing through the court, that is from the day I come here till your husband gets his certificate, he receives a weekly allowance, which will be sufficient, at all events, to keep you from want. It is my duty to take possession of these articles, but—"

"Oh, take them all—every one!" Lina eagerly interposed. "You don't know what comfort you have given me. From what Mr. Glenaen said, I was afraid there would not be a sixpence left for us. He told me you would clear away everything, and that we should have no money for lodgings or food."

"He said so, did he?" demanded her auditor.

"Yes, he assured me, Mr. Storn was ruined, and—"

Here Lina stopped suddenly short, for a look in the man's face told her she was treading on dangerous ground—that, with the rapidity with which such persons' thoughts travel, he had put two and two together, and got an inkling of the truth. She did not know exactly where she had gone wrong, but she felt she had made a false move somehow, and checked herself in the middle of her sentence, with the tell-tale blood flushing her face, and revealing whole histories to the experienced individual who stood before her.

"When you first spoke of Mr. Glenaen," he said, with, perhaps, a sense of her embarrassment, and also with a desire to disabuse her mind of an erroneous impression—"I was about to say that though it was my duty to take possession of these articles of personal jewellery, still I should make it a point to inform the official assignee of the readiness with which all the effects have been resigned, and the facilities which have been afforded me in the discharge of a most disagreeable task. I will also make a report of Mr. Storn's illness, and have no doubt but that every indulgence which can be conceded will be granted under the circumstances."

Having concluded which speech, and finished putting down the articles of furniture in the apartment, and taken a sideway glance at Mr. Storn, and cast an unobserved look of very strange compassion on Mrs. Storn, he bowed himself out of the chamber, followed, however, by Lina, who accompanied him down stairs into the dining-room, when, asking him to be seated, she rang the bell for Janet.

"Janet," she said, when that person made her appearance, "this gentleman has given me great relief; make him as comfortable as possible while he remains. I must leave all that to you."

Then, as courteously as though he had been some pleasant guest, Mrs. Storn wished him "good night," and, taking her lamp from Janet, she passed from the apartment—the messenger holding open the door for her to do so.

Had she been a queen, he could not have treated her with more ceremonious respect than he extended to that lonely woman in her helplessness.

Next day, Mr. Matson came to offer her a home, and whatever assistance lay in his power. "He would have been there earlier," he said, "but had only returned from the north the night before—what could he do for her now?"

"Nothing," answered Lina, piteously, and began to cry.

"Nothing at all?" he asked.

"Oh, no, nothing!" sobbed Lina, "unless, indeed, you could stay here for this one night. The doctor has just gone, and does not seem to think my husband can live till morning, and I don't know what to do. Sometimes, Mr. Matson, it seems to me as if my senses were going."

"You must try to bear up, Mrs. Storn," said her friend gravely; "everything, even his life, is hanging on you at this moment. I will just run down into the city, speak a word to Mary, and then return immediately."

"I have now three children," he added, after a minute's hesitation; "a boy and another girl a week old. But for this, Mary would have come with me;" and hurriedly preventing the sickly congratulation that Lina was trying, with her poor white lips, to utter, he ran down stairs—left the house—hastened off to the city, and within two hours was back again.

"Now, Mrs. Storn, for the patient," were his first words on entering; and for the second time in their acquaintance it appeared to Lina as though he brought a fresher and purer air along with him. A whiff of moral heather seemed wafted through the close, depressing atmosphere of the sick chamber when he crossed its threshold, and, passing to the side of the bed—unskilful doctor and inexperienced nurse though he might be—took the dying man's burning hand in his.

"Mrs. Storn," he said, "you are doing wrong to keep that large fire in the room. I am afraid you have a fashionable doctor attending here."

"He has the largest practice in this part of town," Lina answered.

"So he may have, but he is killing Maurice Storn. A person who prescribes for him as he would for a fine lady or gentleman is worse than useless. I should like to see him. When will he be here again?"

"Not to-night," she said with a sigh.

"Not to-night!" echoed Mr. Matson in amazement. "For

Heaven's sake, then, Mrs. Storn, let us send for somebody else."

"No one else would come," Lina replied, mournfully. "It is the etiquette of the profession not to interfere with another doctor's patient.

"Another humbug," retorted Mr. Matson, pettishly. "Forgive me, Mrs. Storn," he instantly added, "I did not mean that rude remark for you, but for the system that would rather kill a man *en règle* than cure him against etiquette; however, a doctor of some kind we must have. You asked me once to trust you with my wife. Will you trust me now with your husband?"

"Implicitly," she answered.

"Then give me your doctor's name and address," he said; and having jotted both down, he was about to quit the room, when she stopped him.

"Mr. Matson," she said, "can he be cured?"

"That I am not doctor enough to tell," he answered; "but I trust so, with the help of God."

With the help of God! Lina closed the door after Mr. Matson, and then, taking her husband's hand, which he had just relinquished, knelt down by the bedside, and prayed for that help of which John had spoken, baring his head as he did so. She prayed for God's help—for strength—and patience— and submission—and faith. She prayed for His help to cure her husband; and then she rose up firm, and having, with her own hands, put out the fire and cut down the curtains, she commenced waiting for her friend's return.

He came at last. When the twilight was deepening into night, and Lina had lit her lamp and drawn the blinds, she heard him coming up the stairs, and not alone. There were two sets of boots tramping up to the sick room; but there was something in their sound which reminded her of a morning when she had heard two men tramping down that same staircase before, bearing away from her all which remained of Geordie.

The association was more than she could bear; so, to get rid of the idea, she went out on to the landing and met the new comers.

The doctor was a stranger. Mr. Matson explained, that not having found their regular physician at home, he had gone on further, and been so fortunate as to secure Doctor Humphries, who, at this mention of his name, bowed to Mrs. Storn, and then bustled in to see the patient.

He laid his fingers on the pulse, placed his hand on the

heart, looked into Mr. Storn's face, and without a remark of any kind called for ink and paper, pulled a gold pen out of his pocket, and traced two or three hieroglyphics, then handing the prescription to Mr. Matson, bade him get it filled up without delay.

Whilst Messrs. Colke's manager was away fulfilling his orders, Doctor Humphries seemed to have laid all thought of the sick man aside. He amused himself by a critical examination of Lina's lamp, by tasting every bottle of medicine ranged on the mantelpiece, and by an inspection of the few pictures that hung on the wall, filling up the intervals by addressing perfectly irrelevant observations to Mrs. Storn. She would have liked to put some questions to this remarkable individual concerning her husband's present state and future chances of recovery; but walking round and round the room in a heavy top coat buttoned up to the chin, with his hands behind his back, and his thoughts apparently anywhere, he seemed to her so inaccessible that she held her tongue—most probably the very thing, of all others, he desired she should do.

Still she had an odd sort of faith in the doctor's skill. She believed his prescription, whatever it might be, would do her husband good; and she could not help looking at her watch every two or three minutes, to see how long Mr. Matson had been away.

"Has he far to go?" she asked at last.

"No, only the length of three streets," was the reply.

"But all this sending about for doctors and medicines takes time," she said, restlessly.

"Yes; and time is life occasionally, isn't it?"

He acquiesced so readily in her proposition, and seemed to care so little about the special significance it might have in the present case, that Lina grew impatient. She felt she could not sit there much longer and watch his easy promenade and complete tour of inspection without doing something desperate; so she did do something desperate, rose, and left him to pursue his investigations in solitude, while she ran away down into the hall, and opened the door, and stood there listening for Mr. Matson's return.

She had stood once before in the same place with a heavier heart; and as the cool night air blew upon her temples, a sort of ease—spite of her anxiety—(pardon the paradox!) fell upon her spirit.

She might have remained at her post about five minutes, which seemed to her as many days, when Mr. Matson came back with the medicine.

"Did you think I was long?" he said, cheerily. "It seemed to me that I was, and yet I made all the haste I could. Where is Doctor Humphries?"

"He is upstairs physicking himself I know, and amusing himself I hope. He has driven me almost mad, creaking about from table to chimney-piece, and back again; but I suppose, poor man, it is the only exercise he has. Let me look at the medicine.—Oh! Maurice has had none like this before. Let us see what the doctor will do with it;" and she sped on before Mr. Matson like the wind, and delivered the medicine to the physician.

With the same imperturbable indifference which had driven her out of the room, he took the bottle, held it between him and the light, uncorked and tasted it, and having finally, as Lina said afterwards with great disgust, made a perfect laboratory of his stomach, he asked for a table-spoon and wine glass.

Mrs. Storn had both at hand; and having measured the dose, he proceeded, with Mr. Matson's help, to administer it. "After this," he said, "the patient will fall asleep; when he wakens, give him the remainder; and if he is perfectly sensible the second time, all danger is over. Give him, on second wakening, wine and beef tea in moderation. I shall be here first thing to-morrow. Good night."

Mr. Matson accompanied him to the hall. When he returned, the first words he said were—

"Now, Mrs. Storn, can you let me have something to eat, for I left home without dinner, and am very hungry? I am sure you also require something, with a long night before you, and a weary day just ended. May I have a private and confidential chat with Janet?"

"Certainly, everything in the house is yours—that is," she added, recollecting herself, "so far as anything in it belongs to us."

"Ah! there are better days coming, Mrs. Storn," he answered in his cheerful, buoyant tone; "but now for Janet."

Whether it was the result of his conversation with that personage, or the excellence of the coffee, or the speed and goodness of the cookery, never exactly transpired; but Lina was induced, seeing her husband sound asleep, to leave her post and swallow some food, under protest, be it understood; for, like most other women in times of trouble and danger, she seemed to fancy there was some special virtue in fasting.

When Mr. Matson had finished, they went back again into the sick chamber, where Lina sat down beside the bed, whilst her companion took a book and tried to amuse himself by reading.

Hour after hour passed swiftly away. It was midnight, it was dawn, it was morning, and yet Lina never stirred nor moved, till, unclosing her eyes, she awoke with a cry and a start to find the dull, cold light of the winter's day looking at her through the windows.

"Oh, he has not had his medicine," she cried out, between sleeping and waking; but Mr. Matson's voice answered her.

"He is saved!"

"Lina," said her husband, feebly.

It was the first word she had heard him speak rationally since *that* night, and the sound of her name uttered coherently by him seemed to terrify her.

Mr. Matson, observing the scene closely, could not help marvelling that, instead of seizing the weak, emaciated hand which he vainly tried to stretch out towards her, she should almost recoil from contact with it. For a moment she stood looking frightened and stupefied, and the next commenced weeping as though her heart would break.

"Well, I never!" thought Mr. Matson; "the woman is crying just as if she were sorry he had not died;" but he did not express this agreeable idea, only contented himself with remarking that she was "thoroughly knocked up," drew her from the room.

He thought perhaps she was vexed at the *ruse* he had practised, and explained to her that the doctor had considered Mr. Storn's state so critical, that he felt it would be simply an act of charity to make her sleep through the crisis.

"Janet and I watched him the whole night through," he said, "gave him his second dose, and you see the result. He is now ready for your nursing, for as many slops, and as much nourishment as you like to give him." But Lina did not seem in a hurry to avail herself of this suggestion; she buried her head in the sofa pillows, and cried till Mr. Matson thought she really must end in hysterics.

"It's confoundedly odd," he muttered, "I am sure I don't understand her;" but all at once a suspicion of the truth flashed through his mind, and impelled him to exclaim—"For God's sake, Mrs. Storn, whatever it may be that is troubling you, don't give way now. His life depends on you—you can either kill or cure him—do be calm."

And she was. She got up, and dried her eyes, and returned to her husband's bedside, and gave him his food and medicine, and sate with her hand clasped in his for days and nights together. Except a certain quietness of manner, and a desire to escape as much as possible from his surveillance, Mr. Matson could notice nothing particular about her; but these signs and tokens, taken in conjunction with former knowledge, were not lost on Messrs. Colke and Ferres' manager, and he determined that if it were possible he would watch her well.

Nevertheless, spite of all his precautions, she had nearly eluded his vigilance. Coming early one morning to give Mr. Storn, who was now almost off the doctor's hands, and quite well enough to talk about business, some information concerning the cause of the bankruptcy, he met Lina about a dozen steps from her own door. In a flurried, nervous sort of way, she told him she was going to make a few purchases, and seemed so unwilling to accept the offer of his company, that he determined, welcome or unwelcome, she should have it.

He went with her to a dozen different shops. She tried to tire him out by making needless journeys to every tradesman she knew; she went into a linendraper's and tossed over calicoes and muslins for half-an-hour, and at last, finding he was not to be shaken off, she said, as they stood in the street together—

"I am afraid I must now bid you good bye, Mr. Matson; I have another—that is, I am going——"

"Home with me, Mrs. Storn," he finished significantly.

"No, no, not home; I can never go home again, Mr. Matson; don't keep me—don't ask me—for mercy's sake let me go."

"Mrs. Storn," he said firmly, "I must, and I will take you back to your husband. After I have spoken to him I shall not venture to control your movements;" and as he finished he drew her arm within his, and, perfectly regardless of all her entreaties, and expostulations, and prayers to be released, hurried her along the pavement home.

There was a scene of violent struggle, of passionate supplications, of tears, and kneeling in the hall, which Mr. Matson terminated somewhat abruptly by lifting her very unceremoniously in his arms, and carrying her upstairs.

"Mr. Storn," he said, "I have brought you back your wife."

Maurice was sitting in a chair by the fire looking at a letter which he held in his hand, as though stupefied. When Mr. Matson spoke, he lifted his head, and said, "Oh, Lina!"

Next instant she was lying at his feet, grovelling there in the very dust and ashes of her humiliation and her repentance —she, his Lina, his wife.

He called her still his, he raised her up, and held her to his heart, and laid her cold, white cheek to his; and having seen this much, John Matson left them alone together.

What passed between the pair during the interval that followed was never repeated by either, but the burden of the long pent-up confession on the one side, and the agonised pardon on the other, may be gathered from Mr. Storn's last words—

"May God forgive me, Lina, for having neglected my duty, as I forgive you this blow."

CHAPTER XXXIII.

BACK TO THE EAST.

Mr. Storn used the right word when he called the discovery of Lina's secret a blow, for no other expression could have conveyed an idea of the effect her confession produced upon him. To find that through all the time he was toiling and slaving, she, whom he believed true as proven steel, had been struggling with an unholy passion, giving her heart to another, and tampering with the perils of a temptation which scarcely admitted of a hope of deliverance, was a blow struck at the very foundation of that which is the basis of all love—faith; and the man's mind reeled again with the force and suddenness of the shock.

Journeying back as he was at the time by slow degrees to health from the very brink of the grave, he had no strength of body left to help him to bear up against the violence of this new trouble; and after vainly struggling with his sorrow and his weakness, he was obliged to own himself beaten, and go back to bed again, driven there by what the doctor called a most unaccountable relapse.

Unaccountable to him, perhaps, but not to Lina, who sat night and day by her husband's side, feeling, as in an agony of sorrow and remorse, she looked upon that pale, haggard face, that she had learned the staunchness, unselfishness, and nobility of his character all too late; that his worth, which, if she had appreciated it fully in the days gone by, might have made a better woman of her, was only being revealed now to her to show the depth of her own unworthiness. Sitting there through all those weary, wretched hours, Lina, with the light of truth shining on her understanding, saw herself as she really was, a poor, faithless woman, who had blinded and deceived him, who had flung aside his love at the beck of a weakling like herself, who had toyed, and played, and gambled with her virtue, as though her own purity and reputation, and his honour and happiness, were things of no account; who was no more fit to be wife to such a man, than she was deserving of the love that even in the midst of her humiliation he bore her.

The one redeeming point about Lina at this stage of her mental history was, that she felt his superiority and her own abasement; she felt she did not deserve to be permitted the privilege of nursing him; that no reproaches he could have uttered were so eloquent of her error as his silence; that no punishment could have been so severe as the contrast between his generosity and her littleness. She passed through ages of torture, through eternities of mental anguish during the anxious days of that relapse, when she shrunk from letting her hand touch his, and yet when he could not rest tranquil for a moment unless he held it fast.

No doubt he fancied the pressure might prove a guarantee of his unshaken love, of his free and full forgiveness; no doubt he wished to prove to her, even in his sickness and his weakness, how strong and unswerving his protection would be to her in health and in strength. No doubt he feared lest by a look or a gesture he should hurt the heart of one who had so grievously wounded him, for Maurice Storn's was a noble nature; there was not an atom of meanness or littleness in him, and it was as much a part and portion of his character to refrain from even silently upbraiding her then, as it had been in the days gone by, to trust her without a limit to his faith.

And yet every effort he made to heal the wound only drove the probe home deeper. He might spare his wife his reproaches, but he could not ease the pangs of her own self-reproach; and day by day a darker shadow came stealing over her heart, and out of the utter silence that was maintained between them on the subject which lay nearest the souls of both, a sort of night fell upon her, and she spoke and moved, and even looked up with reluctance.

Maurice could not understand her. Slowly struggling back to convalescence, with her soft white hand clasped in his, he was trying, even when too weak to speak, to unravel that most tangled skein of human nature, a woman's mind, wondering what place he held in her affections, and whether still, and in spite of her confession and his forgiveness, of her story of temptation and misery and repentance, she was not sitting thus silent and absorbed because of the love she had borne and bore to Herbert Clyne.

It was not a reflection calculated to cheer the spirits of an invalid, and perhaps it was the wear and tear of this ever-present suspicion which made him at last say—

"Lina, before I leave this bed of sickness, and go out into the world again to work and struggle as before, there is one thing I must know, which your own manner has put in my mind to ask. Answer me, dear, as you would if I were dying, as, perhaps, indeed, I may be, for I am strangely long of getting back my strength—answer me now, truthfully and without reserve, as you may have to do some day—whilst you have been sitting here beside me, have your thoughts not been wandering away from me to him—have you not been wishing for his companionship, and thinking that your life in the future might be lonely without his sinful love?"

"So help me Heaven, Maurice," she answered—and there was a something marvellously startling in the contrast between his quiet, earnest question and her passionate reply, "I have never thought of Herbert Clyne since *that* night with a feeling that I should be afraid or ashamed to show you."

"Then what is the matter, Lina?—Is it that though you have been able to root out that mad affection for him, you cannot take back the love I would not for my life do otherwise than believe you once held in your heart for me?"

"Not take it back!" she echoed; "oh, Maurice! I love you better,—far better now than in the days when you first asked me to be your wife; but I know I have come to understand you too late, and that you can never love me again,—it is impossible you should."

"Are you sure you understand me now, Lina?" he asked, raising her head and looking into the face so altered from what it had been the first time he beheld it; "I think not, or you would know that when my heart changes or swerves from you, it will have ceased beating for ever. I never can say much about what I feel, but all I want to know is, whether you still love me, and me alone, and whether you will be faithful and true to me as I shall be to you?"

"Maurice, I will be faithful and true till death. You may trust me now."

From that day, Maurice Storn got better, and before very long was able to move from the fashionable house in Belgravia to an unfurnished floor which Mr. Matson had taken for them in the City. It was, perhaps, only natural, under the circumstances, for the chemist to decline his friend's invitation for them to make the old house their home till times mended, and John accordingly contented himself with sending such furniture to their lodgings as he knew the Storns would never dream of buying for themselves, whilst Mary's dear, useful fingers sewed up carpets and arranged curtains, and made the bare, comfortless room look habitable and cozy before Lina and her husband came to take possession of them.

There was not a thing forgotten which they were likely to need; a long apprenticeship to poverty had made Mary know precisely the articles which Lina would be most likely to over-look; and with her own hands she spread the table cloth, and set out the tea things, and placed the kettle on the stand ; and then, having seen that there was no solitary item wanting in Lina's bed-chamber, that the room was well aired and the fire burning, she sat down in the parlour, and taking up a paper, commenced to read.

True woman !—she went first to the deaths, births, and marriages, and the fourth wedding she lit on was Herbert Clyne's ; she had known he was married, for Miss Tryphenia had sent her cards, but somehow the printed announcement startled her.

Did Lina know ? The dear, good little wife, who, perhaps, at the bottom of her heart had a very feminine feeling of sympathy for Lina's fault, could not bear that paragraph to be the first greeting her friend found in her new home, so she put the paper aside, and took up a book to amuse herself till their arrival.

It was late when the cab drove to the door, and Mary, follow-ing the married couple up the stairs, declared afterwards to her husband, it was pitiable to see how much his long illness had weakened Mr. Storn, and to notice how grievously his altered fortunes affected him.

Lina, sitting beside him at the tea-table, buttering his toast, cutting up his chop, guarding him from draughts, did not seem to perceive the narrow dimensions of their new abode, nor appear to fret about their changed circumstances ; but Mr. Storn's eyes wandered round the room, noticing the dingy paint and the vulgar paper, and the common fire-place. It was put before him in a tangible form at last, that he had fallen from the topmost rung of fortune's ladder to the ground ; that he had life to begin all over again, with so much less of it left than formerly, that he had climbed so high as just to touch and lose—that he was a ruined man.

Nevertheless, he felt he had something left, which, so long as it pleased God to grant him health, was an indestructible inheritance—intellect ; and he resolved, stretching out his poor, weak hand over the arm of his chair, as if to try its power, that he would make haste and get well to labour, for Lina's sake, once more.

Janet, who stuck to them in their misfortunes, faithful and methodical as ever, removed the tea equipage, and then Mr. Storn, lying full length upon the couch, asked Mrs. Matson if there were such a thing in the house as a newspaper.

"You seem to have remembered everything else a sick man is likely to want," he said with a grateful smile. "Perhaps you have not forgotten that."

It was not in Mary's nature to refuse his request, so she produced the *Times*, and handed it to him with the remark that, as it belonged to the office, she must take it with her when she went; then she and Lina drew their chairs near to the fire, and had a comfortable gossip about household matters, and future plans and present prospects.

"How these coals scorch one's face," Mrs. Storn observed at last, and she pushed back her chair, and held up her hand to protect her cheeks from the blaze.

Just then Mr. Storn dropped the first sheet of the *Times*, and his wife picking it up, said, "It will do nicely for a fan— *faute de mieux.*"

"Have this, dear, instead," said Mary, proffering a book.

"Thank you, this will do beautifully," answered Lina, and talked on, glancing almost unconsciously all the while at what the people wanted, and the moneys found, and the bank notes missing. Suddenly she stopped in the middle of a sentence, and Mary knew she had dropped at last upon the one piece of news in that paper which had any interest for her. Instinctively the one woman, true, faithful, and happy wife, placed her hand on that of the other who had been, and was so miserable, and pressed it tenderly; but Lina's was not a nature to appreciate or reciprocate the sympathy which, though meant in all love and kindness, was yet ill-judged.

Coldly withdrawing her hand, she turned over the paper, and whilst the sales by auction flitted and danced before her eyes, her guest's cheek flushed painfully, and hurt, and grieved, she could, perhaps, scarcely have told why; Mrs. Matson, after a moment's hesitation, rose to go.

Then Lina, all penitence, got up too, and accompanying Mary into the bedroom, showed her, by fifty little acts, that she was sorry for her irritation, and anxious to make amends for it. She would tie on her friend's bonnet, and pick up her gloves, and fasten her veil, and adjust her shawl, and wrap her up warm and snug; and when she had stuck the last pin in its place, she put her arms round her neck and kissed her.

"Mary, dear," she said, "I fear you have been doing too much for us to-day; you look pale and tired."

"I do not feel tired," was the reply, uttered cheerfully enough, though some painful feeling ruffled the usually tranquil face for a minute. "I am not very strong," she added almost in the same breath; "I have never been, and I feel I never shall be."

"You should take care of yourself," urged Mrs. Storn.

"I do," she replied. "I have grown very careful lately; there are four reasons why I should."

"And what may they be?" Lina queried.

"John and the children," Mary replied with a grave smile, and the old thoughtful look Mrs. Storn had noticed at Bow, came into her eyes. "I am getting better, however," she said after a pause, "and whenever the warm weather comes, I mean to be very extravagant, and get money from my husband, and go out of town. Leave him all to himself," Mrs. Matson finished with a brighter glance, "for the first time since our marriage."

"You have never repented that, Mary, have you?" enquired Lina, earnestly.

"Repented! Good gracious! no, it was the happiest event of my life, and John says it was the best day's work he ever did. We were thinking of trying for the Dunmow flitch."

"Do," counselled Lina; "and if you win, give me the half of it."

A shade crossed Mrs. Storn's face as she spoke, but her visitor did not perceive it, for she heard a knock at the hall door, and cried out—

"That's John; I told him not to come, but he thinks I never can take care of myself."

"Mary has been accusing you of disobeying orders," said Mrs. Storn as her old friend came up the stairs; "but I think I shall beg her not to scold you dreadfully this time, for Mr. Storn will be so glad to see you."

"And I am glad to see him back in the city once again," Mr. Matson declared, shaking hands cordially with the bankrupt chemist. "I would rather find you in a larger house, Mr. Storn," he added; "but that is to come yet, and I have proved myself what a great mass of happiness can be packed up in very little space. How did he bear jolting over the stones, Mrs. Storn?" he asked.

"Better than I expected," the convalescent answered for himself. "I am gaining ground, and shall soon be a strong man now—able to commence work again."

"Have you ever thought about what it would be best for

you to do till this bankruptcy question is settled ?" inquired Mr. Matson, as he seated himself beside the sofa.

"Settled, or not, there is no choice left me; I must take a situation of some kind. I suppose you know the estate will not pay five shillings in the pound."

"So I have heard."

"I cannot imagine where all the money went to," Mr. Storn continued. "I am sure the acid always paid fifty per cent. at least; and though our housekeeping was heavy, still it was not too much, considering the amount of our profits. The new experiment certainly swamped us; but till the last day I thought we could pay twenty shillings. Where the money went to puzzles me."

"Do you think Mr. Glenaen took it ?" Mrs. Storn demanded.

"Took it ! My dear Lina, what do you mean ?" asked her husband, in a ruffled tone.

"I mean, do you think it possible Mr. Glenaen did anything with the money you know nothing about ?" she explained.

"Most certainly not. That would have been swindling, a downright act of fraud."

"Nevertheless," here interposed Mr. Matson, "many people imagine Mr. Glenaen has not been acting honourably, either by you or your creditors. There are two or three large houses who I know are determined to give trouble, and I do not anticipate an immediate or favourable certificate. Perhaps I should not have come worrying you to-night about these things; but Mr. Ferres was speaking of you this evening, and asking me what you thought of doing."

"And what interest can it possibly be to him what I mean to do ?" inquired Maurice, shortly.

"He thought, perhaps, till times mended a little, you might like to draw a salary out of our house," said John in an off-hand sort of way. "He fancied you would not care to commence again on your own account immediately, and authorised me to say that, if you decided on taking a situation, they would endeavour to meet your views."

There was a minute's silence—then Mr. Storn said in a low voice—

"Tell Mr. Ferres that I accept his offer, and am grateful for it."

"He attached a condition, however, to the proposal," Mr. Matson explained, "which, perhaps, you may think rather stringent, namely, that whilst you hold your situation, there shall be no speculating or experimenting. He said it was better to have this understood at first, and——"

"It would be more satisfactory for us both hereafter," finished Mr. Storn, as his friend hesitated. "I agree to the condition."

"Thanks," said John Matson, as he rose to go. "Now, Mary, let us be off. The children were crying in the most fearful style before I left home; there was a perfect concert got up by the innocents—a screaming trio. Good night, Mr. Storn. I shall call in and report progress to-morrow."

CHAPTER XXXIV.

UNDER EXAMINATION.

NEXT day but one after Mr. Storn's removal to the city, he managed to crawl over to Basinghall Street and make a formal surrender to the court. Ill enough he looked as he stood before the clerk's desk, waiting for his protection, to convince any one that the medical certificate which had been handed in before, of his unfitness to attend in person, was perfectly correct, and that it was merely bodily weakness, and not mental disinclination, which had prevented his fulfilling the requirements of the law in the very earliest stages of his bankruptcy. In truth, the chemist was growing painfully anxious for the second examination to be concluded. He wanted information as to the actual state of his affairs, which he found he was not going to receive from his partner.

From the time the cyanogen experiments were commenced Mr. Glenaen had taken on himself the office of book-keeper, and Maurice knew no more than the man in the moon where all the money made by the sulphuric acid was gone. He had heard the manufacturer declare with an oath that every copper which came out of the sulphuric chamber was melted in the cyanogen furnaces; but lying on the sofa with a pencil and piece of paper in his hand, Mr. Storn estimated probable gains and actual expenditure, and could not make either one or the other result only in five shillings in the pound for the creditors. He knew his housekeeping expenses had not been unreasonable; he remembered that for the only large private debt he ever incurred he had suffered judgment, and allowed the sheriff's officers to take possession of his private goods; he could not fail to recollect that but for the court allowance he should not have a stick of furniture in his room nor a sovereign in his pocket; it might be, that too much had been spent in

plans and squandered in experiments; but still, if they had
spilt with cyanogen, they had filled with sulphuric acid; and
where the eighty thousand pounds, of which it was said the
estate was deficient, had gone, Mr. Storn confessed was a
mystery to him.

As it seemed to be likewise to the creditors, who proved extremely difficult people to deal with. Opposition after opposition was entered against the bankrupts, and before the day
appointed for hearing the case came round, Maurice perceived
that old friends and customers had changed their tone concerning him, and that reckless expenditure and personal extravagance
were amongst the mildest of the terms applied to the proceedings of the pair lately trading under the firm of Storn, Glenaen,
and Co. He did not understand the aspect of affairs at all;
he saw the balance sheet prepared during his illness by his
partner, and found that while the profits had been large, the
outgoings had been enormous; he beheld lists of debts that
appalled him, entries of payments which were sufficient to have
swamped any business; he found that Glenaen's personal expenses had been nothing to his; and he was almost deranged
when he added up the sums that had been wasted on the experiment that had beggared them.

"It was quite time for us to shut up, Matson," he said dolefully, when he came to the end of the list. "There seems no
mistake in the balance sheet, but still some way, I think, there
ought to be more for the creditors."

Thus it was with a heavy heart he went slowly out on the
appointed morning to face Mr. Commissioner Scourge and the
refractory creditors; he knew the failure of the cyanogen lay
with him, and that he could give no sufficient reason why he
had risked such large sums in trying to perfect it; he had tried
to do right and act honestly, but evil had come and put another
face on his endeavours; he was sorry for having let so many
people in, and he was anxious and nervous about what the
Commissioner, and the assignees, and the creditors might find
to say.

Very reluctantly, therefore, he entered the doors and walked
round the paved square, absently touching each pillar as he
went past; very slowly he ascended the stone staircase, and
paced along the corridor, where he paused for a minute before
entering the mean dirty court where the Commissioner, in a
great wig, sat looking up at the ceiling, apparently perfectly
unconscious that anything was going on around him in which
he had the slightest concern. Occasionally, indeed, he came
down from dream land to the affairs of every-day life, being

pleased to sign documents that were brought to him from time to time, but which had nothing whatever to do with the case before him. He leaned back in his chair and gazed in a state of beatitude at the brown paint of the canopy above his throne, or at the dirty plaster above that, whilst the clerk scratched away over sheets of paper, and the official assignee handed in his report, and the fortunate bankrupt, who was passing without opposition, was swearing, in the happiest manner possible that he had given up everything he owned in the world. Perhaps it was the truth—or perhaps it was not; at all events the creditors did not think him worth powder and shot; and he had his wife's settlement to fall back upon, even if there really were nothing saved out of the general wreck of his own fortunes. He had enough of an estate to pay the bankruptcy expenses, and that was all which materially concerned any one of the individuals present at the scene, on which Maurice Storn, leaning against the counsel's box, and holding his hat in his hand, looked anxiously.

"Shall we get off as well, Glenaen?" he whispered to that worthy, who had just come tramping up the staircase, and who now stood beside his partner mightily shabbily dressed, and appearing like a craft that had met the trade winds of fortune blowing the wrong way, and got its rigging torn to ribbons in the storm. "Shall we get off as well?" said Mr. Storn; to which Gordon Glenaen vouchsafed a gruff,

"What the deuce should hinder us?" by way of reply.

It was not long before the fortunate bankrupt had the pleasure of seeing the commissioner sign the order for his certificate, and his coat brushed Glenaen's as he walked out of court a free man. Immediately after a solicitor rose, and stating that in the case of Storn, Glenaen and Co., bankrupts, he appeared for the creditors—commenced an harangue which lasted for exactly twenty minutes, and concluded with an announcement of his (Mr. Blink's) intention to examine the bankrupts; whereupon Mr. Storn was put in the box, sworn, and the questioning commenced.

Little enough Maurice knew, and the legal gentleman soon found his subtle course of examination was entirely thrown away.

From the time he commenced the experiments in cyanogen, Mr. Storn explained that he had never made a single entry in the company's books. His time was so fully occupied with endeavouring to perfect his scheme, that it was impossible for him to attend to the counting-house portion of the business.

"By virtue of my oath," Mr. Storn proceeded, after having been reminded by the lawyer that he had sworn to tell the whole truth, "I never imagined we were hopelessly insolvent until a few days before the bankruptcy; my partner, for some time previously, had been making heavy complaints of the manner in which the cyanogen experiments were draining the sulphuric business dry; but I knew if the former were successful, we should recover ourselves immediately, and up to the very last I had no reason to anticipate a failure in my plan."

In reply to the solicitor, Mr. Storn went on to say, that he could assign no satisfactory cause for the ill success of his scheme—his plan had answered on a small scale, and he knew no reason why it had not done so on a larger one: if he were able to try again with his present experience, he could not make any material alteration in his method. The scheme had been fairly tried: money and time, and thought, all had been given to the experiment. Cyanogen was a product which had engaged the attention of chemists of all countries. It had been produced in large quantities, but always at a great expense. His, Mr. Storn's endeavour, had been to reduce that expense. In answer to a question from Mr. Blinks, as to what cyanogen was, the chemist replied, that it was a gas, which, when combined with other substances, was used largely for purposes of manufacture. Hitherto it had been produced by the decomposition of animal matter, but his endeavour was to take its most expensive component from the atmosphere. "In other words," explained Mr. Storn, as he thought, in the clearest manner possible, "to solidify the nitrogen forming so large a portion of the air we breathe, and thus get the dearest part of cyanogen for nothing."

Seeing that he might as well, or better, have expounded his meaning to the learned individual before him in Hindoostanee, Mr. Storn then endeavoured to explain his explanation by proceeding thus:—

"To illustrate the case—carbonate of soda, a substance with which everyone must be well acquainted, is a compound of a gas called carbonic acid, and an alkali called soda. Cyanide of potassium is a compound of a gas called cyanogen, and an alkali called potash. In both cases the compound is formed by the union of a gas with a solid—the gas itself becoming solidified by the union."

Of course, after this very lucid explanation, which was about as clear to the person who listened to it as an Indian love song performed in the original, no further question as to the nature of cyanogen could in decency be asked; and accordingly, the lawyer, at whose mystification Mr. Glenaen was internally shaking his sides, professed himself completely enlightened, and proceeded to enquire,

"In what especial branch of manufacture cyanogen was principally used?"

"Dyeing and colour making," answered Mr. Storn.

"And your object was to reduce the cost of its production?"

"Precisely," said Maurice, who had told him this six times before.

"And you attribute your bankruptcy to the failure of this experiment?"

"I know of no other reason which should have brought us here," was the reply; "for, to the best of my belief, there were always large profits returned by the sulphuric acid."

"There, now he has set him off again," thought Mr. Glenaen; and true enough, the word acid was hardly uttered, before Mr. Blinks plunged into chemicals once more.

"What was sulphuric acid?"

"Sulphur and oxygen," answered Mr. Storn, mercifully shortening his reply.

"And you discovered a new method of preparing it?"

"Yes; a much cheaper process than that in general use."

"What is the ordinary process?" persisted Mr. Blinks, who had not the slightest idea he was making a donkey of himself.

"Burning sulphur in a furnace, and combining it in large leaden chambers with the vapours produced by the decomposition of nitrate of potash."

Having obtained which information, the lawyer proceeded to enquire what Mr. Storn's process was. Whereupon up started Mr. Blast, solicitor for the bankrupts, and told Mr. Storn he was not bound to answer that question.

"I have not the slightest intention of doing so," was the chemist's tranquil reply.

"In what essential particular, then," persisted the lawyer, "did your process differ from that ordinarily in use?"

"I discovered a means of economizing nitre," was Maurice's answer.

"And how did you effect that?"

"I appeal to the court," Mr. Storn said, turning to Mr. Commissioner Scourge, "whether I am bound to answer that question."

"Certainly not," was the decision of the court, to which Mr. Blinks bowed his head in angry silence.

"To what purpose is sulphuric acid generally applied?" continued that gentleman, after the little break just chronicled; but before Mr. Storn could reply, the Commissioner enquired the object of the course of examination adopted, stating, at the same time his belief that it was perfectly irrelevant to the case.

"My object was to ascertain the genuineness of the experiments reported to have been tried," answered Mr. Blinks; "but if your honour considers I am wasting the time of the court, I will proceed to the question of accounts."

"You had much better," was his honour's curt reply, and Mr. Blinks proceeded as follows—

"What should you say were the average returns from the sulphuric acid business?"

"I cannot tell," Maurice answered; "for after the acid once got into regular working order, I had nothing whatever to do with the books. This much, however, I can say, positively, that if my creditors were willing to give me back the sulphuric factory at Bow, I would undertake to repay them all, principal and interest, in seven years."

"I dare say you would," muttered Gordon Glenaen to himself; "but why need you be such a fool as to say it?" and he shot a look from under his knitted eyebrows at Storn, which look was caught by Mr. Commissioner Scourge, who from that time forth kept the manufacturer more under inspection than was at all agreeable to the individual so favoured.

And the great man of the court sent one or two glances towards Mr. Storn, who was growing as pale as a corpse, and at last, whilst doing his best to answer the lawyer's finishing questions, lost his voice completely.

"You will perceive," said Mr. Blast, addressing Mr. Blinks, "that Mr. Storn is but just recovering from a dangerous illness."

"I have done with Mr. Storn for the present," was Mr. Blinks' reply, uttered with that suavity of manner for which, when not bullying a witness, he was so famous; and on the strength of this gracious assurance, Mr. Storn very thankfully sat down.

Gordon Glenaen was then sworn and examined.

Had been a manufacturing chemist for years past. Was originally in the employment of Messrs. Colke and Ferres, where he became acquainted with his present partner. Started in business with money partly saved, and partly borrowed from his mother. Repaid the moneys advanced by her within five years from the time of starting in business. Had made sometimes a profit and sometimes a loss. His factory at Bow was not for the special manufacture of any chemical, and, till his partnership with Storn, he was a general, and not a particular manufacturer. Had made chlorine—chlorine was made of

chloride of sodium, peroxide of manganese, and sulphuric acid
—had done a good deal in bichromate of potash, citrate of
iron, citric acid, ferro-prussiate of potash, and muriatic acid;
had made pyroligneous acid, sesqui-carbonate and hydrochlo-
rate of ammonia; and manufactured sulphate of soda, which,
Mr. Glenaen explained, with great *goût*, was made from chloride
of sodium and sulphuric acid—hydrochloric acid being produced during the process.

He strung together every hard name he could think of;
and having, during the course of his examination, mentioned
ferro-prussiate of potash, and chloride of sodium, two or three
times, Mr. Blinks seized on the latter expression, as the most
pronounceable, and enquired " what it was ?"

" Chloride of sodium," repeated Mr. Glenaen, " is muriate
of soda."

" Is there no other name for it, sir ?" interposed the commissioner, sharply.

" No other technical name that I recollect at this moment,"
answered Mr. Glenaen.

" We don't want chemical names, we want English here, if
possible.   What is the every-day name of chloride of sodium ?"

Thus pressed, Mr. Glenaen had no alternative left, but to
inform Mr. Blinks that the other name for chloride of sodium
was common salt—an intimation which raised a titter in the
court, and dimly suggested to Mr. Blinks the idea that, during
his pursuit of knowledge under difficulties, he had been afford-
ing infinite amusement to the individual whom he immediately
after commenced questioning on the subject of accounts.

Mr. Glenaen had found the money for the first sulphuric
experiments, to the extent of, perhaps, fifteen hundred pounds;
did not remember with whom the first mention of partnership originated; never offered to find the money to start the
concern; had not sufficient to have done so; told Mr. Storn
he could get the money, and did get it from his mother; she
had fifteen per cent. for the sums advanced; could not say
whether any, or all, or none of the cash so obtained passed
through his partner's hands; had the highest opinion possible
of Mr. Storn's abilities as a practical and experimental chemist; never took into consideration the fact, that if Mr. Storn
found the brains, and Mrs. Glenaen the money for the experiment, he, Glenaen, individually contributed nothing; thought
that, as his own money helped to test the thing, and as he was
the first to suggest its being attempted, he had a right to some
of the after-profits; in his opinion fifteen per cent. was not a
heavy rate of interest for his mother to draw out of a new con-

cern; nobody else would have advanced the money at all; when the acid began to pay, never suggested to Mr. Storn it would be advisable to reduce the debt to Mrs. Glenaen; thought Mr. Storn able to think about his own affairs for himself; never advised him to do anything, except reduce his personal expenses; instead of Mrs. Glenaen's debt being liquidated, fresh debts were incurred; would swear she had advanced the sum mentioned in the balance-sheet; remembered he was on oath when he said not a sixpence had ever been returned to her; could produce vouchers for all the payments mentioned in the books; would be ruined by this bankruptcy; compelled to relinquish business, and probably take a situation; his mother had a mortgage over his own factory at Bow; could not say when, or on what occasion, the money had been advanced for which she held that mortgage; only knew it was received by the concern; considered his mother a wealthy woman, but concluded that his bankruptcy would cripple her resources materially; knew nothing about his father, nor the source whence Mrs. Glenaen's income was derived; advised Mr. Blinks to go and ask her about it himself; felt no hesitation in saying the cyanogen had ruined them; believed he was justified in spending the amounts mentioned in the balance-sheet; did not know they were insolvent when he contracted the latest debts; had always lived in the simplest manner possible; was unmarried; resided with his mother; sometimes he and she were on good terms, and sometimes they were not; would swear there was no collusion between them in the matter of the debts; did not think the profits of the firm had been divided into kicks and half-pence; knew, at all events, the half-pence had not found their way to him; believed Mr. Storn's failure in the cyanogen experiment might be traced to his son's death; thought his partner's brains had not been worth much since; the last payment of interest to his mother was made ten days before their bankruptcy; did not know then that they should have to pass through the court; had never taken a receipt from his mother for the interest, but could procure a discharge from her; could not recollect stating before that half a year's interest was due to her; if he ever did say so, must have meant before the last payment was made; could not mention, at the moment, in what precise manner the sums advanced by Mrs. Glenaen had been disbursed; they had all been spent about the concern, and had not found their way into his (Glenaen's) pocket; the only way in which he could account for their bankruptcy was, that Mr. Storn did not attend to the business; what he meant by not attending was,

putting his heart in it; would not undertake to swear that
Mr. Storn had not spent eighteen hours out of the twenty-four
at work; thought that very probably he had; did not consider
they had bought their goods in a very dear market; money
spent in chemical plant made no show; the return of the coals
was correct; had purchased coals from different people; sold
the coke; there was not much profit from that; everything
entered in the balance-sheet was correct; had not been keeping
his books for the court; could see no material difference between the books when kept by himself, and the books as kept
by Mr. Storn, except that the debit side was larger; this was
correct; the cyanogen experiment accounted for that; could
not say why, fourteen days after Mr. Storn relinquished the
books, there was a credit of five thousand pounds to Mrs.
Glenaen; did not think, with the balance in hand at time of
commencing the cyanogen, the loan was unjustifiable; remembered now that the reason he took the money then was, because
his mother was willing to lend it, and he did not know whether,
when they wanted the amount, she would be in the same mind;
had thought his mother's command of money singular, but
there were many singular things in the world; if Mrs. Glenaen
were in business, would not object to become partner; thought
the concern, wherever it existed, must be a paying one; on
oath, did not know where her income came from; would like
to know as much as Mr. Blinks; it was not derived from his
factory or Mr. Storn's sulphuric acid; thought it possible the
five thousand pounds in question had not been named to Mr.
Storn; never named money matters to him at all until a short
time before the bankruptcy; as he had made a hit with the
sulphuric acid, thought he would make a hit with the cyanogen,
and grudged no money to perfect it; never considered the
money was not theirs to spend; only knew they were insolvent
by adding up the books the first night the cyanogen failed;
they made two or three attempts after that to perfect the
experiment; Mr. Storn was almost deranged when he found
it a failure; he, Mr. Glenaen, was not in the habit of getting
excited about anything; admitted, in answer to a query to
that effect from Mr. Blinks, that he might be a philosopher,
but thought it was not pleasant to be beggared for all that;
had not made away with any property; had no property, except
his factory, to make away with, and that belonged, by right of
mortgage, to his mother; did not think it likely she would give
it back to him; was not particularly alive to the benefits of
having a mother; it did not appear to have done much for him;
there was a coolness between his mother and himself since the

failure; she thought he should have seen her safe at all events; had never been told by her he had pocketed the money himself; wished Mr. Blinks would examine her, and then, probably, he would get all the information he wanted; thought it a bad business for him he had ever seen Mr. Storn, and was desired by the lawyer to stand down.

Mr. Storn was then recalled; had never inquired what interest Mrs. Glenaen was to receive; never heard of the five thousand advanced so soon after he gave up the management of the books; considered the sulphuric acid had latterly sold at a low rate; had no reason to suspect Mr. Glenaen of dishonesty; never had suspected him; did not suspect him now; was certain his partner had no knowledge of the source whence his mother derived her income; believed, however, she really had one, as her money had started them at Bow; never imagined that money might really belong to Glenaen, and be merely lent nominally by the lady; now the idea was suggested, did not think it probable; had striven to afford every facility to the creditors; was quite willing to work the Bow factory, under inspection; would commence again to-morrow; could get a situation immediately; must do so, as, beyond the Court allowance, he had nothing. So ended Mr. Storn; and Mr. Blinks was pleased to dismiss him prior to commencing his address to the Court. When that was concluded, Mr. Blast had a good deal to urge in behalf of the bankrupts; and when all had said their say, the Commissioner delivered judgment.

The accounts, he opined, were not correct; and he would adjourn the case for three months, in order to give the bankrupts an opportunity of amending their balance sheet.

In the meantime he should order the allowance to be continued to the bankrupt, Storn; but the answers of Glenaen were so unsatisfactory that he should discontinue his allowance—while extending protection to both. He was not satisfied with the bankrupt, Glenaen, who ought, from his position, to have known the firm was hopelessly insolvent. Storn might be, and was to blame, for not inquiring into the state of affairs; but, considering that he had only recently recovered from a dangerous illness, and had attended solely to the experimental part of the business, his honor would make an order for the five pounds a-week, previously allowed, to be continued.

Having so spoken, his honor further intimated, that as it was late, he should not hear any other case; and thus the court closed, while Maurice Storn and Gordon Glenaen walked down the steps together.

"A very nice cleft stick you and your experiments have

put me in," grumbled the latter, as they turned into Gresham Street.

"I am sorry for it," was Maurice's answer; and with a cold good-bye he turned down Prince's Street, while his partner strode along Lothbury, and getting from thence by easy stages, through Bartholomew and Finch Lanes, into Cornhill, hailed a Bow and Stratford omnibus, and chewing the cud of anger and mortification, jolted away along the noisy pavement—Home.

CHAPTER XXXV.

SIR HERBERT CLYNE.

DURING the passage of the three months which Mr. Commissioner Scourge allowed the bankrupts for the amendment of their balance sheet, Maurice Storn, after one or two attempts to cut the Gordian knot of their pecuniary affairs, left the books and accounts to the doctoring of his late partner, and accepting Mr. Ferres' offer, slipped into harness again, and became once more a clerk in the house which he had left to better his condition. He took the counting-house department; Mr. Ferres abdicating in his favour; while John Matson devoted himself more exclusively to the out-door business of the firm. The old salary was about divided between the pair; but Maurice never murmured at the pay. He felt only too thankful to obtain a post likely to provide Lina and himself with daily bread when the court allowance should cease, and he was neither very nice about what he got, nor how he worked. He had gone back to the Maurice Storn of earlier times, and was the same in all respects as before he began his experiments save one—viz.: that where he had been formerly a rising, he was now a disappointed man; yet the disappointment made him work all the harder. Mr. Ferres could not fail to perceive this, and respected him for it.

Work—on the old treadmill from six in the morning till seven, and eight, and nine at night; work on another man's business for another man's benefit, as he had so lately worked and toiled for his own. Work with a weakened body and a heavier heart! Work for a sum he had not hesitated to waste on the simplest of his cyanogen experiments. Work everlasting! but still Maurice Storn never repined; while Lina, though she saw as little of her husband as ever, though poverty had come to her, was happier than she had been during the whole

of their comfortable competence in the city, and unexpected
and fleeting wealth out west. Sitting in her small rooms, sewing. and making, and mending; contriving, in her way, as Mary
Matson had once done in hers, how to make much out of
little; feeling economy a duty, and exertion a necessity, Mrs.
Storn took at last her humble woman's part in the world, and
was contented with it, or, at all events, tried to be; for if ever
her thoughts strayed sorrowfully back to Geordie, or remorse-
lessly and with shame towards Mr. Clyne, she would rise from
her work and busy herself in some little domestic arrangements
till the struggle was over, and she felt she might with safety
trust her heart alone with itself once more.

Changed days those for Lina, when the same black crape
bonnet she had worn in Belgravia was forced to do duty for
months and months together along Fenchurch Street, through
Leadenhall Market, up Gracechurch Street, down Cornhill;
when the city lady had to turn and patch her dresses, and try
to look neat on old materials, and take care of her ribbons, and
sew the fingers of her gloves; when she had to go out and do
her marketing for herself while Janet did her washing at home;
when she forgot to remember that it was disagreeable to be
jostled and stared at, but went straight on through the crowded
city thoroughfares to her object. Changed days those for the
rather fine-ladyish Lina of old, when she was forced to wear
mended shoes, and walk away through the streets without an
escort; when her housekeeping had to be reduced to the nar-
rowest limits in order to pay for the wine which, during that
weary convalescence, had been life to her husband; for the
couch on which he stretched out his tired limbs in the evening;
for the easy chair that stood by the fireplace, and the solitary
table which occupied the centre of their sitting room.

In those days while the court allowance still lasted, Mr.
Storn was trying to save enough to pay off the debts contracted
during his illness, and to buy sufficient to furnish, ever so
plainly, a house of their own; and though all this pinching
might be a change to Mistress Lina, it was yet not an unpleasant one. Her trials had come in the days of their prosperity;
and adversity, which might have proved a test and a trouble to
many a woman, was no trouble to her. Very faithfully in those
days the poor weak, erring wife of old tried to do her duty, and
as a reward for her endeavour, the road of duty was smoothed
under her feet; and but for the memory of that time when she
had so nearly been lost for ever, Lina, spite of her childless
hearth and lonely existence, would have been a very happy
woman.

Once she met Mr. Clyne; she on foot, he in a carriage with his wife by his side. There was a stoppage in King William Street, and as Lina stood waiting to cross, she happened to look at a brougham which was jammed between two omnibuses and a load of hay. As she raised her face, Mr. Clyne's glance lighted upon it, and he turned as white as the ribbons in his wife's bonnet. Mrs. Storn had only time to see that gravely and respectfully he raised his hat, while Tryphenia, brimfull of virtue and assumption, drew herself up and stared haughtily at the woman she had once been only too glad to know, then, with a contemptuous gesture, dragged her shawl over her shoulders, and, leaning back, seemed to profess that the chemist's wife was much too low a person for her even to honour by a look. It all passed in a second, the next the omnibus moved forward, and the brougham followed, while Lina remained standing just where the occurrence found her, unmindful that the street was comparatively clear, and that she could now cross and wend her way home.

"I will take you over, ma'am," said a benevolent sweeper, who had been watching her previous attempts to effect the passage, and who fancied she was a stranger, and timid about the crossings. "I will take you over, don't be afraid, we shall not be run down—please remember the sweeper, ma'am," he finished, as they touched the opposite curb, and the boy stood there thumbing the brim of a disreputable old hat, whilst Lina pulled out her purse and gave him the smallest coin she could find in it.

Changed days those for Lina; perhaps it was some notion of this sort which troubled Mr. Clyne, and made him so silent and abstracted, that the fair Tryphenia was tempted to observe, as they drove along Cannon Street—

"I wonder, Herbert, you, a married man, would bow to that woman. If Mr. Storn approved I suppose it did not much signify to you what you did when you were single, but now the case is different."

"Madam," was Herbert's answer, "had Mrs. Storn been the character you insinuate, you would never have been Mrs. Clyne. Pray spare me any tears," he added in the same breath; "I had hoped that long ago you and I understood one another."

And he sank back in his corner of the carriage, while Tryphenia, in the other, managed to shed real tears of rage and wounded vanity. It was well to be Mrs. Clyne in the present, and Lady Clyne to come; but she would have liked something more—something she had fancied before marriage she could do without a place in her husband's heart, which, she found out before she had been three days a wife, had no room in it for the love of her, or any other woman, save one. So she, though heartless herself, was mortified to find she had no power to fill or warm the heart of another, and for this reason she wept tears of spite, which Mr. Clyne heeded no more than if they had been a shower of drops from a watering pot. He was sick of her tears, and her smiles, and her littleness, and her affectations, and he was not sorry that their six months' tour on the continent had been abruptly terminated, for he felt weary of the companionship of the wife he had chosen, and hoped and trusted that in England their paths would lie more separate; that the burden he had voluntarily laid on his own shoulders, would be lightened for him in the land of his birth.

He had been summoned from abroad by intelligence of the dangerous illness of Sir Hugh Clyne, and leaving Tryphenia in London, he hurried on to the north, arriving at the Falls only a few hours before the old baronet breathed his last. He was weak, but sat propped up with pillows in an arm-chair near the window, looking, with still undimmed eyes, over the park with its noble trees and lordly herds, and at the woods stretching far and far away in the distance, till at last the fresh green of the early summer foliage seemed to touch and mingle with the blue of the early summer sky.

"Well, Herbert," he said, "I am going home to the old vault at last. I suppose you think I have kept you out of your title long enough, and that it is time for me. There, don't look vexed, I did not mean it, boy; you were always the best of our race, and I daresay you would not grudge me a few years of dotage yet. But I don't want to stay—sit down, I have a few words to say to you."

Herbert obeyed, and the old man remained for a few minutes gazing in silence at his nephew.

"I am pleased to know it is you to come after me," he said at length, "and I am glad you will bring a wife home to the old place. I hope you may have children, Herbert, and that for centuries to come the Falls will pass from father to son, and not, as it has been doing, from nephew to nephew's boy. Besides, the nephews are all exhausted now, Herbert, and after you there is none other. Why did you not bring the future Lady Clyne with you, my boy? Ha, does the scent lie in that direction? I am sorry for it, Herbert, and yet I have sometimes thought that a wife we do not love is better than no wife at all. Could you not have found in the length and breadth of England though, some other than a silk merchant's daughter, and wed her with your heart?"

"I have no heart, sir," was Herbert's answer.

"So your ship went to pieces on that sunk rock," Sir Hugh said pityingly. "Well, many a good craft has gone that way before you, and you have done the wisest thing you could to marry; nothing like the new for replacing the old; and yet a new love is worth no more than a new wine, it wants mellowness and strength. Herbert, I am sorry."

Heaven knew so was his listener; but there was no use grieving over the sinful and irretrievable past then, and the young man begged the baronet to change the subject. "My wife and I will travel along very smoothly together I doubt not," he said. "She is young, handsome, accomplished, fit to sit at the head of my table, and rule her house. After all, what more could I expect? We shall never be called upon to endure the test of love, poverty; as for all other things, let them rest."

"Aye, but things do not rest through all the long years of matrimony. I wish you had come to me first; but you married in such a hurry. I suppose the other played you false, Herbert; ah! well, never mind, let her go."

How the man's heart gushed blood at the other's words; how sick he grew while Lina, as he had last seen her—alone in the crowded street—with her dear, beautiful, sorrowful face raised to his came back and stood before his mind's eye. Poor Lina—poor child—in trouble and poverty he pictured her still fighting out the fight of old alone. Let her go! oh! the old baronet might as well have bade him lose memory at once. Let her go; perhaps he might when sense and life went too.

"I have been engaged lately with a correspondence with a Mr. Ferres of London," said Sir Hugh, after a few minutes' silence, "the London partner of that great house of Colke and Ferres, which is pretty well known in this part of the world. He seems a straightforward, business sort of person, and, therefore, as I have no time to attend to the affair properly myself, I must leave you to complete the investigation he asked me to commence. Earnshaw—you know Earnshaw, don't you? It lies about six miles to the north-west of Newcastle—came to me in the natural order of things from my uncle, but he got it from his wife, a Mrs. Maudsley, whose first husband cut his only son out of the property, and left it at the disposal of his widow—who disposed of it some seventy or eighty years since to my uncle, and, as he always understood the son I have mentioned died abroad, he took the estates as a very lucky windfall, which added two thousand a-year to his income. Mr. Ferres now says this young Maudsley did die abroad, it is true, but left behind him two sons, both of whom returned to England, one dying without issue, and the other leaving a son and two daughters. Now it would seem there had been a sort of a saying handed down in the family, that Earnshaw would some day fall in; and the grandson of the original heir took the notion so firmly into his head of there being truth at the bottom of these words, that he spent all the later years of his life hunting after Earnshaw in impossible places, and came at last to be regarded, even by his best friends, as a sort of monomaniac. One of his friends married his daughter, the last of the Maudsle vrace, and she is to be found in some place in the city of London; Storn, I think is the name of her husband. Now, you will see these people, even should they be all, as Mr. Ferres says, lineal descendants of the original Maudsley, have not a shadow of legal claim to this property, but still, I put it to you, Herbert, if they have not a right in equity; the property was willed away from the son at first, and it seems to me this Mrs. Storn has as much right to Earnshaw as you have to the Falls."

"Good Heavens! how the threads of our destiny have been woven in and out together," thought Herbert to himself, and he sat reflecting over the strange communication till his uncle interrupted him by asking what was his opinion of the matter. "Should the two thousand a-year be retained or relinquished, that was the question?"

"Relinquished by all means," said Mr. Clyne, warmly; "my dear sir, if you would do me a personal favour—will this estate back to its rightful owner—a few words would be sufficient."

"Yes, but we must not be rash, Herbert," expostulated the baronet; "we do not know whether this Mrs. Storn be really what she professes to be. Mr. Ferres may be deceived—it would be easy for you to make all the needful enquiries, and then, when quite satisfied, resign the property. It should not be permitted to leave the family without the fullest and strictest investigation of the claim now made. You could do all this—you will have time, I shall not."

"Mr. Storn would not accept this estate from me," Herbert remarked.

"And why not?" demanded the baronet.

"Because," answered his nephew with a painful hesitation, "he is honourable, and I was not."

"Not honourable, Herbert. You, a Clyne—my nephew—the future baronet—say this. What do you mean?—did you do the man an injury—do you owe him money, or lead him into any trouble; not honourable!—what do you mean?"

"I mean, sir, what I say; I have known Mr. Storn for years,

and believe a more upright, honourable man does not breathe; but yet there is that between us which he can never forgive nor forget. For my sake, then, sir, do them this tardy act of justice—he was rich, and made a large sum of money by means of chemistry, but failed not long since, and lost every farthing. You may therefore judge what Earnshaw would be to him, and it would be a relief to me to know he had got it back."

"But I do not like willing such property away in the dark," expostulated Sir Hugh; "and, besides, I do not know the names of any of these people."

"Madeline and Maurice Storn," Herbert informed him, with a lingering tenderness on the first name, which opened up a new volume in his history for the baronet's consideration.

"How old may this Mrs. Storn be?" he enquired.

"Not four-and-twenty, I should say," was Mr. Clyne's reply.

"Did you know her as Miss Maudsley?"

"No; only as Mrs. Storn."

"Humph!" said Sir Hugh, and he leaned back on his pillow and digested the information just received, for many minutes. When he spoke again, it was on a subject foreign to Earnshaw.

"By the bye, Herbert, you will find among my papers a memorandum of an annuity of five hundred a-year, to a relation by marriage of our family. You may find it to your advantage to pay this regularly—she is not a pleasant person to have dealings with—and, if crossed, might be troublesome."

"She!—is there a woman living on you, too? or can it be the same that harassed my father to death."

"Very possibly," was Sir Hugh's reply.

"And am I bound to pay money to her?" exclaimed Herbert, angrily.

"You will find it better to do so," answered the baronet.

"And why must I do this?" asked his nephew.

"I should counsel you not to ask; the story is not a creditable or pleasant one. It will die with her, and, as she is not a very young woman, let us hope the annuity will not have to be paid much longer."

"I do not like working in the dark," said Herbert; "during my father's lifetime, I paid hundred after hundred to some shadow which stood behind him, and now, when I thought the tax was removed, you tell me to pay her five hundred a-year. It is not for the value of the money," Mr. Clyne continued; "but I do not like being kept in ignorance like a child."

"Not even where the child's ignorance is a blessing?"

"No."

"My dear nephew, if you like to obtain the information you

desire, you may easily do so after my death, by declining to pay this annuity: but take a dying man's advice—for the honour of the family—for the sake of your father's memory, make no enquiry, and provoke no explanation."

"Only tell me one thing then, sir," urged Herbert; "is there crime anywhere about this matter?"

"No," answered Sir Hugh; "not exactly crime, but a mistake. Your father was not a bad, but he was a very foolish man. He committed a fatal error once, and by the payment of this annuity, a small, very small share of its consequences fall on you. And now, pray leave me for a little, I am tired."

Towards evening the young man returned to the sick chamber, and found his uncle considerably better.

"You have done me good, Herbert," he said; "I have not felt so well for a month past. I thought I was dying this morning, and now I almost fancy I may live a little while longer. You shake your head, doctor—so be it then—God's will be done."

Still, while his nephew remained in the room, the old man seemed to get better and better.

"I do not think, Herbert, you would be sorry if I did keep you out of your title for a few months yet. Could you not bring Mrs. Clyne down here and take up your home in the old walls, just as if I were really dead and buried? I should like you to live here—somehow I feel strangely well to-night."

"Hadn't I better leave you now, sir?" suggested Herbert; "I fear you are overtaxing your strength."

"Perhaps you are right; yes, you may leave me—only I want to ask a favour before you go. During this sickness I have been trying to study this book," he said, placing his hand on a large Bible that lay on a table; "but I cannot stoop forward, and the volume is more than I am able to hold. Would you mind reading to me? our rector came and offered to do so, but I couldn't stand that, just as if I were a bed-ridden, rheumatic old woman; and though the servants are willing and faithful, their drone would drive me mad. Take it, my boy, you will not grudge the time, I know; and you may find something in the book to guide and steady your own course hereafter. Now, begin."

Almost mechanically, Herbert opened the volume.

"Where shall I commence?" he asked.

"I was reading St. John," answered the baronet; "I ended where you see that mark."

"'Let not your heart be troubled,'" began the young man.

Very distinctly he read out the inspired narrative, without any mock solemnity or mournful gravity ; he spoke the words of truth and promise as he found them, reverently ; and it was a singular scene to see the owner of that large estate, leaning back in his chair and listening to the story written by the humble disciple of old, which assured him of a heritage fairer and lovelier than any earthly territory—an imperishable heritage in the world to come.

When he reached the end of the chapter, Herbert paused, and enquired if his uncle were tired.

"No, please go on ; your voice is like a woman's—soft and low—and yet I can hear every word—pray do not stop."

Thus entreated, Herbert continued, and read chapter after chapter till he reached the end of that gospel.

As he concluded "the world itself could not contain the words that should be written—Amen," he laid his hand on the open volume, and looked at his uncle.

"Thank you, Herbert," said the old man. "Now ring the bell for Hinchcliffe. I will go to bed—good night—and to-morrow we will talk about Earnshaw, and it shall all be as you like."

With a grateful pressure of the wasted hand, Herbert quitted the baronet, and repairing to the apartments which had been assigned to him, and opening a window overlooking the gardens, flung himself into a chair beside the casement to think—

About Lina and Earnshaw, and their past and his own future ; about the wife whom, if he had known her years before, he might then have held to his heart and been proud of his name, and his family, and his lands, for her sake. For hours and hours he remained sunk in reverie—whilst unconsciously his eyes rested on the gardens below, flooded with moonlight, that kept shifting and changing its brightness from place to place.

At last, with a sigh, he rose, and closing the casement, betook himself to bed. Not for hours did he fall asleep, however ; and when, towards morning, he sank into forgetfulness, it was only to be wakened by Hinchcliffe, with the words—

"I am sorry to disturb you, Sir Herbert, but my master is dead."

CHAPTER XXXVI.

THE TWO BARONETS.

THE day after Sir Hugh Clyne's funeral chanced to be that on which the adjourned case of Storn, Glenaen, and Co., bankrupts, came on for hearing; and all unconscious that his own and his mother's movements had been for some time previously under the surveillance of a detective officer, the manufacturer entered the court on the morning appointed, and took his place in the box with the pleasant prospect of a final examination by Mr. Blight.

Nor was his expectation disappointed. During the whole of the previous three months, Mr. Blight, the official assignee, and the creditors generally, had been unable to add a solitary item to their stock of knowledge, and accordingly Mr. Blight was savage, and flung questions at Mr. Glenaen in a manner which might have moved any person, unacquainted with the facts of the case, to pity.

Not a single charge in the ammunition box of legal warfare was left in Mr. Blight's possession when the bankrupt sat down; and although it was that gentleman's firm determination to ask for a further adjournment, in order that Mrs. Glenaen might be produced and examined, he felt some doubts as to whether His Honour would feel inclined to grant his request.

He was vexed, and mortified, and out of temper, and sat listening with a would-be brisk, but really sullen air to the remarks of Mr. Blast, when a man, travel-stained and dusty, entered the court and handed the lawyer a piece of paper. Mr. Blight opened and read, rubbed his eyes, and read again, finally folded up the billet, and sat smiling at one or two of the largest creditors till the lawyer for the bankrupt had concluded his appeal.

Then Mr. Blight rose, and addressing the commissioner, said he must apply for a further adjournment, information having just reached him that the bankrupt, Glenaen, had succeeded to a large property.

"Where?" shouted that individual, and nobody in court doubted the intelligence was as unexpected and sudden to him as to his creditors.

"Pray be silent, sir," said Mr. Blight, while the commissioner asked for further particulars.

"I think it better not to make any statement in open court,

lest some difficulties might be thrown in our way," said Mr. Blight, pompously; "but if your Honour will read that." handing in the note, "I think you will consider yourself justified in granting my request."

Three times His Honour read the missive, which ran as follows:—

"Sir,

"Mrs. Glenaen lays claim to the title and lands of the late Sir Hugh Clyne for her son, the bankrupt; she was Mr. Montague Clyne's first wife, and, consequently, the present Sir Herbert Clyne (so called) and his sister are illegitimate. I will remain in court.

"Yours obediently,
"J. D."

"Do you consider this information reliable?" inquired His Honour.

Mr. Blight considered it especially so.

"Then I will adjourn the case for four days, to enable you to confirm your statement; and if a further adjournment be then required, you can apply for it."

"But," here broke in Glenaen, "I am entitled to no property. It is merely a trick to retard our certificate. I ought to know as much about my own affairs as Mr. Blight, and——"

"If you do not keep silence, sir, I shall commit you for contempt of court," said His Honour, savagely.

"My knowledge of your affairs seems to be much greater than your own," was Mr. Blight's remark to the bankrupt, as he bustled out of the sitting into one of the empty courts, where he had a long and confidential chat with the detective, while Mr. Glenaen lay in wait for him at the foot of the stairs.

"Well, are you going to tell me anything about this precious property?" he enquired, seizing the lawyer, as he was passing out into the street; "what is the use of mystifying about the business? is there a property, or is the whole thing gammon?"

"There is a property, and the thing is not gammon," was Mr. Blight's reply.

"And where is it—what is it—why is it?" persisted the bankrupt.

"Allow me to suggest that you should go and ask your mother," answered the gentleman addressed.

"Yes; and perhaps you would be so obliging as to tell me

where she is to be found at the present moment?" exclaimed her dutiful son

"I could tell you, but I will not," replied Mr. Blight. "It would be a sad thing to forestall the confidences of a mother and son. Good afternoon;" and he jumped into his cab and drove off, while Mr. Glenaen hailed another and went back to Bow.

There he found a special messenger waiting with a missive from Mrs. Glenaen, dated "The Falls," and advising him to join her there immediately. "You are now Sir Gordon Clyne," she wrote, "rightful owner of this property—of every rood of ground, and article of furniture, the late Baronet left behind him. There is not a twig in the shrubberies, nor a picture on the walls, which belongs to Herbert—*Sir* Herbert as they call him—and yet he will not leave the house. It is needful that you should come and make him."

So said Mrs. Glenaen, for it was the hour of her vengeance, and she improved it.

"What have I, or my innocent children, ever done to you," Montague Clyne pleaded once, "that you should track and persecute us thus?" and then the woman answered, and answered truly—

"Because I hate both you and them."

And she did hate them! Ah, heaven, how pitilessly, in the day of her strength, she lorded it over Herbert Clyne! How insolently she moved through the noble rooms, daring anyone to stop her progress, or deny her right. What a galling thing it was for one of pure and ancient blood, who was illegitimate through no sin of anyone belonging to him, to see that low-born, upstart woman laying her hand over park and manor, cottage and hall, field and wood, and drawing everything in, cruelly and relentlessly, to herself.

And she had the right to do all this! Standing in the hall where so lately friends and servants had called him by his new title, she pulled rank and position, wealth, name, and legitimacy from him, and flung him out into the world without a shilling.

She had the power to gather the fruit of his life's promise—to reap the golden grain that had been planted and watched for him—to set her foot on the threshold, and tell him he was an intruder in the house of his kindred, for she was his father's wife, while her son was his elder brother. The man he had looked down on, and sneered at once, was lord and master over him now.

So the solicitors, who made themselves busy about the matter, told Herbert Clyne they feared; and he, with the light of the present falling upon, and explaining the darkness of the past, could only listen and believe.

Nevertheless, he would not leave the old place. It seemed to him that his very presence at the Falls when is uncle died, gave him a sort of right to hold out the citadel against the assaults of all fresh comers. And it was not till the arrival of Sir Gordon Clyne, as Mrs. Glenaen styled her son, that the supplanted baronet felt in very earnestness that his empire had departed from him.

When Mr. Glenaen entered the library, he was received by several of the county magistrates, Lord Neverdon, two or three solicitors, and the rector of Fallwood, who had all been asked to be present at the conference. Apart from the rest, Herbert Clyne stood, with folded arms, gazing from one of the windows, while Mrs. Glenaen entered the room by an opposite door, and greeted her son.

"Mr. Glenaen," commenced Lord Neverdon, when the gentlemen had exchanged bows, "you, or rather your mother for you, have laid claim to the lands and title of the late Sir Hugh Clyne. If you can prove that claim to be just and equitable, my nephew has no desire to throw unnecessary obstacles in the way of your succession. All we want is proof, not mere assertion and angry recrimination, but proof that, first, Mrs. Glenaen was the lawful wife of my brother-in-law, Montague Clyne, and, second, that you are the legitimate child of that marriage."

"I know no more about it, gentlemen, than the man in the moon," was Mr. Glenaen's answer, "and am as anxious as you to hear what my mother has got to say on the subject."

He turned towards her, and so did the rest of the persons assembled. For some strange reason, she hesitated, for the first time since her entrance into the house, to speak. She looked at her son, and then at all the persons present, but remained silent.

"Speak, mother," exclaimed her son, impatiently. "How did you come to be Mr. Clyne's wife, and who am I?"

"You are Montague Clyne's eldest son," she answered, emphatically.

"Then why, in heaven's name, have you called me Glenaen?"

He uttered the words sharply and angrily, and Mrs. Glenaen, glancing round the room at the expectant faces, sought in vain for some form of words that might suit her purpose.

"Because I thought it best, both for you and myself," she said, at last.

"Madam," remarked Lord Neverdon, "we are but wasting time

in these generalities. If you will be so good as to put your statement in some definite form, we can then ascertain its value. Vague assertions are useless. We want to know how you became Mrs. Montague Clyne—when and where your son was born—why you lived apart from Mr. Clyne—and the motives that induced you, for forty years, to relinquish a position which, if you were legally married, belonged to you?"

"We do not wish to make this investigation more disagreeable than can be avoided," added one of the magistrates, "but it is absolutely necessary that we should be put in possession of the facts of the case."

"I was married, then," began Mrs. Glennaen, "forty-five years since, to Montague Clyne. He was poor when the wedding, a private one, took place; and he had only a small fortune then, nor other than the faintest chance of this baronetage, which has now fallen in to his son. I was living with my uncle in this county at the time, but left his house, and, unknown to any of my relatives, married, and went with my husband to London. We lived there for two years as man and wife; and in the parish of St. Clement Danes, Gordon, who now stands before you, was born. His birth is entered in the parish register. We lived very wretchedly. He was cruel and neglectful, and at last we separated by mutual consent. He offered me a thousand pounds—it was almost all he possessed— if I would leave England and take the child with me. I was to have sailed for America in a vessel called the Panama, but I did not go. It went down with all hands. Not a soul, passenger or crew, was saved; and he thought I had gone down also, and was thankful."

Mrs. Glenaen paused in her narrative, but with an impatient gesture Gordon urged her to proceed.

"Years passed away, and Mr. Clyne first came into possession of his cousin's Hampshire property, and then married Lord Neverdon's sister. When I ran short of money, I presented myself before him, was recognised, and bribed to silence. I persuaded him our son was dead—that his secret was safe— that he could, by making me his friend, save his children from illegitimacy. In those days I repaid him the scorn he had flung on me at the time we separated. I gave him no peace— I gave him no rest. I deluded him with promises, and I harassed him to death. For years and years his life was a reproach and a misery—It would have been better for him to have faced the worst at once; but he was too weak a fool, too cowardly a creature, to dare the danger and have it past. He was so weak—so purposeless—"

"Whoever you may be, woman," broke in Herbert Clyne, "remember the man you are speaking of was my father."

"I think Mrs. Glenaen is needlessly digressing," observed one of the magistrates seated near Lord Neverdon. "May I now inquire, madam, the reason why, during all this period, you never claimed for your son and yourself the rank to which, if your story be correct, you were justly entitled?"

"Mrs. Glenaen doubtless had her own good reasons for preferring private to public life," remarked Mr. Chamley, who had been confidential solicitor to Sir Hugh Clyne, and he smiled a bitter, contemptuous smile, which stung the manufacturer, though he scarcely knew why. "With your permission," continued Mr. Chamley, bowing to Lord Neverdon and the assembled magistrates, "I should like to ask Mrs. Glenaen a few questions, which may, perhaps, have the effect of placing the matter in a truer light before you."

"By all means," answered the persons addressed in concert, and thus encouraged, Mr. Chamley proceeded.

"Pray, Mrs. Glenaen, was your character particularly good at the time of your marriage with Mr. Montague Clyne?"

There was a dead silence, during the continuance of which she turned her back towards her son, and looked to her questioner with a rush of blood darkening her face.

"I am waiting for a reply, madam," said the solicitor at last.

"Is there nothing can be done in this matter?" commenced Mr. Glenaen hastily. "Can no compromise be effected? Sir Herbert Clyne, I am willing to listen to any reasonable proposition you may make for settling the affair between ourselves, without the intervention of strangers."

"I either remain in this house Sir Herbert Clyne by right of birth, or I leave it a beggar, Mr. Glenaen," was the young man's answer. "There is nothing in the business *I* am ashamed or afraid to hear."

And he turned again to the window, whilst Mr. Chamley proceeded—

"I suppose, Mrs. Glenaen, I am to receive your silence as an admission that your reputation was not perfectly unsullied. Now I must ask you to tell us with whom you lived during the interval between your separation from Mr. Clyne and his marriage."

"I shall answer no question. I will not be insulted. I—"

"You will please to remember, madam, you have brought these questions on yourself; and that if you decline to answer them here, you must either relinquish all claim to the Falls, or else have them put to you in open court. Was your name never coupled with that of a person called Hindon?"

"It might have been," she reluctantly admitted.

"That was before your marriage; and during the time you were living with Mr. Clyne in London he had reason to suspect the man Hindon had followed you? Was not this so?"

Once again she said that it might have been.

"And he was to have accompanied you to America?"

She assented to the question.

"Did you ever go through the ceremony of marriage with him?"

"Never!" this was emphatic, though the woman's features absolutely writhed as she answered him.

"Yet still you lived together?"

She bowed her head in answer, while Gordon Glenaen rose, and walking to the window where the illegitimate baronet stood, said, laying a finger on his arm,

"Sir Herbert!"

"Well, sir."

"Can we not arrange this matter together?"

"No! I have told you before, there can be no compromise of the affair. I either remain here master and baronet, or I go out a nameless beggar. For the rest you must take the evil with the good. I cannot interfere."

If a devil had possessed him, Mr. Glenaen could not have turned away with a worse expression, nor resumed his seat with an air of haughtier defiance.

As he left Herbert he heard the lawyer say, "In the face of all this, Mrs. Glenaen, how is it possible for any mortal being except yourself to say who your son really is? You say you were Mr. Clyne's wife; you confess you lived for years with Hindon; and we know you have called yourself Mrs. Glenaen ever since your boy was seven years old. Now what can we make of all this, and your son's evident desire to effect a compromise, except that you are trying now to extort money from Sir Herbert Clyne as you did from his father and the late baronet?"

"If you like to dispute my son's claim you can do so," she replied.

"We are aware of that," remarked Lord Neverdon sarcastically.

"But if your nephew wishes to know without further trouble whether or not I was his father's wife, he had better ask Mrs. Storn. I daresay she could tell him about it."

And with this parting blow to Herbert she was passing from the room, when she suddenly paused, and addressing Mr. Chamley, said—"Hindon is not dead. Sir Hugh Clyne took that on trust as he took my word that the boy born and baptized, Montague Clyne's son, had died in infancy. Hindon is not dead, I can furnish you with his address," and she swept out of the room, Gordon following her.

"Mother!" he said, catching hold of her dress as she would have hurried away; and when she felt his hand on her, she paused and turned.

"Mother!" he repeated, and it was a sight to see those two standing in the old picture gallery looking at one another, while the portraits of the Clynes for centuries past frowned on them from the walls.

"Is it true?" he asked.

"That you are Sir Gordon Clyne? raise your eyes to the faces up there," and she pointed to the likenesses of the proud and weak Northumberland Clynes, "and say if you are not of their race, and of their blood. True! to be sure it is."

"I did not mean that," he said. "Is it true what they say of you?"

"A little—not much," was her answer.

"I wish then," he said, "you would return to London, and leave me to arrange this business by myself."

"No," was Mrs. Glenaen's reply; "I will remain mistress here, and should like to see any of them dispute my right."

"So be it then," acquiesced her son, adding sotto voce, "till I am master."

<hr>

CHAPTER XXXVII.

MR. GLENAEN PAYS HIS CREDITORS.

The date at which the manufacturer had mentally specified his mother should resign her regency of his affairs was rather more speedy in its arrival than he had anticipated; and before many months were over he had the pleasure of entering upon his new title, and of surveying the woods and manors of The Falls, from the window out of which Sir Hugh Clyne had looked the day of Herbert's arrival for the last time.

Sir Gordon was a proud man when he drove through the gates and stood in the old place master; a proud man, yet still the same as he had been in the chemical factory at Bow, or under the roof tree of Maurice Storn; and so, before he had been many weeks a baronet, friend and foe found out.

The blot in his escutcheon was his mother; and over that the pair battled royally. Even with him, however, she had the best of it; turning his own confession of debt in the Bankrupt Court against him, and recovering in the matter of Storn, Glenaen, and Company, whose bankruptcy was annulled, twenty thousand pounds from the owner of the Falls, as a golden nest egg towards commencing dowager housekeeping. He had his choice between payment or perjury; and, like a sensible man, he chose the former. Though smarting bitterly under the demands of creditors, who were clamorous to the extent of eighty thousand pounds, nothing could induce him — not even shortness of ready cash—to compromise matters with Mrs. Glenaen and receive her mistress of his house.

The one unmercenary action of Sir Gordon's life was quarrelling with his parent; and if he did sell Earnshaw and Beachwood in order to prevent the necessity of mortgaging the Falls, or truckling under to his mother, there was no one to blame him; not even Maurice Storn, who heard from Mr. Chamley that, had Sir Hugh lived another day, or Herbert succeeded to the property, justice would have been done him.

"I have paid your debts, and the debts you led me into," wrote Sir Gordon, "to the tune of eighty thousand pounds; and if I have sold Earnshaw for forty-five thousand, it does no more than pay your share of the liabilities, if so much. You are now starting in the world again clear, and I trust you may make a better thing of it than formerly."

With which friendly wish Sir Gordon closed the correspondence; and Maurice Storn, laying the letter of his old crony and partner aside, turned him to his daily drudgery again—a beggar.

There was another whom the fact of Sir Hugh dying intestate flung out into the world penniless; one whom we may follow step by step from the uplands of the Falls to the valleys of the South, who had to give up name and position, the title he had been trained to expect, the place he had occupied, the wealth he had possessed, whose mother's fortune returned to her relatives on the maternal side, who, when Sir Gordon drove through the gates of the Falls, would have stood in the dusty high road of life without a friend or sixpence but for the kindness of his uncle, Lord Neverdon, and of his relatives the Kingstons.

By them he was always called Herbert Clyne; and shall we, dear reader, who have travelled with him thus far, be less considerate than they? Let me to the end of this story, which is now—I say it lingeringly—drawing near its close, speak of the weak, tender-hearted man, who has occupied so large a portion of these pages, by the name under which he passed through so

much of life, and of love, and of sorrow, even for Lina's sake—
for her, most miserable woman, who, for weeks after she had
heard of his misfortunes, could do nothing, when her husband
was out of sight, but sit and think, and weep. She feared to
mention his name before Maurice lest he should imagine she
still held in her heart some remnant of the old, unsanctified
love; and yet, in one way or other, Herbert Clyne's affairs
were perpetually presented for her consideration, till, as a
crowning stroke of the caprice of fortune, she heard he had
taken a clerk's situation, at thirty shillings a-week, which John
Matson, at his request, procured for him.

But still she fought the fight of old out bravely, and in the
long run won. She knew it was as dangerous, and as disloyal,
to give him her pity now as it had been to give her love then.
There was another; one who out of the depths of his great
heart had forgiven her fault, that needed all the love, and sympathy, and admiration she had to bestow. Broken in health
and in fortune, what right had she to take a grain of pity from
him to bestow on the man who had striven to injure him?
Was it not her right and her duty to forsake all others and
cleave unto him? and should Lina, even for the sake of womanly
compassion and womanly remorse, make an agony of relinquishing that which it ought to be her pleasure to forget?

Many a struggle Lina had with her own heart before she
could bring herself to believe it was sinful for her to feel sorry
for Mr. Clyne, and long to speak to and comfort him; for she
was a very woman, far indeed from perfection, most proper
reader! yet none, perhaps, the less loveable for that—who
found her way back to honour and virtue—to the serene and
stable happiness of married life, through the paths of penitence
and resolution, through tears, and sighs, and struggles—by the
help, under God, above all things, of work.

Maurice, too, aided her purpose. Silently, yet tenderly, he
led her weary heart to rest. Somehow, in those days, she clung
to him as she had never done before; and it seemed as though
his strong, calm mind exercised the same sort of passive influence over her eager, impulsive nature that a cool hand laid
upon a burning forehead does on the throbbing pain and the
quivering nerves.

Not by words, but by actions, he brought her heart home
again to him. Most thoughtful and loving was he, in those
days of poverty and struggle, for her mental and bodily health
and comfort. Very willingly he would have kept the winds of
heaven from blowing upon her face, but Lina would not let
him be the only labourer. Though it was not possible for her

to add to the general fund, she could still prevent more being drawn from it than was absolutely necessary. She could do with one servant, and market for the household, and put the black ribbon she still wore for Geordie across her plain straw bonnet. She could, with management, dress as neatly, though far less richly than formerly, and work with her own hands the collars and sleeves which made a cheap dress look well. She could keep everything in their home trim and regular, so that no rude evidence of altered fortunes should meet her husband's eye, wherever he turned. Almost unconsciously, Lina, for whom the upholsterers had done these things in the days gone by, looped up curtains, and arranged draperies, disposed furniture in the best positions, and gave a sort of fashionable air even to the little vulgar parlour, off Eastcheap, from whence, before long, they moved to an old-fashioned house, situate in a strange, out-of-the-way nook, in the neighbourhood of Savage Gardens, which, if I recollect rightly, was called Muscovy Court. There she gathered flowers and ornaments about her by degrees, saving and scraping, out of her housekeeping money, to buy all sorts of incongruous articles—this week purchasing tea cups, and the next, stair-carpeting—making little visits of inspection to second-hand book-stalls, whence she bore away chemical volumes for her husband, to replace those he had lost in the general crash. A very busy, useful woman that idle Lina of old became, in the time of their adversity, when she filled her flower-stands with chrysanthemums and laurustinas, instead of camellias and myrtles, when electro-plate had to take the place of silver, and the tumblers and water-cups on the table were not cut, but blown.

She managed and contrived better than poor Mary Matson had ever known how; and she was always at leisure in the evenings, to sit with her husband, and sew while he was reading, and listen when he talked. And now that no human being came between the pair, he absolutely commenced trying fresh experiments before his wife. Laboratory and utensils were gone; but there was a spare closet in the house whence, after dinner, Lina was in the habit of extracting empty Florence flasks, old cards, strings of corks, earthenware pans, and such like articles, with which Maurice was striving to replace the expensive apparatus which had filled his chemical studio at Bow.

With these, set out on a large deal table, Mr. Storn would manipulate, and test, and experimentize for hours; while Lina, who, at first, had not the slightest ghost of a notion of what he was about, learned, by watching his performances, so much of his craft, that she knew when to hand him a clean glass, or a stopper, or a tube; and she was able to make his filters for him, and took all the trouble of washing his vessels off his hands. She dusted his rods and his stirrers, labelled the bottles which were not to be interfered with, wrote down, at his dictation, the results of each separate experiment, and recorded, in the large book he kept for the purpose, the *modus operandi* by which each product was obtained.

Sometimes Mr. Matson came over for tea, and then Mr. Storn could talk about chemical tests, and analyses, and discoveries to somebody who comprehended their meaning—Lina sitting by during the conversation, and thinking that, had it been so always, something in her life might have been different. By means of these little experiments, Mr. Storn was able, after a time, to add considerably to his income. Whenever the concern in the north was in a dilemma, for want of a hint or a formula, Mr. Ferres stated the case to Mr. Storn, who went home, and, eight times out of ten, returned to business next morning with the key to the difficulty, written out, in his pocket; and for these keys he was paid, according to value of product desired, from two to ten guineas on the spot—a great help to the income of any man on a salary; and, before twelve months were over, the chemical apparatus was replenished, and the house filled with better furniture, and the pair settled down to the every-day routine of city life, in comparative competence again.

It was just about this time, in the autumn of the year succeeding that on which Sir Gordon Clyne came into possession of his property, that John Matson entered the house in Muscovy Court, and, without taking a chair, addressed himself to Maurice as follows:

"Pray, Mr. Storn, do you know who it can be that is flooding the London market with your sulphuric acid?"

"No one, I should think," answered Mr. Storn, looking somewhat excited, nevertheless.

"Well, do you suppose that Taylor and Davies could contract for ten thousand carboys, at twenty per cent. lower than Meeden, unless they have some one at their back, in possession of your secret? See, there is the offer. Mr. Ferres is at the counting-house, and sent me round with it. He wants you to come over directly."

"There is only one man in England knows how to make sulphuric acid on my plan," said Mr. Storn, rising, "and that man is Gordon Glenaen. Mr. Ferres offered me half profits, eight months ago, if I would divulge my secret;

but I told him I couldn't do it—I was bound in honour to Glenaen."

"Bound in honour to the arch fiend!" exclaimed Mr. Matson, impetuously; "still you were right," he added, in a quieter tone, next minute; "only, if you find he has played you false, of course you will be at liberty to fight him with his own weapons."

"If I could be but sure!" replied Mr. Storn; "I do not think he would be such a consummate scoundrel! but then, who is it, Matson—who has found this out, besides me?"

"Nobody. It is Mr. Glenaen who supplies these people. But come away. Mr. Ferres is waiting for you. He is as pleased as if he had got a legacy. He thinks you are all his own now. Are you ready?"

"Quite," answered Mr. Storn; and he was leaving the room, when Lina laid her hand on his shoulder, and said—

"You will do nothing rash, Maurice?"

"Trust me, dear," he replied, and next minute was hurrying down Trinity Square to Great Tower Street, then along it to Eastcheap.

Half-an-hour afterwards, one of the office boys came running over, in a state of breathlessness, for razors, a change of linen, and such like indispensables, to be packed ready for Mr. Storn, "who would be at Muscovy Court," he said, "in five minutes."

"Are the things put up, Lina?" she heard him crying, almost before the time mentioned had elapsed. "Be quick, dear, I have not a moment to lose."

She had them all ready. Janet was just cutting some sandwiches, and she was corking a small bottle of wine.

"Did Maurice really mean to go north?"

"Yes, Lina. Mr. Ferres wishes it, and so do I. John Matson will travel with me."

"Oh! I am glad of that," she said—"thankful. Good bye, Maurice. Remember you are to do nothing rash."

"Am I in the habit of being rash?" he asked, laughing, as he took Mr. Matson's arm, and with a farewell nod to his wife walked off towards Fenchurch Street.

At the same hour on the following evening they were posting across a lonely bye-road in Northumberland to the "Clyne Arms," a little wayside public house, which stood about half-a-mile from the principal entrance to the Falls.

"Tea, with rasher of bacon and eggs for two," was Mr. Matson's practical order, when he had paid the post-boy and dismissed the vehicle, and stooping their heads to avoid striking the doorway, the two Londoners entered the best room of the rural inn, and stood looking out of the window till the meal should be prepared.

The "Clyne Arms" was built on a slight eminence, which commanded a view of the house, park, and plantations of the Falls; and the friends remained looking at the place in silence till the sun set behind a hill of pines that bounded the view. He left a glory in the autumnal sky, which cast a strange beauty over the foliage of the trees, and lit up the windows of the old hall, and forced John Matson to say, almost in spite of himself—

"It must have been a hard thing for that young fellow to lose such a place. He is greatly to be pitied."

Mr. Storn might have thought so, but he remained silent.

"Have you heard the separation is final between him and his wife? She could not forgive him for being poor and having no father to speak of, nor herself for having missed Sir Gordon; so she retires to the parental roof with the fortune her godfather gave her when she was married, and the whole family are grieving that Treffy cannot obtain a divorce, which was what she wanted. A nice thing matrimony seems in certain circles—witness Glenaen's mother and the cat-and-dog life poor Mr. Clyne and the Honourable Frances led together. Ah! let us be thankful—here comes the bacon!"

To which Mr. Matson did ample justice; but his companion could not eat. He pushed aside his plate, and sat with his head resting on his hand, thinking about all the old partnership days, and the long years during which he and the baronet had been close friends and allies.

"I hardly believe, Matson," he began at last, "that Glenaen could be such an unprincipled scoundrel. I hope it is some one else. I should not like to have to think so ill of him."

"We shall soon know certainly whether he makes it himself," answered Mr. Matson, pouring out another cup of tea. "If he have no factory here, he must have sold the secret to some of the great northern houses. Although possible, I do not consider it at all probable that anyone else has discovered your process; and as for Glenaen's principles, I should not rate their market value at a farthing a-pound. We ought, both of us, though, to style the man Sir Gordon. I hear he is as touchy about being called Mr., as a newly-married lady at being addressed as Miss."

Maurice made no answer. He only moved his head a little, and looked at Mr. Matson, who replied to the look with a laughing—

"Yes, indeed, I have finished at last. I suppose you thought

I was going to eat all night. Now I will start off on a slight tour of inspection.''

While he was away, Mr. Storn drew a chair to the window, and remained looking out through the gathering darkness at the Falls. He thought about Lina and the illegitimate Clyne; about the days, and the weeks, and the years, he had left her alone and deprived her of his confidence, in order to give it to the man who now owned the lordly property, and who had proved himself—as bankrupt and as baronet—to have so mean and small a soul.

Then he went over the pros and cons of the sulphuric acid, and had almost decided his late partner was guilty, when John Matson re-entered the room and said,

"Well, Mr. Storn, he has a factory. '

"Where ?" demanded the chemist.

"Some place in the grounds; but we shall soon know all about it; for I chanced to meet with a fellow whom Sir Gordon kicked off the premises, and who, I think, would shoot him, if he were not afraid of being hung. We had better leave word it is uncertain at what hour we may return. There is no saying what might happen to detain us. The man I speak of will take us to the spot; so now come along, we shall net the old fox yet. Have a glass of wine first, though—you are shaking like a leaf;" and he ordered a bottle, and poured out half a tumbler for his friend, who drank it off at a draught, and then declared he was ready. Away they went, through the grounds and winding walks of the baronet's estate, guided by a long, evil-looking Northumbrian, who spoke never a word, but stalked on before them till they reached the upland at the back of the house. On they went, higher still, and further away from the dwelling, until, in the very thickest part of the pine plantation, they came on a small cleared space, over one half of which Mr. Glenaen had built his factory.

"There it is, where he makes his 'spurriments as he calls them," whispered their conductor, and for a moment the two strangers paused, sniffing the air.

"Well, what do you say he is making ?" demanded Mr. Matson at last.

"He is trying the cyanogen," answered Mr. Storn; and his face was a sight to behold, with the moonlight streaming down on his pale cheeks and gleaming eyes. "Come here, my man, I want to speak to you," he added, pulling the guide back amongst the trees. "If you will get me over the factory to-night— through every inch of it—I will give you ten pounds for your trouble. Can you do it ?"

"How long will you wait?" demanded the other, after a moment's reflection.

"Till morning, if you like," was the answer.

"And you won't touch anything?"

"Not an article. I only want to know what Mr.—I mean Sir Gordon—is doing. I suspect he is trying to rob me, and I wish to see whether there is any likelihood of his succeeding."

"Well, I will do my best then. Come back here in three hours' time, and we will see. Ten pounds, you say?"

"Paid now, if you like," acquiesced the chemist.

"No, no—I'll take your word for it," answered the man, moving away; but returning again immediately, he added—"Perhaps you had as well give me half now. I might have to show it."

Maurice instantly placed ten sovereigns in his open hand; and then, passing his arm through Mr. Matson's, drew him away from the spot. "In three hours," he muttered—"in three hours I shall know all."

Unless a man be making love, or trying to raise money to meet a bill before bank hours are over, three hours do not fly away on rapid wings; and so the waiters discovered. Nevertheless they did glide into the past somehow; and at the time appointed Storn and his friend stood waiting for their conductor at the place agreed on.

"I fear he has played us false," said Mr. Storn at last. "I wish I had kept the money."

"He will come, never fear," answered Mr. Matson; and even as he spoke the man appeared from the other side of the building, beckoning them to approach.

The door of the factory was partly open, and the next moment they found themselves inside. "Now make haste," said the man in a whisper; "he may come here at any moment."

"Give me your lantern," was Maurice's reply; and he walked through the place, looking at this back and that preparation; he gave only one glance to each item, and when he had gone over the whole factory, he said, in a tone of intense disappointment, "Is this all?"

"The sulphuric acid is here clear enough," remarked Mr. Matson.

"Yes; but I cannot exactly discover what he is trying with the other, and I must know."

"On my word then, I don't see how you are to do it," returned the other.

"I have done here, my friend," said Mr. Storn, without paying the smallest attention to Mr. Matson's remark; "and now

you must take me down by the house, close to it, you understand."

"Very well," acquiesced the man; and away he went brush-
ing through the copse, in a manner which might have alarmed
the keepers, had Sir Gordon kept any, but he did not. It was
not till they stood close beside the building, that their guide
made any pause or halt; but then he suddenly stopped in a
small belt of plantation, and looked enquiringly at his companions.

"Wait for me," Maurice said, stealing out from the spot
where the others stood, and cautiously gaining a better point
of observation. In one of the furthermost towers he saw a
light gleaming from an upper window—all the rest of the house
was in darkness; for a moment he watched it anxiously, then
a figure passed between it and the glass; then the light burnt
brightly again, and Mr. Storn, whose eyes and nose were as
sharp as those of a dog, was on the scent again.

He would have climbed the pyramids then—the determination which had beggared was supporting him now. He never
thought about how he was to get up; he only saw the light
shining high above his head—the thing was to be done—the
watchword of old almost involuntarily passed his lips, and the
next moment he was springing like a squirrel or a burglar, to
his object.

Age, ivy, and iron girders favoured the chemist's purpose;
but nothing favoured him so much as his own indomitable will;
up, not painfully and slowly, but rapidly and silently, he went;
hands, feet, teeth, all pressed into the service; and so at last,
with one great effort, he clutched the sill. That, and a spout
running down through the ivy, completed his success; he could
peep into the room, see what his enemy was about, and after a
time drop safely down again.

Little did the baronet, poring over his chemicals, guess whose
eyes were noting his failure—whose heart was throbbing with
joy at his disappointment.

"He can't do it, Matson—he never will do it," was Mr.
Storn's triumphant announcement. "Here, my fine fellow, is
a trifle extra for you; I would give you more, but I have only
enough left to pay my fare back to London. You have done
me a great service to-night—you have enabled me to beat him."

"And will you beat him?" was the question.

"As thoroughly as ever he was beaten in his life, and with
his own weapons too," answered Maurice.

"Well, I'm more glad of that than of the money," said the
man; and nothing further passed between them, except a few

enquiries concerning the modes of operation pursued at the factory, which Mr. Storn made on the principle of having full value out of his informant.

"Now, Matson," said the chemist, "I must see this baronet in the morning, first thing."

"Very well, go and sleep on your intention till then," answered his friend; the result of which piece of advice was, that Mr. Storn never awoke till it was nearly ten o'clock the following day.

"You should have called me," he said to his friend; and then swallowing a cup of tea, and eating a slice or two of toast, he started off for the Falls, accompanied by his ally, who was curious to see the matter out.

"Sir Gordon was not at home," the footman affirmed, and Maurice was ready to swear with vexation. Mr. Matson, however, ascertained that he had gone to a meet of the Fallwood hounds, and was to be found at Lord Clenstone's; and thither accordingly the friends proceeded.

"Quite a gay sight," remarked Mr. Matson, when a turn in the drive brought them in sight of the house, before which a cavalcade of riders was drawn up. "Who would have thought when Gordon Glenaen used to be lounging about in the old factory coat, that he would ever go out, like a second Nimrod, hunting, dressed out, moreover, in tops and scarlet?—a glorious sight! See, Storn, there he is."

"Where?" asked Maurice, eagerly; and Mr. Matson answered,—"In the centre of that left hand knot of horsemen. Now, remember you must be calm—you will be calm."

"Trust me," was the reply; and they proceeded till they came close to a number of equestrians, who eyed them strangely, as birds of a foreign feather.

"I wish to speak to one of your party, gentlemen," said Maurice, noticing this, and raising his hat. "Perhaps you will kindly allow me to pass up to where he is—Sir Gordon Clyne."

There was an instantaneous reining aside of steeds, and amid a good deal of prancing and curvetting, not to speak of rearing and kicking in the back ground, Maurice Storn made his way up to the baronet.

"Sir Gordon Clyne," he said; and that individual turning, recognized him instantly.

"Ah! Storn," he said, "how are you—very glad to see you —when did you come?" and he drew in his horse with one hand, while he held out the other to his old crony and partner.

"Excuse me, sir," answered Maurice, "but you and I never

shake hands again; I came down here to satisfy myself as to whether you were the individual who was flooding the London market with my sulphuric acid; and I find not only that you have robbed me of my rightful share of that discovery, but that also you are trying to forestall me with the cyanogen."

"There is some great mistake here," said the baronet; "you must have been most grossly misinformed. If you will call at my place this evening, I am sure I can satisfy you that you have been deceived. I assure you I have never acted otherwise than fairly towards you; come to dinner this evening, and I will then hear what you have to say."

"You shall hear what I have to say now," was the reply. "I will not enter your doors, and I will listen to no false excuses,—I knew there was only one man in England who could make sulphuric acid on my principle, and I knew that man was yourself. I come now to tell you I will let Ferres have the secret for nothing if he likes, and I will drive you out of the trade if it beggars me again. As for the other experiment, you have not brains enough to perfect it; I watched you last night addling yourself over impossibilities, still trying to cheat me, and I now assure you, Sir Gordon Clyne, that in this also I will baffle you. I did not imagine till last night, you were such a thorough scoundrel as you have proved yourself."

" Complimentary phrases seem to be the fashion, Mr. Storn," said the ci-devant manufacturer; "however, I need not ask at whose instigation you have come here—Mr. Matson and I have an old grudge—for the rest, you have not forgotten your old knack of playing the spy. If all accounts be true, if you had watched chemical manufacturers a little less, and your wife a little more, it would have been better for your purse and her honour."

He had barely uttered the last words, before Storn's grasp was on his throat. In vain he struck, kicked, and struggled. Almost ere he knew what his adversary was about, Maurice had dragged him from the saddle to the ground, where, seizing his riding whip, he belaboured the proprietor with might and main.

Standing amongst the huntsmen, bareheaded, he thrashed the baronet as if his life depended on the operation; and it was not until some of the gentlemen, flinging themselves to the ground, dragged him by main force from his victim, that Sir Gordon, with face swollen and bleeding, was able to get up and confront his opponent, who, almost foaming with rage, would have flown at him again, but for the vice-like strength of the hands that held him.

"You shall answer for this," said the baronet, as he limped from the scene of action.

"Is this what you call being calm?" whispered Mr. Matson, as they stood in the centre of a group of excited individuals, who had not been able to make head or tail of the whole affair, except that hard words and harder knocks had been going.

In a few sentences Mr. Matson explained the true state of the case, and then Lord Clenstone came forward and declared, after such a serious assault, he, as a magistrate, could not permit Mr. Storn to depart; "he must remain in my house," he said, "till we have decided what course to pursue."

The result of this detention was, that Mr. Storn being brought before a full bench of magistrates, was fined five pounds, and dismissed with that and a long-winded lecture from the president.

"I must ask some gentleman present to lend me the amount," said the defendant, looking round the crowded court; "I have not got so much money left."

It was mortifying to Sir Gordon to see the instantaneous response this appeal met with—scarcely a gentleman in the place failing to draw out his purse and offer the required amount.

"Thank you all," said Mr. Storn, taking the five pounds from a person who stood close beside him, and declining the other loans; "I trust the magistrates will not consider I mean to be impertinent when I say I never paid any money with so much pleasure in my life. I am sure it will gratify my kind friends here to know I am about to return to town to make sulphuric acid, and to take the trouble of perfecting my experiment off Mr. Glennaen's hands."

"Let me be partner with you then," said the young man who had just pulled out his purse. "I am Mr. Colke's son—Colke and Ferres—you know."

CHAPTER XXXVII.

JOHN MATSON'S TROUBLE.

THE well-known house of Colke and Ferres had two men at its head who were much too wise to permit the new firm of Colke and Storn to part company from them; and, accordingly, when Augustus Colke and Maurice Storn entered into possession of a fine new factory at Lee, it was pretty generally understood in chemical circles that the money for the young had been derived from the old concern; and that the North of England and the North of London manufacturers were, to a certain extent, partners together.

This was a great lift for Maurice Storn; by a fortunate chain of circumstances he was raised at once from the purgatory of bankruptcy to the seventh heaven of chemical prosperity; and for the second time in his life he struck out boldly and bravely for opulence to win it. True, the sulphuric acid was no longer a monopoly, for Sir Gordon Clyne sold the secret to the highest bidder he could find; but still the highest bidder was, after all, only one opponent in the market, and, by an improvement in the process, Maurice soon found he was able to sell at a shade more profit than the new comer. And, besides, sulphuric acid was not the only arrow left in his quiver; he had ways and means of producing alum, extract of carthamus, tartaric acid, and various dyes, cheaper than any other man in Great Britain; and though the great cyanogen experiment still remains an unreached El Dorado—a mine of gold to be searched for and worked by any who may be so fortunate as to hit upon the secret the German chemist carried out of life with him—wealth came to the new firm in a few years, and the world went well with them.

It was a splendid phalanx of chemical standing and chemical knowledge which, allied together under the name of two distinct firms, defied all the manufacturers of England to distance it in the market; and there was not a chemist in the kingdom in whom the name of Storn failed to excite respect.

"The first experimental and practical chemist of the day," he was styled by the first minds of the country, and thus the man's dream of fame was realized at last.

Meanwhile John Matson's salary was raised; and after some hesitation, and much consultation between Mr. Colke, senior, and Mr. Ferres, it was eventually decided that the person who had worked so well for them as clerk might be safely raised to the rank of managing partner.

Directly Maurice told his wife this news she went to the old house to congratulate her friend.

Mary was lying on the sofa, holding a book in her hand, the pages of which were blotted with her tears; but it was getting dusk, and Lina did not perceive that the eyes of the dear, faithful woman were red and swollen with weeping.

"I am so glad, Mary," she began; and she sat down beside the sofa, and spoke her rejoicings out almost in a breath; pausing at last in wonderment at Mrs. Matson's silence to say—

"Are you not glad, too?"

"No," Mary answered, "I do not care."

"Not care! why, what in the world is the matter? Not care about what will give your husband so much pleasure?"

"It will not give him pleasure to-morrow," the poor wife cried out. "Oh! Mrs. Storn, I have been afraid for a long time, but now I am sure I shall die soon."

"Die soon!" Lina repeated the words mechanically.

"Yes, I have been getting weaker and weaker every day for a long time. For weeks, except when John was in the house, I have hardly moved from this sofa, and so at last I sent for a doctor: he is just gone, and he says what I thought."

Lina could not answer: she remained silent, with Mary's hand clasped in hers, thinking over every little incident that confirmed what Mrs. Matson stated. For months Mary had been constantly "tired." Even Mr. Storn had noticed how pale and thin Matson's wife was getting; and then Lina's thoughts wandered back to the old time at Bow, when she could not get her visitor to whisper what was troubling her.

Had she felt the shadow of the angel's wings then? and was there anything more than the fancy of a sick woman now? She had no apparent disease. Might not change of air and scene and good advice work wonders? Mrs. Matson had youth on her side; and her friend tried to comfort her with the assurance that youth and good nursing could cure any disease. "Even the vapours, dear," added Lina, "which I think is the worst complaint you are labouring under at present."

Mary shook her head sorrowfully. "Do you remember," she said, "asking me once long ago what I was constantly reading good books for?"

"Yes, I recollect perfectly."

"And do you remember what I told you in reply?"

"That you wanted to know something of the country where you were going; and I said, we were all going there, I hoped, though not immediately."

"Ah! but I am, dear," poor Mary answered. "My father died just the same way, you could not have told he was ill. I do not think he ever had an hour's pain first or last, but he just wasted away and away, and died. So I am going, I feel it."

"Have you told Mr. Matson this?" Lina inquired.

"No, not yet, but I must. I mean to speak to him to-night. He will not be glad about the partnership then. Poor John, he will not care about money ever again, and we were so happy together. Oh! Mrs. Storn, are not you sorry for us both?"

Sorry for her, who wouldn't have been? for the gentle, loving woman, who had so much to bind her to life that she had tried to shut her eyes to the coming of death, hating to look upon the face of the spectre that brings such rest to most.

Sorry for her! Lina could not speak, could not answer. She only laid her cheek on the pillow, and drew the poor face, wet with tears, close to hers and kissed it. Thus the two remained till Mr. Matson entered, when Mary looked up and spoke to him without a change in her voice that Lina could detect—cheerfully, lovingly—the same true wife as ever.

"Are you not well this evening, Mary?" John asked, after he had spoken to Mrs. Storn, and stirred the fire, and lightened the room a little. "Are not you well?"

"What makes you think I am ill?" she inquired.

"It is such an unusual thing to see you lying on the sofa," he answered.

"I often lie on the sofa, though you may not see me," she replied. "I get tired."

"Tired, little wife!" he exclaimed. "You are always talking about being tired now. What is the matter? what should you prescribe for her, Mrs. Storn?"

"To get out of London," Lina promptly replied.

It was more the manner than the matter of this answer that made John look at his wife anxiously.

"Do you think you want change, Mary?" he asked. "Do you really feel ill?—have you any pain?"

"No; I do not feel very ill, and I have no pain; but I am tired, love—tired and weak."

"But that is not right," he said. "You ought not to be tired, and you have been growing pale and thin latterly. What is the matter, my own wife? Had we not better have some advice at once?"

He was stooping over her as he spoke, and she put her arms round his neck and drew his face close to hers, and pushed his hair back from his forehead, keeping silence all the time.

"You do not answer, love," he said at last. "I should like to send for a doctor at once. This ought not to go on. I think I shall just run round and see if Dr. Poclet is at home. Do not you agree with me, Mrs. Storn, Mary should have some little thing to put her to rights? Let me go, dear. I will be back directly."

But she would not. She held him there tight, whilst she answered—"Wait a moment. I have something to tell you."

"What is it, dear?" he asked, tenderly and anxiously.

"Dr. Poclet was here to-day."

"Well, love—"

" And he says—oh! John, John, how can I tell you——"

She had no need. He fell on his knees beside the sofa, and, whilst she rained tears over him, laid his head on her breast and groaned aloud. During the minute he remained thus, all she had been to him during the years of their married life, as wife, friend, comforter, counsellor, crowded into his mind, and he felt he could not part from her. Mary should not, Mary must not die. He said this, clasping her close to his heart; and the hopeful spirit of old, now it had got the weight of that dreaded confidence removed from it, bounded up again; and she, who but an hour previously had been assuring Lina her doom was fixed, was the first to echo her husband's words, and believe, even in spite of knowledge, that she would be cured.

Poor Mary, dear Mary, smiling and crying at one and the same moment—she told him she would get strong again for his sake; and laying her down on the sofa pillows, Mr. Matson repaired to the counting-house to tell his trouble to his principal and request his advice.

It was soon given—" Consult the best physician in London, and do with her whatever he tells you," Mr. Ferres answered concisely; and accordingly, next day Mr. Matson took his wife to the most eminent doctor he could hear of, who asked her a few questions, felt her pulse, wrote a prescription, recommended change of air and cheerful society, and was very polite and very civil in bowing the pair out.

Mary took his medicine and went to Torquay, begging so hard, however, at the end of six weeks, to be permitted to return home, that Lina, who had accompanied her, wrote to Mr. Matson that she thought his wife would really be better in London.

By slower and shorter stages than those by which she had gone down, the invalid returned to the city. It was hardly to be told how she wasted away. The passage from life to death was so tedious and imperceptible, that it was only by looking back at the time when she had been able to go about that her friends knew she was getting worse.

Lying on the sofa in that house to which Lina had come home a bride, with John's strong arms circling her, and striving to hold her back, Mary glided on nearer and nearer to the great sea. There was no disguise, no delusive hope about the matter now. She was dying, and they both knew it, and clung to each other while she remained, like two in a doomed ship that stand side by side waiting for the vessel to go to pieces.

It was the ship of their lives that was among the breakers now; and Mr. Ferres, who knew—no one better—what a wife the dying woman had been to John, took his work almost entirely on himself, and allowed the pair to spend the last days together.

Oh! ye who scoff and sneer at the state ordained by God—who call its happiness apocryphal, and only its troubles sure—who say that marriage is a cure for love—who deny that men are constant and women true—I would that you could have witnessed the agony of that parting, if only to convince you that it is possible for a man, after years of matrimony, to cling to his wife, and for her to feel that the sting of death was only to be found in leaving him.

"Mrs. Storn will take charge of the children, John, and I should like her to do so till they grow up, if you have no objection," Mary said one day, speaking faintly, and with half-closed eyes.

"It shall be as you wish," he answered.

"I feel very tired," she said, after a minute's silence.

He laid her head on his shoulder, passing his arm round her waist, whilst Mrs. Storn hurried to the table to reach some restorative. Carefully she counted the drops, but never administered them. Mary had spent her last strength in twining her hand about her husband's neck, and something in her attitude arrested Mrs. Storn's progress.

For a moment she stood looking at the pair in doubt, till John, struck by a sudden fear, held his breath to listen, then he raised her head and saw a change had come.

"Look here, Mrs. Storn," he whispered, as though he could disturb the sleep into which she had fallen. "Look at Mary."

"It is over," Lina answered, and she would have led him away and taken the charge of the corpse on herself; but with a great cry he bade her not touch Mary, praying her for God's sake to leave them alone together.

Upon this, Mrs. Storn went away into the bed-chamber, where, in about half-an-hour, John Matson followed, bearing that which had been his wife in his arms.

He would not let a creature touch her but himself. He permitted Mrs. Storn to make all the arrangements for the funeral, sitting beside the body all the time, straightening her hair, and strewing the flowers, and laying her in her coffin with his own hands. They could not get him away from the room; he did not make any complaint, or express any sorrow, he only sat still beside the bed, praying them to leave him alone with her.

When the day arrived for the funeral, he took Mr. Storn's arm, and entered the carriage with him, whilst the hearse moved slowly on to Abney Park Cemetery. There they laid her lovingly, solemnly; everybody who had ever been intimate with John Matson having assembled to show their respect and esteem for his wife. Herbert Clyne had seen her married—he came to see her buried; and after all was over, Mr. Storn hung behind for a moment, and thinking, perhaps, of what the world had said, and might say of his own wife, shook hands with Mary's old friend, and walked with him down to the gate.

Before noon it was all over—dust to dust, ashes to ashes—and John Matson went back to the house that from thenceforth was desolate unto him.

Lina was there, sitting in the room where she had died; and when Mr. Matson saw her, he abruptly left the apartment, returning, however, in a few minutes, with his children.

"Take them away, please," he said; "you know it was her wish."

"Should you not like them to remain here for a few days?" she ventured,—"I will stay too."

"No, I would rather they went now."

"And shall I go also?" Lina enquired.

"Yes; I do not know what to say about all you have done for me in your life, but you can do nothing more for me now—nor for her ever. I would rather be alone."

She took his hand in hers, and pressed it pityingly; then, gathering the two youngest to her heart, she bade the other follow, and quitted the old city house, leaving John Matson alone with his trouble.

CHAPTER XXXVIII.

CONCLUSION.

OUT at Enfield—about a mile from the town, and almost close to the grand old Chase—Maurice Storn made a permanent home for himself at last.

A pleasant home! It comes up before my mind's eye, as I write, though it is so long since I looked upon the old-fashioned house, with its small casements, and many gables, with its pointed door-ways, and curious corridors, and unexpected stairs.

Can I not see the conservatory half concealed by trees, and the lawn, with its drooping willows, and dark Portuguese laurels, and the grand old trees, and the sparkling fountain, and the winding walks, leading away to that sheet of water where the swans swam about from morning till night, in great state and majesty; but, as it appeared to me, without the least object in the world.

Can I not—pausing for a moment, and leaving this busy hive of London, while I think—bring the whole scene before me just as I saw it last, with the summer sun shining down upon it, and making rainbow colours in the gushing waters?

Cool and secluded—a place a man might like to live and die in—a haven of rest for the evening of life—a pleasant retreat from the bustle and noise of London—if I could choose a home for myself, it would be that old-fashioned mansion to which Maurice Storn conveyed his wife and their adopted children, when the world prospered abundantly with him once again, and good at last came forth out of evil.

He made himself busy there, as it was in his nature to make himself busy everywhere; building a laboratory within the grounds, and driving very diligently over to Lee, where young Mr. Colke lived, and ostensibly managed the factory for his partner.

When the day's work was over, and the chemist returned from his experiments, or from town, he would take the children on to the lawn, and play and romp with them, or else he would walk round the lake with Lina, projecting this improvement, and talking of that discovery, taking his youth, as it were, at the wrong end of his life, yet enjoying it none the less for all that, for he was happy in his wife, and in his home, happy in the loving heart that gave him now no divided allegiance, but found its best happiness in atoning for the errors of the past—for the wretched years and the miserable misunderstandings of their earlier married life.

There never was a shade on Lina's face, save when some stranger might unwittingly touch the old, old sore, by speaking of Mary's children as hers. Then the wound inflicted by Geordie's death began to bleed afresh, and it needed all the strength of her determined will to stop that drop, dropping of bitterness down upon her heart.

As for Maurice, sometimes he could not help but pause in the midst of his tests and analyses, to ask himself to what purpose his labour, to what end his toil?

If he added acre to acre, and thousand to thousand, where would his wealth, and his name, and his position go?

To have been a father and to be childless—to have thought to build up a house, and then, when it was almost completed, see the corner-stone swept away from his edifice, it was hard to bear, hard to think of; but still Maurice Storn, watching John Matson, and seeing how little, after all, children can compensate a man's heart for the loss of his wife—did bear up bravely, and thanked God, from the bottom of his soul, that He had been merciful to his need, and left him for the evening of his life, a woman whose truth and purity he would not have doubted for a moment—his own still beautiful Lina.

How he trusted her; how sure he was her errors had been of his, not her causing, may be gathered from the fact, that one afternoon, a short time before Mr. Clyne sailed for a far distant colony, where his uncle had procured him an appointment, he allowed Herbert to come down to their house, and saying, "Lina, I have brought an old friend to bid you good bye"— never thought, as many a one would have done, of watching how the pair met, of noticing how his wife looked, or listening if Herbert's voice quivered.

He welcomed the poor dethroned, illegitimate aristocrat into his doors with, perhaps, as sincere a feeling of pity as he ever felt for any human being, and forgot, or remembered only as a thing of the far, far past, that the man who sat there so poor in wealth, and birth, and worldly consideration had once, in his day of leisure and superiority, tried to injure him.

And after dinner, when they all went out on to the lawn, and down the winding walk to the water, Maurice dropped behind for a moment or two with the children, who were feeding the swans, while Lina and Herbert paced slowly and silently along the path together.

At last he paused and said, looking first back at his host, and then at the children, and then round the place, so awfully silent, so intensely calm, that its very stillness oppressed and deafened him :—

"Mrs. Storn, are you happy now ?"

"Perfectly," she answered, slowly and thoughtfully, yet with that old rush of waters flooding her heart for a moment too.

"I thank God for that," he answered; but he turned his eyes away to the setting sun as he spoke, and they were dim.

Dim with the memory of hopes, sinful though they might be —blasted; with the aim, and the end, and the happiness of his life gone. Dim with the agony of a heart that had erred in loving her; but that still, throughout all time, and changes, and chances, could never love another. Dim with the thoughts of that home and that rest, never destined for him, with the recollection of his fool's paradise in the past—with the certainty of the remorseful, objectless future that stretched out so drearily before him in a foreign land.

Dim for a moment, but he did not show Lina that film; and it was only by an indescribable softening of his voice, by a tone which touched the old chord in Lina's heart, that she knew what he was thinking of. Going over the old tragedy again, with a consciousness of its termination; treading the boards of life's weary stage with an agonized memory of the conclusion he had arrived at; pacing over, step by step, the whole of the road they had trod together, looking fearfully forth into the future which he knew he must travel alone. The whole thing came and passed through Herbert's mind in a moment, and was reflected by the strange sympathy of old in Lina's heart. The next Mr. Storn rejoined them, and noticing his wife looked pale, drew her arm within his, and pressed it, when he felt how she clung to him then as she ought to have done, Heaven help them both, in the days of that awful temptation which was past.

They went into the house, and when the twilight came stealing on, Mr. Clyne rose, with an effort, and said it was time for him to go. There was just light enough left in the room for Mr. Storn to perceive how the man's glance turned despairingly round the apartment, taking in every article of furniture, every picture, every ornament; the very covering of the sofa on which Lina sat, the landscape hanging above her head, the folds of the black silk dress, the wreaths of her luxuriant hair; Mr. Storn could not avoid noticing how almost unconsciously his visitor's eye took in these details; stamping them on his memory, that he might add another daguerreotype to the dreary gallery to which he was everlastingly letting his fancy wander up and down, in agony of spirit and in bitterness of soul.

Very slowly Mrs. Storn got up to bid him good bye; for the life of her she could not help trembling from head to foot, and the hand she extended was cold and clammy. For a moment he held it irresolute, then, with a deprecating look at Mr. Storn, stooped and kissed it. "Farewell for the last time in this world, Mrs. Storn," he said; "we shall never meet again."

Lina tried to speak, but she could not do it. She opened her lips, but was unable to utter a single sentence. She felt him release her hand, and saw him leave the room, and strove to cry out that she had something to say; but not a word reached Herbert's ear, for the cruel hand of old was clutching her heart and choking her.

Maurice walked down the drive with his guest. Neither of them spoke a word till, having reached the gate, Mr. Storn paused and said—

"I do not know, Mr. Clyne, whether I have done wisely in bringing you here to-day. I thought it might, perhaps, be better for you both to see each other once again; but I fear I judged wrong, so far, at least, as you are concerned. Still it may, perhaps, be a comfort for you to remember hereafter, that whatever injury you may once have tried to inflict on me, we parted friends now."

And as he spoke, Mr. Storn stretched out that honest hand of his, and laid it in that of the man who had so nearly robbed him of his life's most precious jewel. " Good bye, Mr. Clyne, and God speed you !"

For a moment Mr. Clyne's hand closed on the one thus given —for an instant his pride and his manhood struggled with his feelings ; but then it was all over, and Herbert Clyne, burying his face in his hands, and leaning forward on the gate, was sobbing like a child.

Very gently Mr. Storn let his grief have its way, and then, taking him by the arm, he talked to him as though he had been his son or his brother.

Right and wrong—the sin, the shame, and the sorrow—the great peril from which Lina had been saved almost by a miracle —the fearful temptation to which she had been subjected— Mr. Storn spoke of these things boldly, and yet most kindly, standing there under the shadow of his own trees with Herbert for the first and the last time.

Nor, in the course of that long and painful conversation, did he spare himself. He confessed that, but for his own neglect, he believed the evil never would have come upon them. He was not lenient either to his own conduct or to that of his visitor ; but it was touching to hear how lovingly and trustingly he spoke of his wife. He seemed to think that the two men should bear the blame between them, leaving her free and clear in the transaction. To him she was pure as an angel of light. If for a moment her foot had faltered on the earth, it was only because his protecting arm had been withdrawn from her support. There was a something so beautiful, so almost sublime in the man's unwavering faith and unshaken love, that Herbert Clyne felt his spirit bow down before the power of Mr. Storn's calm, mental superiority, and acknowledged that, had they both been free, and standing before Lina suitors for her hand, Maurice, and not he, ought to have been her chosen husband.

Much passed between the pair that night standing in the gathering darkness—much of advice, and encouragement, and forgiveness on Mr. Storn's part—much of sorrow and repentance on that of Mr. Clyne.

It was one of those rare occasions in life on which men speak all that is in their hearts freely and without reserve— when words are uttered and resolutions made which, though they may never be spoken of afterwards, are not forgotten, but influence the life and the conduct thenceforth for ever ; and at last the interview ended with a cordial shake hands and good bye—Herbert Clyne walking away from that place which he was to see no more, in a far more manly and healthy state of mind than that in which he had entered it.

When Maurice reached home, he found Lina lying on the sofa all in the dark. Her head was aching, she said ; and accordingly Maurice drew a chair close to her side, and took one of her hands in his, and drew her to his heart. Then she began to cry, very softly at first, as if afraid of grieving him, but afterwards, when she found he only stroked her hair and kissed her forehead, and did not try to stop her tears, she wept as if her heart would break.

And he never bade her to be comforted—he let the stream flow on as long as it would, unchecked ; but then, when the grief was exhausted, and the channel dry, and her nervousness departed, he drew her nearer still to his breast, and told her the burden of what had passed between himself and Mr. Clyne.

As he finished, Lina put her arm round his neck, and drew his head down, and kissed him tremblingly ; but, oh! with what trust and thankfulness! And thus the great cloud of their life was cleared away ; and the husband and wife, without an unexchanged thought between them, were right at last.

It was a strange fancy which made Herbert Clyne, in his after-years, study for a doctor. Every leisure moment, from the time the notion seized him, was devoted to reading for his profession ; and when, at last, he gave up his appointment, and got his diploma, no cleverer general practitioner could have been found in the colony, than the quondam man about town.

Not long after he quitted England, Mrs. Clyne died, but he never married again. It might be a punishment for his crime, that the man with such a clinging, loving woman's nature, should never know what it was to have a fond wife nestling in his heart—should never return to any, save a lonely hearth—should never see the old, quiet peaceful home-dream of his earlier manhood realized.

As for John Matson, when he grew a very rich and prosperous man, he tore himself, for his children's sakes, away from the old city mansion, and bought a property, and took his girls and his boy from Mrs. Storn, who gave them up to their rightful owner, holding, however, still a kind of property in them.

Their mother, they always called her—and well they might, for she abundantly discharged a mother's duty towards them ; and for a time, after they went away, the house seemed lonely to both Lina and her husband.

That soon wore off, however, for Mrs. Storn had never really taken them into her heart as her own. In her sight they had always been adopted. They had never, for an instant, usurped Geordie's place in her affections; and though Mary's living children might be taken from her, no human being could intermeddle with the old, sanctified, and privileged grief of having given birth to a living child, and lost him.

Besides, the girls did not reside far off, and they came and told her their little troubles, and placed their difficulties in her hands to straighten for them; and, after a time, they weaned their father somewhat from his trouble, and fringed the dark cloud of his life with gold.

But there was no real balm in Gilead for Mr. Glenaen's former manager. Years after her death, he was mourning for his wife, as Rachel of old "mourned for her children, and refused to be comforted." His boy and girls were good and tender, but they were not Mary to him. Riches came, but they could not bring her back to life. He had buried his heart in her grave, and her death seemed to have destroyed all sense of enjoyment in him. He never, however, forgot the duties he owed to the children she had left him, and for their sakes struggled on, when, for his own, he might have ceased working altogether.

Wealth and position came to him in due time. He made money, and invested it judiciously. There was scarcely a thing he turned his hand to which failed—scarcely a purchase he concluded that did not yield him cent. per cent. Richer, perhaps, than Mr. Storn, though less famous, he bought properties, and lived in good style, and took rank among the county families. Yet there was a something mournfully suggestive in hearing, as Maurice Storn did once, John Matson say, with that formerly cheerful, but now subdued voice of his—

"Times have changed with me since I lived in the garret, in Coleman Street. I am now a chemical manufacturer in the city, and a gentleman in Herts. But, ah me! for the old times of struggle and poverty to come back again once more."

THE END.

BRADBURY AND EVANS, PRINTERS, WHITEFRIARS.